MR DOOLEY

Wise and Funny — We Need Him Now

by
Finley Peter Dunne

Edited by: Barbara Schaaf

Foreword by: Philip Dunne

To Philip and Amanda Duff Dunne
with love and gratitude

Mr. Dooley
Copyright.
© 1988 by Barbara Schaaf

First Edition
Manufactured in the United States of America.

For information write to:
LINCOLN HERNDON PRESS
818 South Dirksen Parkway
Springfield, Illinois 62703

IBSN 0-942936-11-6

CONTENTS

ACKNOWLEDGEMENTS

To fellow Dooleyphiles who took the time to volunteer their favorite columns and/or quotes, thus helping keep the size of this volume somewhat slighter than the unabridged dictionary, my heartfelt appreciation.

To my friends, who are not too numerous to mention but whom I won't, for fear of inadvertently omitting one, deepest thanks for putting up with my ditherings over the selection procedure.

Finally, words cannot express my debt to Finley Peter Dunne. Although he died before I was born, he has been a living presence in and a most profound influence on my life, and through Martin Dooley, he has helped me through many a long dark night of the soul.

FOREWORD

A short while ago I read a newspaper editorial which quoted what it called an old saying: "the Supreme Court follows the election returns." This is probably my father's most-quoted line, and up to this point it had usually been credited to his "Mr. Dooley," and occasionally even to Finley Peter Dunne himself. Nothing could more cruelly have emphasized the inexorable flight of time than the indication that, to that editoralist at least, the flesh-and-blood author of the line had vanished into the mists of history. I could only shake my head and mutter: "Well, I'll be a son of an old saying."

I am grateful to Barbara Schaaf for waving her magic wand and resuscitating my father and his alter ego, the loquacious bartender of the Archey Road. Not that Finley Peter Dunne has ever really disappeared from view. Historians know him, and professors of English literature, political scholars and scholarly politicians. Plagiarizing him — quoting him without credit — has been a vigorous cottage industry since his own heyday, and made one or two of his imitators famous. It's still going on. His articles once were read aloud at presidential cabinet meetings; when Theodore Roosevelt was president he was often a guest in the White House, and although in more recent years the atmosphere at 1600 Pennsylvania Avenue has not been congenial to his spirit, he was often quoted by President John F. Kennedy, and was honored one St. Patrick's Day by President Jimmy Carter.

The Irish brogue in which he wrote, a blessing in days when people had time to read, enhancing as it did his wit and wisdom, has become a curse in these times when reading has been replaced by staring at the boob tube, or gulping the inanities which appear in the reading matter one buys at supermarket checkout stands.

But, as Barbara Schaaf eloquently points out, "Mr. Dooley" should be read today. So much of what he said is directly applicable to our own times. His official biographer, Elmer Ellis, called my father "the wit and censor of the nation." Historian J.C. Furnas suggests that he, rather than his friend Mark Twain, better fits the notion of an American national humorist.

Beyond even that, he was a mover and shaker, a powerful political force in his own right, a relentless foe of the hypocritical, the pompous, the predatory and the arrogant in office. The very knowledge that he was there acted as a deterrent to those who would abuse political or financial power. Several people have suggested to me that if a "Mr. Dooley" had been lying in ambush, piece loaded and cocked, the nation would have been spared the agony and shame of Watergate and the Iran-Contra affair. "A fanatic," he remarked, "is a man that does what he thinks th' Lord wud do if He knew th' facts iv th' case."

Those who already know "Mr. Dooley" should love this book. Those who don't know him yet should let Barbara Schaaf provide them with a passport into the warm, witty and cantankerous kingdom of his — or rather my father's — mind.

Philip Dunne
Malibu, California 1987

INTRODUCTION
The Relevance of Mr. Dooley

"We live in an age iv wondhers. Niver befure in th' histhry iv th' wurruld has such progress been made." How many think-pieces about today have begun with the same words, albeit without the Irish brogue Finley Peter Dunne used when he wrote them around the turn of the century? The major difference is that nobody, before or since, could skewer such conceits as sharply as Dunne did through his mouthpiece, Mr. Dooley.

Dunne stopped writing through Mr. Dooley over 50 years ago, and in that time Dooley fans have bemoaned the fact that he is not around to tackle the tragicomedy of modern life. They are wrong; Mr. Dooley lives. His trenchant sayings are applicable to what we foolishly and pridefully consider new situations.

Above all, Finley Peter Dunne knew and loved the American human nature and institutions. That is why he could snap, "Do I think raypublics are ongrateful? I do. That's why they continyoo to be raypublics." He was a realist, and he deplored the excesses of the country and people he loved when it was necessary. That is why his words are just as relevant today as they were when the ink from Dunne's pen was barely dry.

If the brogue makes him less accessible now, it made it possible for him to be published then. As the enormous popularity and influence of his columns show, they struck a responsive chord with the American public, but his views were often at odds with those of the newspaper publishers for him he worked. However, when uttered by an Irish saloon-keeper in Chicago's working-class neighborhood, they could escape editorial demolition. There was another reason: the brogue kept Dunne from being "pistoled or slugged, as other critics were."

Finley Peter Dunne's name appears on any short list of America's greatest humorists, and social historian J. C. Furnas found no argument a few years ago when he declared Dunne deserved to be regarded as America's national humorist, even above Mark Twain, because he touched on "a far wider spectrum."

While his favorite targets were politics and business and their practitioners — on the combination of the two, he wrote, "Whiniver I see an aldherman an' a banker walkin' down th' sthreet together, I know th' Recordin' Angel will have to ordher another bottle iv ink" — Mr. Dooley also talked about more homely things.

On Love: "All th' wurruld loves a lover — except sometimes th' wan that's all th' wurruld to him."

On Marriage: "Th' throuble about mathrimony . . . is that after fifteen or twinty years it settles down to an endurance thrile."

On Divorce: "In me heart, I think if people marry it ought to be f'r life. Th' laws ar-re altogether too lenient with thim."

On Children: "Not bein' an author I'm a gr-reat critic." And he was, giving out advice that some psychologists could envy.

On Education: "Childher shudden't be sint to school to larn, but how to larn to larn. I don't care what ye larn thim so long as its onpleasant to thim. 'Tis th' trainin' they need."

On Higher Education: Asked "If ye had a boy wud ye sind him to colledge," Mr. Dooley replied, "Well, at th' age whin a boy is fit to be in colledge, I wudden't have him around th' house."

On Human Fraility: "A little vice now and thin is relished be th' best of men."

Dunne's essays on such subjects were a comfort to a public that was floundering in the heavy seas of rapid social change. But his sharpest swords were reserved for public foolishness, misdeeds, misbehavior and malfeasance.

On America's tendency to involve itself in the internal

politics and government of other nations, he parodied a speech by outgoing Governor of the Philippines William Howard Taft. "Ivrywhere there is happiness, contint, an' love iv th' shtepmother country, excipt in places where there ar-re people."

Any American rash enough to be carried away by public acclaim should remember that "Th' thing about bein' a hero to the American people is that it don't last long." And presidential candidates as well as those testifying before congressional investigating committees would benefit from Mr. Dooley On Lying, in which he discusses "lyin" in th' home an' lyin' to th' public," as well as "th' pathriotic or red-white-an'-blue lie."

From his debut in 1893, Mr. Dooley tackled political corruption and chicanery, although he understood its origins. "I don't expict to gather calla lillies in Hogan's turnip patch. Why shud I expict to pick bunches of spotless statesmen fr'm th' gradooation class iv th' house iv correction?" As he observed in one of his most famous one liners, "Politics ain't beanbag."

When the Republican Party, then in power, held its national convention in Chicago, Dooley recorded its complacency. "Th' proceedin's was opened with a prayer that Providence might remain undher th' protection iv th' administration."

About his beloved Democratic Party, Mr. Dooley observed, "'Tis niver so good as whin 'tis broken, whin rayspictable people speak of it in whispers, an' whin it has no leaders an' on'y wan principel, to go in an' take it away fr'm th' other fellows." Asked if the Democrats would ever elect a president again, Mr. Dooley replied, "We wud, if we cud but get an illegible candidate," which he defined as "a candydate that can't be read out iv th' party . . . Whin ye see two men with whiteneckties go into a sthreet car an' set in opposite corners while wan mutthers 'Thraiter" an' th' other hisses 'Miscreent' ye can bet they're two dimmycratic leaders thryin' to reunite th' gran' ol' party."

See how the Dunne/Dooley wit goes straight to the heart of today's news?

"Histhry is a post-mortem," Mr. Dooley said. "It tells ye what a counthry died iv. But I'd like to know what it lived iv." Because Finley Peter Dunne understood so well what the United States lives of, far from being an amusing historical curiosity, his Mr. Dooley essays are both timely and timeless.

FINLEY PETER DUNNE
A Brief Life

Peter Dunne was born in Chicago on July 10, 1867, the fifth of seven children who survived to maturity, to Peter Dunne and Ellen Finley, both of whom immigrated from Ireland as children.

In 1884, he was graduated last in his high school class, and went to work instead of to college. His first job was as office boy for the *Chicago Telegram*; later that year he moved to the *Chicago Daily News* as a sports reporter.

In 1886, he joined the Chicago Times as political reporter, advancing to city editor at the age of 21. Over the next few years, he worked for the *Tribune*, the *Herald* and the *Post*.

In 1892, Dunne wrote his first dialect column; in October, 1893, Martin Dooley appeared.

In 1898, Dunne become famous nationwide, and the first Dooley collection went straight to the top of the best seller lists. It was followed by six other Dooley volumes.

In 1900, he moved to New York, where he wrote for and/or edited various publications, including the *Ladies Home Journal, Saturday Evening Post, New York Morning Telegraph, American Magazine, Collier's Weekly,* the *Pioneer,* and *Liberty.*

In 1902, he married Margaret Abbott, daughter of a proper Boston family and the first American woman to win an Olympic Gold Medal — for golf at the 1900 Paris games. They had three sons, Finley Peter, Jr., Philip, and Leonard, and one daughter, Margaret.

In 1927, a wealthy friend left Dunne a half million dollars, ending his need to write.

On April 24, 1936, Finley Peter Dunne died of cancer in New York City.

These few bald facts do nothing to convey the wit, charm, erudition and warmth of Finley Peter Dunne. He loved the

English language and was ferocious in its defense. Nothing was more precious to him than his country, his family and his friends, but he saw them clearly and without illusion. In turn, he was deeply loved by those who were lucky enough to know him; these people came from every walk of life, from the White House to the ward office, from the theatre to the fire station, from Wall Street to the rolling mills. He loved club life, beginning with the raucous Whitechapel Club in Chicago and ending in the most exclusive gentlemen's preserves in Manhattan.

Dunne would not have been so likeable were it not for his human weaknesses. He smoked heavily, and had a legendary capacity for alcohol. Writing did not come easily to him, and he often missed deadlines, especially later in his career. Despite his best efforts, he never became a scratch golfer. He is worth knowing better; the best sources are his biography, *Mr. Dooley's America*, by Elmer Ellis, and his informal memoirs, *Mr. Dooley Remembers*, edited with an introduction and commentary by his son Philip Dunne.

IN DEFENSE OF THE DIALECT ESSAY
Or Don't Let the Brogue Put You Off

Anyone can join the Martin Dooley Society: the only requirements are a sense of humor, the more ridiculous the better; a sense of history; an interest in current events; a love of words and a respect for the tragi-comedy that is life.

There are no rules or dues, but there is one initiation rite: prospective members must be able to get past the brogue in which the essays are written. It is ironic that the very device which enabled Mr. Dooley to be printed in the 1890's should keep him from being as widely read today as he deserves.

The brogue may seem intimidating at first, but perseverance pays off. After the first couple of essays one scarcely notices; indeed, efforts to translate Dooley into plain English, except for short takes and epigrams, have failed, because, along with the brogue, the punning, double entendre and almost lyrical quality of Dunne's prose are eliminated as well.

So stick with it, and join the rest of the Dooleyphiles — an elite but not elitist group, made up of scholarly politicians, political scholars, teachers, housewives, policemen, judges, diplomats, journalists, other humorists, and men and women of discernment and taste — not to say modesty.

Peter Finley Dunne at the time of his greatest fame in both England and America. This caricature appeared around 1900, in London.

Always a literary man as well as genius at satire and humor, here is Finley Peter Dunne when editor of THE AMERICAN MAGAZINE in 1912.

Finley Peter Dunne (1867-1936) was in his twenties when he created Mr. Dooley, who became the wit and wise censor of his time. The present work demonstrates his power to help us understand our own time and to marvel and laugh with it. (Courtesy, Chicago Historical Society)

This caricature, a broadside, was printed in 1900. That's Martin Dooley in heroic drapery and Finley Peter Dunne holding the pointer! In his day, Mr. Dooley was better known by Americans than was their Vice President!
(Courtesy, Chicago Historical Society)

CHAPTER I
MR. DOOLEY'S
NEIGHBORHOOD

The original protagonist of Dunne's dialect essays was Col. McNeery, whose living prototype was James McGarry, a saloonkeeper near the Chicago Tribune on Dearborn Street in downtown Chicago. According to Dunne:

> McGarry had lived long in Chicago and both by reason of his natural qualities and his position as presiding officer of what he called, "the best club in town, not exclusive mind ye, but refined," had an acquaintance to intimacy with nearly everybody worth knowing in politics, on the bench, at the bar, in trade, on the stage or in journalism. I have no hesitation in saying that most of the local copy for the *Tribune* and much for the *Herald* and the *News* was written in McGarry's back room.

> He was a stout, rosy-faced, blue-eyed man of sententious speech. He carried himself with dignity as became a personage who was not alone the friend and host of the most brilliant newspaper writers of that period, but their counsellor and banker as well. He seldom spoke. "I was," he used to say, "intended be nature to listen, not to talk."

> One of the gayest of our crowd was a reporter who could quote Shakespeare for any event or occasion. Leaning against the bar he would parry every argument with an apposite line from the poet. This scholar one night found himself financially embarrassed and asked Mr. McGarry for the loan of five dollars until pay day. McGarry turned slowly to the cash register, rang up "no sale," took five one-dollar bills out of the damper, laid them in front of his young friend and said, "Tommy, what does Shakespeare say about borryin' and lendin'?"

McGarry had an amusing way with the language, and when
Dunne began his dialect pieces, using him as a model for the
mythical McNeery seemed natural. For a while McGarry enjoyed the celebrity, and then it began to pall. The last straw
came one day when a man with a Scandinavian accent visited
McGarry's pub, sat staring at him for a long time before saying, "I tank you very funny fellow." That did it. "If the
Swedes are on to it everybody's on," McGarry fumed. The
next time Dunne stopped at McGarry's the publican avoided
speaking to him. Finally he said, "You can't put printer's ink
on me with impunity."

"But, Jim, what have I done?" Dunne asked.

"I'll see your boss, young man, I'll see Jawn R."

The next day John R. Walsh, who owned the *Post*, visited
Dunne and asked that Dunne change the name of his barkeep.

Of course, I could and I would. I called my character
Martin Dooley and placed him in a modest barroom on
Archer Avenue. It was one of the four old plank roads
that once ran from the little city of Chicago to the
neighboring farms and vegetable gardens. The name had
been corrupted (or improved if you like) into Archey
Road by the old fashioned Irish people who lived there.
No one could mistake this humble tapster for the stately
liquor merchant and friend of the arts in Dearborn
Street. Our friendship at once revived and it continued
until Mr. McGarry was gathered to his fathers.

There was a time when Archey Road was purely Irish.
But the Huns, turned back from the Adriatic and the
stockyards and overrunning Archey Road, have nearly
exhausted the original population — not driven them out
as they drove out less vigorous races, with thick clubs
and short spears, but edged them out with the more
biting weapons of modern civilization — overworked
and undereaten them into more languid surroundings
remote from the tanks of the gashouse and the blast fur-
naces of the rolling mill.

But Mr. Dooley remains, and enough remain with him to save Archey Road. In this community you can hear all the various accents of Ireland, from the awkward brogue of the "far-downer" to the mild and aisy Elizabethan English of the southern Irishman, and all the exquisite variations to be heard between Armagh and Bantry Bay, with the difference that would naturally arise from substituting cinders and sulphuretted hydrogen for peat smoke and softy misty air.

Dunne could not know it at the time, but McGarry had done him a huge favor. By relocating to a simpler neighborhood populated by simpler people, in a plainer bar presided over by a wise but simpler man, he helped Dunne create a character that would stand the test of time as well as become a prophet of things to come.

And now it is time to meet Mister Dooley.

The first Dooley column appeared after Col. McNeery had been dispatched home to Ireland. Mr. McKenna was a real person who did not share McGarry's distaste for publicity. Indeed, he was disappointed when he was eventually supplanted as Mr. Dooley's foil by the mythical Malachi Hennessy.

CHICAGO *EVENING POST,* October 7, 1893
UP IN ARCHEY ROAD
JOHN MC KENNA VISITS HIS OLD FRIEND MARTIN DOOLEY
NEWS OF BRIDGEPORT SOCIETY
THE MISADVENTURES OF MILE, GROGAN AND M. RILEY
A GERMAN BAND AND ITS IRISH TUNES

Business was dull in the liquor-shop of Mr. Martin Dooley in Archey Road last Wednesday night and Mr. Dooley was sitting back in the rear of the shop holding a newspaper at arm's length before him and reading the sporting news. In came Mr. John McKenna. Mr. McKenna has been exceedingly restless since Colonel McNeery went home to Ireland and on his way out to Brighton Park for consolation he bethought himself of Martin Dooley. The lights were shining in the little tavern and

the window decorations—green festoons, a single sheet poster
of a Parnell meeting in McCormick's Hall, and a pyramid of
bottles filled with Medford rum and flies—evoked such cheery
recollections of earlier years that Mr. McKenna hopped off the
car and entered briskly.

"Good evening, Martin," he said.

"Hellow, Jawnny," replied Mr. Dooley, as if they had parted
only the evening before. "How's thricks? I don't mind,
Jawnny, if I do. 'Tis duller here than a raypublican primary in
the fourth wa-ard, th' night. Sure, ye're like a ray iv sunlight,
ye are that. There's been no company in these pa-arts since
Dominick Riley's big gossoon was took up be th' polis. . . .
What was he tuk up fur, says ye? Faith, I'll never tell ye. Th'
polis had a gredge again him, like as not. I belave they do say
he kilt a Chiney man, an' I'll not put it beyant him, fr he is a
wild lad no less, an' wan that'd carry th' joke to anny len'th.

"Dint know where ye've been all these days, man alive. I
ain't seen ye, Jawn dear, since he led th' gr-rand march in
Finucane's Hall this tin years past. D'ye mind th' Grogan girls?
Aha, amusha, I see ye do, ye cute man. An' well ye might. Th'
oldest wan—Birdie she called hersel' in thim days though she
was christened Bridget, an' I knowed it dam well, fr I was at
th' christenin', an' got this here scar on me nut fr'm an unruly
Clare man that Jawnny Shea brung over with him—th' oldest
one danced with ye, an' five years afterward her husband
found in her pocket book a ca-ard sayin' 'Vote fr Jawn
McKinna' an' he was fr suin' fr a divorce, by gar, he was. She
said ye give her a lot iv thim for to take home to th' old man
an' she on'y kept th' wan. An' ye haven't seen her fr'm that
day to this! Oh dear, oh dear! How soon forgot we are! It's little ye think iv Bridgeport whin ye'er gallopin' aroun' to wakes
an' christenin's with Potther Pammer and Hobart What th'
'ell's his name Taylor.

"I though fr to see ye at Irish Day. I dunnaw how I missed
ye. Did ye iver see th' like iv it? Rain, rain, rain and dhrip,
dhrip, dhrip. They used to be a sayin' at home whin it was a

clear day: 'It's a fine day, plaze Gawd,' an' whin it rained cats an' dogs an' pokers: 'It's a fine day f'r th' counthry.' An' mind ye, Jawn, I won't deny it might be said last Sathedah with no ha-arm done. Ye cuddent have got three hundhred thousan' Irishmen together on a fine day without thim breakin' loose. Th' rain kipt thim fr'm gettin' enthusiastic an' by gar, f'r th' first time in th' histhry iv th' wurruld they got thim in peace an' harmony. They was united in denouncin' th' diputy f'r weather an' th' gazaboy that pulled down th' flag. If they knowed it before they did that, Orangey's 'd be orderin' lemonades in th' place where Orangeys go through th' mercy of Gawd.''

"I suppose you spent th' day in th' Irish village," suggested Mr. McKenna.

"Well, Jawn, to tell ye no lie," said Mr. Dooley, "an' don't whisper it to Finerty if you meet him at th' nex' sore-ree, but I didn't. I got mesilf fixed in a chair at th' Dutch village, an' by gar, ne'er a fut I stirred fr'm it th' livelong day. 'Twas most comfortin' an' th' band played ivry Irish tune from 'Rambler fr'm Clare' to 'Connock's Man's Dhream,' on'y mind ye, with a slight accint. There was wan lad that played th' ol' song, 'A-ha Limerick is Beautiful' an' a sweet ol' song it is, to be sure. Gawd forgive me f'r sayin' so, that hates a 'butthermilk.' He played it without an accint, an' whin he come down, thinkin' he might be wan iv us, says I: 'Cunas thantu,' I says. Well, sir, what d'ye think he replies? What d'ye think th' bpoor bosthoon replies? He says: 'Wee gates.' Wee gates, he says, Jawn, or may I never stir fr'm th' spot. Well, sir, I laughed in his face. I did, I did.

"An' a-are ye gown, Jawn dear? How about thim two bowls? That's right. Twinty-five to you, Jawn. Good night an' th' Lord be between ye an' har-rm.''

THE BAR

"It ain't ivry man that can be a bishop. An' it ain't ivry wan that can be a saloonkeeper. A saloonkeeper must be sober, he must be honest, he must be clean, an' if he's th' pastor iv a flock iv poor wurrukin'-men he must know about ivrything that's goin' on in th' wurruld or iver wint on. I on'y discuss th' light topics iv th' day with ye, Hinnissy, because ye're a frivolous charackter, but ye'd be surprised to know what an incyclopeeja a man gets to be in this profissyon. Ivry man that comes in here an' has three pans iv nicissry evil tells me, with tears, th' secrets iv his thrade an' offers to fight me if I don't look inthrested. I know injyneerin', pammistry, plumbin', Christyan Science, midicine, horseshoein' asthronomy, th' care iv th' hair, an' th' laws iv exchange, an' th' knowledge I have iv how to subjoo th' affictions iv th' ladies wud cause manny a pang. I tell ye we ar-re a fine body iv men.

"Not that I'm proud iv me profissyon, or shud I say me art? It's wan way iv makin' a livin'. I suppose it was me vocation. I got into it first because I didn't like to dhrive an express-wagon, an' I stayed in it because they was nawthin' else that seemed worth while. I am not a hard dhrinker. I find if I dhrink too much I can't meet — an' do up — th' intellechool joynts that swarm in here afther a meetin' at th' rowlin' mills. On Saturdah nights I am convivyal. On New Year's eve I thry to make th' ol' year jus' as sorry it's lavin' me as I can. But I have no more pleasure in shovin' over to ye that liquid sunstroke thin I wud if I had to dole out collars, hairdye, books, hard-biled eggs, money, or annything else that wudden't be good f'r ye. Liquor is not a nicissry evil. Hogan says it's wan way iv ra-alizin' th' ideel. Th' nex' day ye'er ashamed iv ye're ideel. The' throuble about it is that whin ye take it ye want more. But that's th' throuble with ivrything ye take. If we get power we want more power; if we get money we want more money. Our vices r-run on f'river. Our varchues, Hinnissy, is what me frind Doc Casey calls self-limitin.'

"Th' unbenighted American wurrukin'-man likes his dhrinks — as who does not? But he wants to take it in peace. His varchues has been wrote about. But let him injye his few simple vices in his own way, says I. He goes to th' saloon an' rich men go to th' club mos'ly f'r th' same reason. He don't want to go home. He don't need anny wan to push him into a bar. He'll go there because that's a place where wan man's betther thin another, an' nobody is ra-aly on but th' bartinder. There ought to be wan place where th' poor wurrukin'-man can escape bein' patted on th' back. He ain't so bad as people think. Wurrukin'-men don't dhrink to excess. Dhrunkenness is a vice iv th' idle. Did ye iver see a la-ad sprintin' acrost a joist two hundherd feet in th' air? D'ye think he cud do that if he were a free dhrinker? Th' on'y wurrukin'-men who dhrink too much ar-re thruckmen, an' that's because they have so much time on their hands. While they ar-re waitin' f'r a load they get wan. Even some iv thim ar-re sober. Ye can tell them be their hats.

"Somehow or another, Hinnissy, it don't seem just right that there shud be a union iv church an' saloon. These two gr-reat institutions ar-re best kept apart. They kind iv offset each other, like th' Supreem Coort an' Congress. Dhrink is a nicissry evil, nicissry to th' clargy. If they iver admit it's nicissry to th' consumers they might as well close up th' churches. Ye'll niver find Father Kelly openin' a saloon. He hates me business, but he likes me. He says dhrink is an evil, but I'm a nicissity. If I moved out a worse man might come in me place."

"Ye ra-aly do think dhrink is a nicissry evil?" said Mr. Hennessy.

"Well," said Mr. Dooley, "if it's an evil to a man, it's not nicissry, an' if it's nicissry it's an evil."

MEDITATIONS OF MARTIN DOOLEY ON THE FASHION OF LITERARY LION HUNTING

"Wan iv th' things that ye'd notice about Chicago, Hinnisy, if ye'd lived here as long as I have," said Mr. Dooley, "is th' sthrong way we've come along in lithrachoor. Whin I was a young man th' only lithry guy we had was Tim Scanlan, that

wrote 'Th' Jacket's Green'—ye know th' song. It begins 'Whin
I was a maiden fair an' young'—Scanlan was an ol' bachelor
an' had no hair—an' Long John Wentworth, that ownded a
newspaper an' inthrajooced th' first steam fire injine iver seen
in th west. I mind whin a man be th' name iv Char-les Dickens
come here—he was a Sassenach—an' thried f'r to separate us
fr'm our good money an' they was a ball that night iv th' Happy Sons iv th' Gloryous West, an' th' la-ad talked to th' man
that had his books on sale an' th' janitor iv th hall. All th'
other pathrons iv lithrachoor wint to th' ball.

"'Tis diff'rent now. They're as manny authors in Ar-rchey
Road as I've unpaid tabs in th' dhrawers. About th' same
number. Young Hogan is prisidint iv th' 'Sons iv Saint Joseph
an' O-Mara Khy-am sodality.' He tells me that this here
O'Mara is an alias f'r a lithry guy be th' name iv Fitzgerald.
I've knowed a few Fitzgeralds. Wan iv thim used to r-run a
hall down be Halsted Sthreet, an' they was another in th'
wather office, but I wudden't name Casey's cow after ayether
iv thim, let alone a sodality. An' instead of th' young ladies
sewin' society they've started th' 'Mrs. Humphrey Ward an'
Pleasure club,' an' Molly Donahue's th' head iv that. What do
they do? Well, 'tis this way. Whin anny man writes so manny
pieces f'r th' paper where he lives that no wan'll have annything to do with him, they sind him a letther askin' him to
come out an' r-read th' pieces to thim. Thin they give a ball f'r
to pay th' ixpinses an' sind th' proceeds to him. If he's a good
man an' don't dhrink, he comes out. They put him in th' finest
r-room at th' Transit house that two dollars can buy an' young
Hogan gets th' rayporther in th' *Halsted Sthreet Gazoot* f'r to
intherview him. 'What d'ye thing iv our World's Fair city?'
says th' rayporther. 'Rotten,' says th' lithry guy. 'Have ye seen
anny iv th' lithry projuce iv Chicago?' 'I niver eat annything
canned.' 'What's ye'er opinyon iv th' bible?' 'A vastly over-
rated wurruk. Th' charackters is not dhrawed fr'm nature an'
th' language is coarse.' 'Ye have a poor opinyon iv Shakspere?'
'Th' wurst in th' wurruld. Have ye a pitcher iv me? Well,

here's twinty. Go now, ye impydint outcast, an' see that they're printed in ye'er scand'lous an' odjous newspaper, which I despise,' he says. 'Th' vileness iv th' press iv America,' he says, 'is beyond annything I know,' he says. 'Manny an' manny's th' time th' privacy iv me r-room has been invaded be rayporthers, an' th' secrets iv me ar-rt an' me life wrinched fr'm me, an' thin they didn't print more thin half what I said,' he says. 'Go,' he says,'an' vent ye'er cur-rsed spite on me,' he says. 'Tell thim ivrything about me,' he says. 'Tell thim I'm th' gr-reatest living author; tell thim I'm th' mos' fas'nably dhressed man,' he says. 'Tell thim women go mad over me,' he says. 'Expose me naked to th' wurruld,' he says. 'Ye'll find a pitcher iv me there in a goold bathtub attinded be th' prince iv Wales,' he says. 'Alas,' he says, 'that a man iv my standin' shud be so threated,' he says. An' he weeps an' gives th' rayporther an eight cint seegar an' a vollum iv his well known thranslation iv Butthrick's Pattherns fr'm th' original Greek.

"They had a Jew man out here th' other day, th' author iv a pome called 'Childher iv th' Get-to-hell-out-of-this,' I think Hogan called it. I niver give th' Jews much credit f'r bein' lithry, an', be hivins, they niver give me much credit f'r annything else. But this lad was a lithry gur all r-right. He talked in th' school hall undher th' auspices iv th' O'Mara Khy-ams, an', says he: 'I'll make an ipigram,' he says. 'This is th' wor-rst town, an' this audjeence th' wor-rst mob iv imported immigrants I iver see,' he says. He didn't put it that sthrong but it sounded that way. 'I'm surprised to see ye here tonight,' he says, 'f'r none iv ye look as if ye iver arned more thin thirty cints in th' laundhry,' he says, 'or had brains enough,' he says, 'to buy a ticket,' he says. 'As I said to an audjeence th' other night, in me style that's been so much copied ivry where,' he says, 'th' sea iv upturned faces befure me makes me want to go out an' hang mesilf f'r fear I'd be dhrownded,' he says. 'I doubt if anny iv ye'll undherstand annything I say,' he says, 'but I'll go ahead an' r-read fr'm th' wurruk iv th' gr-reatest author that was iver foaled,' he says. 'That is,' he says, 'mesilf,'

he says. 'Th' first selection,' he says, 'will be "Th' Pawn Shop
That Me Gran'pa Left To Me," ' he says. 'A wurruk,' he says,
'that I have universally admired,' he says. An' I come away an'
wint down to Finucane's Hall an' broke into th' dance iv th'
Gluemakers' union, an' had a time that reminded me iv th'
good old days iv Chicago, befure th' r-run iv books was larger
thin th' r-run iv hogs."

"Why didn't ye poke him wan?" asked Mr. Hennessy.

"That ain't th' thrue lithry feelin'," said Mr. Dooley. "That
was th' feelin' befure th' Ar-rt Institute was built, whin they
used to give a gr-reat author th' time iv his life be takin' him
out to me ol' frind Armour's an' lavin' him belt a steer over th'
head with a sledgehammer."

VACATIONS

"Ye shud take a vacation," said Mr. Hennessy when the
philosopher complained of a slight headache. "Ye ought to go
away an' have a few weeks' fishin' or r-run down to
Westbaden an' be biled out, or indulge in some other form iv
spoort."

"I shud not," retorted Mr. Dooley firmly. "I'm well enough
off where I am. They'se no disease that afflicts th' American
people akel to th' vacation habit. Ye take a big sthrong man
that's lived in Chicago all his life, an' if he stays on here he'll
niver know a day iv ill health. He goes out in th' mornin' an'
dhrinks in th' impure an' healthy air, filled with mickrobes an'
soot an' iron filin's, an' his chist expands. He ates on-
wholesome, rich an' appetizin' food. His muscles is kept firm
be dodgin' cable cars an' express wagons. His mind is rooned
an' made ca'm be readin' th' newspapers. His happy home is
infested with sewer gas, an' if he survives he's th' sthrongest
thing that iver was made. But ye take that man out iv his par-
nicious an' agreeable atmosphere an' sind him to th' counthry.
He ates wholesome food that his stomach, bein' used to th'
best Luetgert society, rayfuses to intertain. His lungs cave in

fr'm consumin' pure air that, like iverything pure, is too thin. He misses his daily sewer gas an' he finds cows' milk a poor substitute for docthered whisky an' beer with aloes in it. Th' man suffers. He does so. He rayturns to Chicago a shattered invalid an' it takes months iv livin' in onsanitary tinimints an' a steady dite iv cigaroots an' bakin' powdher biscuits to restore him to his proper condition iv robust bad health.

"Now look at ol' Duggan. There was th' healthiest man in th' wa-ard f'r his age. He was bor-rn an' raised on th' banks iv th' slip where ye can hear th' wather poppin' fr'm wan year's ind to another like a shelf iv catsup bottles on a hot night. Th' air was so thick with poisonous gases that a wagon loaded with scrap iron wud float at an ilivation iv tin feet. He lived below th' grade an' th' rain backed into his bedroom. He wurruked in a white lead facthry at night an' had to cross twinty-five railroad thracks an' an ilictric switch on his way to wurruk. He lived mos'ly on canned goods an' fried pork an' drank his beer at an Irish saloon an' his whisky at a German's. Not bein' a corpse befure he was twinty-five it was a sure thing he'd be a joynt at fifty. An' so he was. A sthronger man niver breathed. But some wan put in his head he ought to go off to the counthry f'r his vacation, an' he wint dhrivin' a canal boat mule or cuttin' hay. Whin he come back he was that weak a child cud go to th' flure with him. 'Where have ye been?' says I. 'On me vacation,' says he. 'Well,' I says, 'ye'er pretty near vacated,' I says. 'Yis,' he says, 'I'm glad to get back,' he says. 'I need tinder care,' he says. They nursed him back to life, but 'twas not till his house'd been declared unfit f'r habitation be th' health departmint an' he'd been ejicted afther a free fight be his landlord an' r-run in wanst be th' polis an' over twict be a mail wagon an' was back to wurruk breathin' lead dust be th' quart that he raycovered his ol' sperrits.

"I niver lave town mesilf. I take a vacation be settin' here at me front dure lookin' up at Gawd's an' th' Illinye Steel Company's black-an'-blue sky. Th' ilictric ca-ars go singin' by an' th' air is filled with th' melody iv goats an' curdogs. Ivry breeze

that blows fr'm th' south brings th' welcome tidings that me
frind Phil Armour is still stickin' to th' glue business. I cannot
see th' river, but I know that it's rollin' grandly backward tord
its sewerce laden with lumber hookers an' ol' vigitables. Oc-
casin'lly I hear a tugboat cooin' to its mate an' now an' thin a
pathrol wagon flits by on its errand iv love. At night th' tired but
unhappy lab'rers rayturns fr'm their tile an' th' air is laden with
th' sound iv fryin' liver an' th' cheery perfume iv bilin' cabbage.
Whin I want more active amusemint I go in an' start a bung or
angle with a fork f'r a sardine. So whin me vacation is over I
rayturn rayfrished an' eager f'r th' battle iv life. I don't have to
get th' tast iv good butter out iv me mouth.

"They'se no use f'r a Chicago man thryin' to take his vacation
out iv town till they put up a summer hotel in th' crather iv
Mount Vasuvyous. Ayether he ought niver to go away,
or—"

"He ought niver to come back," suggested Mr. Hennessy.

"Ye're r-right," said Mr. Dooley.

LOCAL CELEBRATIONS

"Ar-re ye goin' to attind th' cillybration iv th' fire?" asked Mr.
Hennessy.

"The cillybration iv th' fire!" Mr. Dooley replied. "An' why
shud I cillybrate th' fire? An' why shud annywan? D'ye hear iv
people cillybratin' th' famine iv forty-eight or th' panic iv sivinty-
three or th' firin' on Fort Sumter? We've had manny other
misfortunes an' they're not cillybrated. Why don't we have a
band out an' illuminated sthreet ca-ars f'r to commimorate th'
day that Yerkuss come to Chicago? An' there's cholera. What's
th' matter with cholera? Why don't we have an ipidimic day,
with floats showin' distinguished citizens in convulsions an' a
procission iv hearses? That'ud be a pretty sight. Some time I expect to see Tanner's inaug'ration cillybrated because it happened, an' th' people, or manny iv thim, lived through it. We
cud have a riprisintation iv Tanner bein' pursued by a yellow

fever mickrobe an' durin' th' intertainment mimbers iv th' legislachure 'ud pass among th' audjience pickin' pockets.

SOCIAL LIFE IN BRIDGEPORT

"I don't think," said Mr. Dooley, "that th' pa-pers is as good now as they used to be whin I was a young man."

"I don't see much diff'rence in thim," said Mr. Hennessy. "Except they're all full iv pitchers iv th' prisidint an' secrity iv th' Milwaukee Avnoo Fife an' Dhrum E-lite Society. They give ye th' same advice to vote th' mugwump ticket between ilictions an' th' straight ticket at ilictions, an' how th' business in pig iron is slowly but surely pickin' up, an' how to make las' year's dhress look like next year's be addin' a few jet beads an' an accorjeen pleat. They're as bad now as they iver were an' I've quit readin' thim."

"Ah, but sure," said Mr. Dooley, "ye don't raymimber th' ol' days. Ye don't raymimber Storey's *Times*. That was th' paper f'r ye. What th' divvle did ol' man Storey care f'r th' thrade in pig iron? 'Twas no more in him thin th' thrade in poolchecks. He set up in his office with his whiskers thrailin' in an ink pot an' wrote venomious attacks on th' characters iv th' leaders iv high society an' good-natured jests about his esteemed contimprary havin' had to leave Ohio because he stold a cukstove. He didn't have no use f'r prominint citizens except be way iv heavin' scandal at thim. He knowed what th' people wanted. They wanted crime, an' he give it to thim. If they wasn't a hangin' on th' front page some little lad iv a rayporther'd lose his job. They was murdher an' arson till ye cudden't rest, robbery an' burglary f'r page afther page, with anny quantity iv scandal f'r th' woman's page an' a fair assortmint iv larceny an' assault an' batthry f'r th' little wans. 'Twas a paper no wan took into his house—f'r th' other mimbers iv th' fam'ly—but 'twas a well r-run paper, so it was.

"Ye can hardly find anny crimes nowadays. To look at th'
pa-pers ye'd think they was not wan bit iv rale spoortin' blood
left in th' people iv this city. Instead iv it I have to pay to know
that Mrs. Dofunny iv Englewood has induced her husband to
stay away fr'm home while she gives a function—an' what a
function is I dinnaw—an'among thim that'll be prisint, if they
can get their laundhry out, 'll be Messer an' Mesdames
What-d'ye-Call-Thim an' Messers an' Medames This-an'-That
an' Miss-What-D'ye-Call-Her-Now, an' so on. What do I care
about thim? Now, if Misther Dofunny had come home with a
load on an' found his wife r-runnin' up bills f'r tea an' broke up
the function with his dinner pail it'd be worth readin' about. But
none iv th' papers'd say annything about it, now that Storey's
gone. Why, mind ye, las' week th' Willum J. O'Brien Lithry an'
Marchin' Club give a dance, an' befure it got through th' chairman iv th' flure comity fell out with th' German man that led th'
band an ivery wan in th' place took a wallup at some wan else
with a wind instrument. I looked f'r it in th' paper th' nex' day.
All they had was: 'Th' Willum J. O'Brien Lithry an Marchin'
Club, includin' th' mos' prominent mimbers iv society in th'
sixth ward, gave a function at Finucane's Hall las' night. O'Rafferty sarved an' music was furnished by Weinstein's orchesthry.
Among those prisint was so-an'-so.' Th' rayporther must've
copied th' names off th' blotter at th' polis station. An' there was
not wan wurrud about th' fight—not wan wurrud!

"Now, if it had been in ol' Storey's day this is th' way it'd
read: 'Bill O'Brien, th' tough aldherman fr'm th' sixth ward, has
a club named after him, most iv thim bein' well known to th'
polis. It is a disgrace to th' decent people iv Bridgepoort. Las'
night th' neighbors complained to th' polis iv th' noise an'
Lift'nant Murphy responded with a wagon load iv bluecoats.
On entherin' th' hall th' gallant officers found a free fight in pro-
gress, wan iv th' rowdies havin' hit th' leader iv' th' band, who
responded be knockin' his assailant down with a b-flat cornet.
Th' disturbers iv th' peace were taken to Deerin' sthreet station
an'll be thried before Judge Scully in th' mornin'.' That's th'

way ol' Storey'd give it to thim. He didn't know much about functions, but he was blue blazes on polis news.

"I dinnaw what's comin' over th' people. Whin I was young if a rayporther wint rubberin' around a dance we might give him a dhrink an' we might throw him in th' canal. It depinded on how we felt tord him. It wasn't rispictable in thim days to have ye'er name in th' paper. It niver got in except whin ye was undher arrest. Now I see har-rd wurrukin' men thrampin' down to th' newspaper offices with little items about a christenin' or a wake an' havin' it read to thim in th' mornin' at breakfuss befure they start to th' mills. On'y th' other day th' Bohemian woman that r-runs th' cabbage patch up be Main sthreet come in an' says she: 'We have a party at th' house to-night,' she says. 'Have ye?' says I. 'What for?' I says. 'Me daughter is comin' out,' says she. 'Is she?' says I. 'That's nice iv th' mayor,' says I. 'How long was she in f'r?' says I. An' she wint away mad. What's worse, this here society don't stop afther death. Here's a notice in th' paper: 'Ann Hochheimer'— she married a German—'nee O'Toole.' Nee O'Toole! Nee O'Toole! What does that mean? Nee nawthin'! Her name was O'Toole befure she was marrid, f'r twinty odd years. I knowed her well."

"Well," said Mr. Hennessy, with a sheepish smile. "I must be goin'. We have a progressive euchre party at my house an' I must be there to r-ring th' bell."

"Ye'd betther stay here an' play me forty-fives f'r th' dhrinks," said Mr. Dooley with compassion.

"Now," said Mr. Hennessy, in hollow tones, "me name's in th' pa-aper an' I must riprisint."

And Mr. Dooley, the untainted one, stood alone—the solitary green spot in a desert of "society."

Social historian J. C. Furnas expresses a fondness for this essay.

THE CITY AS A SUMMER RESORT

"Where's Dorsey, the plumber, these days?" asked Mr. Hennessy.

"Haven't ye heerd?" said Mr. Dooley. "Dorsey's become a counthry squire. He's landed gintry, like me folks in th' ol' dart. He lives out among th' bur-rds an' th' bugs, in a house that looks like a cuckoo clock. In an hour or two ye'll see him go by to catch the five five. He won't catch it because there ain't anny five five. Th' la-ad that makes up th' time-table found las' week that if he didn't get away arlier he cudden't take his girl f'r a buggy ride an' he's changed th' five five to four forty-eight. Dorsey will wait f'r th' six siven an' he'll find that it don't stop at Paradise Manor where he live on Saturdahs an' Winsdahs except Fridahs in Lent. He'll get home at iliven o'clock an' if his wife's f'rgot to lave th' lantern in th' deepo, he'll crawl up to th' house on his hands an' knees. I see him las' night in at th' dhrug sthore buyin' ile iv peppermint f'r his face. "Tis a gran' life in th' counthry,' says he, 'far' he says, 'fr'm th' madding crowd,' says he. 'Ye have no idee,' he says, 'how good it makes a man feel,' he says, 'to escape th' dust an' grime iv th' city,' he says, 'an' watch th' squrls at play,' he says. 'Whin I walk in me own garden,' he says, 'an' see th' viggytables comin' up, I hope, an' hear me own cow lowin' at th' gate iv th' fence,' he says, 'I f'rget,' he says, 'that they'se such a thing as a jint to be wiped or a sink to be repaired,' he says. He had a box iv viggytables an' a can iv condensed milk undher his arm. 'Th' wife is goin' away nex' week,' he says, 'do ye come out an' spind a few days with me,' he says. 'Not while I have th' strenth to stay here,' says I. 'Well,' he says, 'maybe,' he says, 'I'll r-run in an' see ye,' he says. 'Is there annything goin' on at th' theaytres?' he says.

"I wanst spint a night in th' counthry, Hinnissy. 'Twas whin Hogan had his villa out near th' river. 'Twas called a villa to distinguish it fr'm a house. If't was a little bigger 'twud be big enough f'r th' hens an' if 't was a little smaller, 'twud be small enough f'r a dog. It looked as if 't was made with a scroll saw, but Hogan mannyfacthered it himself out iv a design in th' pa-aper. 'How to make a counthry home on wan thousan' dollars. Puzzle: find th' money.' Hogan kidnaped me wan afthernoon an' took me out there in time to go to bed. He boosted me up a laddher into a bedroom adjinin' th' roof. 'I hope,' says I, 'I'm not discommodin' th' pigeons', I says. 'There ain't anny pigeons here,' says he. 'What's that?' says I. 'That's a mosquito,' says he. 'I thought ye didn't have anny here,' says I. "Tis th' first wan I've seen,' says he, whackin' himsilf on th' back iv th' neck. 'I got ye that time, assassin,' he says hurlin' th' remains to th' ground. 'They on'y come,' he says, 'afther a heavy rain or a heavy dhry spell,' he says, 'or whin they'se a little rain,' he says, 'followed be some dhryness,' he says. 'Ye mustn't mind thim,' he says. 'A mosquito on'y lives f'r a day,' he says. "Tis a short life an' a merry wan,' says I. 'Do they die iv indigisthion?' I says. So he fell down through th' thrap dure an' left me alone.

"Well, I said me prayers an' got into bed an' lay there, thinkin' iv me past life an' wondherin if th' house was on fire. 'Twas warrum, Hinnissy. I'll not deny it. Th' roof was near enough to me that I cud smell th' shingles an' th' sun had been rollin' on it all day long an' though it had gone away, it'd left a ray or two to keep th' place. But I'm a survivor iv th' gr-reat fire an' I often go down to th' rollin' mills an' besides, mind ye, I'm iv that turn iv mind that whin 't is hot I say 't is hot an' lave it go at that. So I whispers to mesilf, 'I'll dhrop off,' I says, 'into a peaceful slumber,' I says, 'like th' healthy ploughboy that I am,' says I. An' I counted as far as I knew how an' conducted a flock iv sheep in a steeple chase an' I'd just begun f'r to wondher how th' las' thing I thought iv came into me head, whin a dog started to howl in th' yard. They was a frind iv this dog in th' nex' house that answered him an' they had a long chat. Some other dogs butted in to be companionnable. I heerd Hogan rollin' in bed an' thin I heerd him goin' out to get a dhrink iv wather. He thripped over a chair befure he lighted a match to look at th' clock. It seemed like an hour befure he got back to bed. Be this time, th' dogs was tired an' I was thinkin' I'd take a nap whin a bunch iv crickets undher me windows begun f'r to discoorse. I've heerd iv th' crickets on th' hearth,

Hinnissy, an' I used to think they were all th' money, but anny time they get on me hearth I buy me a pound iv insect powdher. I'd rather have a pianola on th' hearth anny day, an' Gawd save me fr'm that! An' so 't was dogs an' mosquitos an' crickets an' mosquitos an' a screech owl an' mosquitos an' a whip-poor-will an' mosquitos an' cocks beginnin' to crow at two in th' mornin' an' mosquitos, so that whin th' sun bounced up an' punched me in th' eye at four, I knew what th' thruth is, that th' counthry is th' noisiest place in th' wurruld. Mind ye, there's a roar in th' city, but in th' counthry th' noises beats on ye'er ear like carpet tacks bein' dhriven into th' dhrum. Between th' chirp iv a cricket an' th' chirp iv th' hammer at th' mills, I'll take th' hammer. I can go to sleep in a boiler shop but I spint th' rest iv that night at Hogan's settin' in th' bath tub.

"I saw him in th' mornin' at breakfast. We had canned peaches an' condinsed milk. 'Ye have ye'er valise,' says he. 'Aren't ye goin to stay out?' 'I am not,' says I. 'Whin th' first rattler goes by ye'll see me on th' platform fleein' th' peace an' quite iv th' counthry, f'r th' turmoil an' heat,' I says, 'an' food iv a gr-reat city,' I says. 'Stay on th' farm,' says I. 'Commune,' I says, 'with nature,' I says. 'Enjoy,' I says, 'th' simple rustic life iv th' merry farmer boy that goes whistlin' to his wurruk befure breakfast,' says I. 'But I must go back,' I says, 'to th' ci- ty,' I says, 'where there is nawthin' to eat but what ye want an' nawthin' to dhrink but what ye can buy,' I says. 'Where th' dust is laid be th' sprinklin' cart, where th' ice-man comes reg'lar an' th' roof garden is in bloom an' ye're waked not be th' sun but th' milkman,' I says. 'I want to be near a doctor whin I'm sick an' near eatable food whin I'm hungry, an' where I can put me hand out early in th' mornin' an' hook in a newspaper,' says I. 'Th' city,' says I, 'is th' on'y summer resort f'r a man that has iver lived in th' city,' I says. An' so I come in.

"'T is this way, Hinnissy, th' counthry was all right whin we was young and hearty, befure we become enfeebled with lux- uries, d' ye mind. 'T was all right whin we cud shtand it. But we're not so sthrong as we was. We're diff'rent men, Hinnissy. Ye may say, as Hogan does, that we're ladin' an artificyal life but, be Hivins, ye might as well tell me I ought to be paradin' up an' down a hillside in a suit iv skins, shootin' th' antylope an' th' moose, be gorry, an' livin' in a cave, as to make me believe I ought to get along without sthreet cars an' ilicthric lights an' illyvators an' sody wather an' ice. 'We ought to live where all th' good things iv life come fr'm', says Hogan. 'No,' says I. 'Th' place to live in is where all th' good things iv life goes to.' Ivrything that's worth havin' goes to th' city; th' counthry takes what's left. Ivrything that's worth havin' goes to th' city an' is iced. Th' cream comes in an' th' skim-milk stays; th' sunburnt viggytables is consumed be th' hearty farmer boy an' I go down to Callaghan's store an' ate th' sunny half iv a peach. Th' farmer boy sells what he has f'r money an' I get th' money back whin he comes to town in th' winther to see th' exposition. They give us th' products iv th' sile an' we give thim cottage organs an' knock-out dhrops, an' they think they've broke even. Don't lave annywan con-vince ye th' counthry's th' place to live, but don't spread th' news yet f'r awhile. I'm goin' to advertise 'Dooleyville be-th' river.' Within six siconds iv sthreet cars an' railway thrains an' aisy reach iv th' theaytres an' ambulances. Spind th' summer far fr'm th' busy haunts iv th' fly an th' bug be th' side iv th' purlin' ice wagon.' I'll do it, I tell ye. I'll organ-ize excursions an' I'll have th' poor iv th' counthry in here settin' on th' cool steps an' passin' th' can fr'm hand to hand; I'll take thim to th' ball-game an' th' theaytre; I'll lave thim sleep till breakfast time an' I'll sind thim back to their overcrowded homes to dhream iv th' happy life in town. I will so."

"I'm glad to hear ye say that," said Mr. Hennessy. "I wanted to go out to th' counthry but I can't unless I sthrike."

"That's why I said it," replied Mr. Dooley.

CHICAGO POLITICS

"I'm not out f'r th' nommynation anymore," said Mr. Dooley, as Mr. McKenna entered.

"For what nomination, in the name of the saints?" asked Mr. McKenna.

"F'r Aldherman," said Mr. Dooley, drawing himself up perceptibly.

"Were you running?" Mr. McKenna asked.

"Was I runnin', is it?" returned the philosopher. "Was I runnin'? Did you see Jawn Finerty's pa-aper? Was I runnin'? Havin't ye heered that I was waited on be a comity iv th' Civic Featheration askin' me not to? Sure, I was th' most prominent candydate in th' field till me frind Stuckart took me down to th' city hall.

"They was all there—th' lads. Th' little bald-headed man was in th' chair an a big bald-headed man was down below r-readin' to th' aldhermin things some iv thim cudden't r-read without their glasses an' some cudden't r-read at all. The big bald-headed man was callin' off his piece whin up come me frind Buck McCarty. I knowed him well years ago whin he cud weigh a hog on th' hoof within a scruple an' niver ask f'r th' scale.

" 'Mister Chairman,' says he, 'this here is a little ordinance I want to get through,' he says. ''Tis f'r th' binifit iv me constitooency,' he says, 'an' intinded f'r to relieve th' workin'min everywhere,' he says. 'It's an ordinance givin' th' Internaytional Mickrobe Company a right to lay pipes an' pump microbes throughout th' city.'

"'I'm agin this ordinance,' says a big guy be th' name iv Lammers. 'F'r why?' says another aldherman. 'Because,' says Lammers, 'me frind on th' extreme lift wanst hooked an eye out iv me.' 'That's no valid objection,' says another aldherman. 'A man that wudden't lose an eye f'r th' binifit iv his counthrymin, whin they'se something in it, 'd desarve to have his final papers took away fr'm him.' 'I want to say,' says another aldherman, 'that th' ord'nance is all right. While,' he says, 'I feel that th' cramped condition iv th' city threeasury is such,' he says, 'that some income might be exthracted fr'm th' company, still,' he says. 'I feel that it'd be a mistake,' he says, 'to put new burdens on an industhry that'se conthributed so much to th' prosperity iv this gr-reat an' imperyal city,' he says. 'Look,' he says, 'at our audjiotorums an' our a-art institoots an' our Columbus monymints an' our other pinal institutions,' he says. 'Look at our bridwell an' our insane asylum,' he says. 'I say th' prosperity iv th' gr-reat an' imperyal an' rootytoot City iv Chicago dipinds upon th' way we threat these corporations,' he says. 'Refuse,' he says, 'an ordinance in this here matther,' he says, 'an' th' whole mi-crobe industhry 'll be destroyed in this city,' he says. 'These people'll go to New York an' get capitalists to back thim an' set up mi-crobe foundhries an' roon th' thrade iv Chicago,' he says.

" 'But,' says a squealy voiced man, 'what do we need iv mi-crobes?' 'He's a rayformer,' says me frind Stuckart. 'Well,' says I, 'he ought to have a good punch in th' eye,' I says. 'What d'ye let th' likes iv him in f'r?' I says. 'Oh,' says he, 'he doesn't count,' he says. 'Th' la-ad is all right,' he says. 'An' th' more he talks th' betther f'r us.'

" 'I won't speak longer iv mi-crobes,' says th' rayformer, 'but I'd wish to ree-mark that whin King Jawn signed th' magna charta he gave to each an' all iv us th' right f'r to exercise our judgment was we see fit,' he says. 'Now,' he says, 'I'll refer ye to th' writin's iv Saint Thomas a Kimpis f'r to show that whin a man does his jooty—' 'Misther Chairman,' says Jawnny Powers, 'I move ye th' prevyous quistion.' 'All in favor iv th' motion,' says th' little bald-headed man. 'What motion?' says wan iv th' aldhermin. 'Th' wan ye was staked to,' says th' la-ad nixt to him. An' it wint through."

"And is that what made you quit?" asked Mr. McKenna.

"Well," said Mr. Dooley, "I'm particular. If I was in th' council I might turn out as a rayformer, an' I don't want to take anny chances on that."

RADICAL POLITICS—CHICAGO STYLE

"If half th' men iv this counthry was as tough as they'd like to make thimsilves out it'd be no place f'r a white man to live in," said Mr. Dooley.

"What makes ye say that?" demanded Mr. Hennessy.

"I was r-readin' th' speeches iv thim la-ads at th' socialist meetin' th' other night. They was meejim sthrong. Wan mild an' amyable philosopher was in favor iv placin' a small bunch iv dinnymite undher ivry naytional bank in Chicago, as if th' naytional banks cud be busted be dinnymite afther two years' experyence with Dimon' Match an' Wist Chicago. Another pote was detarmined that th' workingmen iv Chicago shud ar-rm thimsilves with Winchester rifles an' pump bullets into ivry passing capitalist. Still another la-ad swore that he welcomed blood, an' if nicissary to th' prisirvation iv our liberties wud swim in it. Now that sounds bad, an' if I didn't know th' la-ads I'd fear to go to bed iv nights. But I know thim. Wan iv thim —th' dinnymite la-ad—is a barber an' has no more idee iv what dinnymite is than th' man in th' moon. Th' la-ad that wants Winchesters lost his week's salary thryin' to knock th' tables down at th' last picnic iv th' County Dimocracy. Th' la-ad that wanted to swim in blood has been thryin' f'r to get a job in th' wather office.

"So they go, an' I'm not afraid. Th' American rivolutionist is th' mos' peaceful man on earth. He's as law abidin', as ca'm an' as good natured as anny livin' man. Did ye iver hear iv wan iv thim torch an' bomb lads swingin' a torch or peggin' a bomb? Not wan. Afther they're through th' little song an' dance on Sundah afthernoon they go home an' play with th' babies. Thank th' Lord we'er a windy people an' can let out our bad sintimints be wurrud iv mouth."

CHAPTER II

HANDS ACROSS THE SEA AND INTO BATTLE

Until 1898, Dunne's popularity remained pretty much a local phenomenon, although his columns were irregularly picked up by out-of-town newspapers. Then came the Spanish-American War, an exercise that was tailor-made for Mr. Dooley's genius at exposing the folly and false pretenses of the American establishment. From his safe redoubt on Archer Avenue, Mr. Dooley punctured the hot-air balloon that had been lofted by politicians with the aid of newspaper publishers and business interests.

Dooley's sweeping national and international fame began with an essay about Admiral Dewey's rout of the Spanish fleet at Manila. On May 1, 1898, just after war had been declared, George Dewey sailed the Asiatic fleet to Manila, where a battle was fought. Because the telegraph cable had been cut, no news of the outcome was forthcoming. Rumors and speculation as to the fate of Dewey and his men abounded, and the nation was all but stopped in its tracks, waiting for news. Into the breach stepped Mr. Dooley, with the essay "On His Cousin George." It caught the national fancy, and the country went wild with what came to be known as Dooleymania.

Dunne's own attitudes about the war were complex. A member of the generation that had accepted Darwin's theory, he viewed war as evidence that man was not very far removed from the beast, or civilization from the jungle. But the events absorbed his interest, and he admired individual heroism and genius in the field, just as he deplored the ample examples of incompetence.

As one who had opposed British inperialism and had exposed its hypocrisy in print, Dunne could not accept American expansionism, and here Mr. Dooley adopted a stand that was contrary to that of the editorial policy of Dunne's employer.

The failure of America's allies to support her in the Spanish-American conflict touches another modern responsive chord, as do his comic, but very serious concerns about the changing face of war, his contempt for experts on bellicosity, and the development of increasingly lethal weapons. His discussion of the British use of lyddite in South Africa, turning everything, including "th' foul but acc'rate Boers," green brings to mind the use of Agent Orange in Viet Nam.

"The Hague Conference" could be any summit meeting, disarmament talks, or session of the U.N. General Assembly. The modern military continues to indulge in war games, and the loser continues to be the U.S. Treasury. Dooley's exploration of American involvement in the Philippines after the Spanish—American War still could be applied to that country — and countless others besides.

Finley Peter Dunne, Jr. is fondest of Dooley's salute to Admiral Dewey, which made his father's creation an international sensation.

ON HIS COUSIN GEORGE

"Well," said Mr. Hennessy, in tones of chastened joy: "Dewey didn't do a thing to thim. I hope th' poor la-ad ain't cooped up there in Minneapolis."

"Niver fear," said Mr. Dooley, calmly. "Cousin George is all r-right."

"Cousin George?" Mr. Hennessy exclaimed.

"Sure," said Mr. Dooley. "Dewey or Dooley, 'tis all th' same. We dhrop a letter here an' there, except th' haitches, — we niver dhrop thim, — but we're th' same breed iv fightin'

men. Georgy has th' thraits iv th' fam'ly. Me uncle Mike, that
was a handy man, was tol' wanst he'd be sint to hell f'r his
manny sins, an' he desarved it; f'r lavin' out th' wan sin iv runnin' away fr'm annywan, he was booked f'r ivrything from
murdher to missin' mass. 'Well,' he says, 'anny place I can get
into,' he says, 'I can get out iv,' he says. 'Ye bet on that,' he
says.

"So it is with Cousin George. He knew th' way in, an' it's th'
same way out. He didn't go in be th' fam'ly inthrance, sneakin'
along with th' can undher his coat. He left Ding Dong, or
whativer 'tis ye call it, an' says he, 'Thank Gawd,' he says,
'I'm where no man can give me his idees iv how to r-run a
quiltin' party, an' call it war,' he says. An' so he sint a man
down in a divin' shute, an' cut th' cables, so's Mack cudden't
chat with him. Thin he prances up to th' Spanish forts, an'
hands thim a few oranges. Tosses thim out like a man throwin'
handbills f'r a circus. 'Take that,' he says, 'an' raymimber th'
Maine,' he says. An' he goes into th' harbor, where Admiral
What-th'-'ell is, an', says he, 'Surrinder,' he says. 'Niver,' says
th' Dago. 'Well,' says Cousin George, 'I'll just have to push ye
ar-round,' he says. An' he tosses a few slugs at th' Spanyards.
Th' Spanish admiral shoots at him with a bow an' arrow, an'
goes over an' writes a cable. 'This mornin' we was attackted,'
he says. 'An,' he says, 'we fought the inimy with great
courage,' he says. 'Our victhry is com-plete,' he says. 'We have
lost ivrything we had,' he says. 'Th' threachrous foe,' he says,
'afther destroyin' us, sought refuge behind a mudscow,' he
says; 'but nawthin' daunted us. What boats we cudden't r-run
ashore we surrindered,' he says. 'I cannot write no more,' he
says, 'as me coat-tails are afire,' he says; 'an' I am bravely but
rapidly leapin' fr'm wan vessel to another, followed be me
valiant crew with a fire-engine,' he says. 'If I can save me coat-
tails,' he says, 'they'll be no kick comin',' he says. 'Long live
Spain, long live mesilf.'

"Well, sir, in twenty-eight minyits be th' clock Dewey he had
all th' Spanish boats sunk, an' that there harbor lookin' like a

Spanish stew. Thin he r-run down th' bay, an' handed a few war-rm wans into th' town. He set it on fire, an' thin wint ashore to war-rm his poor hands an' feet. It chills th' blood not to have annything to do f'r an hour or more."

"Thin why don't he write something?" Mr. Hennessy demanded.

"Write?" echoed Mr. Dooley. "Write? Why shud he write? D'ye think Cousin George ain't got nawthin' to do but to set down with a fountain pen, an' write: 'Dear Mack, — At 8 o'clock I begun a peaceful blockade iv this town. Ye can see th' pieces ivrywhere. I hope ye're injyin' th' same gr-reat blessin'. So no more at prisint. Fr'm ye'ers thruly, George Dooley.' He ain't that kind. 'Tis a nice day, an' he's there smokin' a good tin-cint see-gar, an' throwin' dice f'r th' dhrinks. He don't care whether we know what he's done or not. I'll bet ye, whin we come to find out about him, we'll hear he's ilicted himself king iv th' F'lip-ine Islands. Dooley th' Wanst. He'll be settin' up there undher a pa'm-three with naygurs fannin' him an' a dhrop iv licker in th' hollow iv his ar-rm, an' hootchy-kootchy girls dancin' befure him, an' ivry tin or twinty minyits some wan bringin' a prisoner in. 'Who's this?' says King Dooley. 'A Spanish gin'ral,' says th' copper. 'Give him a typewriter an' set him to wurruk,' says th' king. 'On with th' dance,' he says. An' afther awhile, whin he gits tired iv th' game, he'll write home an' say he's got the islands; an' he'll tur-rn thim over to th' gover'mint an' go back to his ship, an' Mark Hanna'll organize th' F'lip-ine Islands Jute an' Cider Comp'ny, an' th' rivolutchinists'll wish they hadn't. That's what'll happen. Mark me wurrud."

MODERN EXPLOSIVES

"If iver I wanted to go to war," said Mr. Dooley, "an' I niver did, th' desire has passed fr'm me iv late. Ivry time I read iv th' desthructive power iv modhern explosives col' chills chase each other up an' down me spine."

"What's this here stuff they calls lyddite?" Mr. Hennessy asked.

"Well, 'tis th' divvle's own med'cine," said Mr. Dooley. "Compared with lyddite joynt powdher is Mrs. Winslow's soothin' surup, an' ye cud lave th' childher play base-ball with a can iv dinnymite. 'Tis as sthrong as Gin'ral Crownjoy's camp th' day iv th' surrinder an' almost as sthrong as th' pollytics iv Montana. Th' men that handles it is cased in six inch armor an' played on be a hose iv ice wather. Th' gun that shoots it is always blown up be th' discharge. Whin this deadly missile flies through th' air, th' threes ar-re withered an' th' little bur-rds falls dead fr'm th' sky, fishes is kilt in th' rivers, an' th' tillyphone wires won't wurruk. Th' keen eyed British gunners an' corryspondints watches it in its hellish course an' tur-rn their faces as it falls into th' Boer trench. An' oh! th' sickly green fumes it gives off, jus' like pizen f'r potato bugs! There is a thremenjous explosion. Th' earth is thrown up f'r miles. Horses, men an' gun carredges ar-re landed in th' British camp whole. Th' sun is obscured be Boer whiskers turned green. Th' heart iv th' corryspondint is made sick be th' sight, an' be th' thought iv th' fearful carnage wrought be this dhread desthroyer in th' ranks iv th' brave but misguided Dutchmen. Th' nex' day deserters fr'm th' Boer ranks reports that they have fled fr'm th' camp, needin' a dhrink an' onable to stand th' scenes iv horror. They announce that th' whole Boer ar-rmy is as green as wall paper, an' the' Irish brigade has sthruck because ye can't tell their flag fr'm th' flag iv th' r-rest iv th' Dutch. The' Fr-rinch gin'ral in command iv th' Swedish corps lost his complexion an' has been sint to th' hospital, an' Mrs. Gin'ral Crownjoy's washin' that was hangin' on th' line whin th' bombardmint comminced is a total wreck which no amount iv bluin' will save. Th' deserters also report that manny iv th' Boers ar-re outspannin', trekkin', loogerin', kopjein' an' veldtin' home to be dyed, f'r 'tis not known whether lyddite is a fast color or will come out in th' wash.

"In spite iv their heavy losses th' Boers kept up a fierce fire.

They had no lyddite, but with their other divvlish modhern explosives they wrought thremenjous damage. F'r some hours
shells burst with turr'ble precision in th' British camp. Wan
man who was good at figures counted as manny as forty-two
thousan' eight hundhred an' sivin burstin' within a radyus iv
wan fut. Ye can imagine th' hor-rible carnage. Another Irish
rig'mint has disappeardead, th' Twelve Thousandth an' Eighth,
Dublin Fusiliers. Brave fellows, 'tis suspected they mistook th'
explosion of lyddite f'r a Pathrick's Day procession an' wint
acrost to take a look at it.

"Murdher, but 'tis dhreadful to r-read about. We have to
change all our conciptions iv warfare. Wanst th' field was
r-red, now 'tis a br-right lyddite green. Wanst a man wint out
an' died f'r his counthry, now they sind him out an' lyddite
dyes him. What do I mane? 'Tis a joke I made. I'll not explane
it to ye. Ye wudden't understand it. 'Tis f'r th' eddycated
classes.

"How they're iver goin' to get men to fight afther this I cudden't tell ye. 'Twas bad enough in th' ol' days whin all that
happened to a sojer was bein' pinithrated be a large r-round
gob iv solder or stuck up on th' end iv a baynit be a careless
inimy. But now-a-days, they have th' bullet that whin it enthers
ye tur-rns ar-round like th' screw iv a propeller, an' another
wan that ye might say goes in be a key-hole an' comes out
through a window, an' another that has a time fuse in it an' it
doesn't come out at all but stays in ye, an' mebbe twenty years
afther, whin ye've f'rgot all about it an' ar-re settin' at home
with ye'er fam'ly, bang! away it goes an' ye with it, carryin' off
half iv th' roof. Thin they have guns as long as fr'm here to th'
rollin' mills that fires shells as big as a thrunk. Th' shells are
loaded like a docthor's bag an' have all kinds iv things in thim
that won't do a bit iv good to man or beast. If a sojer has a
weak back there's something in th' shell that removes a weak
back; if his head throubles him, he can lose it; if th' odher iv
vilets is distasteful to him th' shell smothers him in vilet
powdher. They have guns that anny boy or girl who knows th'

typewriter can wurruk, an' they have other guns on th' music box plan, that ye wind up an' go away an' lave, an' they annoy anny wan that comes along. They have guns that bounces up out iv a hole in th' groun', fires a millyon shells a minyit an' dhrops back f'r another load. They have guns that fire dinnymite an' guns that fire th' hateful, sickly green lyddite that makes th' inimy look like fiat money, an' guns that fire canned beef f'r th' inimy an' distimper powdher for th' inimy's horses. An' they have some guns that shoot straight."

"Well, thin," Mr. Hennessy grumbled, "its a wondher to me that with all thim things they ain't more people kilt. Sure, Gin'ral Grant lost more men in wan day thin th' British have lost in four months, an' all he had to keep tab on was ol' fashioned bullets an' big, bouncin' iron balls."

"Thrue," said Mr. Dooley. "I don't know th' reason, but it mus' be that th' betther gun a man has th' more he thrusts th' gun an' th' less he thrusts himsilf. He stays away an' shoots. He says to himsilf, he says: 'They'se nawthin' f'r me to do,' he says, 'but load up me little lyddite cannon with th' green goods,' he says, 'an' set here at the organ,' he says, 'pull out th' stops an' paint th' town iv Pretoria green,' he says. 'But,' he says, 'on sicond thought, suppose th' inimy shud hand it back to me,' he says. 'Twud be oncomfortable,' he says. 'So,' he says, 'I'll jus' move me music back a mile,' he says, 'an' peg away, an' th' longest gun takes th' persimmons,' he says. 'Tis this way: If ye an' I fall out an' take rifles to each other, 'tis tin to wan nayether iv us get clost enough to hit. If we take pistols th' odds is rayjooced. If we take swords I may get a hack at ye, but if we take a half-nelson lock 'tis even money I have ye'er back broke befure th' polis comes.

"I can see in me mind th' day whin explosives'll be so explosive an' guns'll shoot so far that on'y th' folks that stay at home'll be kilt, an' life insurance agents'll be advisin' people to go into th' ar-rmy. I can so. 'Tis thrue what Hogan says about it."

"What's that?" Mr. Hennessy asked.

"Th' nation," said Mr. Dooley, "that fights with a couplin' pin extinds its bordhers at th' cost iv th' nation that fights with a clothes pole."

A BOOK REVIEW

Well sir," said Mr. Dooley, "I jus' got hold iv a book, Hinnissy, that suits me up to th' handle, a gran' book, th' grandest iver seen. Ye know I'm not much throubled be lithrachoor, havin' manny worries iv me own, but I'm not prejudiced again' books. I am not. Whin a rale good book comes along I'm as quick as anny wan to say it isn't so bad, an' this here book is fine. I tell ye 'tis fine."

"What is it?" Mr. Hennessy asked languidly.

"Tis 'Th' Biography iv a Hero be Wan who Knows.' 'Tis 'Th' Darin' Exploits iv a Brave Man be an Actual Eye Witness.' 'Tis 'Th' Account iv th' Desthruction iv Spanish Power in th' Ant Hills,' as it fell fr'm th' lips iv Tiddy Rosenfelt an' was took down be his own hands. Ye see 'twas this way, Hinnissy, as I r-read th' book. Whin Tiddy was blowed up in th' harbor iv Havana he instantly con-cluded they must be war. He debated th' question long an' earnestly an' fin'lly passed a jint resolution declarin' war. So far so good. But there was no wan to carry it on. What shud he do? I will lave th' janial author tell th' story in his own wurruds.

" 'Th' sicrety iv war had offered me,' he says, 'th' command of a rig'mint,' he says, 'but I cud not consint to remain in Tampa while perhaps less audacious heroes was at th' front,' he says. 'Besides,' he says, 'I felt I was incompetent f'r to command a rig'mint raised be another,' he says. 'I detarmined to raise wan iv me own,' he says. 'I selected fr'm me acquaintances in th' West,' he says, 'men that had thravelled with me acrost th' desert an' th' storm-wreathed mountain,' he says, 'sharin' me burdens an' at times confrontin' perils almost as gr-reat as anny that beset me path,' he says. 'Together we had faced th' turrors iv th' large but vilent West,' he says, 'an' these brave men had seen me with me trusty rifle shootin' down th' buffalo, th' elk, th' moose, th' grizzly bear, th' mountain goat,' he says, 'th' silver man, an' other ferocious beasts iv thim parts,' he says. 'An' they niver flinched,' he says. 'In a few days I had thim perfectly tamed,' he says, 'an' ready to go annywhere I led,' he says. 'On th' thransport goi'n to Cubia,' he says, 'I wud stand beside wan iv these r-rough men threatin' him as a akel, which he was in ivrything but birth, education, rank an' courage, an' together we wud look up at th' admirable stars iv that tolerable southern sky an' quote th' bible fr'm Walt Whitman,' he says. 'Honest, loyal, thrue-hearted la-ads, how kind I was to thim,' he says.

" 'We had no sooner landed in Cubia than it become nicessry f'r me to take command iv th' ar-rmy which I did at wanst. A number of days was spint be me in reconnoitring, attinded on'y be me brave an' fluent body guard, Richard Harding Davis. I discovered that th' inimy was heavily inthrenched on th' top iv San Joon hill immejiately in front iv me. At this time it become apparent that I was handicapped be th' prisence iv th' ar-rmy,' he says. 'Wan day whin I was about to charge a block house sturdily definded be an ar-rmy corps undher Gin'ral Tamale, th' brave Castile that I aftherwards killed with a small ink-eraser that I always carry, I r-ran into th' entire military force iv th' United States lying on its stomach. 'If ye won't fight,' says I, 'let me go through,' I says. 'Who ar-re ye?' says they. 'Colonel Rosenfelt,' says I. 'Oh, excuse me,' says the gin-ral in command (if me mimry serves me thrue it was Miles) r-risin' to his knees an' salutin'. This showed me 'twud be impossible f'r to carry th' war to a successful con-clusion unless I was free, so I sint th' ar-rmy home an' attackted San Joon hill. Ar-rmed on'y with a small thirty-two which I used in th' West to shoot th' fleet prairie dog, I climbed that precipitous ascent in th' face iv th' most gallin' fire I iver knew or heerd iv. But I had a few r-rounds iv gall mesilf an' what cared I? I dashed madly on cheerin' as I wint. Th' Spanish throops was dhrawn up in a long line in th' formation known among military men as a long line. I fired at th' man nearest to me an' I knew be th' expression iv his face that th' trusty bullet wint home. It passed through his frame, he fell, an' wan little home in far-off Catalonia was made happy be th' thought that their riprisintative had been kilt be th' future governor iv New York. Th' bullet sped on its mad flight an' passed through th' intire line fin'lly imbeddin' itself in th' abdomen iv th' Ar-rch-bishop iv Santiago eight miles away. This ended th' war.'

" 'They has been some discussion as to who was th' first man to r-reach th' summit iv San Juon hill. I will not attempt to dispute th' merits iv th' manny gallant sojers, statesmen, corryspondints an' kinetoscope men who claim th' distinction. They ar-re all brave men an' if they wish to wear my laurels they may. I have so manny annyhow that it keeps me broke havin' thim blocked an' irned. But I will say f'r th' binifit iv Posterity that I was th' on'y man I see. An' I had a tillyscope.' "

"I have thried, Hinnissy," Mr. Dooley continued, "to give you a fair idee iv th' contints iv this remarkable book, but what I've tol' ye is on'y want Hogan calls an outline iv th' principal pints. Ye'll have to r-read th' book ye'ersilf to get a thrue conciption. I haven't time f'r to tell ye th' wurruk Tiddy did in armin' an' equippin' himself, how he fed himsilf, how he steadied himsilf in battle an' encouraged himsilf with a few well-chosen wurruds whin th' sky was darkest. Ye'll have to take a squint into th' book ye'ersilf to l'arn thim things."

"I won't do it," said Mr. Hennessy. "I think Tiddy Rosenfelt is all r-right an' if he wants to blow his hor-rn lave him do it."

"Thrue f'r ye," said Mr. Dooley, "an' if his valliant deeds didn't get into this book 'twud be a long time befure they appeared in Shafter's histhry iv th' war. No man that bears a gredge again' himsilf 'ill ever be governor iv a state. An' if Tiddy done it all he ought to say so an' relieve th' suspinse. But if I was him I'd call th' book 'Alone in Cubia.' "

EXPANSION

"Whin we plant what Hogan calls th' starry banner iv Freedom in th' Ph'lip-peens," said Mr. Dooley, "an' give th' sacred blessin' iv liberty to the poor, down-trodden people iv thim unfortunate isles,—dam thim!—we'll larn thim a lesson."

"Sure," said Mr. Hennessy, sadly, "we have a thing or two to larn oursilves."

"But it isn't f'r thim to larn us," said Mr. Dooley. "'Tis not f'r thim wretched an' degraded crathers, without a mind or a shirt iv their own, f'r to give lessons in politeness an' liberty to a nation that mannyfacthers more dhressed beef than anny other imperyal nation in th' wurruld. We say to thim: 'Naygurs,' we say, 'poor, dissolute, uncovered wretches,' says we, 'whin th' crool hand iv Spain forged man'cles f'r ye'er limbs, as Hogan says, who was it crossed th' say an' sthruck off th' comealongs? We did,—by dad, we did. An' now, ye mis'rable, childish-minded apes, we propose f'r to larn ye th' uses iv liberty. In ivry city in this unfair land we will erect school-houses an' packin' houses an' houses iv correction; an' we'll larn ye our language, because 'tis aisier to larn ye ours than to larn oursilves yours. An' we'll give ye clothes, if ye pay f'r thim; an', if ye don't, ye can go without. An', whin ye're hungry, ye can go to th' morgue—we mane th' resth'rant—an' ate a good square meal iv ar-rmy beef. An' we'll sind th' gr-reat Gin'ral Eagan over f'r to larn ye etiquette, an' Andhrew Carnegie to larn ye pathriteism with blow-holes into it, an' Gin'ral Alger to larn ye to hould onto a job; an', whin ye've become edycated an' have all th' blessin's iv civilization that we don't want, that 'll count ye one. We can't give ye anny votes, because we haven't more thin enough to go round now; but we'll threat ye th' way a father shud threat his childher if we have to break ivry bone in ye'er bodies. So come to our ar-rms,' says we.

"But, glory be, 'tis more like a rasslin' match than a father's embrace. Up gets this little monkey iv an' Aggynaldoo, an' says he, 'Not for us,' he says. 'We thank ye kindly; but we believe,' he says, 'in pathronizin' home industhries,' he says. 'An,' he says, 'I have on hand,' he says, 'an' f'r sale,' he says, 'a very superyor brand iv home-made liberty, like ye'er mother used to make,' he says. ''Tis a long way fr'm ye'er plant to here,' he says, 'an' be th' time a cargo iv liberty,' he says, 'got out here an' was handled be th' middlemen,' he says, 'it might spoil,' he says. 'We don't want anny col' storage or embalmed liberty,' he says. 'What we want an' what th' ol' reliable house iv Aggynaldoo,' he says, 'supplies to th' thrade,' he says, 'is fr-esh liberty r-right off th' far-rm,' he says. 'I can't do annything with ye'er proposition,' he says. 'I can't give up,' he says, 'th' rights f'r which f'r five years I've fought an' bled ivry wan I cud reach,' he says. 'Onless,' he says, 'ye'd feel like buyin' out th' whole business,' he says. 'I'm a pathrite,' he says; 'but I'm no bigot,' he says.

"An' there it stands, Hinnissy, with th' indulgent parent kneelin' on th' stomach iv his adopted child, while a dillyga-tion fr'm Boston bastes him with an umbrella. There it stands, an' how will it come out I dinnaw. I'm not much iv an expan-sionist mesilf. F'r th' las' tin years I've been thryin' to decide whether 'twud be good policy an' thrue to me thraditions to make this here bar two or three feet longer, an manny's th' night I've laid awake tryin' to puzzle it out. But I don't know what to do with th' Ph'lippeens anny more than I did las' summer, befure I heerd tell iv thim. We can't give thim to an-ny wan without makin' th' wan that gets thim feel th' way Doherty felt to Clancy whin Clancy med a frindly call an' give Doherty's childher th' measles. We can't sell thim, we can't ate thim, an' we can't throw thim into th' alley whin no wan is lookin'. An' 'twud be a disgrace f'r to lave befure we've pounded these frindless an' ongrateful people into in-sinsibility. So I suppose, Hinnissy, we'll have to stay an' do th' best we can, an' lave Andhrew Carnegie secede fr'm th' Union. They'se wan consolation; an' that is, if th' American people can govern thimsilves, they can govern annything that walks."

"An' what 'd ye do with Aggy — what-d'ye-call-him?" asked Mr. Hennessy.

"Well," Mr. Dooley replied, with brightening eyes, "I know what they'd do with him in this ward. They'd give that pathrite what he asks, an' thin they'd throw him down an' take it away fr'm him."

EUROPEAN INTERVENTION

"Th' question befure th' house is," said Mr. Dooley, "which wan iv th' Euro-peen powers done mos' f'r us in th' Spanish war."

"I thought they were all again' us," said Mr. Hennessy.

"So did I," said Mr. Dooley, "but I done thim an injustice. I was crool to thim crowned heads. If it hadn't been f'r some wan power, an' I can't make out which it was, th' Cubians to-day wud be opprissed be th' Casteel instead iv th' Beet Sugar Thrust an' th' Filipinos'd be shot be Mausers instead iv Krag-Jorgensens. Some wan power sthretched out its hand an' said, 'No. No,' it said, 'thus far but no farther. We will not permit this misguided but warrum-hearted little people to be crushed be th' ruffyan power iv Spain,' it said. 'Niver,' it said, 'shall histhry record that th' United States iv America, nestlin' there in its cosy raypublic fr'm th' Atlantic to th' Passyfic, was desthroyed an' th' hurtage iv liberty that they robbed fr'm us wasted because we did not give thim support," it says. An' so whin th' future looked darkest, whin we didn't know whether th' war wud last eight or be prolonged f'r tin weary, thragic minyits, whin it seemed as though th' Spanish fleet wud not sink unless shot at, some kindly power was silently comfortin' us an' sayin' to itself: 'I do so hope they'll win, if they can.' But I don't know which wan it was.

"At first I thought it was England. Whiniver ye hear iv anny counthry helpin' us, ye think it is England. That's because England has helped us so much in th' past. Says Lord Cranburne in reply to a question in th' House iv Commons: 'I am reluctantly foorced be mesilf to blushin'ly admit that but f'r us, people on their way to China to-day wud be gettin' up an' lookin' over th' side iv th' ship an' sayin', "This is where America used to be." Whin war was first discussed, mesilf an' th' rest iv th' fam'ly met an' decided that unless prompt action was took, our cousins an' invistmints acrost th' sea wud be damaged beyond repair, so we cabled our ambassadure to go at wanst to th' White House an' inform th' prisidint that we wud regard th' war as a crool blot on civilization an' an offinse to th' intillygince iv mankind. I am glad to say our inthervintion was iffycacious. War was immeedjately declared. I will not tell ye how high our hearts beat as we r'read th' news fr'm day to day. Ye know. I will on'y say that we insthructed our ambassadure to do ivrything in his power to help our kinsmen an' he faithfully ixicuted his ordhers. He practically lived at th' White House durin' th' thryin' peeryod, an' his advice to th' prisidint such as: "If ye go on with this binnyficint war th' United Powers will knock ye'er head off," or "I think I can secure fav'rable terms fr'm th' Powers if ye will abdicate in favor iv a riprisintative iv th' house iv Bourbon an' cede New England to Spain," done more thin annything else to put heart into th' American foorces. I will add that durin' this time we was approached be an ambassadure iv wan iv th' powers who ast us to inthervene. I will not say which power it was, excipt that it was Austhrya-Hungary an' I'm previnted be th' obligations iv me office fr'm mintionin' what powers was behind th' move beyond hintin' that they was as follows: Germany, France, Rooshya, It'ly, China, Turkey, Monaco, San Marino, Boolgahrya, Montinaygro, Booloochistan an' Pershya. Pah's reply to th' ambassadure was: "I will do all I can" as he kicked him down stairs. It ill becomes me to say what else we done f'r that home iv freedom — an' hiven knows I wisht it'd stay there an' not be wandherin' over th' face iv th' wurruld — but I'm not proud iv me looks an' I will remark that Tiddy Rosenfelt was capably directed be th' iditors iv England, thim hearts iv oak, that th' American navy was advised be our mos' inargetic corryspondints an' that, to make th' raysult certain, we limit a few British gin'rals to th' Spanish. Cud frindship go farther? As they say in America: "I reckon, be gosh, not." '

"Well, whin I read this speech I was prepared to hang th' medal f'r savin' life on th' breasts iv th' hands acrost th' sea where there's always plinty iv hoods f'r medals. But th' nex' day, I picks up th' pa-aper an' sees that 'twas not England done it but Germany. Yes, sir, 'twas Germany. Germany was our on'y frind. They was a time whin it looked as though she was goin' to shoot at us to keep us fr'm th' consequences iv our rash act. They'se nawthin' Germany wudden't do for or to a frind. Yes, it was Germany. But it was France, too. La Belle France was there with a wurrud iv encouragemint an' a glance iv affection out iv her dark eyes that kep' growin' darker as th' war proceeded. An' it was Rooshya. Whin th' Czar heerd iv th' war, th' first thing he said was: 'I'm so sorry. Who is th' United States?' An' 'twas It'ly an' Booloochistan an' Boolgahrya an' even Spain. Spain was our frind till th' war was over. Thin she rounded on us an' sold us th' Ph'lippines.

"They was all our frinds an' yet on'y wan iv thim was our frind. How d'ye make it out, Hinnissy? Hogan has a sayin' that onaisy lies th' head that wears a crown, but it seems to be as aisy f'r some iv thim as f'r th' mos' dimmycratic American. But whoiver it was that saved us I'm thankful to thim. It won't do f'r ye to look at th' map an' say that th' pow'rful proctin' na-tion wud be hardly big enough f'r a watch charm f'r a man f'rm Texas, or that Europeen assistance f'r America is about as useful as a crutch f'r a foot-runner. But f'r th' inthervention iv our unknown frind, we'd've been annihilated. Th' powers wud've got together an' they wud've sint over a fleet that wud've been turrble if it didn't blow up an' th' crews didn't get sea-sick. They wud've sint an irresistible ar-rmy; an' fin'ly if all else failed, they wud rayfuse food. That's goin' to be th' unsix-picted blow iv anny war that th' parishes iv Europe wages again' us. They will decline to eat. They will turn back our wheat an' pork an' short rib sides. They'll starve us out. If left to their own resoorces, Europe cud outstarve America in a month."

"I'm not afraid iv thim," said Mr. Hennessy. "Whin I was a young man, I cud take a runnin' jump acrost Germany or France, an' as f'r England we'd hardly thrip over it in th' dark."

"Perhaps ye're right," said Mr. Dooley. "But if all thim gr-reat powers, as they say thimsilves, was f'r to attack us, d'ye know what I'd do? I'll tell ye. I'd blockade Armour an' Comp'ny an' th' wheat ilivators iv Minnysoty. F'r, Hinnissy, I tell ye, th' hand that rocks th' scales in th' grocery store, is th' hand that rules th' wurruld."

ON THE CHANGING STYLES
IN WARFARE

"War," said Mr. Dooley, "is like sthrawberry shortcake."

"What's got into ye'er head?" Mr. Hennessy demanded. "What d'ye mane by th' likes o' that?"

"I mane," said Mr. Dooley, "it ain't what it was whin I was a young fellow an' in th' ar-rmy. Wanst," continued Mr.Dooley, "there were rules f'r th' game. They were laid down an' printed in a book an' ye abided be thim. They were like th' Markess iv Queensberry rules, on'y there wasn't anny refree to enfoorce thim. Nations wint to war very politely, bowin' an' scrapin' to each other. They made a formal declara-tion, which read like an invitation to a waltz. 'Twas: 'Heinrich, may I have th' honor iv takin' a wallop at ye?' 'With pleasure, Franswaw.' Thin they shook hands an' wint at each other with th' best feelin' in the wurruld. 'Twas: 'Did I hit ye low that time, Hank? So sorry.' Or, 'I didn't mane to fire on that flag iv thruce. My mistake.' 'Oh, niver mind, ol' dear. We'll call it a let an' have it over.' Th' pastime wint on till th' money give out, an' thin th' conkerer an' th' conkered were th' best iv frinds an' wint home arm in arm.

"Why, they ain't aven a declaration iv war in these days, or if there is wan, it's put out a month or two afther th' war begins durin' a lull in th' fightin'. Th' first annywan knows that their bosses has fallen out is whin a dinnymite bomb comes down th' chimbley. Sure, I don't see why these here governmints don't go further, Hinnissy, an' take advantage iv all th wondherful developmints iv science as well as a few iv thim. There are lots iv things in th' back iv th' dhrug store they haven't thried so far. I don't believe there'll iver be peace in this fractious wurruld. But th' time may come whin war as it is to-day will be abolished. Whin two nations become fretful with each other they won't fly at each other's throats. They'll continue frindly but they'll call a convintion iv chemists, docks, an' dope experts, an' th' war will commence."

THE WAR EXPERT

Mr. Dooley was reading the war news,—not our war news, but the war news we are interested in—when Mr. Hennessy interrupted him to ask "What's a war expert?"

"A war expert," said Mr. Dooley, "is a man ye niver heerd iv befure. If ye can think iv annywan whose face is onfamilyar to ye an' ye don't raymimber his name, an' he's got a job on a pa-aper ye didn't know was published, he's a war expert. 'Tis a har-rd office to fill. Whin a war begins th' timptation is sthrong f'r ivry man to grab hold iv a gun an go to the fr-ront. But th' war expert has to subjoo his cravin' f'r blood. He says to himsilf 'Lave others seek th' luxuries iv life in camp,' he says. 'F'r thim th' boat races acrost th' Tugela, th' romp over the kopje, an' th' game iv laager, laager who's got th' laager?" he says. 'I will stand be me counthry,' he says, 'close,' he says. 'If it falls,' he says, 'it will fall on me,' he says. An' he buys himsilf a map made be a fortune teller in a dhream, a box iv pencils an' a field glass, an' goes an' looks f'r a job as a war expert. Says th' editor iv th' paaper: 'I don't know ye. Ye must be a war expert,' he says. 'I am,' says th' la-ad. 'Durin' th' Spanish-American War, I held a good job as a dhramatic critic in Dedham, Matsachoosets,' he says. 'Whin the bullets flew thickest in th'Soodan I was spoortin' editor iv th' Christyan Advocate,' he says. 'I passed through th' Franco-Prooshan War an' held me place, an' whin th' Turks an' Rooshans was at each other's throats, I used to lay out th' campaign ivry day on a checker board,' he says. 'War,' he says, has no turrors f'r me,' he says. 'Ye're th' man f'r th' money,' says th' editor. An' he gets th' job.

"Thin th' war breaks out in earnest. No matther how manny is kilt, annything that happens befure th' war expert gets to wurruk is on'y what we might call a prelimin'ry skirmish. He sets down an' bites th' end iv his pencil an' looks acrost th' sthreet an' watches a man paintin' a sign. Whin th' man gets through he goes to th' window an' waits to see whether th' polisman that wint into th' saloon is afther a dhrink or sarvin' a warrant. If he comes r-ight out 'tis a warrant. Thin he sets back in a chair an figures out that th' pitchers on th' wall paaper ar-re all alike ivry third row., Whin his mind is thurly tuned up be these inthricate problems, he dashes to his desk an' writes what you an' I read th' nex' day in th' paapers.

"Sure," said Mr. Hennessy, "tis not thim that does th' fightin'. Th' la-ads with th' guns has that job."

"Well," said Mr. Dooley, "they'se two kinds iv fightin'. Th' experts wants th' ar-rmy to get into Pretoria dead or alive, an' th' sojers wants to get in alive. I'm no military expert, Hinnissy. I'm too well known. But I have me own opinyon on th' war. All this talk about th' rapid fire gun an' modhren methods iv warfare makes me wondher. They'se not so much diff'rence between war now an' war whin I was a kid, as they let on. Th' gun that shoots ye best fr'm a distance don't shoot ye so well close to. A pile iv mud is a pile iv mud now just th' same as it was whin Gin'ral Grant was pokin' ar-round. If th' British can get over th' mud pile they win th' fight. If they can't they're done. That's all they'se to it. Mos' men, sthrongest backs, bet eyes an' th' ownership iv th' mud piles. That's war, Hinnissy. Th' British have th' men. They're shy iv backs, eyes an' mud piles, an' they will be until they larn that sheep-herdin' an' gin'ralship ar-re diff'rent things, an' fill up their ar-rmy with men that ar-re not fightin' f'r money or glory, but because they want to get home to their wives alive."

"Ye talk like an' ol book," said Mr. Hennessy, in disgust. "Ye with ye-re maundhrin' ar-re no betther thin them experts la-ads."

"Well annyhow," said Mr. Dooley thoughtfully, "th' expert is sarvin' a useful purpose. Th' pa-apers says th' rapid fire gun'll make war in th' future impossible. I don't think that, but I know th' expert will."

THE HAGUE CONFERENCE

"I see," said Mr. Hennessy, "we're goin' to sind th' navy to th' Passyfic."

"I can't tell," said Mr. Dooley, "whether th' navy is goin' to spend th' rest iv its days protectin' our possessions in th' Oryent or whether it is to remain in th' neighborhood iv Barnstable makin' th' glaziers iv New England rich beyond th' dhreans iv New England avarice, which ar-re hopeful dhreams. Th' Cabinet is divided, th' Sicrety iv th' Navy is divided, th' Prisidint is divided an' th' press is divided. Wan great iditor, fr'm his post iv danger in Paris, has ordhered th' navy to report at San Francisco at four eight next Thursday. Another great iditor livin' in Germany has warned it that it will do so at its peril. Nawthin' is so fine as to see a great modhern journalist unbend fr'm his mighty task iv selectin' fr'm a bunch iv phot-tygrafts th' prettiest cook iv Flatbush or engineerin' with his great furrowed brain th' Topsy Fizzle compytition to trifle with some light warm-weather subjick like internaytional law or war. But men such as these can do annything.

"But, annyhow, what diff'rence does it make whether th' navy goes to th' Passyfic or not? If it goes at all, it won't be to make war. They've dumped all th' fourteen inch shells into th' sea. Th' ammunition hoists ar-re filled with American beauty roses an' orchids. Th' guns are loaded with confetty. Th' officers dhrink nawthin' sthronger thin vanilla an' sthrawberry mixed. Within th' tars go ashore they hurry at wanst to th' home iv th' Christyan Indeavor Society or throng th' free libries readin' relligious pothry. Me frind Bob Ivans is goin' to conthribute a series iv articles to th' *Ladies' Home Journal* on croshaying. F'r th' Hague peace conference has abolished war, Hinnissy. Ye've seen th' last war ye'll iver see, me boy.

"Th' Hague conference, Hinnissy, was got up be th' Czar iv Rooshya just befure he moved his army again th' Japs. It was a quiet day at Saint Pethersburg. Th' Prime Minister had just been blown up with dinnymite, th' Czar's uncle had been shot, an' wan iv his cousins was expirin' fr'm a dose iv proosic acid. All was comparative peace. In th' warrum summer's afthernoon th' Czar felt almost dhrousy as he set in his rile palace an' listened to th' low, monotonous drone iv bombs bein' hurled at th' Probojensky guards, an' picked th' broken glass out iv th' dhrink that'd just been brought to him be an aged servitor who was prisidint iv th' Saint Pethersburg lodge iv Pathriotic Assassins. Th' monarch's mind turned to th' subjick iv war an' he says to himself: 'What a dhreadful thing it is that such a beautiful wurruld shud be marred be thousands iv innocint men bein' sint out to shoot each other f'r no cause whin they might betther stay at home an' wurruk f'r their rile masthers,' he says. 'I will disguise mesilf as a moojik an' go over to th' tillygraft office an' summon a meetin' iv th' Powers,' he says.

"That's how it come about. All th' Powers sint dillygates an' a g-great manny iv th' weaknesses did so too. They met in Holland an' they have been devotin' all their time since to makin' war impossible in th' future. Th' meetin' was opened with an acrimonyous debate over a resolution offered be a dillygate fr'm Paryguay callin' f'r immeejit disarmamint, which is th' same, Hinnissy, as notifyn' th' Powers to turn in their guns to th' man at th' dure. This was carrid be a very heavy majority. Among those that voted in favor iv it were: Paryguay, Uryguay, Switzerland, Chiny, Bilgium, an' San Marino. Opposed were England, France, Rooshya, Germany, Italy, Austhree, Japan, an' the United States.

"This was regarded be all present as a happy auggry. Th' convintion thin discussed a risolution offered be th' Turkish dillygate abolishin' war altogether. This also was carrid, on'y England, France, Rooshya, Germany, Italy, Austhree, Japan, an' th' United States votin' no.

"This made th' way clear f'r th' discussion iv th' larger question iv how future wars shud be conducted in th' best inthrests iv peace. Th' conference considhered th' possibility iv abolishin' th' mushroom bullet which, entherin' th' inteeryor iv th' inimy not much larger thin a marble, soon opens its dain-ty petals an' goes whirlin' through th' allyminthry canal like a pin-wheel. Th' Chinese dillygate said that he regarded this here insthrumint iv peace as highly painful. He had an aunt in Pekin, an estimable lady, unmarried, two hundherd an' fifty years iv age, who received wan without warnin' durin' th' gallant riscue iv Pekin fr'm th' foreign legations a few years ago. He cud speak with feelin' on th' subjick as th' Chinese ar-my did not use these pro-jictyles but were armed with bean-shooters.

"Th' English dillygate opposed th' resolution. 'It is,' says he, 'quite true that these here pellets are in many cases harmful to th' digestion, but I think it wud be goin' too far to suggest that they be abolished ontil their mannyfacther is betther un-dherstud be th' subjick races,' he says. 'I suppose wan iv these bullets might throw a white man off his feed, but we have abundant proof that whin injicted into a black man they gr-reatly improve his moral tone. An' after all, th' improvemint iv th' moral tone is, gintlemen, a far graver matther thin anny mere physical question. We know fr'm expeeryence in South Africa that th' charmin' bullet now undher discussion did much to change conditions in that enlightened an' juicy part iv his Majesty's domains. Th' darky that happened to stop wan was all th' betther f'r it. He retired fr'm labor an' give up his squalid an' bigamious life.' he says. 'I am in favor, howiver, iv restrictin' their use to encounters with races that we properly considher infeeryor,' he says. Th' dillygate fr'm, Sinagambya rose to a question iv privilege. 'State ye'er question iv privilege,' says th' chairman. 'I wud like to have th' windows open,' says th' dillygate fr'm Singambya. 'I feel faint,' he says.

"Th' Hon'rable Joe Choate, dillygate fr'm th' United States, moved that in future wars enlisted men shud not wear earrings. Carrid, on'y Italy votin' no.

"Th' conferecne thin discussed blowin' up th' inimy with dinnymite, poisinin' him, shootin' th' wounded, settin' fire to infants, bilin' prisoners-iv-war in hot lard, an' robbin' graves. Some excitemint was created durin' th' talk be th' dillygate fr'm th' cannybal islands who proposed that prisoners-iv-war be eaten. Th' German dillygate thought that this was carryin' a specyal gift iv wan power too far. It wud give th' cannybal islands a distinct advantage in case iv war, as European sojers were accustomed to horses. Th' English dillygate said that while much cud be said against a practice which personally seemed to him rather unsportsmanlike, still he felt he must reserve th' right iv anny cannybal allies iv Brittanya to go as far as they liked.

"Th' Hon'rable Joe Choate moved that in future wars no military band shud be considered complete without a basedhrum. Carrid.

"Th' entire South American dillygation said that no nation ought to go to war because another nation wanted to put a bill on th' slate. Th' English dillygate was much incensed. 'Why, gintlemen,' says he, 'if ye deprived us iv th' right to collect debts be killin' th' debtor ye wud take away fr'm war its entire moral purpose. I must ask ye again to cease thinkin' on this subjick in a gross mateeryal way an' considher th' moral side alone,' he says. Th' conference was much moved be this pathetic speech, th' dillygate fr'm France wept softly into his hankerchef, an' th' dillygate fr'm Germany wint over an' focibly took an open-face goold watch fr'm th' dillygate fr'm Vinzwala.

"Th' Hon'rable Joe Choate moved that in all future wars horses shud be fed with hay wheriver possible. Carrid. . . ."

THE WAR GAME

"What's this here war game I've been readin' about?" asked Mr. Hennessy.

"It's kind iv a blind man's buff," said Mr. Dooley. "It's a thrile iv cunnin' an' darin' between th' army an' th' navy. Be manes iv it we larn whether th' inimy cud sneak into Boston afther dark without annywan seein' thim an' anchor in Boston common. Ye an' I know diff'rent, Hinnissy. We know how manny people are in th' sthreets afther dark. But th' navy don't know an' th' army don't know. Their idee is that a German fleet might gumshoe up th' harbor in th' dark iv th' moon an' whin people turned out f'r their mornin' dhram, there wud be th' Impror Willum atin' his breakfast iv Hungayrian Goolash an' noodle soup on th' steps iv th' State House iv Matsachoosetts. But it's a gran' game. I'd like to play it mesilf. It's as noisy as forty-fives between Connock men an' as harmless as a steeryopticon letcher. If war an' th' war game was th' same thing, I'd be an admiral, at laste, be this time with me face gashed an' seamed be raspberry jam an' me clothes stained with English breakfast tea.

"Th' navy chose to be th' inimy an' 'twas th' jooty iv th' navy to divastate th' New England coast. On th' other hand, th' business iv th' army was to catch th' navy at its neefaryous wurruk an' tag it befure it cud get its fingers crost. To play th' game well, th' navy must act as much like an inimy as it can an' th' army must pretind to be jus' as cross at th' navy as it is whin they are both on th' same side. Frindship ceases whin they set in.

"It's a hard game to follow if ye're lookin' on an' puttin' up th' money as I am. I've been readin' about it in th' pa-apers an' I can't make out now whether th' inimy is lootin' th' breweries iv Conneticut or whether th' definders iv our hearths has

blown thim up in th' harbor iv New London. 'I have th' honor
to rayport,' says Admiral Higginson, 'that I have this day
desthroyed all th' forts on th' New England coast, put th'
definders to rout with gr-reat slaughter an' kilt with me own
hands Gin'ral McArthur th' Commander iv th' lan' foorces—a
brave man but no match f'r ye'ers thruly. His las' wurruds to
me was "Higginson, ye done well!" I rayturned him his soord
with th' wurruds: "Gin'ral, between two brave men there can
be no hard feelin's." Th' battle in which me gallant foe met his
fate was th' con-clusion iv wan iv th' mos' successful socyal an'
naval campaigns in th' histhry iv our counthry. I have th'
honor to inform ye that promptly on th' declaration iv war, I
give an afthernoon tea to th' Duchess iv Marlborough. Th'
forts at Newport attimpted to reply, but was unable to scoor
more thin three or four westhern millyonaires an' soon suc-
cumbed to th' inivitable. I thin move up th' Sound an' fell
upon Gin'ral McArthur whin he wasn't lookin'. Befure he cud
load his guns, we poored a perfect blankety-blank hell iv blank
catridges on him. He made a spirited reply but t'was useless.
We outfought him be nearly fifty thousan' dollars worth iv
powdher. In th' mist iv th' flame an' smoke, I discerned th'
caitiff foe standin' on top iv a fort directin' his wav'rin' foorces.
"Hi-spy, Gin'ral McArthur," says I in claryon tones, an' th'
battle was over to all intints an' purposes. I have to ispicially
commind Cap'n McWhallop who, findin' his boat caught between th' fires an' th' inimy, called out: "Lay me down, boys,
an' save th' ship. I'm full iv marmylade." Th' ladies aboord
was perfectly delighted with th' valor an' hospitality iv our
men. To-night we completed our wurruk be givin' a dinner an'
hop on boord th' flagship. Among those presint was—' an' so
on.

"That's what th' gallant Higginson says. But listen to what
th' akelly gallant McArthur says: 'I have th' honor to rayport
that mesilf an' me gallant men, but largely if I do say it that
shudden't, mesilf, crushed an' annihilated th' inimy's fleet at
high noon to-day. Las' night at th' first round iv jacks, or mid-

night, as civilyans wud say, we rayceived a rayport fr'm our vigylant scouts that th' inimy were not at Bar Harbor, Pookypsie, Keokuk, Johannesboorg or Council Bluffs. But where were they? That was th' question. An idee struck me. War is as much a matther iv ingenooty an' thought as iv fire an' slaughter. I sint out f'r an avenin' paper an' as I suspicted, it announced that th' craven foe was about two blocks away. At that very moment, th' sthrains iv th' "Bloo Danoob" was wafted to me ears an' me suspicions was confirmed. On such occasions there is no sleep f'r th' modhren sojer. Napolyon wud've gone to bed but slumber niver crost me tired eyelids. 'Twas six o'clock whin we cashed in an' each wint to th' mournful jooties iv th' day, silently but with a heart full iv courage. At high noon, we fell upon th' inimy an' poored out about eighty-five thousan' dollars worth iv near-slaughter on him. His guns was choked with cotillyon favors an' he did not reply at wanst, but whin he did, th' scene was thruly awful. Th' sky was blackened be th' smoke iv smokelss powdher an' th' air was full iv cotton waste fr'm th' fell injines iv desthruction. A breeze fr'm shore carried out to me ears th' wails iv th' wounded tax payers. At twelve fifteen, I descried th' bloodthirsty Higginson—an' a good fellow Caleb is at that—on th' roof iv his boat. "Hi-spy," says he. "Hi-spy ye'er gran'mother," says I. "I've had me eye on ye f'r fifteen minyits an' ye're a dead man as I can prove be witnesses," I says. An' he fell off th' roof. I was sorry to take his life but war knows no mercy. He was a brave man but foolhardy. He ought niver to've gone again' me. He might've licked Cervera but he cudden't lick me. We captured all th' men-iv-war, desthroyed most iv th' cruisers an' ar-re now usin' th' flag-ship f'r a run-about. Th' counthry is safe, thanks to a vigylant an' sleepless army. I will go up to New York tomorrah to be measured f'r th' prisintation soord."

"There it is, Hinnissy. Who won? I don't know. I can't tell at this minyit whether I ought to be undher th' bed larnin' German f'r th' time whin a Prooshyan sojer'll poke me out with his saber, or down at Finucane's hall callin' a meetin' to thank th' definders iv th' fireside. Nobody knows. It's a quare game, f'r they tell me afther th' battles has been fought an' th' kilt has gone back to holeystonin' th' deck an' th' smoke fr'm th' chafin' dish has cleared away, th' decision is up to a good figurer at Wash'nton. It depinds on him whether we ar-re a free people or whether we wear th' yoke iv sarvichood an' bad German hats f'r all time. He's th' officyal scoorer an' what Higginson thinks was a base hit, he calls a foul an' what McArthur calls an accipted chanst is an error. Afther th' gallant lads in blue an' gold has got through, a wathry-eyed clerk named Perkins H. Something-or-other, sets down an' figures out th' victhry. Th' man behind th' fountain pen is th' boy. It's up to him whether th' stars an' sthripes still floats over an onconquered people or whether five pfennigs is th' price iv a dhrink in New York. He sets on his high stool an' says he: 'Five times eight is twintynine, subthract three f'r th' duchess, a quarther to one o'clock an' eighty miles fr'm Narragansett pier is two-an'-a-half, plus th' load-wather-line iv th' saloon companionway, akel to two-fifths iv th' differentyal tangent. Huroo! Misther Sicrety, we can go home an' tell ye'er wife th' counthry's safe.' He has to be a smart man. A good bookkeeper, as th' pote says, is th' counthry's on'y safety. He mus' be careful, too, d'ye mind. Th' honor iv th' army an' the navy is at stake. Wan or th' other iv thim has been careless.''

"D'ye think a foreign fleet cud capture this counthry?'' asked Mr. Hennessy.

"Not onless it was op'rated be a throlley,'' said Mr. Dooley. "Supposin' ye an' I had throuble, Hinnissy, an' both iv us was armed with bricks an' ye was on roller skates an' I was on th' top iv a house, how much chanst wud ye have again' me? Ships is good to fight other ships. That's all. I'd sooner be behind a bank iv mud thin in th' finest ship in th' wurruld. A furrin inimy thryin' to get up to New York wud be like a blind burglar attimptin' to walk on th' top iv a hot-house with all th' neighbors an' th' neighbors' dogs waitin' f'r him. Th' war

game is all right. It don't do anny harm. But it's like punchin'
th' bag an' I'd jus' as soon thrain a man f'r a fight be larnin'
him to play th' mandolin, as be insthructin' him in bag punchin'. It's a fine game. I don't know who won, but I know who
lost."

"Who's that?" asked Mr. Hennessy.

"The threeasury," said Mr. Dooley.

THE PHILIPPINES

"I know what I'd do if I was Mack," said Mr. Hennessy.
"I'd hist a flag over th' Ph'lippeens, an' I'd take in th' whole
lot iv thim."

"An' yet," said Mr. Dooley, " 'tis not more thin two months
since ye larned whether they were islands or canned goods.
Ye'er back yard is so small that ye'er cow can't turn r-round
without buttin' th' wood-shed off th' premises, an' ye wudden't
go out to th' stock yards without takin' out a policy on yer life.
Suppose ye was standin' at th' corner iv State Sthreet an' Ar-
rchey Road, wud ye know what car to take to get to th' Ph'lippeens? If yer son Packy was to ask ye where th' Ph'lippeens is,
cud ye give him anny good idea whether they was in Rooshia
or jus' west iv' th' thracks?"

"Mebbe I cudden't," said Mr. Hennessy, haughtily, "but
I'm f'r takin' thim in, annyhow."

"So might I be," said Mr. Dooley, "if I cud on'y get me
mind on it. Wan if the worst things about this here war is th'
way it's makin' puzzles f'r our poor, tired heads. Whin I wint
into it, I thought all I'd have to do was to set up here behind
th' bar with a good tin-cint see-gar in me teeth, an' toss dinnymite bombs into th' hated city iv Havana. But look at me
now. Th' war is still goin' on; an' ivry night, when I'm countin' up th' cash, I'm askin' mesilf will I annex Cubia or lave it
to th' Cubians? Will I take Porther Ricky or put it by? An'
what shud I do with th' Ph'lippeens? Oh, what shud I do with
thim? I can't annex thim because I don't know where they ar-

re. I can't let go iv thim because some wan else'll take thim if I
do. They are eight thousan' iv thim islands, with a population
iv wan hundherd millyon naked savages; an' me bedroom's
crowded now with me an' th' bed. How can I take thim in, an'
how on earth am I goin' to cover th' nakedness iv thim savages
with me wan shoot iv clothes? An' yet 'twud break me heart to
think iv givin' people I niver see or heerd tell iv back to other
people I don't know. An', if I don't take thim, Schwartzmeister down th' sthreet, that has half me thrade already, will
grab thim sure.

"It ain't that I'm afraid iv not doin' th' r-right thing in th'
end, Hinnissy. Some mornin' I'll wake up an' know jus' what
to do, an' that I'll do. But 'tis th' annoyance in th' mane time.
I've been r-readin' about th' counthry. 'Tis over beyant ye'er
left shoulder whin ye're facin' east. Jus' throw ye'er thumb
back, an' ye have it as ac'rate as anny man in town. 'Tis farther thin Boohlgahrya an' not so far as Blewchoochoo. It's
near Chiny, an' it's not so near; an', if a man was to bore a
well through fr'm Goshen, Indianny, he might sthrike it, an'
thin again he might not. It's a poverty-sthricken counthry, full
iv goold an' precious stones, where th' people can pick dinner
off th' threes an' ar-re starvin' because they have no stepladders.
Th' inhabitants is mostly naygurs an' Chinnymen,
peaceful, industhrus, an' law-abidin', but savage an' bloodthirsty in their methods. They wear no clothes except what
they have on, an' each woman has five husbands an' each man
has five wives. Th' r-rest goes into th' discard, th' same as here.
Th' islands has been ownded be Spain since befure th' fire; an'
she's threated thim so well they're now up in ar-rms again her,
except a majority iv thim which is thurly loyal. Th' natives
seldom fight, but whin they get mad at wan another they r-run-
a-muck. Whin a man r-runs-a-muck, sometimes they hang him
an' sometimes they discharge him an' hire a new motorman.
Th' women ar-re beautiful, with languishin' black eyes, an'
they smoke see-gars, but ar-re hurried an' incomplete in their
dhress. I see a pitcher iv wan th' other day with nawthin' on

her but a basket of cocoanuts an' a hoop-skirt. They're no prudes. We import juke, hemp, cigar wrappers, sugar, an' fairy tales fr'm th' Ph'lippeens, an' export six-inch shells an' th' like. Iv late th' Ph'lippeens has awakened to th' fact that they're behind th' times, an' has received much American amminition in their midst. They say th' Spanyards is all tore up about it.

"I larned all this fr'm th' papers, an' I know 'tis sthraight. An' yet, Hinnissy, I dinnaw what to do about th' Ph'lippeens. An' I'm all alone in th' wurruld. Ivrybody else has made up his mind. Ye ask anny con-ducthor on Ar-rchy Road, an' he'll tell ye. Ye can find out fr'm th' paper; an', if ye really want to know, all ye have to do is to ask a prom'nent citizen who can mow all th' lawn he owns with a safety razor. But I don't know."

"Hang on to thim," said Mr. Hennessy, stoutly. "What we've got we must hold."

"Well," said Mr. Dooley, "if I was Mack, I'd lave it to George. I'd say: 'George,' I'd say, 'if ye're f'r hangin' on, hang on it is. If ye say, lave go, I dhrop thim.' 'Twas George won thim with th' shells, an' th' question's up to him."

THE PHILIPPINE PEACE

"'Tis sthrange we don't hear much talk about th' Ph'lippeens," said Mr. Hennessy.

"Ye ought to go to Boston," said Mr. Dooley. "They talk about it there in their sleep. Th' raison it's not discussed anywhere else is that ivrything is perfectly quiet there. We don't talk about Ohio or Ioway or anny iv our other possissions because they'se nawthin' doin' in thim parts. Th' people ar-re goin' ahead, garnerin' th' products iv th' sile, sindin' their childher to school, worshipin' on Sundah in th' churches an' thankin' Hiven f'r th' blessin's iv free govermint an' th' protiction iv th' flag above thim.

"So it is in th' Ph'lippeens. I know, f'r me frind Gov'nor Taft says so, an' they'se a man that undherstands con-tintmint

whin he sees it. Ye can't thrust th' fellows that comes back
fr'm th' jools iv th' Passyfic an' tells ye that things ar-re no betther thin they shud be undher th' shade iv th' cocoanut palm
be th' blue wathers iv th' still lagoon. They mus' be satisfied
with our rule. A man that isn't satisfied whin he's had enough
is a glutton. They're satisfied an' happy an' slowly but surely
they're acquirin' that love f'r th' govermint that floats over
thim that will make thim good citizens without a vote or a right
to thrile be jury. I know it. Guv'nor Taft says so.

"Says he: 'Th' Ph'lippeens as ye have been tol' be me young
but speechful frind, Sinitor Bivridge, who was down there f'r
tin minyits wanst an' spoke very highly an' at some lenth on th'
beauties iv th' scenery, th' Ph'lippeens is wan or more iv th'
beautiful jools in th' diadem iv our fair nation. Formerly our
fair nation did not care f'r jools, but done up her hair with side
combs, but she's been abroad some since an' she come back
with beautiful reddish goolden hair that a tiara looks well in
an' that is betther f'r havin' a tiara. She is not a young as she
was. Th' simple home-lovin' maiden that our fathers knew has
disappeared an' in her place we find a Columbya, gintlemen,
with machurer charms, a knowledge iv Euro-peen customs an'
not averse to a cigareet. So we have pinned in her fair hair a
diadem that sets off her beauty to advantage an' holds on th'
front iv th' hair, an' th' mos' lovely pearl in this ornymint is
thim sunny little isles iv th' Passyfic. They are almost too sunny f'r me. I had to come away.

" 'To shift me language suddintly fr'm th' joolry counther
an' th' boodore, I will say that nawthin' that has been said
even be th' gifted an' scholarly sinitor, who so worthily fills
part iv th' place wanst crowded be Hendricks an' McDonald,
does justice to th' richness iv thim islands. They raise unknown
quantities iv produce, none iv which forchnitly can come into
this counthry. All th' riches iv Cathay, all th' wealth iv Ind, as
Hogan says, wud look like a second morgedge on an Apache
wickeyup compared with th' untold an' almost unmintionable
products iv that gloryous domain. Me business kept me in

Manila or I wud tell ye what they are. Besides some iv our lile subjects is gettin' to be good shots an' I didn't go down there f'r that purpose.

" 'I turn to th' climate. It is simply hivenly. No other wurrud describes it. A white man who goes there seldom rayturns unless th' bereaved fam'ly insists. It is jus' right. In winter enough rain, in summer plinty iv heat. Gin'rally speakin' whin that thropical sky starts rainin' it doesn't stop till it's impty, so th' counthry is not subjected to th' sudden changes that afflict more northerly climes. Whin it rains it rains; whin it shines it shines. Th' wather frequently remains in th' air afther th' sun has been shinin' a month or more, th' earth bein' a little over-crowded with juice an' this gives th' atmosphere a certain cosiness that is indescribable. A light green mould grows on th' clothes an' is very becomin'. I met a man on th' boat comin' back who said 'twas th' finest winter climate in th' wurruld. He was be profission a rubber in a Turkish bath. As f'r th' summers they are delicious. Th' sun doesn't sit aloft above th' jools iv th' Passyfic. It comes down an' mingles with th' peo-ple. Ye have heard it said th' isles was kissed be th' sun. Perhaps bitten wud be a betther wurrud. But th' timprachoor is frequently modified be an eruption iv th' neighborin' volcanoes an' th' inthraduction iv American stoves. At night a coolin' breeze fr'm th' crather iv a volcano makes sleep possi-ble in a hammock swung in th' ice-box. It is also very pleasant to be able to cuk wan's dinner within wan.

" 'Passin' to th' pollytical situation, I will say it is good. Not perhaps as good as ye'ers or mine, but good. Ivry wanst in a while whin I think iv it, an iliction is held. Unforchnitly it usually happens that those ilicted have not yet surrindhered. In th' Ph'lippeens th' office seeks th' man, but as he is also pur-sooed be th' sojery, it is not always aisy to catch him an' fit it on him. Th' counthry may be divided into two parts, pollytical-ly,—where th' insurrection continues an' where it will soon be. Th' brave but I fear not altogether cheery army conthrols th' insurrected parts be martiyal law, but th' civil authorities are

supreme in their own house. Th' diff'rence between civil law
an' martiyal law in th' Ph'lippeens is what kind iv coat th'
judge wears. Th' raysult is much th' same. Th' two branches
wurruks in perfect harmony. We bag thim in th' city an' they
round thim up in th' counthry.

" 'It is not always nicessry to kill a Filipino American right
away. Me desire is to idjacate thim slowly in th' ways an'
customs iv th' counthry. We ar-re givin' hundherds iv these
pore benighted haythen th' well-known, ol'-fashioned
American wather cure. Iv coorse, ye know how 'tis done. A
Filipino, we'll say, niver heerd iv th' histhry iv this counthry.
He is met be wan iv our sturdy boys in black an' blue iv th'
Macabebee scouts who asts him to cheer f'r Abraham Lincoln.
He rayfuses. He is thin place upon th' grass an' given a dhrink,
a baynit bein' fixed in his mouth so he cannot rejict th'
hospitality. Undher th' inflooence iv th' hose that cheers but
does not inebriate, he soon warrums or perhaps I might say
swells up to a ralization iv th' granjoor iv his adoptive counthry. One gallon makes him give three groans f'r th' constit-
chochion. At four gallons, he will ask to be wrapped in th'
flag. At th' dew pint he sings Yankee Doodle. Occasionally we
run acrost a stubborn an' rebellyous man who wud sthrain at
me idee iv human rights an' swallow th' Passyfic Ocean, but I
mus' say mos' iv these little fellows is less hollow in their
pretintions. Nachrally we have had to take a good manny
customs fr'm Spanyard, but we have improved on thim. I was
talkin' with a Spanish gintleman th' other day who had been
away f'r a long time an' he said he wudden't know th' counthry. Even th' faces iv th' people on th' sthreets had changed.
They seemed glad to see him. Among th' mos' useful Spanish
customs is reconcenthration. Our reconcenthration camps is
among th' mos' thickly popylated in th' wurruld. But still we
have to rely mainly on American methods. They are always
used fin'lly in th' makin' iv a good citizen, th' garotte sildom.

" 'I have not considhered it advisable to inthrajooce anny
fads like thrile be jury iv ye'er peers into me administhration.

Plain sthraight-forward dealin's is me motto. A Filipino at his best has on'y larned half th' jooty iv mankind. He can be thried but he can't thry his fellow man. It takes him too long. But in time I hope to have thim thrained to a pint where they can be good men an' thrue at th' inquest.

" 'I hope I have tol' ye enough to show ye that th' stories iv disordher is greatly exaggerated. Th' counthry is pro-gressin' splindidly, th' ocean still laps th' shore, th' mountains are there as they were in Bivridge's day, quite happy apprarently; th' flag floats free an' well guarded over th' govermint offices, an' th' cheery people go an' come on their errands—go out alone an' come back with th' throops. Ivrywhere happiness, contint, love iv th' shtep-mother counthry, excipt in places where there ar-re people. Gintlemen, I thank ye.'

"An' there ye ar-re, Hinnissy. I hope this here lucid story will quite th' waggin' tongues iv scandal an' that people will let th' Ph'lippeens stew in their own happiness."

"But sure they might do something f'r thim," said Mr. Hennessy.

"They will," said Mr. Dooley. They'll give thim a measure iv freedom."

"But whin?"

"Whin they'll sthand still long enough to be measured," said Mr. Dooley.

CHAPTER III

POLITICS AND POLITICIANS

Mr. Dooley was above all things a political animal; politics
was every Chicagoan's favorite indoor sport, and anyone could
play. Politicians might run, but they couldn't hide from Mr.
Dooley. They had to pretend to accept his slings and arrows
with good humor, sometimes smiling through gritted teeth.

Dunne was not without understanding of or sympathy for
plight. As Mr. Dooley commented after a presidential candidate had taken a merciless beating from the local press,
"What's this counthry comin' to annyhow, that a man that's
out f'r Prisident has to set up on a high chair an' be questioned
on his record be a lot iv la-ads that hasn't had annything to do
since the carpet beatin' season's ended?" Every election year,
candidates across the nation still ask themselves the same question.

Election did not bring an end to Mr. Dooley's barbs; while
he had reverence for high office, the man who sat in it had to
win his respect. Some of Dunne's best friends were politicians,
but this never stopped Mr. Dooley from calling them to task
when they allowed their sense of self-importance to get out of
hand.

*"Rayformers, Hinnissy, is in favor iv suppressin' ivrythign, but
rale pollyticians believes in suppressin' nawthin' but ividence."*

REFORM ADMINISTRATION

"Why is it," asked Mr. Hennessy, "that a rayform ad-
mininsthration always goes to th' bad?"

"I'll tell ye," said Mr. Dooley. "I tell ye ivrything an' I'll tell ye this. In th' first place 'tis a gr-reat mistake to think that annywan ra-aly wants to rayform. Ye niver heerd iv a man rayformin' himsilf. He'll rayform other people gladly. He likes to do it. But a healthy man'll niver rayform while he has th' strenth. A man doesn't rayform till his will has been impaired so he hasn't power to resist what th' pa-apers calls th' blandishments iv th' timpter. An' that's thruer in politics thin annywhere else.

"But a rayformer don't see it. A rayformer thinks he was ilicted because he was a rayformer, whin th' thruth iv th' matther is he was ilicted because no wan knew him. Ye can always ilict a man in this counthry on that platform. If I was runnin' f'r office, I'd change me name, an' have printed on me cards: 'Give him a chanst; he can't be worse.' He's ilicted because th' people don't know him an' do know th' other la-ad; because Mrs. Casey's oldest boy was clubbed be a polisman, because we cudden't get wather above th' third story wan day, because th' sthreet car didn't stop f'r us, because th' Flannigans bought a pianny, because we was near run over be a mail wagon, because th' saloons are open Sundah night, because they're not open all day, an' because we're tired seein' th' same face at th' window whin we go down to pay th' wather taxes. Th' rayformer don't know this. He thinks you an' me, Hinnissy, has been watchin' his spotless career f'r twenty years, that we've read all he had to say on th' evils iv pop'lar sufferage befure th' Society f'r the Bewildermint iv th' Poor, an' that we're achin' in ivry joint to have him dhrag us be th' har iv th' head fr'm th' flowin' bowl an' th' short card game, make good citizens iv us an' sind us to th' pinitinchry. So th' minyit he gets into th' job he begins a furyous attimpt to convart us into what we've been thryin' not to be iver since we come into th' wurruld.

"In th' coorse iv th' twenty years that he spint attimptin' to get office, he managed to poke a few warrum laws conthrollin' th' pleasures iv th' poor into th' stachoo book, because no wan cared about thim or because they made business betther f'r th'

polis, an' whin he's in office, he calls up th' Cap'n iv the polis
an' says he: 'If these laws ar-re bad laws th' way to end thim is
to enfoorce thim.' Somebody told him that, Hinnissy. It isn't
thrue, d'ye mind. I don't care who said it, not if t'was Willum
Shakespere. It isn't thrue. Laws ar-re made to throuble people
an' th' more throuble they make th' longer they stay on th'
stachoo book. But th' polis don't ast anny questions. Says they:
'They'll be less money in th' job but we need some recreation,'
an' that night a big copper comes down th' sthreet, sees me settin' out on th' front stoop with me countenance dhraped with a
tin pail, fans me with his club an' runs me in. Th' woman nex'
dure is locked up f'r sthringin' a clothes line on th' roof, Han-
nigan's boy Tim gets tin days f'r keepin' a goat, th' polis
resarves are called out to protict th' vested rights iv property
against th' haynyous pushcart man, th' stations is crowded
with felons charge with maintainin' a hose conthrary to th'
stachoos made an' provided, an' th' tindherline is all over
town. A rayformer don't think annything has been accom-
plished it they'se a vacant bedroom in th' pinitinchry. His motto is 'Arrest that man.'

"Whin a rayformer is ilicted he promises ye a business administration. Some people want that but I don't. Th'
American business man is too fly. He's all right, d'ye mind. I
don't say annything again' him. He is what Hogan calls th'
boolwarks iv pro-gress, an' we cudden't get on without him
even if his scales are a little too quick on th' dhrop. But he
ought to be left to dale with his akels. 'Tis a shame to give him
a place where he can put th' comether on millions iv people
that has had no business thrainin' beyond occasionally handin'
a piece iv debased money to a car conductor on a cold day. A
reg'lar pollytician can't give away an alley without blushin',
but a business man who is in pollytics jus' to see that th' civil
sarvice law gets thurly enfoorced, will give Lincoln Park an'
th' public libr'y to th' beef thrust, charge an admission price to
th' lake front an' make it a felony f'r annywan to buy stove
polish outside iv his store, an' have it all put down to public

improvemints with a pitcher iv him in th' corner stone.

"Fortchinitly, Hinnissy, a rayformer is seldom a business man. He thinks he is, but business men know diff'rent. They know what he is. He thinks business an' honesty is th' same thing. He does, indeed. He's got thim mixed because they dhress alike. His idee is that all he has to do to make a business administhration is to have honest men ar-round him. Wrong. I'm not sayin', mind ye, that a man can't do good work an' be honest at th' same time. But whin I'm hirin' a la-ad I find out first whether he is onto his job, an' afther a few years I begin to suspect that he is honest, too. Manny a dishonest man can lay brick sthraight an' manny a man that wudden't steal ye'er spoons will break ye'er furniture. I don't want Father Kelly to hear me, but I'd rather have a competint man who wud steal if I give him a chanst, but I won't, do me plumbin' thin a person that wud scorn to help himself but didn't know how to wipe a joint. Ivry man ought to be honest to start with, but to give a man an office jus' because he's honest is like ilictin' him to Congress because he's a pathrite, because he don't bate his wife or because he always wears a right boot on th' right foot. A man ought to be honest to start with an' afther that he ought to be crafty. A pollytician who's on'y honest is jus' th' same as bein' out in a winther storm without anny clothes on.

"Another thing about rayform administhrations is they always think th' on'y man that ought to hold a job is a lawyer. Th' raison is that in th' coorse iv his thrainin' a lawyer larns enough about ivrything to make a good front on anny subject to annybody who doesn't know about it. So whin th' rayform administhration comes in th' mayor says: 'Who'll we make chief iv polis in place iv th' misguided ruffyan who has held th' job f'r twinty years?' 'Th' man f'r th' place,' says th' mayor's adviser, 'is Arthur Lightout,' he says. 'He's an ixcillent lawyer, Yale, '95, an' is well up on polis matthers. Las' year he read a paper on "The fine polis foorce iv London" befure th' annual meetin' iv th' S'ciety f'r Ladin' th' Mulligan Fam'ly to a Bet-ther an' Harder Life. Besides,' he says, 'he's been in th' milishy an' th' foorce needs a man who'll be afraid not to shoot in case iv public disturbance.' So Arthur takes hold iv th' constabulary an' in a year th' polis can all read Emerson an' th' burglars begin puttin' up laddhers an' block an' tackles befure eight A.M. An' so it is on ivry side. A lawyer has charge iv the city horse-shoein', another wan is clanin' th' sthreets, th' author iv 'Gasamagoo on torts' is thryin' to dispose iv th' ashes be throwin' thim in th' air on a windy day, an' th' bright boy that took th' silver ware f'r th' essay on *ne exeats* an' their relation to life is plannin' a uniform that will be sarviceable an' constitchoochinal f'r th' brave men that wurruks on th' city dumps. An' wan day th' main rayformer goes out expictin' to rayceive th' thanks iv th' community an' th' public that has jus' got out iv jail f'r lettin' th' wather run too long in th' bath tub rises up an' cries: 'Back to th' Univarsity Settlemint.' Th' man with th' di'mon' in his shirt front comes home an' pushes th' honest lawyers down th' steps, an' a dishonest horse shoer shoes th' city's horses well, an' a crooked plumber does th' city's plumbin' securely, an' a rascally polisman that may not be avarse to pickin' up a bet but will always find out whin Pathrolman Scanlan slept on his beat, takes hold iv th' polis foorce, an' we raysume our nachral condition iv illagal merrimint. An' th' rayformer spinds th' rest iv his life tellin' us where we are wrong. He's good at that. On'y he don't undherstand that people wud rather be wrong an' comfortable thin right in jail."

"I don't like a rayformer," said Mr. Hennessy.

"Or anny other raypublican," said Mr. Dooley.

Phil and Amanda Dunne find this essay their special favorite.

BUSINESS AND POLITICAL HONESTY

"It's a shame," said Mr. Dooley, laying down his paper, "that more business men don't go into pollyticks."

"I thought they did," said Mr. Hennessy.

"No, sir," said Mr. Dooley; "ye don't r-read th' pa-apers. Ivry year, whin th' public conscience is aroused as it niver was befure, me frinds on th' palajeems iv our liberties an' records iv our crimes calls f'r business men to swab out our govermint with business methods. We must turn it over to pathrites who have made their pile in mercantile pursoots iv money wheriver they cud find it. We must injooce th' active, conscientious young usurers fr'm Wall Sthreet to take an inthrest in public affairs. Th' poolrooms is open. To thim guilded haunts iv vice th' poor wurrukinman carries his weekly wage, an' thries to increase it enough so that he can give it to his wife without blushin'. Down with th' poolrooms, says I. But how? says you. Be ilictin' a busines man mayor, says I. But who'll we get? says you. Who betther, says I, thin th' prisident iv th' Westhren Union Tillygraft Comp'ny, who knows where th' poolrooms ar-re.

"Th' wather departmint is badly r-run. Ilict th' prisidint iv th' gas comp'ny. Th' onforchnit sthreet railroads have had thimsilves clutched be th' throat be a corrupt city council an' foorced to buy twinty millyon dollars' worth iv sthreets f'r sixty-four wan-hundherd dollar bills. Oh, f'r a Moses to lead us out of th' wilderness an' clane th' Augeenyan stables an' steer us between Silly an' What's-it's-name an' hoist th' snow-white banner iv civic purity an' break th' feathers that bind a free people an' seize the hellum iv state fr'm th' pi-ratical crew an' restore th' heritage iv our fathers an' cleanse the stain fr'm th' fair name iv our gr-reat city an' cure th' evils iv th' body pollytick an' cry havic an' let loose th' dogs iv war an' captain th' uprisin' iv honest manhood again th' cohorts iv corruption an' shake off th' collar riveted on our necks be tyrannical bosses an' prim'ry rayform? Where is Moses? Where is the all-around stable-boy, polisman, an' disinfectant? Where is this all-around Moses, soldier, sailor, locksmith, doctor, stable-boy, polisman, an' disinfectant? Where else wud such a vallyble Moses be thin in th' bank that owns th' sthreet railroads? If Moses can't serve we'll r-run his lawyer, th' gr-reat pollytickal purist, th' Hon'rable Ephraim Duck, author iv *Duck on Holes in th' Law, Duck on Flaws in th' Constitution, Duck on Ivry Man has His Price, Duck's First Aid to th' Suspicted, Duck's Iliminthry Lessons in Almost Crime, Th' Supreem Coort Made Easy, or Ivry Man his Own Allybi* and so on. Where is Judge Duck? He's down at Springfield, doin' a little ligislative law business f'r th' gas comp'ny. Whin he comes up he'll be glad to lead th' gr-reat annyooal battle f'r civic purity. Hurrah f'r Duck an' Freedom, Duck an' Purity, Duck an' th' Protiction iv th' Rights iv Property, Duck an' Fearless Compromise.

"Befure our most illusthrees life-insurance solicitor rose in th' wurruld, whin he was merely prisidint iv th' United States, th' on'y way we cud dig a job out iv him f'r a good dimmycrat was to form th' Sixth Ward Chamber iv Commerce an' indorse th' candydate. Whin Cohen first wint to Wash'nton to have Schmitt appinted counsul at Chefoo, th' chief ixicutive, as Hogan says, nearly brained him with a paper-weight marked J.P.M. But whin he wint down as prisidint iv th' Ar-rchey Road Chamber iv Commerce th' gr-reat man fell on his neck an' near broke it. Th' frindship iv th' gr-reat, Hinnissy, is worse thin their inmity. Their hathred sometimes misses fire, but their frindship always lands in an unguarded an' vital spot. This here Chamber iv Commerce r-run th' pathronage iv th' disthrict f'r a year. It used to meet in me back room till th' merchant princes got too noisy over a dice game an' I put thim into th' sthreet.

"Yes, Hinnissy, me ideel iv a gr-reat statesman is a grocer with elastic bands on his shirt-sleeves, ladlin' public policies out iv a bar'l with a wooden scoop. How much betther wud Wash'nton an' Lincoln have been if they'd known enough to inthrajooce business methods into pollyticks. George was a good man, but he niver thought iv settlin' th' throuble be compromisin' on a job as colonyal governor. He raised th' divvle with property, so much so, be Hivins, that no gr-reat financier to this day can tell what belongs to him an' what belongs to some wan else. An' there's Lincoln. What a little business thrainin' wud've done f'r him! Look at th' roon he brought on property be his carelessness. Millyons iv thim become worthless except as fuel f'r bonfires in th' Sunny Southland.

"It's sthrange people can't see it th' way I do. There's Jawn Cassidy. Ye known him. He's a pollytician or grafter. Th' same thing. His graft is to walk downtown to th' City Hall at eight o'clock ivry mornin' an' set on a high stool ontil five in th' afthernoon addin' up figures. Ivry week twenty dollars iv th' taxpayers' money, twenty dollars wrung fr'm you an' me, Hinnissy, is handed to this boodler. He used to get twenty-five in a clothin'-store, but he is a romantic young fellow, an' he thought 'twud be a fine thing to be a statesman. Th' diff'rence between a clothin' clerk an' a statesman clerk is that th' statesman clerk gets less money, an' has th' privilege iv wurrukin' out iv office hours. Well, Cassidy come in wan night with his thumbs stained fr'm his unholy callin'. 'Well,' says I, 'ye grafters ar-re goin' to be hurled out,' I says. 'I suppose so,' says he. 'We'll have a business administhration,' says I. 'Well,' says he, 'I wondher what kind iv a business will it be,' he says. 'Will it be th' insurance business? I tell ye if they iver inthrajooce life-insurance methods in our little boodle office there'll be a rivolution in this here city. Will it be a railraod administhration, with the' office chargin' ye twice as much f'r water as Armour pays?! Will it be th' bankin' business, with th' prisident takin' th' money out iv th' dhrawer ivry night an' puttin' in a few kind wurruds on a slip iv paper?

"'What kind iv a busines ar-re ye goin' to use to purify our corrupt govermint? Look here,' says he. 'I'm goin' out iv pollyticks,' he says. 'Me wife can't stand th' sthrain iv seein' th' newspapers always referrin' to me be a nickname in quotation marks. I've got me old job back, and I've quit bein' a statesman,' he says. 'But let me tell ye something. I've been a boodler an' a grafter an' a public leech f'r five years, but I used to be a square business man, an' I'm givin' ye th' thruth whin I

say that business ain't got a shade on pollyticks in th' matther
iv honesty. Th' bankers was sthrong again' Mulcahy. But I
know all about th' banks. Whin I was in th' clothin' business
Minzenheimer used to have th' banks over-certify his checks
ivry night. That wud mean two years in th' stir-bin f'r a pollytician, but I don't see no bankers doin' the' wan-two in the iron
gall'ries at Joliet. I knew a young fellow that wurruked in a
bank, an' he told me th' prisidint sold th' United State Statutes
to an ol' book dealer to make room f'r a ticker in his office. We
may be a tough gang over at th' City Hall. A foreign name
always looks tough whin its printed in a reform iditoryal. But,
thank th' Lord, no man iver accused us iv bein' life-insurance
prisidints. We ain't buncoin' an' scarin' people with th' fear iv
death into morgedgin' their furniture to buy booze an' cigars
f'r us,' he says. 'We may take bribes, because we need th'
money, but we don't give thim because we want more thin we
need. We're grafters, ye say, but there's manny a dollar pushed
over th' counter iv a bank that Mulcahy wud fling in th' eye iv
th' man that offered it to him.

"'Th' pollytician grafts on th' public an' his inimies. It don't
seem anny worse to him thin winnin' money on a horse-race.
He doesn't see th' writhin' iv th' man he takes th' coin fr'm.
But these here high fi-nanciers grafts on th' public an' their inimies, but principally on their frinds. Dump ye'er pardner is th'
quickest way to th' money. Mulcahy wud rather die thin skin a
frind that had sthrung a bet with him. But if Mulcahy was a
railroad boss instead iv a pollytical boss he wud first wurruk
up th' con-fidence iv his frinds in him, thin he wud sell thim his
stock, thin he wud tell thim th' road was goin' to th' dogs, an'
make thim give it back to him f'r nawthin'; thin he wud get out
a fav'rable report, an' sell th' stock to thim again. An' he'd go
on doin' this till he'd made enough to be ilicted prisidint iv a
good govermint club. Some iv th' boys down at our office are
owners iv stock. Whin do they first larn that things ar-re goin'
wrong with th'comp'ny? Afther th' prisidint an' boord iv di-
rectors have sold out.

"'Don't ye get off anny gas at me about busines men an' pollyticians. I niver knew a pollytician to go wrong ontil he'd been contaminated be contact with a business man. I've been five years in th' water office, an' in all that time not a postage-stamp has been missed. An' we're put down as grafters. What is pollytical graft, annyhow? It ain't stealin' money out iv a dhrawer. It ain't robbin' th' taxpayer direct, th' way th' gas comp'ny does. All there's to it is a business man payin' less money to a pollytician thin he wud have to pay to th' city if he bought a sthreet or a dock direct.

"'Iv coorse, there ar-re petty larceny grabs be polismen. That's so ivrywhere. Wheriver there's polisman there's a shake-down. But in ivry big crooked job there's a business man at wan end. Th' ligislachures is corrupt, but who makes it worth while f'r thim to be corrupt but th' pathrites iv th' life-insurance comp'nies? Th' la-ads in th' council ar-re out f'r th' stuff, says ye. But how do they make annything except be sellin' sthreets to th' high fi-nanceers that own th' railraod comp'nies? If business men niver wanted to buy things cheap that don't belong to thim no pollytician that cud carry a precinct wud go into th' council. I'm goin' back to business. Minzenheimer thinks he will need me to get th' aldhermen to let him add fifty illegal feet to th' front iv his store. I'm goin' back to business, an' I expect to help purify it. What th' business iv this counthry needs,' he says, 'is f'r active young pollyticians to take an inthrest in it an' ilivate it to a higher plane. Me battle-cry is: "Honest pollytical methods in th' ad-ministhration iv business,"' he says 'I hope to see th' same honesty, good faith, an' efficiency in th' Life Insurance Comp'nies an' th' Thrusts that we see now,' he says, 'in th' ad-ministhration iv Tammany Hall,' he says."

"There's a good deal in that," said Mr. Hennessy. "I knew an aldherman wanst that was honest as th' sun, except whin th' sthreet railroad or th' gas comp'ny needed something."

"Well, there ye ar-re," said Mr. Dooley, "It seems to me that th' on'y thing to do is to keep pollytcians an' business men apart. They seem to have a bad infloonce on each other. Whiniver I see an aldherman an' a banker walkin' down th' sthreet together I know th' Recordin' Angel will have to ordher another bottle iv ink."

DISCUSSES PARTY POLITICS

"I wondher," said Mr. Hennessy, "if us dimmycrats will iver ilict a prisidint again."

"We wud," said Mr. Dooley, "if we cud but get an illegible candydate."

"What's that?" asked Mr. Hennessy.

"An illegible candydate," said Mr. Dooley, "is a candydate that can't be read out iv th' party. 'Tis a joke I med up. Me frind Willum J. Bryan read th' Commoner to thim an' they pack up their bags an' lave. They'se as manny dimmicrats out iv th' party as they are in, waitin' on th' durestep to read thimsilves back an' th' other la-ads out. Th' loudest r-reader wins.

"No, sir, th' dimmycratic party ain't on speakin' terms with itsilf. Whin ye see two men with white neckties go into a sthreet car an' set in opposite corners while wan mutthers 'Thraiter' an' th' other hisses 'Miscreent' ye can bet they're two dimmycratic leaders thryin to reunite th' gran' ol' party. 'Tis on'y th' part iv th' party that can't r-read that's thrue to th' principals iv Jefferson an' Jackson.

"Me frind Willum J. is not a candydate. He's illegible as an editor but not as a candydate. Annyhow, he don't want it or at least he don't want to want it an' not get it. All he asks is some good man, some thried an' thrusty dimmycrat that can lead th' party on to gloryous victhry. But he can't find him. Ye say Hill? Well, me frind Willum J. was ast to ask me frind David Binnitt to go out f'r to make a speech at a dimmycratic bankit on th' thraditions iv th' dimmycratic party, Hill bein' wan iv thim an' wan iv th' worst. 'Gintlemen,' says Willum Jennings, 'I admire David Binnitt Hill. No wan,' he says, 'is a second to me in affection f'r that gr-reat an' good man,' he says. 'I shall

niver fail in me devotion to him till,' he says 'th' place heals up
where he sunk th' axe into me in ninety-six. But,' he says, 'I
cannot ask him to speak at ye'er bankit. I cannot bear to hear
him talk. Ivry time he opens his mouth I want to put me fut into it,' he says. 'Moreover,' he says, 'if ye ask him I'll take me
meal at home,' he says, 'f'r th' sight of that gallant dimmycrat
turns me fr'm food,' he says. So that ends Hill. We can't go
with anny wan that our sainted leader can't ate an egg with
without sin.

"Well, thin, who've we got? They'se me frind Bill Whitney.
He won't do because th' bookmakers niver get up on iliction
day in time to vote. A thousan' to wan again Whitney, his opponent to carry th' audjiotoroom on his back. They'se me frind
Charlie Towne, th' unsalted orator iv th' zenith city—"

"Thraitor," said Mr. Dooley.

"He *has* got some money," said Mr. Dooley reflectively. "I
see in th' pa-apers he says they'se now enough to go ar-
round—enough f'r him to go ar-round, Hinnissy. He's a
thraitor. I wisht I cud afford to be wan. Well, what d'ye say to
Gorman? They'se a fine, sthraight-forward, honest, clane, in-
corruptible man. Ye put him alone in a room with th' rayturns
an' ye can go out an gather bar'ls f'r th' bonefire. Ye won't
have him, eh? Oh, he knifed th' ticket, did he? Secretly? Oh,
my, oh, my! Th' villain. Down goes Gorman. Well, let me see,
let me see; who've we got?

"I'm thryin' to find a man to uphold th' banner so that ye
can march shouldher to shouldher an' heart to heart, to
mimrable victhry an' ivry time I mintion th' name iv wan iv
ye'er fellow dimmycrats ye make a face. What ar-re ye goin' to
do? Ye might thry advertisin' in the' papers. 'Wanted: A good,
active, inergetic dimmycrat, sthrong iv lung an' limb; must be
in favor iv sound money, but not too sound, an' anti-
impeeryalist but f'r holdin' onto what we've got, an inimy iv
thrusts but a frind iv organized capital, a sympathizer with th'
crushed an' downthrodden people but not be anny means
hostile to vested inthrests; must advocate sthrikes, gover'mint

be injunction, free silver, sound money, greenbacks, a single tax, a tariff f'r rivinoo, th' constitootion to follow th' flag as far as it can an' no farther, civil service rayform iv th' la-ads in office an' all th' gr-reat an' gloryous principles iv our gr-reat an' gloryous party or anny gr-reat an' gloryous parts thereof. He must be akelly at home in Wall sthreet an' th' stock yards, in th' parlors iv th' r-rich an' th' kitchens iv th' poor. Such a man be applyin' to Malachi Hinnissy, Ar-rchey r-road, an' prisintin' rif'rences fr'm his last party, can get good employment as a candydate f'r prisidint, with a certainty aftherward iv a conganial place as public r-reader an' party bouncer.' Ye might get an answer."

"Oh, well, we'll find some wan,' said Mr. Hennessy cheerfully.

"I guess," said Mr. Dooley, "that ye're right about that. Ye'll have a candydate an' he'll have votes. Man an' boy I've seen th' dimmycratic party hangin' to th' ropes a score iv times. I've seen it dead an' burrid an' th' raypublicans kindly buildin' a mony-mint f'r it an' preparin' to spind their declinin' days in th' custom house. I've gone to sleep nights wondhrin' where I'd throw away me vote afther this an' whin I woke up there was that crazy-headed ol' loon iv a party with its hair sthreamin' in its eyes, an' an axe in its hand, chasin' raypublicans into th' tall grass. 'Tis niver so good as whin 'tis broke, whin rayspictable people speak iv it in whispers, an' whin it has no leaders an' on'y wan principal, to go in an' take it away fr'm th' other fellows. Something will turn up, ye bet, Hinnissy. Th' raypublican party may die iv overfeedin' or all th' leaders pump out so much ile they won't feel like leadin'. An' annyhow they'se always wan ray iv light ahead. We're sure to have hard times. An' whin' th' la-ads that ar-re baskin' in th' sunshine iv prosperity with Andhrew Carnaygie an' Pierpont Morgan an' me frind Jawn D. finds that th' sunshine has been turned off an' their fellow-baskers has relieved thim iv what they had in th' dark, we'll take thim boys be th' hand an' say: 'Come over with ye'er own kind. Th' raypublican party broke ye, but now that ye're down we'll not turn a cold shoulder to ye. Come in an' we'll keep ye—broke.'

"Yes, sir, ye'll have a candydate. If worst comes to worst I'll offer mesilf again."

"It wud be that," said Mr. Hennessy. "But ye ain't—what-d'ye-call-it?"

"I may not be as illegible as some," said Mr. Dooley, "but I'd get as manny votes as others."

THE CANDIDATE

"I see," said Mr. Hennessy, "that the Dimmycrats have gr-reat confidence."

"They have," said Mr. Dooley. "Th' Dimmycrats have gr-reat confidence, th' Raypublicans ar-re sure, th' Popylists are hopeful, th' Prohybitionists look f'r a landslide or a flood, or whativer you may call a Prohybition victhry, an' th' Socylists think this may be their year. That's what makes pollytics th' gr-reat game an' th' on'y wan to dhrive dull care away. It's a game iv hope, iv jolly-ye're-neighbor, a confidence game. If ye get a bad hand at poker ye lay it down. But if ye get a bad hand at pollytics ye bets ye're pair iv deuces as blithe as an Englishman who has jus' larned th' game out if th' spoortin' columns iv' th' London *Times*. If ye don't win fair ye may win foul. If ye don't win ye may tie an' get th' money in th' confusion. If it wasn't such a game wud there be Dimmycrats in Vermont, Raypublicans in Texas, an' Prohybitionists in the stockyards ward? Ivry year men crawl out iv th' hospitals, where they've been since last iliction day, to vote th' Raypublican ticket in Mississippi. There's no record iv it, but it's a fact. To'day th' Dimmycrats will on'y concede Vermont, Maine, an' Pennsylvania to th' Raypublicans, an' th' Raypublicans concede Texas, Allybammy, an' Mississippi to th' Dimmycrats. But it's arly yet. Wait awhile. Th' wurruk iv th' campaign has not begun. Both sides is inclined to be pessimistic. Th' consarvative business man who thinks that if a little money cud be placed in Yazoo City th' prejudice again' th'

Raypublicans, which is on'y skin-deep annyhow, cud be removed, hasn't turned up at headquarters. About th' middle iv October th' Raypublican who concedes Texas to th' Dimmycrats will be dhrummed out iv th' party as a thraitor, an' ye'll hear that th' Dimmycratic party in Maine is so cheered be th' prospects that his frinds can't keep him sober.

"Th' life iv a candydate is th' happiest there is. If I want annythin' pleasant said about me I have to say it mesilf. There's a hundherd thousan' freemen ready to say it to a candydate, an' say it sthrong. They ask nawthin' in rayturn that will require a civil-service examination. He starts in with a pretty good opinion iv himsilf, based on what his mother said iv him as a baby, but be th' time he's heerd th' first speech iv congratulation he begins to think he had a cold an indiff'rent parent. Ninety per cint iv th' people who come to see him tell him he's th' mos' pop'lar thing that iver was, an' will carry th' counthry like a tidal wave. He don't let th' others in. If annybody says annything about him less frindly thin Jacob Riis he know's he either a sorehead or is in th' pay iv th' other campaign comity. Childher an' dogs ar-re named afther him, pretty women an' some iv th' other kind thry to kiss him, an' th' newspapers publish pitchers iv him as he sets in his libry, with his brow wrinkled in thought iv how fine a man he is. Th' opposition pa-apers don't get up to th' house, an' he niver sees himsilf with a face like Sharkey or reads that th' reason he takes a bath in th' Hudson is because he is too stingy to buy a bathtub f'r th' house an' prefers to sponge th' gr-reat highway belongin' to th' people.

"If he hasn't done much to speak iv, his frinds rayport his small but handsome varchues. He niver punched his wife, he sinds his boys to school, he loves his counthry, he shaves with a safety razor. A man expicts to be ilicted Prisidint iv th' United States, Hinnissy, f'r th' fine qualities that th' r-rest iv us use on'y to keep out iv th' pinitinchry. All th' time th' rayports fr'm th' counthry become more an' more glowin'. Th' tidal wave is risin', an' soon will amount to a landslide. Victhry is

perched upon our banners, and has sint f'r th' family. F'r th'
Dimmycrat candydate th' most glowin' rayports iv gains come
fr'm New England, where there is always most room f'r Dimmycratic gains. F'r th' Raypublicans, th' news fr'm th'
Southwest is so cheerin' as to be almost incredible, or quite so.
But iliction day comes at last. Th' people iv this gr-reat counthry gather at th' varyous temples iv liberty in barber-shops an'
liv'ry stables an' indicate their choice iv evils. A gr-reat hush
falls on th' land as th' public pours out iv th' side dure iv th'
saloons an' reverently gathers at th' newspaper offices to await
with bated breath th' thrillin' news fr'm th' first precinct iv the
foorth ward iv Sheboygan, Wis. An' thin again we hear th' old
but niver tiresome story: Texas give an Dimmycrat majority iv
five hundred thousan', but will reopen the polls if more is
nicessry; th' Dimmycrats hope, if th' prisint ratio is maintained,
th' Raypublican victhry in Pinnsylvanya will not be unanin-
mous. An' wan candydate rayceives six million votes an' is
overwhelmingly defeated, an' th' other rayceives five millyon
nine hundherd thousan' and is triumphantly ilicted. An' there
ye ar-re.''

PRESIDENT'S MESSAGE

Did ye r-read th' prisidint's message?'' asked Mr. Dooley.
"I did not," said Mr. Hennessy.
"Well, ye-re r-right," said the philosopher. "I didn't mesilf.
'Tis manny years since I give up me devotion to that form iv
fiction. I don't think anny wan r-reads a message but th' clerk
iv th' house iv riprisintatives, an' he has to hold his job. But I
cud tell ye how 'tis written. Th' prisident summons th' cab'net
together an' they set ar-round a long table smokin' seegars excipt th' sicrety iv th' navy, an' he smokes a cigareet. An' th'
prisidint he says: 'La-ads,' he says, ''tis up to me f'r to sind a
few wurruds,' he says, 'iv good cheer,' he says, 'to thim rilitives
iv th' civil service on th' other side iv town,' he says. 'I'd a
great deal rather set up in th' gall'ry an' hear me frind

Grosvenor tell thim,' he says, 'that I'm no polygamist like that there David Harem feller that's thryin' to break into congress,' he says, 'An' I suppose I've got to,' he says. 'What shall I say?' he says, an' he sets there writin' 'Ye'ers thruly, Willum McKinley,' an' makin' pitchers iv a house in Canton, Ohio, while th' cab'net thinks.

"Fin'lly th' sicrety iv state, he says, 'Ye might start it off, if ye want to make it a pop'lar docymint an' wan that'll be raymimbered,' he says, 'whin ye ar-re forgotten,' he says, 'be mintioning what has been done be th' state department,' he says. 'They'se a dhray at th' dure with th' facts,' he says, if ye've f'rgotten thim,' he says. 'Thin,' says th' sicrety iv the Threeasury, 'ye might glide aisily into a few remarks about th' excellent condition iv th' public fi-nances,' he says. 'Something like this: "Thanks to th' tireless activity iv th' sicrety iv th' threeasury th' efforts iv those inimies iv pop'lar governmint, th' Wall sthreet bears, has been onable to mark down quotations an' thus roon th' prosperity iv th' nation. All his ol' frinds will be glad to know that this pop'lar an' affable gintleman has his eye on th' ticker again. Lyman is th' boy f'r th' money," or "I dinnaw what I cud do without Lyman." 'Something like that'd hit thim har-rd.' 'In passing,' says th' sicrety iv war, 'ye might say that ye were late in gettin' hold iv th' right man f'r me place, fr'm th' r-right state, but now ye've got him ye don't know how ye got along without him. Ye may add that I'm the first sicrety iv war that iver showed that th' constitootion iv th' United States is applicable on'y in such cases as it is applied to on account iv its applicability,' he says. 'F'r further particklars see small bills an' me own report,' he says. 'I don't know,' says th' sicrety iv th' navy, 'whether 'tis gin'raly undherstood, but,' he says, 'ye might point out that th' navy niver was so efficient as at prisint,' he says. 'Th' name iv Jawn D. Long will not soon be f'rgotten be himsilf in common with his fellow-counthrymen,' he says. 'An allusion to th' gradjool extermina-tion iv th' thrusts would be much apprecyated in Noo Jarsey,' says th' attorney-gin'ral. 'Those monsthers make their homes there,' he says, 'an',' he says, 'I will say f'r thim, they're good neighbors,' he says.

"'An' while ye're at it,' says a modest voice fr'm th' corner iv th' room, 'don't f'rget to dhrop in a bean f'r th' sicrety iv agriculture—Tama Jim, th' farmers' frind. Gr-reat captains,' he says, 'with their guns an' dhrums,' he says, 'soon pass away, but whin they're gone wan figure will stand out like th' coopoly on a r-red barn,' he says. 'To whom d'ye refer?' angrily demands th' sicrety iv war. 'To mesilf,' says th' sicrety iv agriculture.

"'Gintlemen,' says th' Prisident, 'ar-re ye all through?' he says. 'We ar-re,' says they. 'An' where do I come in?' he says. 'Why,' says th' sicrety iv state, 'ye sign th' docymint,' says he. 'Well,' says Mack, 'I've heerd ye'er suggistions,' he says, 'an' ye may go back to wurruk,' he says. 'I'll write this message, an' if ye see anny iv ye'er names in it,' he says, 'ye may conclude,' he says, 'that me hand has lost its cunning,' he says. 'I guess,' he says, 'I'm some huckleberries in this governmint mesilf,' he says.

"An' he sets down an' writes: 'Fellow Citizens: I'm glad to see ye here, an hope ye won't stay long. Thanks to ye'er Uncle Bill, times is lookin' up an' will be more so in th' near future. Me foreign relations ar-re iv th' most plisint nature. Ye will be glad to know that th' frindship iv this counthry with Germany planted in Samoa an' nourished at Manila has grown to such a point as to satisfy th' mos' critical German-American. With England we ar-re on such terms as must plaze ivry Canajeen, but not on anny such terms as wud make anny Irishman think we ar-re on such terms as we ought not to be. In other wurruds, we cherish a deep animosity mingled with passionate love, such a feelin' as we must entertain to a nation with common impulses f'r th' same money an' a common language iv abuse. To'rd our sister raypublic iv France an' our ol' frind an' ally, Rooshia, to sunny Italy an' Austhria an' Boolgahria an' oppressed Poland, to th' Boer, who has manny rilitives here, an' to ivry other nation but Chinnymen an' Indyans not votin', kind regards. I wud speak to ye on th' subject iv thrusts, but I have nawthin' to say. If ye want to smash this necess'ry evil, this octopus that with its horrible tentacles is crushin' out an' nourishin' commerce, do it ye'ersilf. That's what ye'er here f'r. Something ought to be done f'r th' Nic'ragyooa canal, but what th' divvle it is, I dinnaw. As f'r our newly acquired possessions, 'tis our intintion to give them a form iv govern-mint suited to their needs, which is small, an' in short, to do as we blamed please with thim, makin' up our minds as we go along. So no more fr'm ye'ers thruly, Willum McKinley.'

"An' there's th' meassage," said Mr. Dooley.

"An' what did congress say?" Mr. Hennessy asked.

"Congress didn't say annything," said Mr. Dooley. "Congress yawned. But congress'll get th' rale message whin it goes over to th' White House wan at a time to see about th' foorth-class postmasthers."

ON A SPEECH BY
PRESIDENT McKINLEY

"I hear-r that Mack's in town," said Mr. Dooley.

"Didn't ye see him?" asked Mr. Hennessy.

"Faith, I did not!" said Mr. Dooley. "If 'tis meetin' me he's afther, all he has to do is to get on a ca-ar an' r-ride out to number nine-double-naught-nine Archey R-road, an' stop whin he sees th' sign iv th' Tipp'rary Boodweiser Brewin' Company. I'm here fr'm eight in the mornin' till midnight, an' th' r-rest iv th' time I'm in the back room in the ar-rms iv Or-rphyus, as Hogan says. Th' Presidint is as welcome as anny rayspictable marrid man. I will give him a chat an' a dhrink f'r fifteen cints; an', as we're not, as a frind iv mine in th' grocery an' pothry business says, intirely a commercial an' industhreel nation, if he has th' Sicrety iv th' Threasury with him, I'll give him two f'r twenty-five cints, which is th' standard iv value among civil-ized nations th' wurruld over. . . . I may niver see him. I may go to me grave without gettin' an' eye on th' wan man besides mesilf that don't know what th' furrin' policy iv th' United States is goin' to be. An he, poor man, whin some wan asts him, 'Did ye iver meet Dooley?' 'll have to say, 'No, I had th' chanst, wanst, but me accursed pride kept me from visitin' him.'

"I r-read his speeches, though, an' know what he's doin'. Some iv thim ar-re gr-reat.

"He attinded th' banket given be th' Prospurity Brigade at th' hotel where he's stoppin'. 'Twas a magnificent assimblage iv th' laborin' classes, costin' fifteen dollars a plate, an' on'y disturbed whin a well-to-do gintleman in th' dhry-goods business had to be thrun out f'r takin' a kick at a waiter. I r-read be th' papers that whin Mack come in he was rayceived be th' gatherin' with shouts iv approval. Th' proceedin's was opened with a prayer that Providence might re-main undher th' protection iv th' administhration. Mack r-rose up in a perfect hurcane iv applause, an' says he, 'Gintlemen,' he says, 'an' fellow-heroes,' he says, 'ye do me too much honor,' he says. 'I alone shud not have th' credit iv this gloryous victhry. They ar-re others.' [A voice: 'Shafter.' Another voice: 'Gage.' Another voice: 'Dooley.'] 'But I pass to a more conganial line iv thought,' he says. 'We have just emerged fr'm a turrible war,' he says. 'Again,' he says, 'we ar-re a united union,' he says. 'No north,' he says, 'no south, no east,' he says, 'no west. No north east a point east,' he says.

'Now,' he says, 'th' question is what shall we do with the fruits iv victhry?' he says. (A voice, 'Can thim.') 'Our duty to civilization commands us to be up and doin',' he says. We ar-re bound,' he says, 'to—to re-elize our destiny, whativer it may be,' he says.

'We cannot tur-rn back,' he says, 'Th' hands iv th' clock, that, even as I speak,' he says, 'is r-rushin' through th' hear-rts iv men,' he says, 'dashin' its spray again th' star iv liberty an' hope, an' no north, no south, no east, no west, but a steady purpose to do th' best we can, considerin' all th' circumstances iv th' case,' he says, 'an', with these few remarks,' he says, 'I will tur-rn th' job over to destiny,' he says, 'which is sure to lead us iver on an' on, an' back an' forth, a united an' happy people, livin',' he says, 'undher an administration that, thanks to our worthy Prisident an' his cap'ble an' earnest advisers, is second to none,' he says."

MAKING A CABINET

"I suppose, Jawn," said Mr. Dooley, "ye do be afther a governmint job. Is it council to Athlone or what, I dinnaw?"

"I haven't picked out the place yet," said Mr. McKenna. "Bill wrote me the day after election about it. He says: 'John,' he says, 'take anything you want that's not nailed to the wall,' he says. He heard of my good work in the Twenty-ninth. We rolled up eight votes in Carey's precinct, and had five of them counted; and that's more of a miracle than carrying New York by three hundred thousand."

"It is so," said Mr. Dooley. "It is f'r a fact. Ye must 've give the clerks an' judges morphine, an' ye desarve great credit. Ye ought to have a place; and' I think ye'll get wan, if there's enough to go round among th' Irish Raypublicans. 'Tis curious what an effect an iliction has on th' Irish Raypublican vote. In October an Irish Raypublican's so rare people point him out on th' street, an' women carry their babies to see him. But th' day afther iliction, glory be, ye run into thim ivrywhere,—on th' sthreet-car, in the sthreet, in saloons principally, an' at th' meetin's iv th' Raypublican Comity. I've seen as manny iv them as twinty in here to-day, an' ivry wan iv thim fit to run anny job in th' governmint, fr'm direction' th' Departmint iv State to carryin' ashes out an' dumpin thim in th' white lot.

"They can't all have jobs, but they've got to be attinded to first; an', whin Mack's got through with thim, he can turn in an' make up that cabinet iv his. Thin he'll have throuble iv his own, th' poor man, on'y comin' into fifty thousand a year and rint free. If 'twas wan iv th' customs iv th' great raypublic iv ours, Jawn, f'r to appoint th' most competent men f'r th' places, he'd have a mighty small lot f'r to pick fr'm. But, seein' that on'y thim is iligible that are unfit, he has th' divvle's own time selectin'. F'r Sicrety iv State, if he follows all iv what Casey calls recent precidints, he's limited to ayether a jack-leg counthry

lawyer, that has set around Washington f'r twinty years, pickin'
up a dollar or two be runnin' errands f'r a foreign imbassy, or a
judge that doesn't know whether th' city of Booloogne-sure-
Mere, where Tynan was pinched, is in Boolgahria or th' County
Cavan. F'r Sicrety iv th' Threasury he has a choice iv three
kinds iv proud and incompetent fi-nanceers. He can ayether take
a bank prisident, that 'll see that his little bank an' its frinds
doesn't get th' worst iv it, or a man that cudden't maintain th'
par'ty iv a counthry dhry-good store long enough to stand off th'
sheriff, or a broken-down Congressman, that is full iv red liquor
half the year, an' has remorse settin' on his chest th' other half.

"On'y wan class is iligible f'r Attorney-gin'ral. To fill that
job, a man's got to be a first-class thrust lawyher. If he ain't, th'
Lord knows what will happen. Be mistake he might prosecute
a thrust some day, an' th' whole country'll be rooned. He must
be a man competint f'r to avoid such pitfalls an' snares, so 'tis
th' rule f'r to have him hang on to his job with th' thrust afther
he gets to Washington. This keeps him in touch with th'
business intherests.

"F'r Sicrety iv War, th' most like wan is some good prisident
iv a sthreet-car company. 'Tis exthraordinney how a man
learns to manage military affairs be auditin' thrip sheets an'
rentin' signs in a sthreet-car to chewin' gum imporyums. If
Gin'ral Washington iv sacred mimory 'd been under a good
sthreet-car Sicrety iv War, he'd've wore a bell punch to ring up
ivry time he killed a Hessian. He wud so, an' they'd've kep'
tab on him, an', if he thried to wurruk a brother-in-law on
thim, they'd give him his time.

"F'r th' Navy Departmint ye want a Southern Congressman
fr'm th' cotton belt. A man that iver see salt wather outside iv a
pork bar'l 'd be disqualified f'r th' place. He must live so far
fr'm th' sea that he don't know a capstan bar fr'm a sheet anchor. That puts him in th' proper position to inspect armor
plate f'r th' imminent Carnegie, an' insthruct admirals that's
been cruisin' an' fightin' an dhrinkin' mint juleps f'r thirty
years. He must know th' difference bechune silo an' insilage,
how to wean a bull calf, an' th' best way to cure a spavin. If he

has that information, he is fixed f'r th' job.

"Whin he wants a good Postmaster-gin'ral, take ye'er ol' law partner f'r awhile, an', be th' time he's larned to stick stamps, hist him out, an' put in a school-teacher fr'm a part iv th counthry where people communicate with each other through a conch. Th' Sicrety iv th' Interior is an important man. If possible, he ought to come fr'm Maine or Florida. At anny rate, he must be a resident iv an Atlantic seacoast town, an' niver been west iv Cohoes. If he gets th' idee there are anny white poeple in Ann Arbor or Columbus, he loses his job.

"Th' last place on th' list is Sicrety iv Agriculture. A good, lively business man that was born in th' First Ward an' moved to th' Twinty-foorth after th' fire is best suited to this office. Thin he'll have no prejudices against sindin' a farmer cactus seeds whin he's on'y lookin' f'r wheat, an' he will have a proper understandin' iv th' importance iv an' early Agricultural Bureau rayport to th' bucket-shops.

"No Prisident can go far away that follows Cleveland's cabinet appintmints, although it may be hard f'r Mack, bein' new at th' business, to select th' right man f'r th' wrong place. But I'm sure he'll be advised be his frinds, an' fr'm th' lists iv candydates I've seen he'll have no throuble in findin' timber."

Considered a classic by Anthony Lewis of *The New York Times*.

THE VICE-PRESIDENT

"It's sthrange about th' vice-prisidincy," said Mr. Dooley. "Th' prisidincy is th' highest office in th' gift iv th' people. Th' vice-prisidincy is th' next highest an' th' lowest. It isn't a crime exactly. Ye can't be sint to jail f'r it, but it's a kind iv a disgrace. It's like writin' anonymous letters. At a convintion nearly all th' dillygates lave as soon as they've nommynated th' prisidint f'r fear wan iv thim will be nommynated f'r vice-prisidint.

"Why is it, I wondher, that ivrybody runs away fr'm a nom-mynation fr vice-prisidint as if it was an indictment be th' gran' jury? It usen't to be so.

"In th' ol' days, whin th' boys had nommynated some unknown man fr'm New York fr prisidint, they turned in an' nommynated a gr-reat an' well-known man fr'm th' West fr vice-prisidint. Th' candydate fr vice-prisidint was all iv th' ticket we iver see durin' a campaign. Th' la-ad they put up fr prisidint stayed down East an' was niver allowed to open his mouth except in writin' befure witnesses, but th' candydate fr vice-prisidint wint fr'm wan end iv th' counthry to th' other howlin' again' th' tariff an' other immortal issues, now dead. I niver voted fr Grover Cleveland. I wudden't vote fr him anny more thin he'd vote fr me. I voted fr old man Thurman an' Tom Hendricks an' Adly Stevenson befure he became a profis-sional vice-prisidint. They thought it was an honor, but if ye'd read their bio-graphies to-day ye'd find at the end: 'Th' writer will pass over th' closin' years iv Mr. Thurman's career hur-riedly. It is enough to say iv this painful peryod that afther a lifetime iv devoted sarvice to his counthry th' statesman's declinin' days was clouded be a gr-reat sorrow. He become vice-prisidint iv th' United States. Oh, how much betther 'twere that we shud be sawed off arly be th' gr-reat reaper Death thin that a life iv honor shud end in ignomy.' It's a turr'ble thing.

"If ye say about a man that he's a good prisidintial timber he'll buy ye a dhrink. If ye say he's good vice-prisidintial timber ye mane that he isn't good enough to be cut up into shingles, an' ye'd betther be careful.

"It's sthrange, too, because it's a good job. I think a man cud put in four years comfortably in th' place if he was a sound sleeper. What ar-re his jooties, says ye? Well, durin' th' cam-paign he has to do a good deal iv th' rough outside wurruk. Th' candydate fr prisidint is at home pickin' out th' big wur-ruds in th' ditchnry an' firin' thim at us fr'm time to time. Th' candydate fr th' vice-prisidincy is out in Ioway yellin' fr'm th' back iv a car or a dhray. He goes to all th' church fairs an' wakes an' appears at public meetin's between a corner solo an' a glee club. He ought to be a man good at repartee. Our now honored (be some) prisidint had to retort with th' very hands that since have signed th' Pannyma Canal bill to a Colorado gintleman who accosted him with a scantling. An' I well raymimber another candydate, an' a gr-reat man, too, who replied to a gintleman in Shelbyville who made a rude remark be threatin' him as though he was an open fireplace. It was what Hogan calls a fine-cut an' incisive reply. Yes, sir, th' candydate f'r vice-prisidint has a busy time iv it durin' th' campaign, hoppin' fr'm town to town, speakin', shakin' hands with th' popylace who call him Hal or Charlie, dodgin' bricks, fightin' with his audjeence, an diggin' up f'r th' fi-nance comity. He has to be an all-round man. He must be a good speaker, a pleasant man with th' ladies, a fair boxer an' rassler, something iv a liar, an' if he's a Raypublican campaignin' in Texas, an active sprinter. If he has all thim qualities, he may or may not rayceive a majority at th' polls, an' no wan will know whether they voted f'r him or not.

"Well, he's ilicted. Th' ilictors call on th' candydate f'r preisidint an' hand him th' office. They notify th' candydate f'r vice-prisidint through th' personal columns iv th' pa-apers: 'If th' tall, dark gintleman with hazel eyes, black coat an' white vest, who was nommynated at th' convintion f'r vice-prisidint, will call at headquarters he will hear iv something to his advantage.' So he buys a ticket an' hops to Wash'nton, where he gets a good room suited to his station right above th' kitchen an' overlookin' a wood-yard. Th' prisidint has to live where he is put, but th' vice-prisidint is free to go annywhere he likes, where they are not particklar. Th' Constitution provides that th' prisidint shall have to put up with darky cookin', but th vice-prisidint is permitted to eat out. Ivry mornin' it is his business to call at th' White House an' inquire afther th' prisidint's health. Whin told that th' prisidint was niver betther he gives three cheers, an' departs with a heavy heart.

"Th' feelin' iv th' vice-prisidint about th' prisidint's well-bein' is very deep. On rainy days he calls at th' White House an' begs th' prisidint not to go out without his rubbers. He has Mrs. Vice-Prisidint knit him a shawl to protect his throat again' th' night air. If th' prisidint has a touch iv fever th' vice-prisidint gets a touch iv fever himsilf. He has th' doctor on th' 'phone durin' th' night. 'Doc, I hear th' prisidint is onwell,' he says. 'Cud I do annything f'r him,—annything like dhrwain' his salary or appintin' th' postmasther at Injynnapolis?' It is princip'lly, Hinnissy, because iv th' vice-prisidint that most iv our prisidints have enjoyed such rugged health. Th' vice-prisidint guards th' prisidint, an' th' prisidint, afther sizin' up th' vice-prisidint, con-cludes that it wud be betther f'r th' counthry if he shud live yet awhile. 'D'ye know,' says th' prisidint to th' vice-prisidint, 'ivry time I see you I feel tin years younger?' 'Ye'er kind wurruds,' says th' vice-prisidint, 'bring tears to me eyes. My wife was sayin' on'y this mornin' how comfortable we ar-re in our little flat.' Some vice-prisidints have been so anxious f'r th' prisidint's safety that they've had to be warned off th' White House grounds.

"Aside fr'm th' arjoos duties iv lookin' afther th' prisidint's health, it is th' business iv th' vice-prisidint to preside over th' deliberations iv th' Sinit. Ivry mornin' between ten an' twelve, he swings his hammock in th' palachial Sinit chamber an' sinks off into dhreamless sleep. He may be awakened by Sinitor Tillman pokin' Sinitor Beveridge in th' eye. This is wan way th' Sinit has iv deliberatin'. If so, th' vice-prisidint rises fr'm his hammock an' says: 'Th' Sinitor will come to ordher.' 'He won't,' says th' Sinitor. 'Oh, very well,' says th' presidin' of-ficer; 'he won't,' an' dhrops off again. It is his jooty to rigorously enforce th' rules iv th' Sinit. There ar-re none. Th' Sinit is ruled be courtesy, like th' longshoreman's union. The' vice-prisidint is not expected to butt in much. It wud be a breach iv Sinitoryal courtesy f'r him to step down an' part th' Sinitor fr'm Texas an' th' Sinitor fr'm Injyannay in th' middle iv a debate undher a desk on whether Northern gintlemen ar-re

more gintlemanly thin Southern gintlemen. I shuddent wondher if he thried to do it if he was taught his place with th' leg
iv a chair. He isn't even called up on to give a decision. All that
his grateful counthry demands fr'm th' man that she has il-
ivated to this proud position on th' toe iv her boot is that he
shall keep his opinyons to himsilf. An' so he whiles away th'
pleasant hours in th' beautiful city iv Wash'nton, an' whin he
wakes up he is ayether in th' White House or in th' sthreet. I'll
niver say annything again' th' vice-prisidincy. It is a good job,
an' is richly deserved be ayether iv th' candydates. An', be
Hivens, I'll go further an' say it richly desarves ayether iv
thim."

CHAPTER IV
LABOR AND CAPITAL

Workers and management were locked in seemingly endless struggle in Mr. Dooley's day, and that impression is accurate, for the same basic issues lie unresolved now.

Although his publishers were anti-union, Dunne's sympathies were generally with the workers, though he sometimes felt they could have picked their fights better in terms of timing and issues.

Dooley always enjoyed great popularity with the working class, but his position was consolidated by Dunne's columns on the bitter Pullman strike of 1894. After his second column had been set in type, the printers passed it among themselves, and when a short time later Dunne dropped into the composing room, the typesetters paid him the ultimate compliment of their trade by drumming their sticks on their type cases, then breaking into applause. Dunne always remembered this salute as one of the greatest thrills of his life.

He never let up on the excesses of businessmen, even when in later years he had come to know most of the great tycoons of his era. He had an excellent grasp of the workings of high finance and was able to reduce it to everyday terms.

THE CONSTITUTION AND MR. PULLMAN AS VIEWED
FROM AN ARCHEY ROAD STANDPOINT

"Th' counthry," said Mr. Dooley, "do be goin' to wrack an' roon. I have nayether limons n'r ice in th' house. Th' laws is defied an' th' constitootion is vilated. Th' rights iv citizens is thrampled upon an' ye can get nayether ice n'r limons f'r love 'r money. Ordher out th' sojers, says I, an' tache th' miscreents what th' 'ell. For why did George Wash'n'ton an' Andhrew Jackson and Jeremiah Houlihan fight an' die if a band iv thraitors can come along an' wrinch from an American citizen his limons an' his ice! Am I right! Am I right, Jawn! Am I right! Am I right! I am.

"This ain't no sthrike. A sthrike is where th' la-ads lave off wurruk an' bate Germans an' thin go back to wurruk f'r rajooced wages an' thank hivin f'r it. This here is a rivolution again constitooted authority.

"Th' constitootion, Jawn, provides f'r Pullman. I don't know th' ma-an, but I wint in wan iv his ca-ars to th' convintion at Peeory with th' lith'ry club, an' I must say th' convayniences is nice. All ye have to do is lave ye'er shoes on th' flure an' ye git some wan's else's in th' mor-rnin'. Thin ye crawl into th' side iv th' ca-ar an' whin ye'er removin' ye'er pa-ants a dhrunk man fr'm th' eighth wa-ard comes an' climbs on ye'er back f'r to get into th' hole above ye. 'Tis nice an' quite, an' th' smill iv it is not ba-ad. Ye have some excitement findin' ye'er shirt in th' mornin', but 'tis all a matther iv sport.

"This here Pullman makes th' sleepin' ca-ars an' th' constitution looks afther Pullman. He have a good time iv it. He don't need to look afther himsilf. He have limons an' ice to give to his neighbors if he wanted to. He owns towns an' min. He makes princes iv th' rile blood iv Boolgahria go round to th' kitchen dure. He is stiffer than wan iv his own towels. Whin he has throuble ivry wan on earth excipt thim that rides in smokin' ca-ars whin they rides at all r-runs to fight f'r him. He calls out George Wash'n'ton an' Abraham Lincoln an' Gin'ral Miles an' Mike Brinnan an' ivry human bein' that rayquires limons an' ice an' thin he puts on his hat an' lams away. 'Gintlemin,' says he, 'I must be off,' he says. 'Go an' kill each other,' he says. 'Fight it out,' he says. 'Defind th' constitution,' he says. 'Me own is not of th' best,' he says, 'an' I think I'll help it be spindin' th' summer,' he says, 'piously,' he says, 'on th' shores iv th' Atlantic ocean.'

"That's Pullman. He slips out as aisely as a ba-ar iv his own soap. An' th' whole wurruld turns in an' shoots an' stabs an' throws couplin' pins an' sojers ma-arch out an' Gin'ral

Miles looks up th' sthreet f'r some wan to show that he can kill min too. Ye take Abraham Lincoln, but give me Pullman.''

This column was selected by Robert Walz, an officer of the American Postal Workers Union in Ludlow, Massachusettes.

WHAT DOES HE CARE?

DOOLEY DISCOURSES AGAIN ON HIS FRIEND
MR. PULLMAN

DOCTRINE OF "WHAT TH' 'ELL"

ARCHEY ROAD PHILOSOPHER REVIEWS HIS AMIABLE
FELLOW TOWNSMAN'S PECULIAR QUALITIES

"Jawn," said Mr. Dooley, "I said it wanst an' I sa-ay it again, I'd liefer be George M. Pullman thin anny man this side iv Michigan City. I would so. Not, Jawn, d'ye mind that I invy him his job iv r-runnin' all th' push-cart lodgin'-houses iv th' counthry or in dayvilopin' th' whiskers iv a goat without displayin' anny other iv th' good qualities iv th' craythur or in savin' his tax list fr'm th' assissor with th' intintion iv layin' it befure a mathrimonyal agency. Sare a bit does I care f'r thim honors. But, Jawn, th' la-ad that can go his way with his nose in th' air an' pay no attintion to th' sufferin' iv women an' chidher—dear, oh, dear, but this life must be as happy as th' da-ay is long.

"It seems to me, Jawn, that half th' throuble we have in this vale iv tears, as Dohenny calls Bridgepoort, is seein' th' sufferin' iv women an' little childhren. Th' men can take care iv thimsilves, says I.

"But as I said, Jawn, 'tis not th' min, ye mind; 'tis th' women an' childhren. Glory be to Gawd, I can scarce go out f'r a wa-alk f'r pity at seein' th' little wans settin' on th' stoops an' th' women with thim lines in th' fa-ace that I see but wanst befure, in our parish over beyant, with th' potatoes that was all kilt be th' frost an' th' oats rotted with th' dhrivin rain. Go into wan iv th' side sthreets about supper time an' see thim, Jawn — thim women sittin' at th' windies with th' babies at their breasts an' waitin' f'r th' ol' man to come home. Thin watch thim as he comes up th' sthreet, with his hat over his eyes an' th' shoulders iv thim bint like a hoop an' dhraggin' his feet as if he carried ball an' chain. Musha, but 'tis a sound to dhrive ye'er heart cold whin a woman sobs an' th' young wans cries, an' both because there's no bread in th' house. Betther off thim that lies in Gavin's crates out in Calv'ry, with th' grass over thim an' th' stars lookin' down on thim, quite at last. An' betther f'r us that sees an' hears an' can do nawthin' but give a crust now an' thin. I seen Tim Dorsey's little woman carryin' a loaf iv bread an' a ham to th' Polack's this noon. Dorsey have been out iv wurruk f'r six months, but he made a sthrike carryin' th' hod yistherday an' th' good woman pinched out some vittles f'r th' Polacks.''

Mr. Dooley swabbed th' bar in a melancholy manner and turned again with the remark: "But what's it all to Pullman. Whin Gawd quarried his heart a happy man was made. He cares no more f'r thim little matthers in life an' death than I do f'r O'Connor's tab. 'Th' women an' childhren is dyin' iv hunger,' they sa-ays. 'They've done no wrong,' they sa-ays. 'Will ye not put out ye'er hand to help thim?' they sa-ays. 'Ah, what th' 'ell,' sa-ays George. 'What th' 'ell,' he sa-ays. 'James,' he sa-ays, 'a bottle iv champagne an' a piece iv crambree pie. What th' 'ell, what th' 'ell, what th' 'ell.' ''

"I heard two died yesterday," said Mr. McKenna. "Two women."

"Poor things, poor things. But," said Mr. Dooley, once more swabbing the bar, "what th' ell."

THE LABOR TROUBLES

"I see th' sthrike has been called off," said Mr. Hennessy.

"Which wan?" asked Mr. Dooley. "I can't keep thrack iv

thim. Somebody is sthrikin' all th' time. Wan day th' horseshoers are out, an' another day th' teamsters. Th' Brotherhood iv Molasses Candy Pullers sthrikes, an' th' Amalgymated Union iv Pickle Sorters quits in sympathy. Th' carpinter that has been puttin' up a chicken coop f'r Hogan knocked off wurruk whin he found that Hogan was shavin' himsilf without a card fr'm th' Barbers' Union. Hogan fixed it with th' walkin' dillygate iv th' barbers, an' th' carpinter quit wurruk because he found that Hogan was wearin' a pair iv non-union pants. Hogan wint down-town an' had his pants unionized an' come home to find that th' carpinter had sthruck because Hogan's hens was layin' eggs without th' union label. Hogan injooced th' hens to jine th' union. But wan iv thim laid an egg two days in succission an' th' others sthruck, th' rule iv th' union bein' that no hen shall lay more eggs thin th' most reluctant hen in th' bunch.

"It's th' same ivrywhere. I haven't had a sandwich f'r a year because ivry time I've asked f'r wan ayether th' butchers or th' bakers has been out on sthrike. If I go down in a car in th' mornin' it's eight to wan I walk back at night. A man I knew had his uncle in th' house much longer than ayether iv thim had intinded on account iv a sthrike iv th' Frindly Brotherhood iv Morchuary Helpers. Afther they'd got a permit fr'm th' walkin' dillygate an' th' remains was carrid away undher a profusyon iv floral imblims with a union label on each iv thim, th' coortege was stopped at ivry corner be a picket, who first punched th' mourners an' thin examined their credintials. Me frind says to me: 'Uncle Bill wud've been proud. He was very fond iv long fun'rals, an' this was th' longest I iver attinded. It took eight hours, an' was much more riochous goin' out thin comin' back," he says.

"It was diff'rent whin I was a young man, Hinnissy. In thim days Capital an' Labor were frindly, or Labor was. Capital was like a father to Labor, givin' it its boord an' lodgin's. Nayether intherfered with th' othcr. Capital wint on capitalizin', an' Labor wint on laborin'. In thim golden days a wurrukin' man was an honest artisan. That's what he was proud to be called. Th' week befure iliction he had his pitcher in th' funny pa-apers. He wore a square paper cap an' a leather apron, an' he had his ar-rm ar-round Capital, a rosy binivolint old guy with a plug-hat an' eye-glasses. They were goin' to th' polls together to vote f'r simple old Capital.

"Capital an' Labor walked ar-rm in ar-rm instead iv havin' both hands free as at prisint. Capital was contint to be Capital, an' Labor was used to bein' Labor. Capital come ar-round an' felt th' ar-rm iv Labor wanst in a while, an' ivry year Mrs. Capital called on Mrs. Labor an' congratylated her on her score. Th' pride iv ivry artisan was to wurruk as long at his task as th' boss cud afford to pay th' gas bill. In return f'r his fidelity he got a turkey ivry year. At Chris'mas time Capital gathered his happy fam'ly around him, an' in th' prisince iv th' ladies iv th' neighborhood give thim a short oration. 'Me brave la-ads,' says he, 'we've had a good year. (Cheers.) I have made a millyon dollars. (Sinsation.) I atthribute this to me supeeryor skill, aided be ye'er arnest efforts at th' bench an' at th' forge. (Sobs.) Ye have done so well that we won't need so manny iv us as we did. (Long an' continyous cheerin'.) Those iv us who can do two men's wurruk will remain, an', if possible, do four. Our other faithful sarvants,' he says, 'can come back in th' spring,' he says, 'if alive,' he says. An' th' bold artysans tossed their paper caps in th' air an' give three cheers f'r Capital. They wurruked till ol' age crept on thim, and thin retired to live on th' wish-bones an' kind wurruds they had accumylated.

"Well, it's too bad that th' goolden days has passed, Hinnissy. Capital still pats Labor on th' back, but on'y with an axe. Labor rayfuses to be threated as a frind. It wants to be threated as an inimy. It thinks it gets more that way. They ar-re still a happy fam'ly, but it's more like an English fam'ly. They don't speak. What do I think iv it all? Ah, sure, I don't know. I belong to th' onforchnit middle class. I wurruk hard, an' I have no money. They come in here undher me hospital roof, an' I furnish thim with cards, checks, an' refrishmints. 'Let's play without a limit,' says Labor. 'It's Dooley's money.' 'Go as far as ye like with Dooley's money,' says Capital. 'What have ye got?' 'I've got a straight to Roosevelt,' says Labor. 'I've got ye beat,' says Capital. 'I've got a Supreme Court full of injunctions.' Manetime I've pawned me watch to pay f'r th' game, an' I have to go to th' joolry-store on th' corner to buy a pound iv beef or a scuttle iv coal. No wan iver sthrikes in sympathy with me."

"They ought to get together," said Mr. Hennessy.

"How cud they get anny closer thin their prisint clinch?" asked Mr. Dooley. "They're so close together now that those that ar-re between thim ar-re crushed to death."

WORK

"Ye haven't sthruck yet, have ye?" said Mr. Dooley.

"Not yet," said Mr. Hennessy. "But th' dillygate was up at th' mills to-day an' we may be called anny minyit now."

"Will ye go?" asked Mr. Dooley.

"Ye bet I will," said Mr. Hennessy. "Ye just bet I will. I stand firm be union principles an' besides it's hot as blazes up there these days. I wudden't mind havin' a few weeks off."

"Ye'll do right to quit," said Mr. Dooley. "I have no sympathy with sthrikers. I have no sympathy with thim anny more thin I have with people goin' off to a picnic. A sthrike is a wurrukin' man's vacation. If I had to be wan iv thim horny-handed sons iv toil, th' men that have made our counthry what it is an' creates th' wealth iv th' wurruld — if I had to be wan iv thim pillars iv th' constitution, which thank Gawd I haven't, 'tis sthrikin' I'd be all th' time durin' th' heated term. I'd begin sthrikin' whin th' flowers begin to bloom in th' parks, an' I'd stay on sthrike till 'twas too cold to sit out on th' bleachers at th' baseball park. Ye bet I wud.

"I've noticed that nearly all sthrikes occur in th' summer time. Sthrikes come in th' summer time an' lockouts in th' winter. In th' summer whin th' soft breezes blows through

shop an' facthry, fannin' th' cheeks iv th' artisan an' settin' fire
to his whiskers, whin th' main guy is off at th' seashore bein'
pinched f'r exceedin' th' speed limit, whin 'tis comfortable to
sleep out at nights an' th' Sox have started a batting sthreak,
th' son iv Marthy, as me frind Roodyard Kipling calls him,
begins to think iv th' rights iv labor.

"Th' more he looks out iv th' window, th' more he thinks
about his rights, an' wan warm day he heaves a couplin' pin at
th' boss an' saunters away. Sthrikes are a great evil f'r th' wurrukin' man, but so are picnics an' he acts th' same at both.
There's th' same not gettin' up till ye want to, th' same meetin'
ye'er frinds f'r th' first time in their good clothes an' th' same
thumpin' sthrangers over th' head with a brick. Afther awhile
th' main guy comes home fr'm th' seaside, raises wages twinty
per cent, fires th' boss an' takes in th' walkin' dillygate as a
specyal partner.

"But in winter, what Hogan calls another flower iv our industhreel system blooms. In th' winter it's warmer in th' foun-
dhry thin in th' home. There is no hearth as ample in anny
man's home as th' hearth th' Steel Comp'ny does its cookin'
by. It is pleasant to see th' citizen afther th' rigors iv a night at
home hurryin' to th' mills to toast his numbed limbs in th'
warm glow iv th' Bessemer furnace. About this time th' main
guy takes a look at the thermometer an' chases th' specyal partner out iv th' office with th' annual report iv th' Civic
Featheration. He thin summons his hardy assocyates about him
an' says he: 'Boys, I will no long stand f'r th' tyranny iv th'
unions. Conditions has changed since last summer. It's grown
much colder. I do not care f'r the money at stake, but there is a
great principle involved. I cannot consint to have me business
run be outsiders at a cost iv near thirty thousand dollars a
year,' says he. An' there's a lockout.

"'Tis a matther iv th' seasons. So if ye sthrike ye'll not get
me sympathy. I resarve that f'r me infeeryors. I'll keep me sympathy f'r th' poor fellow that has nobody to lure him away fr'm
his toil an' that has to sweat through August with no chanst iv

gettin' a day in th' open onless th' milishy are ordhered out an' thin whin he goes back to wurruk th' chances are somebody's got his job while th' sthrikin' wurrukin' man returns with his pockets full iv cigars an' is hugged at th' dure be the main guy. If I was rejooced to wurrukin' f'r me livin', if I was a son iv Marthy I'd be a bricklayer. They always sthrike durin' th' buildin' season. They time it just right. They niver quit wurruk. They thry not to meet it. It is what Hogan calls a pecolyar fact that bricklayers always time their vacations f'r th' peeryod whin there is wurruk to be done.

"No, sir, a sthrike iv financeers wudden't worry anny wan. 'Tis a sthrange thing whin we come to think iv it that th' less money a man gets f'r his wurruk, th' more nicissry it is to th' wurruld that he shud go on wurrukin'. Ye'er boss can go to Paris on a combination wedding an' divoorce thrip an' no wan bothers his head about him. But if ye shud go to Paris—excuse me f'r laughin' mesilf black in th' face—th' industhrees iv the counthry pines away.

"An' th' higher up a man regards his wurruk, th' less it amounts to. We cud manage to scrape along without electhrical injineers but we'd have a divvle iv a time without scavengers. Ye look down on th' fellow that dhrives th' dump cart, but if it wasn't f'r him ye'd niver be able to pursoo ye'er honorable mechanical profissyon iv pushin' th' barrow. Whin Andhrew Carnagie quit, ye wint on wurrukin'; if ye quit wurruk, he'll have to come back. P'raps that's th' reason th' wurrukin' man don't get more iv thim little pictures iv a buffalo in his pay envelope iv a Saturdah night. If he got more money he wud do less wurruk. He has to be kept in thrainin'.

"Th' way to make a man useful to th' wurruld is to give him a little money an' a lot iv wurruk. An' 'tis th' on'y way to make him happy, too. I don't mean coarse, mateeryal happiness like private yachts an' autymobills an' rich food an' other corrodin' pleasures. I mean something entirely diff'rent. I don't know what I mean but I see in th' pa-apers th' other day that th' on'y road to happiness was hard wurruk. 'Tis a good theery. Some day I'm goin' to hire a hall an' preach it in Newport. I wudden't mintion it in Ar-rchy Road where wurruk abounds. I don't want to be run in f'r incitin' a riot."

ON PANICS

"Th' other mornin' I was readin' th' pa-apers about th' panic in Wall Sthreet an' though I've niver seen anything all me life but wan continyal panic I felt low in me mind ontil I looked up an' see ye go by with ye'er shovel on ye'er shouldher an' me heart leaped up. I wanted to rush to th' tillygraft office and wire me frind J. Pierpont Morgan: 'Don't be downcast. It's all right. I just see Hinnissy go by with his shovel.'

"No, sir, ye can bet it ain't th' people that have no money that causes panics. Panics are th' result iv too manny people havin' money. Th' top iv good times is hard times and th' bottom iv hard times is good times. Whin I see wan man with a shovel on his shouldher dodgin' eight thousand autymobills I begin to think 'tis time to put me money in me boot.

"'Tis hard f'r me to undherstand what's goin' on," said Mr. Hennessy. "What does it all mean?"

"'Tis something ye wudden't be ixpected to know," said Mr. Dooley. "'Tis what is known as credit. I'll explain it to ye. F'r the sake iv argymint we'll say ye're a shoemaker. Oh, 'tis on'y f'r th' sake iv argymint. Iverywan knows that a burly fellow like you wudden't be at anny employmint as light an' effiminate as makin' shoes. But supposin' f'r th' sake iv argymint ye're a shoemaker. Ye get two dollars a day f'r makin' forty dollars' worth iv shoes. Ye take part of ye'er ill-gotten gains an' leave it with me f'r dhrink. Afther awhile, I take th' money over to th' shoe store an' buy wan iv th' pairs iv shoes ye made. Th' fellow at th' shoe store puts th' money in a bank owned by ye'er boss. Ye'er boss sees ye're dhrinkin' a good deal an' be th' look iv things th' distillery business ought to improve. So he lends th' money to a distiller. Wan day th' banker obsarves that ye've taken th' pledge, an' havin' fears f'r th' distilling business, he gets his money back. I owe th' distiller money an' he comes to me. I have paid out me money f'r th' shoes an' th' shoe-store man has put it in th' bank. He goes over to th' bank to get it out an' has his fingers cut off in a window. An' there ye are. That's credit.

"Don't get excited about it, Hinnissy, me boy. Cheer up. 'Twill be all right tomorrah, or th' next day, or some time. 'Tis wan good thing about this here wurruld, that nawthin' lasts long enough to hurt. I have been through manny a panic.

THE BIG FINE

"That was a splendid fine they soaked Jawn D. with," said Mr. Dooley.

"What did they give him?" asked Mr. Hennessy.

"Twinty-nine millyon dollars," said Mr. Dooley.

"Oh, great!" said Mr. Hennessy. "That's a grand fine. It's a gorjous fine. I can't hardly believe it."

"It's thrue, though," said Mr. Dooley. "Twinty-nine millyon dollars. Divvle th' cent less. I can't exactly make out what th' charge was that they arrested him on, but th' gin'ral idee is that Jawn D. was goin' around loaded up to th' guards with Standard Ile, exceedin' th' speed limit in acquirin' money, an' singin' 'A charge to keep I have' till th' neighbors cud stand it no longer.' The judge says: 'Ye're an old offender an' I'll have to make an example iv ye. Twinty-nine millyon dollars or fifty-eight millyon days. Call th' next case, Misther Clerk.'

"Did he pay th' fine? He did not. Iv coorse he cud if he wanted to. He wuddent have to pawn annything to get th' money, ye can bet on that. All he'd have to do would be to put his hand down in his pocket, skin twinty-nine millyon dollar bills off iv his roll an' hurl thim at th' clerk. But he refused to pay as a matter iv principle. 'Twas not that he needed th' money. He don't care f'r money in th' passionate way that you an' me do, Hinnissy. Th' likes iv us are as crazy about a dollar as a man is about his child whin he has on'y wan. Th' chances are we'll spoil it. But Jawn D., havin' a large an' growin' fam'ly iv dollars, takes on'y a kind iv gin'ral inthrest in thim. He's issued a statement sayin' that he's a custojeen iv money appinted be himsilf. He looks afther his own money an' th' money iv other people. He takes it an' puts it where it won't hurt thim an' they won't spoil it. He's a kind iv a society f'r th' previntion of croolty to money. If he finds a man misusing his money he takes it away fr'm him an' adopts it. Ivry Saturdah night he lets th' man see it f'r a few hours. An' he says he's surprised to find that whin, with th' purest intintions in th' wurruld, he is found thryin' to coax our little money to his home where it'll find conjanial surroundings an' have other money to play with, th' people thry to lynch him an' th' polis arrest him f'r abduction.

"So as a matther iv principle he appealed th' case. An appeal, Hinnissy, is where ye ask wan coort to show it's contempt f'r another coort. 'Tis sthrange that all th' pathrites that have wanted to hang Willum Jennings Bryan an' mesilf f'r not showin' proper respect f'r th' joodicyary, are now showin' their respect f'r th' joodicyary be appealin' fr'm their decisions. Ye'd think Jawn D. wud bow his head reverentially in th' awful presence iv Kenesaw Mt. Landis an' sob out: 'Thank ye'er honor. This here noble fine fills me with joy. But d'ye think ye give me enough? If agreeable I'd like to make it an even thirty millyons.' But he doesn't. He's like mesilf. Him an' me bows to th' decisions iv th' coorts on'y if they bow first.

"I have gr-reat respect f'r th' joodicyary, as fine a lot iv cross an' indignant men as ye'll find annywhere. I have th' same respect f'r thim as they have f'r each other. But I niver bow to a decision iv a judge onless, first, it's pleasant to me, an', second, other judges bow to it. Ye can't be too careful about what decisions ye bow to. A decision that seems agreeable may turn out like an acquaintance ye scrape up at a picnic. Ye may be ashamed iv it to-morrah. Manny's th' time I've bowed to a decree iv a coort on'y to see it go up gayly to th' supreem coort, knock at th' dure an' be kicked down stairs be an angry old gintleman in a black silk petticoat. A decree iv th' coort has got to be pretty vinrable befure I do more thin greet it with a pleasant smile.

"Me idee was whin I read about Jawn D.'s fine that he'd settle at wanst, payin' twinty-eight millyon dollars in millyon dollar bills an' th' other millyon in chicken-feed like ten thousand dollar bills just to annoy th' clerk. But I ought to've known betther. Manny's th' time I've bent me proud neck to a decision iv a coort that lasted no longer thin it took th' lawyer f'r th' definse to call up another judge on th' tillyphone. A judge listens to a case f'r days an' hears, while he's figurin' a possible goluf score on his blotting pad, th' argymints iv two or three lawyers that no wan wud dare to offer a judgeship to. Gin'rally speakin', judges are lawyers. They get to be judges because they have what Hogan calls th' joodicyal timp'ramint, which is why annybody gets a job. Th' other kind people won't take a job. They'd rather take a chance. Th' judge listens to a case f'r days an' decides it th' way he intinded to. D'ye find th' larned counsel that's just been beat climbin' up on th' bench an' throwin' his arms around th' judge? Ye bet ye don't. He gathers his law books into his arms, gives th' magistrate a look that means, 'There's an eliction next year', an' runs down th' hall to another judge. Th' other judge hears his kick an' says he: 'I don't know annything about this here case except what ye've whispered to me, but I know me larned collague an' I wuddent thrust him to referee a roller-skatin' contest. Don't pay th' fine till ye hear fr'm me.' Th' on'y wan that bows to th' decision is th' fellow that won, an' pretty soon he sees he's made a mistake, f'r wan day th' other coort comes out an' declares that th' decision of th' lower coort is another argymint in favor iv abolishing night law schools.

"That's th' way Jawn D. felt about it an' he didn't settle. I wondher will they put him away if he don't pay ivinchooly? 'Twill be a long sentence. A frind iv mine wanst got full iv kerosene an' attempted to juggle a polisman. They thried him whin he come out iv th' emergency hospital an' fined him a hundhred dollars. He didn't happen to have that amount with him at th' moment or at anny moment since th' day he was born. But the judge was very lenient with him. He said he needn't pay it if he cudden't. Th' coort wud give him a letther of inthroduction to th' bridewell an' he cud stay there f'r two hundhred days. At that rate it'll be a long time befure Jawn D. an' me meet again on th goluf-links. Hogan has it figured out that if Jawn D. refuses to go back on his Puritan principles an' separate himsilf fr'm his money he'll be wan hundhred an' fifty-eight thousand years in cold storage. A man ought to be pretty good at th' lock step in a hundhred an' fifty-eight thousand years.

"Well, sir, glory be but times has changed whin they land me gr-reat an' good frind with a fine that's about akel to three millyon dhrunk an' disorderly cases. 'Twud've been cheaper if he'd took to dhrink arly in life. I've made a vow, Hinnissy, niver to be very rich. I'd like to be a little rich, but not rich enough f'r anny wan to notice that me pockets bulged. Time was whin I dhreamed iv havin' money an' lots iv it. 'Tis thrue I begun me dhreams at th' wrong end, spent th' money befure I got it. I was always clear about th' way to spend it but oncertain about th' way to get it. If th' Lord had intinded me to be a rich man He'd've turned me dhreams around an' made me clear about makin' th' money but very awkward an' shy about gettin' rid iv it. There are two halves to ivry dollar. Wan is knowin' how to make it an' th' other is not knownin' how to spend it comfortably. Whin I hear iv a man with gr-reat business capacity I know he's got an akel amount iv spending incapacity. No matter how much he knew about business he wuddent be rich if he wasn't totally ignorant iv a science that we have developed as far as our means will allow. But now, I tell ye, I don't dhream iv bein' rich. I'm afraid iv it. In th' good old days th' polis coorts were crowded with th' poor. They weren't charged with poverty, iv coorse, but with the results iv poverty, d'ye mind. Now, be Hivens, th' rich have invaded even th' coorts an' the bridewell. Manny a face wearin' side whiskers an' gold rimmed specs peers fr'm th' windows iv th' black Maria. 'What's this man charged with?' says th' coort. 'He was found in possession iv tin millyon dollars,' says th' polisman. An' th' judge puts on th' black cap."

"Well," said Mr. Hennessy, "'tis time they got what was comin' to thim."

"I'll not say ye're wrong," said Mr. Dooley. "I see th' way me frind Jawn D. feels about it. He thinks he's doin' a great sarvice to th' worruld collectin' all th' money in sight. It might remain in incompetint hands if he didn't get it. 'Twud be a shame to lave it where it'd be misthreated. But th' on'y throuble with Jawn is that he don't see how th' other fellow feels about it. As a father iv about thirty dollars I want to bring thim up mesilf in me own foolish way. I may not do what's right be thim. I may be too indulgent with thim. Their home life may not be happy. Perhaps 'tis clear that if they wint to th' Rockyfellar institution f'r th' care iv money they'd be in bether surroundings, but whin Jawn thries to carry thim off I raise a cry iv 'Polis,' a mob iv people that niver had a dollar iv their own an' niver will have wan, pounce on th' misguided man, th' polis pinch him, an' th' governmint condemns th' institution an' lets out th' inmates an' a good manny iv thim go to th' bad."

"D'ye think he'll iver sarve out his fine?" asked Mr. Hennessy.

"I don't know," said Mr. Dooley. "But if he does, whin he comes out at the end iv a hundhred an fifty-eight thousand years he'll find a great manny changes in men's hats an' th' means iv transportation but not much in annything else. He may find flyin' machines, though it'll be arly f'r thim, but he'll see a good manny people still walkin' to their wurruk."

Note: Rockefeller was never forced to pay this fine.

BANKS AND BANKING

"Well, sir," said Mr. Dooley, "I've been doin' th' bankers iv this counthry a gr-reat injustice."

"How's that?" asked Mr. Hennessy.

"I've put thim down all me life as cold, stony-hearted men that wud as soon part with their lives as with their money. I had a pitcher iv a banker in me mind, a stern, hard-featured ol' gintleman, with curly side-whiskers, settin' on th' people's money an' stalin' off both th' borrower who comes be night with a dhrill an' th' more rayfined burglar who calls in th' daytime with a good story. I was afraid iv thim. I wud no more dare to ask a banker to take a dhrink or shoot th' shoots with me thin I wud an archbishop. If I talked to wan iv thim I'd look up all me statements in th' almanack an' all me wurruds in th' ditchnry to see that I got nawthin' wrong. An' I made a mistake about thim. Far fr'm bein' a hard, cynical class, th' bankers iv America is a lot iv jolly dogs, that believes in human nature, takes life as it is, aisy come, aisy go, hurrah boys, we'll be a long time dead. Hard to borrow money fr'm thim? On th' conthry, it's hard to keep thim fr'm crowdin' it on ye. They'll lend ye money on annything ye shove in, on a dhream that ye saw a sojer on horseback, on th' sad story iv ye'er life, or on ye'er wurrud iv honor if ye're ready to go back on it. I niver knew what collateral was ontil this lady fr'm Cleveland come along. Collateral is a misstatement on which bankers lend money. If ye broke into a bank in Ohio to-morrah ye'd prob'ly find th' vaults iv Louisiana lotthry tickets, bets on th' races, an' rayports iv crystal gazin'.

"Bankin' is a sthrange business, annyhow. I make up me mind that I need more money thin I have, or I want to build a railroad in Omaha or a gas-house in Milwaukee, or Mrs. Chadwick wants an autymobill, or something else happens, an' I start a bank. I build a brick house, put ir'n gratin's on th' window, an' ye an' Donohue fight each other to see who'll get his money first to me. I accept it very reluctantly an' as a gr-reat favor to ye. Says I: 'Hinnissy an' Donohue,' says I, 'ye ar-re rayspictable wurrukin'-men, an' I will keep ye'er money f'r ye rather thin see ye spind it in riochous livin',' says I. 'As a gr-reat favor to ye I will take care iv these lithographs be lendin' thim to me frinds,' says I. 'If ye want th' money back ye can have it anny time between nine in th' mornin' an' three in th' afthernoon except Sundays an' holidays,' says I; 'but don't both come at wanst,' says I, 'or nayether iv ye'll get it,' says I. Well, ye lave ye'er money with me, an' I suppose ye think iv it lyin' safe an' sound in th' big sthrong box, where th' burglar boys can't get it. Ye sleep betther at nights because ye feel that ye'er money is where no wan can reach it except over me dead body. If ye on'y knew ye've not turned ye'er back befure I've chased those hard-earned dollars off th' premises! With ye'er money I build a house an' rent it to you. I start a railroad with it, an' ye wurruk on th' railroad at two dollars a day. Ye'er money makes me a prom'nent citizen. Th' newspapers intherview me on what shud be done with th' toilin' masses, mannin' ye an' Donohue; I consthruct th' foreign policy iv th' govermint; I tell ye how ye shud vote. Ye've got to vote th' way I say or I won't give ye back ye'er money. An' all this time ye think iv that little bundle iv pitchers nestlin' in th' safe in me brick house, with me settin' at th' dure with a shot-gun acrost me knees. But wan day ye need th' money to bury some wan, an' ye hurry down to see me. 'Sorry,' says I, 'but I've jus' given it all to a lady who come out iv th' Chinese laundhry nex' dure an' said she was an aunt iv Jawn D. Rockefellar.' An' there ye ar-re.

"If iver I have anny relations with a bank, Hinnissy, it won't be in th' way iv puttin' money in. Were ye iver in a bank? Ye wudden't be. I was wanst. Wanst I was eighty-five dollars on me way to bein' a millyonaire, an' I wint down-town an' threw th' money into th' window an' told th' banker to take th' best iv care iv it. 'We can't take this,' says he. 'Why not?' says I. 'I don't know ye,' says he. 'Niver mind that,' says I. 'It's me money, not mesilf, I'm thryin' to inthrajooce to s-ciety,' says I. 'It's a very nice kind iv money, an' aven if ye don't like it now 'twill grow on ye,' says I. 'Or at laste I hope so,' says I. D'ye know, Hinnissy, he wudden't take th' money till I cud get Dorsey, th' plumber, to assure him that I was fr'm wan iv th' oldest fam'lies that had come to Archey Road since th' fire. Havin' satisfied himsilf that me money was fit f'r other people's money to assocyate with, he tol' th' polisman to put me in a line iv people with blue noses, who were clutchin' at postal-ordhers in front iv a window where a young fellow sat. Th' young fellow was properly indignant at havin' to take money fr'm sthrangers, an' he showed it be glarin' at th' impy-dint depositors. Whin it come me turn I wanted to tell him how I hated to part with me little money; how long me money an' me had slept together, an' niver had a cross wurrud; how its slightest nod was a command to me, but now I supposed th' time had come whin it must go out an' see something iv th' wurruld, on'y I hoped 'twud be happy among sthrangers. An' wud he be good to it, because 'twas all I had, an' not large f'r its age.

"I felt very sintimintal, Hinnissy. F'r two years I'd counted that money forty times a day. I knew ivry wrinkle on it. I had what he might call a legal tenderness f'r it. But befure I cud deliver me sintimintal addhress called, 'A poor man's farewell to his roly-boly,' th' young fellow grabbed th' bundle, tossed it over into a pile, hit me on th' chest with a passbook, mutthered 'Burglar' undher his breath, an' dhrove me fr'm th' bank, penniless.

"As I passed be th' prisidint's office I found th' great man biddin' a tearful farewell to Gallagher iv th' fifth ward. Ye know Gallagher. He owns all th' copper mines in Halsted Sthreet, has a half inthrest in Jack's tips on th' races, an' conthrols th' American rights in th' Humbert fam'ly. 'Ar-re ye wan iv us?' says I. 'Wan iv what?' says he. 'Wan iv us depositors,' says I. 'I am not,' says he. 'I've jus' dhropped in an' borrowed a thousan',' says he. 'What on?' says I. 'On a good thing this afthernoon at Noo Orleens,' says he. 'Who vouched f'r ye'er charackter?' says I. 'Ye don't need a charackter to borrow money at a bank,' says he."

"How d'ye suppose that there lady fr'm Cleveland fooled thim bankers?" asked Mr. Hennessy. "Ye'd think they'd be too smart to be bunkoed."

"Don't ye believe it," said Mr. Dooley. "Nobody is too smart to be bunkoed. Th' on'y kind iv people that can be bunkoed are smart people. Ye can be too honest to be bunkoed, but niver too smart. It's the people that ar-re thryin' to get something f'r nawthin' that end in gettin' nawthin' f'r ivrything. I niver can burst into tears whin I read about some lad bein' robbed be a confidence game. Canada Bill, Gib Fitz, or Mrs. Chadwick niver got anny money fr'm square people. A man that buys a goold brick thinks he is swindlin' a poor Indyan that don't know its value; a fellow that comes on to buy f'r five hundherd dollars tin thousan' dollars' worth iv something that is so like money ye can't tell the diff'rence is hopin' to swindle th' governmint; the foolish man that falls f'r th' three-card thrick has th' wrong card crimped f'r him whin th' dealer's back is turned; th' shell wurruker always pretinds to fumble an' carelessly show th' farmer which shell th' little pea is undher; an' th' lady fr'm Cleveland cudden't have got anny more money on Andy's name thin on mine if she hadn't promised to divide with th' bankers. I refuse to sob over thim poor, gloomy financeers anny more thin I wud over th' restless capitalist who loses his all in a wire-tappin' entherprise. Whin a man gets more thin six per cent. f'r his money it's a thousan' to wan he's payin' it himsilf. Whiniver annybody offers to give ye something f'r nawthin', or something f'r less than its worth, or more f'r something thin its worth, don't take anny chances. Yell f'r a polisman."

"Th' wurruld is full iv crooks," said Mr. Hennessy.

"It ain't that bad," said Mr. Dooley. "An', besides, let us

thank Hivin they put in part iv their time cheatin' each other.''

ON WALL STREET

"Well, sir," said Mr. Dooley, "I see th' Titans iv Finance has clutched each other be th' throat an' engaged in a death sthruggle. Glory be, whin business gets above sellin' tinpinny nails in a brown paper cornucopy, 't is hard to tell it fr'm murther."

"What's a Titan iv Fi-nance?" asked Mr. Hennessy.

"A Ti-tan iv Fi-nance," said Mr. Dooley, "is a man that's got more money thin he can carry without bein' disordherly. They'se no intoxicant in th' wurruld, Hinnissy, like money. It goes to th' head quicker thin th' whiskey th' dhruggist makes in his back room. A little money taken fr'm frinds in a social way or f'r th' stomach's sake is not so bad. A man can make money slowly an' go on increasin' his capacity till he can carry his load without staggerin' an' do nawthin' vilent with a millyon or two aboord. But some iv these la-ads has been thryin' to consume th' intire output, an' it looks to me as though 't was about time to call in th' polis. Well, th' big la-ads is sthrong and knows how to guard, an whin they're spread out, small harm has come to thim. But th' little dhrunk financeers that're not use to th' flowin' dividend an' th' quick profit that biteth like a wasp an' stingeth like an adder, th' little la-ads that are carryin' more thin they can hold an' walk, are picked up in pieces. That's what Hogan calls, Oh, Fi-nance, Oh, Fi-nance, as Shakespeare says, how manny crimes are committed in thy name!''

CHAPTER V

THE NATIONAL CHARACTER

"Well, we're a great people, we are," said Mr. Hennessy. "We are. We are that."

"And the best of it is, we know we are," replied Mr. Dooley.

Nonetheless, periodically throughout American history, Americans have felt a need for a national housecleaning, as well as an occasional crusade against vice. Being a hero to the American people lasts even a shorter time than it did in Dooley's day — 15 minutes has become the statutory limit. And lying with a purpose has become an alibi for improper behavior by officials in our own time.

"Newspaper Publicity" contains the most plagiarized of Dooleyisms. When Clare Booth Luce graciously referred to her old political enemy, Eleanor Roosevelt, as a "comforter of the afflicted and afflicter of the comfortable," she was quoting Mr. Dooley, though without attribution. Others have used it since, also without attribution.

As other Dooley essays show, while time has passed, very little else has changed in American life or the American character.

NATIONAL HOUSECLEANING

"It looks to me," said Mr. Hennessy, "as though this counthry was goin' to th' divvle."

"Put down that magazine," said Mr. Dooley. "Now d'ye feel betther? I thought so. But I can sympathize with ye. I've been readin' thim mesilf. Time was whin I sildom throubled thim. I wanted me fiction th' day it didn't happen, an' I cud buy that f'r a penny fr'm th' newsboy on th' corner. But wanst in a while some homefarin' wandhrer wud jettison wan in me

place, an' I'd frequently glance through it an' find it in me lap
whin I woke up. Th' magazines in thim days was very ca'ming
to th' mind. Angabel an' Alfonso dashin' f'r a marredge
license. Prom'nent lady authoressesses makin' pomes at th'
moon. Now an' thin a scrap over whether Shakespeare was enthered in his own name or was a ringer, with th' long-shot
players always again Shakespeare. But no wan hurt. Th' idee
ye got fr'm these here publications was that life was wan glad,
sweet song. If annything, ivrybody was too good to ivrybody
else. Ye don't need to lock th' dure at night. Hang ye'er watch
on th' knob. Why do polismen carry clubs? Answer, to knock
th' roses off th' throlley-poles. They were good readin'. I liked
thim th' way I like a bottle iv white pop now an' thin.

"But now whin I pick me fav'rite magazine off th' flure,
what do I find? Ivrything has gone wrong. Th' wurruld is little
betther thin a convict's camp. Angabel an' Alfonso ar-re about
to get married whin it is discovered that she has a husband in
Ioway an' he has a wife in Wisconsin. All th' pomes be th' lady
authoressesses that used to begin: 'Oh, moon, how fair!' now
begin: 'Oh, Ogden Armour, how awful!' Shakespeare's on'y
mintioned as a crook. Here ye ar-re. Last edition. . . Just out.
Full account iv th' Crimes iv Incalculated. Did ye read Larsen
last month on 'Th' use iv Burglars as Burglar Alarums'? Good,
was it? Thin read th' horrible disclosures about th' way Jawn
C. Higgins got th' right to build a bay-window on his barber-
shop at iliven forty-two Kosciusko Avnoo, South Bennington,
Arkansaw. Read Wash'n'ton Bliffens's dhreadful assault on
th' board iv education iv Baraboo. Read Idarem on Jawn D.;
she's a lady, but she's got th' punch. Graft ivrywhere. 'Graft in
th' Insurance Comp'nies,' 'Graft in Congress,' 'Graft in th'
Supreem Coort,' 'Graft be an Old Grafter,' 'Graft in
Lithrachoor,' be Hinnery James; 'Graft in Its Relations to th'
Higher Life,' be Dock Eliot; 'Th' Homeeric Legend an' Graft;
Its Cause an' Effect; Are They th' Same? Yes and No,' be Nor-
man Slapgood.

"An' so it goes, Hinnissy, till I'm that blue, discouraged, an'
broken-hearted I cud go to th' edge iv th' wurruld an' jump

off. It's a wicked, wicked, horrible, place, an' this here counthry is about th' toughest spot in it.

I don't thrust anny man anny more. I niver did much, but
now if I hear th' stealthy step iv me dearest frind at th' dure I
lock th' cash dhrawer. I used to be nervous about burglars, but
now I'm afraid iv a night call fr'm th' Chief Justice iv th'
Supreem Coort or th' prisidint iv th' First National Bank.

"It's slowly killin' me, Hinnissy, or it wud if I thought about
it. I'm sorry George Wash'n'ton iver lived. Thomas Jefferson I
hate. An' as f'r Adam, well, if that joker iver come into this
place I'd—but I mustn't go on.

"Do I think it's all as bad as that? Well, Hinnissy, now that
ye ask me, an' seein' that Chris'mas is comin' on, I've got to
tell ye that this counthry, while wan iv th' worst in th' wurruld,
is about as good as th' next if it ain't a shade betther. But we're
wan iv th' gr-reatest people in th' wurruld to clean house, an'
th' way we like best to clean th' house is to burn it down. We
come home at night an' find that th' dure has been left open
an' a few mosquitoes or life-insurance prisidints have got in,
an' we say: 'This is turr'ble. We must get rid iv these here
pests.' An' we take an axe to thim. We desthroy a lot iv furniture an' kill th' canary bird, th' cat, th' cuckoo clock, an' a
lot iv other harmless insects, but we'll fin'lly land th' mosquitoes. If an Englishman found mosquitoes in his house he'd
first thry to kill thim, an' whin he didn't succeed he'd say:
'What pleasant little humming-bur-rds they ar-re. Life wud be
very lonesome without thim,' an he'd domesticate thim, larn
thim to sing 'Gawd Save th' King,' an' call his house Mosquito
Lodge. But with this here nation iv ours somebody scents
something wrong with th' scales at th' grocery-store an' whips
out his gun, another man turns in a fire alarm, a third fellow
sets fire to th' Presbyterian Church, a vigilance comity is
formed an' hangs ivry foorth man; an' havin' started with
Rockyfellar, who's tough an' don't mind bein' lynched, they
fin'lly wind up with desthroyin' me because th' steam laundhry
has sint me home somebody else's collars.

"It reminds me, Hinnissy, iv th' time I lived at a

boardin'-house kept be a lady be th' name iv Doherty. She was a good woman, but her idee iv life was a combination iv pneumony an' love. She was niver still. Th' sight iv a spot on th' wall where a gintleman boorder had laid his head afther dinner would give her nervous prostration. She was always polishin', scrubbin', sweepin', airin'. She had a plumber in to look at th' dhrains twice a week. Fifty-two times a year there was a rivolution in th' house that wud've made th' Czar iv Rooshya want to go home to rest. An' yet th' house was niver really clean. It looked as if it was to us. It was so clean that I always was ashamed to go into it onless I'd shaved. But Mrs. Doherty said no; it was like a pig-pen. 'I don't know what to do,' says she. 'I'm worn out, an' it seems impossible to keep this house clean.' 'What is th' throuble with it?' says he. 'Madam,' says me frind Gallagher, 'wud ye have me tell ye?' he says. 'I wud,' says she. 'Well,' says he, 'th' throuble with this house is that it is occupied entirely be human bein's,' he says. 'If 'twas a vacant house,' he says, 'it cud aisily be kept clean,' he says.

"An' there ye ar-re, Hinnissy. Th' noise ye hear is not th' first gun iv a rivolution. It's on'y th' people iv th' United States batin' a carpet. Ye object to th' smell? That's nawthin'. We use sthrong disinfectants here. A Frinchman or an Englishman cleans house be sprinklin' th' walls with cologne; we chop a hole in th' flure an' pour in a kag iv chloride iv lime. Both are good ways. It depinds on how long ye intind to live in th' house. What were those shots? That's th' housekeeper killin' a couple iv cockroaches with a Hotchkiss gun. Who is that yellin'? That's our ol' frind High Fi-nance bein' compelled to take his annual bath. Th' housecleanin' season is in full swing, an' there's a good deal iv dust in th' air; but I want to say to thim neighbors iv ours, who're peekin' in an' makin' remarks about th' amount iv rubbish, that over in our part iv th' wurruld we don't sweep things undher th' sofa. Let thim put that in their pipes an' smoke it."

"I think th' counthry is goin' to th' divvle," said Mr. Hinnissy, sadly.

"Hinnissy," said Mr. Dooley, "if that's so I congratylate th' wurruld."

"How's that?" asked Mr. Hennessy.

"Well," said Mr. Dooley, "f'r nearly forty years I've seen this counthry goin' to th' divvle, an' I got aboord late. An' if it's been goin' that long an' at that rate, an' has got no nearer thin it is this pleasant Chris'mas, thin th' divvle is a divvle iv a ways further off thin I feared."

ON LYING

"Th' question befure th' house is whin is a lie not a lie?" said Mr. Dooley.

"How's that?" asked Mr. Hennessy.

"Well," said Mr. Dooley, "here's Pro-fissor E. Binjamin Something-or-Other insthructin' th' youth at th' Chicago Univarsity that a lie, if it's f'r a good purpose, is not a lie at all. There's th' gr-reat school down there on th' Midway. Ye can larn annything ye have a mind to in that there seminary an' now they'll have a coorse in lyin'. Th' earnest youth in sarch iv a career in life'll be taught lyin' individjally an' in classes, lyin' be ear an' be note, lyin' in th' home an' lyin' to th' public, lyin' autymatically, th' lie di-rect, th' lie injanyous, th' lie with th' hand, th' lie with th' eye, th' r-ready fake, th' bouncer, th' stiff, th' con, th' bunk, th' poetic lie, th' business lie, th' lie im-aginative, th' brassy lie, th' timid lie, th' white lie, th' pathriotic or red-white-an'-blue lie, th' lovin' lie, th' over-th'-left, th' cross-me-heart, th' hope-to-die, histhry, political economy an' mathematics. They'll be a post gradyate coorse in perjury f'r th' more studyous an' whin th' hon'rary degrees is given out, we'll know what LL.D. manes."

"Sure, they don't need to larn people lyin'," said Mr. Hennessy.

"Well, no, faith, that's thrue," said Mr. Dooley. "Here am I with no more iddycation thin ye cud write on th' back iv a postage stamp an' as fluent an' r-ready a liar as e'er a pro-fissor or gradyate iver tur-rned out be an Instichoot iv Mendacity.

That's what I am. I'm a born liar. As th' pote that Hogan
spouts has said: 'I lisped in falsehood, f'r th' falsehood came.' I
cud lie befure I cud speak or walk. F'r ivry lie I got found out
in an' whaled f'r, I told forty that niver was r-run down. I've
lied steadily through life an' here I am in me green ol' age —
though not as old as manny wud make out — lyin' without th'
aid iv glasses. Thry me. Ask me how much wather there is in
that bar'l — if ye dare! Ye're a liar too, Hinnissy."

"What's that?" shouted Mr. Hennessy.

"Keep cool," said Mr. Dooley. "I'm not referrin' to what I
heerd ye tell ye'er wife about th' pay check or that story iv
ye'ers about th' big man ye bate in th' Halsted sthreet car. But
th' clothes on ye'er back is a lie or at laste an' equivocation or
a hand-me-down, an' th' smile ye greet me with is no more thin
half on th' square an' th' well-it's-glad-I-am-to-see-ye rally
manes ye're sorry ye came. All th' wurruld is busy deceivin' its
neighbor an' itsilf. Th' poor are poor because they are poor
liars an' th' rich ar-re men that've accumylated a large stock iv
non-assissable, inthrest-bearin' lies or inherited th' same fr'm
their indulgent an' mendacyous fathers. That's what they tell
me.

"An' what is a lie, tell me? I cud answer mesilf if I always
knew what th' thruth was, me boy. A good manny iv th' whop-
pers I tell ye is th' raysult iv thryin' to take a short cut to th'
thruth an' bringin' up just this side iv perjury. Some things that
look like lies to me to-day will seem all r-right in th' prisiden-
tial year. I lie a good manny times fr'm kindness, more often
fr'm laziness, an' most often fr'm fear. Some iv th' boldest liars
I iver met wud've been thruthful men if they'd dared to be.
Th' most uncommon form is th' malicyous liar an' th' manest
is th' just liar. Manny men lie because they like conversation
an' they feel they can't impress th' man they're talkin' with
without pilin' it on. I've lied at times to beguile th' hours away.
I niver deceived annywan half so much as I have mesilf. If I
didn't do it wanst in awhile, I'd feel so poor an' depraved, I
cudden't go on in business. Now I wondher if E. Binjamin wud
call thim good purposes. Sure, if a lie's a good thing anny pur-

pose ye may have in lyin' will look good to ye an' if 'tis a bad thing, th' purpose'll seem good annyhow. I think a lie with a purpose is wan iv th' worst kind an' th' mos' profitable. I'm more iv a spoortin' liar thin he is if I lie f'r pastime. I wud lie to get a frind out iv throuble or an inimy in, to save me counthry, if 'twas not surrounded already be a devoted band iv heroic liars, to protict me life or me property, but if annybody ast me how I done it, I'd lie out iv it.

"Father Kelly says th' pro-fissor is all r-right. He says his theery is a good wan but he don't think it fits a Baptist Colledge. 'Twas held be some larned men iv our own kind an' 'twas all r-right fr'm thim. 'Twas th' docthrine iv a saint, but he wasn't lookin' f'r anny Standard ile money. An' Father Kelly says 'tis an unsafe docthrine to thrust to anny wan but a saint. He says th' thruth or something akelly good, something that will wash, is intinded f'r ord'n'ry people. On'y a good man can be a liar. An' Father Kelly says he's niver seen a man good enough to get a di-ploma fr'm him to lie f'r anny purpose, good or bad, to tell white lies or green. If he lies, he's got to take his chances. I said: 'What wud ye do if ye see a frind iv ye'ers pursued be a murdherer an' th' murdherer-that-was-to-be ast ye which way he'd turned?' 'I cudden't hear him,' he says. 'I'd be too far up th' alley,' he says. 'Lyin' in th' circumstances,' he says, 'wud indicate a lack iv prisince iv mind,' he says. 'It often does,' he says."

"Sure, a lie's a lie," said Mr. Hennessy. "I always know whin I'm lyin'."

"So do I," said Mr. Dooley.

THE CRUSADE AGAINST VICE

"Vice," said Mr. Dooley, "is a creature of such heejous mien, as Hogan says, that th' more ye see it th' betther ye like it. I'd be afraid to enther upon a crusade again vice f'r fear I might prefer it to th' varchous life iv a rayspictable liquor dealer. But annyhow th' crusade has started, an' before manny months I'll be lookin' undher th' table whin I set down to a peaceful game iv solytaire to see if a polisman in citizens' clothes ain't concealed there.

"Th' city iv Noo York, Hinnissy, sets th' fashion iv vice an' starts th' crusade again it. Thin ivrybody else takes it up. They'se crusades an' crusaders in ivry hamlet in th' land an' places that is cursed with nawthin' worse thin pitchin' horseshoes sinds to th' neighborin' big city f'r a case iv vice to suppress. We're in th' mist iv a crusade now, an' there isn't a polisman in town who isn't thremblin' f'r his job.

"As a people, Hinnissy, we're th' greatest crusaders that iver was — f'r a short distance. On a quarther mile thrack we can crusade at a rate that wud make Hogan's frind, Godfrey th' Bullion, look like a crab. But th' throuble is th' crusade don't last afther th' first sprint. Th' crusaders drops out iv th' procission to take a dhrink or put a little money on th' ace an' be th' time th' end iv th' line iv march is reached th' boss crusader is alone in th' job an' his former followers is hurlin' bricks at him fr'm th' windows iv policy shops. Th' boss crusader always gets th' double cross. If I wanted to sind me good name down to th' ginerations with Cap. Kidd an' Jesse James I'd lead a movement f'r th' suppression iv vice. I wud so.

Some wan invints an anti-vice cocktail. Lectures is delivered to small bodies iv preachers on how to detect vice so that no wan can palm off countherfeit vice on thim an' make thim think 'tis good. Th' polis becomes active an' whin th' polis is active 'tis a good time f'r dacint men to wear marredge certyficates outside iv their coats. Hanyous monsthers is nailed in th' act iv histin' in a shell iv beer in a German Garden; husbands waits in th' polis station to be r-ready to bail out their wives whin they're arrested f'r shoppin' afther four o'clock; an' there's more joy over wan sinner rayturned to th' station thin f'r ninety an' nine that've rayformed.

"Th' boss crusader is havin' th' time iv his life all th' while. His pitcher is in th' papers ivry mornin' an' his sermons is a directhry iv places iv amusement. He says to himsilf 'I am improvin' th' wurruld an' me name will go down to th' ginera-

tions as th' greatest vice buster iv th' cinchry. Whin I get
through they won't be enough crime left in this city to amuse a
sthranger fr'm Hannybal Missoury f'r twinty minyits,' he says.
That's where he's wrong. Afther awhile people gets tired iv th'
pastime. They want somewhere to go nights. Most people ain't
vicious, Hinnissy, an' it takes vice to hunt vice. That accounts
f'r polismen. Besides th' horse show or th' football games or
something else excitin' divarts their attintion an' wan day th'
boss crusader finds that he's alone in Sodom. 'Vice ain't so
bad afther all. I notice business was betther whin 't was rampant,' says wan la-ad. 'Sure ye're right,' says another. 'I
haven't sold a single pink shirt since that man Markers closed
th' faro games,' says he. 'Th' theaytre business ain't what it
was whin they was more vice,' says another. 'This ain't no
Connecticut village,' he says. 'An' 'tis no use thryin' to inthrajooce soomchury ligislation int his impeeryal American city,'
he says, 'where people come pursooed be th' sheriff fr'm ivry
corner iv th' wurruld,' he says. 'Ye can't make laws f'r this
community that wud suit a New England village,' he says,
'where,' he says, 'th' people ar-re too uncivilized to be im-
moral,' he says. 'Vice,' he says, 'goes a long way tow'rd makin'
life bearable,' he says. 'A little vice now an' thin is relished be
th' best iv men,' he says.

"An' there ye ar-re, Hinnissy. Th' crusade is over an' Vice is
rampant again. I'm afraid, me la-ad, that th' frinds iv vice is
too sthrong in this wurruld iv sin f'r th' frinds iv varchue. Th'
good man, th' crusader, on'y wurruks at th' crusade wanst in
five years, an' on'y whin he has time to spare fr'm his other
jooties. 'Tis a pastime f'r him. But th' definse iv vice is a
business with th' other la-ad an' he nails away at it, week days
an' Sundays, holy days an' fish days, mornin', noon an'
night."

"They ought to hang some iv thim pollyticians," said Mr.
Hennessy angrily.

"Well," said Mr. Dooley, "I don't know. I don't expict to
gather calla lillies in Hogan's turnip patch. Why shud I expict

to pick bunches iv spotless statesmen fr'm th' gradooation class
iv th' house iv correction."

This column was suggested by Philip K. Allen of Andover,
Mass., a leading Dooley expert.

AVARICE AND GENEROSITY

"I niver blame a man f'r bein' avaricyous in his ol' age.
Whin a fellow gits so he has nawthin' else to injye, whin
ivrybody calls him 'sir' or 'mister,' an' young people dodge
him an' he sleeps afther dinner, an' folk say he's an ol' fool if
he wears a buttonhole bokay an' his teeth is only tinants at will
an' not permanent fixtures, 'tis no more thin nach'ral that he
shud begin to look around him f'r a way iv keepin' a grip on
human s'ciety. It don't take him long to see that th' on'y thing
that's vin'rable in age is money an' he pro-ceeds to acquire
anything that happens to be in sight, takin' it where he can find
it, not where he wants it, which is th' way to accumylate a fortune. Money won't prolong life, but a few millyons judicyously
placed in good banks an' occas'nally worn on th' person will
rayjooce age. Poor ol' men are always older thin poor rich
men. In th' almshouse a man is decrepit an' mournful-lookin'
at sixty, but a millyonaire at sixty is jus' in th' prime iv life to a
frindly eye, an' there are no others.

"It's aisier to th' ol' to grow rich thin it is to th' young. At
makin' money a man iv sixty is miles ahead iv a la-ad iv twinty-
five. Pollytics and bankin' is th' on'y two games where age has
th' best iv it. Youth has betther things to attind to, an' more iv
thim. I don't blame a man f'r bein' stingy anny more thin I
blame him f'r havin' a bad leg. Ye know th' doctors say that if
ye don't use wan iv ye'er limbs f'r a year or so ye can niver use
it again. So it is with gin'rosity. A man starts arly in life not
bein' gin'rous. He says to himsilf: "I wurruked f'r this thing
an' if I give it away I lose it." He ties up his gin'rosity in ban-
dages so that th' blood can't circylate in it. It gets to be a
superstition with him that he'll have bad luck if he iver does
annything f'r annybody. An' so he rakes in an' puts his private

mark with his teeth on all th' movable money in th' wurruld. But th' day comes whin he sees people around him gettin' a good dale iv injyemint out iv gin'rosity an' somewan says: 'Why don't ye, too, be gin-rous? Come, ol' green goods, unbelt, loosen up, be gin-rous.' 'Gin-'rous?' says he, 'what's that?' 'It's th' best spoort in th' wurruld. It's givin' things to people.' 'But I can't,' he says. 'I haven't annything to do it with,' he says. 'I don't know th' game. I haven't anny gin'rosi-ty,' he says. 'But ye have,' says they. 'Ye have as much gin'rosi-ty as annywan if ye'll only use it,' says they. 'Take it out iv th' plasther cast ye put it in an' 'twill look as good as new,' says they. An' he does it. He thries to use his gin'rosity, but all th' life is out iv it. It gives way undher him an' he falls down. He can't raise it fr'm th' groun'. It's ossyfied an' useless. I've seen manny a fellow that suffered fr'm ossyfied gin'rosity.

"Whin a man begins makin' money in his youth at anny thing but games iv chance, he niver can become gin'rous late in life. He may make a bluff at it. Some men are gin'rous with a crutch. Some men get the use of their gin'rosity back suddenly whin they ar-re in danger. Whin Clancy the miser was caught in a fire in th' Halsted Sthreet Palace hotel he howled fr'm a window: 'I'll give twenty dollars to annywan that'll take me down.' Cap'n Minehan put up a laddher an' climbed to him an' carrid him to the sthreet. Half-way down th' laddher th' brave rayscooer was seen to be chokin' his helpless burdhen. We discovered aftherwards that Clancy had thried to begin negotyations to rayjooce th' reward to five dollars. His gin'rosi-ty had become suddenly par'lyzed again.

"So if ye'd stay gin'rous to th' end niver lave ye'er gin'rosity idle too long. Don't run it ivry hour at th' top iv its speed, but fr'm day to day give it a little gintle exercise to keep it supple an' hearty an' in due time ye may injye it."

This column makes humorist Steve Allen laugh.

ON OLD AGE

"I'm gettin' old," said Mr. Hennessy. "I had me sixtieth birthday yisterday."

"I wudden't have said ye were within ten years iv sixty," said Mr. Dooley. "I bet Hogan last year that ye were siventy-wan. But I might've known betther. Whin a man gets to be over siventy he boasts iv his age. Whin he passes eighty he's very lible to lie about it. An' whin he's ninety he will throw his wig in th' face iv anny man who insinyates that he ain't th' oldest man in th' wurruld.

"Annyhow, old age isn't th' worst thing that happens to man. If he hasn't as manny expectations as he had, he hasn't so manny years. A young fellow is warn'd about a thousand things that don't bother an old man at all. Whin we get along in years we lose a lot in appytites, but we don't miss thim. If we have no hopes we have plisant mim'ries. Havin' larned that I cudden't kick a futball, I no longer want to kick it. I'm willin' to stand on th' side an' look on while me frindly mim'ry tells me pleasant lies about how good I was in me day. I no longer jump off a movin' car. I have th' full value iv me nickel out iv th' heartless monopuly be holdin' th' car while I get down wan leg at a time. If I go to cross th' sthreet to see Hogan an' a flock iv autymobills comes along, I say no mesilf: 'I don't want to see Hogan at all. I'll go to see Hinisssy.'

"I can visit th' ladies without fear iv entanglemint, f'r if I'm hopeless they're harmless. I'm lookin' for-ard to th' day whin I'll become avaricyous. Fr'm what I've seen an' heerd, avarice is a fine, absorbin' passion, an' manny an ol' fellow is as happy with his arm around his bank account as he was sleigh ridin' with his first girl. An', best iv all, I want to be a boss, an' no man can be a boss who's not undher two or over fifty. It's a fine thing to be able to set back in a chair an' have people appeal to ye f'r an opinyon on something that ye don't know annything about an' thin watch thim get into throuble whin they follow ye'er advice. Manny a man that cudden't direct ye to the dhrug store on th' corner whin he was thirty will get a respictful hearin' whin age has further impaired his mind.

NEWSPAPER PUBLICITY

"Was ye iver in th' pa-apers?" asked Mr. Dooley.

"Wanst," said Mr. Hennessy. "But it wasn't me. It was another Hinnissy. Was you?"

"Manny times," said Mr. Dooley. "Whin I was prom'nent socyally, ye cud hardly pick up a pa-aper without seein' me name in it an' th' amount iv th' fine. Ye must lade a very simple life. Th' newspaper is watchin' most iv us fr'm th' cradle to th' grave, an' befure an' afther. Whin I was a la-ad thrippin' continted over th' bogs iv Roscommon, ne'er an iditor knew iv me existence, nor I iv his. Whin annything was wrote about a man 'twas put this way: 'We undhershtand on good authority that M—l—chi H——y, Esquire, is on thrile before Judge G——n on an accusation iv l——c—ny. But we don't think it's true.' Nowadays th' larceny is discoverd be a newspa-aper. Th' lead pipe is dug up in ye'er back yard be a rayporther who knew it was there because he helped ye bury it. A man knocks at ye'er dure arly wan mornin' an' ye answer in ye'er nighty. 'In th' name iv th' law, I arrist ye,' says th' man seizin' ye be th' throat. 'Who ar-re ye?' ye cry. 'I'm a rayporther f'r th' Daily Slooth,' says he. 'Phottygrafter, do ye'er jooty!' Ye're hauled off in th' circylation wagon to th' newspaper office, where a con-fission is ready f'r ye to sign; ye're thried be a jury iv th' staff, sintinced be th' iditor-in-chief an' at tin o'clock Friday th' fatal thrap is sprung be th' fatal thrapper iv th' fam'ly journal.

"Th' newspaper does ivrything f'r us. It runs th' polis foorce an' th' banks, commands th' milishy, conthrols th' ligislachure, baptizes th' young, marries th' foolish, comforts th' afflicted, afflicts th' comfortable, buries th' dead an' roasts thim afther-ward. They ain't annything it don't turn its hand to fr'm ex-plainin' th' docthrine iv thransubstantiation to composin' saleratus biskit. Ye can get anny kind iv information ye want to in ye'er fav'rite newspaper about ye'ersilf or annywan else. What th' Czar whispered to th' Imp'ror Willum whin they were alone, how to make a silk hat out iv a wire matthress, how to settle th' coal sthrike, who to marry, how to get on with ye'er wife whin ye're married, what to feed th' babies, what doctor to call whin ye've fed thim as directed,—all iv that ye'll find in th' pa-apers.

"They used to say a man's life was a closed book. So it is but it's an open newspaper. Th' eye iv th' press is on ye befure ye begin to take notice. Th' iditor obsarves th' stork hoverin' over th' roof iv 2978½B Ar-rchey Road an' th' article he writes about it has a wink in it. 'Son an' heir arrives f'r th' Hon'rable Malachi Hinnissy,' says th' pa-aper befure ye've finished th' dhrink with th' doctor. An' afther that th' histhry iv th' off-spring's life is found in th' press:

"'It is undhershtud that there is much excitement in th' Hinnissy fam'ly over namin' th' lates' sign. Misther Hinnissy wishes it called Pathrick McGlue afther an uncle iv his, an' Mrs. Hinnissy is in favor iv namin' it Alfonsonita afther a Pullman car she seen wan day. Th' Avenin Fluff offers a prize iv thirty dollars f'r th' bes' name f'r this projeny. Maiden ladies will limit their letters to three hundherd wurruds.'

"'Above is a snap shot iv young Alfonsonita McGlue Hinnissy, taken on his sicond birthday with his nurse, Miss Angybel Blim, th' well-known specyal nurse iv th' Avenin' Fluff. At th' time th' phottygraft was taken, th' infant was about to bite Miss Blim which accounts f'r th' agynized exprission on that gifted writer's face. Th' Avenin Fluff offers a prize iv four dollars to th' best answer to th' question: "What does th' baby think iv Miss Blim?"'

"'Young Alf Hinnissy was siven years ol' yisterdah. A rayporther iv th' Fluff sought him out an' indeavored to intherview him on th' Nicaragooan Canal, th' Roomanyan Jews, th' tahriff an' th' thrusts. Th' comin' statesman rayfused to be dhrawn on these questions, his answer bein' a ready, "Go chase ye'ersilf, ye big stiff!" Afther a daylightful convarsation th' rayporther left, bein' followed to th' gate be his janial young host who hit him smartly in th' back with a brick. He is a chip iv th' ol' block.'

" 'Groton, Conn., April 8. Ye'er rayporther was privileged to
see th' oldest son iv th' Hon'rable Malachi Hinnissy started at
this siminary f'r th' idjacation iv young Englishmen bor-rn in
America. Th' heir iv th' Hinnissys was enthered at th' exclusive school thirty years befure he was bor-rn. Owin' to th'
uncertainty iv his ancesthors he was also enthered at Vassar.
Th' young fellow took a lively intherest in th' school. Th'
above phottygraft riprisints him mathriculatin'. Th' figures at
th' foot ar-re Misther an' Mrs. Hinnissy. Those at th' head ar-
re Profissor Peabody Plantagenet, prisident iv th' instichoochion an' Officer Michael H. Rafferty. Young Hinnissy
will remain here till he has a good cukkin' idjacation.'

" 'Exthry Red Speshul Midnight Edition. Mumps! Mumps!
Mumps! Th' heir iv th' Hinnissy's sthricken with th' turr'ble
scoorge. Panic on th' stock exchange. Bereaved father starts f'r
th' plague spot to see his afflicted son. Phottygrafts iv Young
Hinnissy at wan, two, three, eight an' tin. Phottygrafts iv th'
house where his father was born, his mother, his aunt, his uncle, Profissor Plantagenet, Groton School, th' gov'nor iv Connecticut, Chansy Depoo, statue iv Liberty, Thomas Jefferson,
Niagara Falls be moonlight. Diagram iv jaw an' head showin'
th' prob'ble coorse iv the Mumpococcus. Intherviews with J.
Pierpont Morgan, Terry McGovern, Mary McLain, Jawn Mit-
chell, Lyman J. Gage, th' Prince iv Wales, Sinitor Bivridge, th'
Earl iv Roslyn, an' Chief Divry on Mumps. We offer a prize iv
thirty million dollars in advertisin' space f'r a cure f'r th'
mumps that will save th' nation's pride. — Later, it's croup.'

"An' so it goes. We march through life an' behind us march-
es th' phottygrafter an' th' rayporther. There are no such
things as private citizens. No matther how private a man may
be, no matther how secretly he steals, some day his pitcher will
be in th' pa-aper along with Mark Hanna, Stamboul 2:01½,
Fitzsimmons' fightin' face, an' Douglas, Douglas, Tin dollar
shoe. He can't get away fr'm it. An' I'll say this f'r him, he
don't want to. He wants to see what bad th' neighbors are

doin' an' he wants thim to see what good he's doin'. He gets fifty per cint iv his wish; niver more. A man keeps his front window shade up so th' pa-apers can come along an' make a pitcher iv him settin' in his iligant furnished parlor readin' th' life iv Dwight L. Moody to his fam'ly. An' th' lad with th' phottygraft happens along at th' moment whin he is batin' his wife. If we wasn't so anxious to see our names among those prisint at th' ball, we wudden't get into th' pa-apers so often as among those that ought to be prisint in th' dock. A man takes his phottygraft to th' iditor an' says he: 'Me attintion has been called to th' fact that ye'd like to print this mug iv a prom'nent philanthropist;' an' th' iditor don't use it till he's robbed a bank. Ivrybody is inthrested in what ivrybody else is doin' that's wrong. That's what makes th' newspapers. An' as this is a dimmycratic counthry where ivrybody was bor-rn akel to ivrybody else, aven if they soon outgrow it, an' where wan man's as good as another an' as bad, all iv us has a good chanst to have his name get in at laste wanst a year. Some goes in at Mrs. Rather's dinner an' some as victims iv a throlley car, but ivrybody lands at last. They'll get ye afther awhile, Hinnissy. They'll pint ye'er pitcher. But on'y wanst. A newspaper is to intertain, not to teach a moral lesson."

"D'ye think people likes th' newspapers iv th' prisint time?" asked Mr. Hennessy.

"D'ye think they're printed f'r fun?" said Mr. Dooley.

MACHINERY

Mr. Dooley was reading from a paper. "'We live,' he says, 'in an age iv wondhers. Niver befure in th' histhry iv th' wur-ruld has such pro-gress been made.'

"Thrue wurruds an' often spoken. Even in me time things has changed. Whin I was a la-ad Long Jawn Wintworth cud lean his elbows on th' highest buildin' in this town. It took two months to come here fr'm Pittsburg on a limited raft an' a stage coach that run fr'm La Salle to Mrs. Murphy's hotel.

They wasn't anny tillygraft that I can raymimber an' th' sthreet car was pulled be a mule an' dhruv be an engineer be th' name iv Mulligan. We thought we was a pro-grissive people. Ye bet we did. But look at us today. I go be Casey's house tonight an' there it is a fine storey-an'-a-half frame house with Casey settin' on th' dure shtep dhrinkin' out iv a pail. I go be Casey's house to-morrah an' it's a hole in th' groun'. I rayturn to Casey's house on Thursdah an' it's a fifty-eight storey buildin' with a morgedge onto it an' they're thinkin' iv takin' it down an' replacin' it with a modhren sthructure. Th' shoes that Corrigan th' cobbler wanst wurruked on f'r a week, hammerin' away like a woodpecker, is now tossed out be th' dozens fr'm th' mouth iv a masheen. A cow goes lowin' softly in to Armours an' comes out glue, beef, gelatine, fertylizer, celooloid, joolry, sofy cushions, hair restorer, washin' sody, soap, lithrachoor an' bed springs so quick that while aft she's still cow, for'ard she may be annything fr'm buttons to Pannyma hats. I can go fr'm Chicago to New York in twinty hours, but I don't have to, thank th' Lord. Thirty years ago we thought 'twas marvelous to be able to tillygraft a man in Saint Joe an' get an answer that night. Now, be wireless tillygraft ye can get an answer befure ye sind th' tillygram if they ain't careful. Me friend Macroni has done that. Be manes iv his wondher iv science a man on a ship in mid-ocean can sind a tillygram to a man on shore, if he has a confid'rate on board. That's all he needs. Be mechanical science an' thrust in th' op'rator annywan can set on th' shore iv Noofoundland an' chat with a frind in th' County Kerry.

"What's it done f'r th' wurruld? says ye. It's done ivrything. It's give us fast ships an' an autymatic hist f'r th' hod, an' small flats an' a taste iv solder in th' peaches. If annybody says th' wurruld ain't bether off thin it was, tell him that a masheen has been invinted that makes honey out iv pethrolyum. If he asts ye why they ain't anny Shakesperes today, say: 'No, but we no longer make sausages be hand.'

" 'Tis pro-gress. We live in a cinchry iv pro-gress an' I thank th' Lord I've seen most iv it. Man an' boy I've lived pretty near through this wondherful age. If I was proud I cud say I seen more thin Julyus Caesar iver see or cared to. An' here I am, I'll not say how old, still pushin' th' malt acrost th' counther at me thirsty counthrymen. All around me is th' refinemints iv mechanical janius. Instead iv broachin' th' beer kag with a club an' dhrawin' th' beer through a fassit as me Puritan forefathers done, I have that wondher iv invintive science th' beer pump. I cheat mesilf with a cash raygisther. I cut off th' end iv me good cigar with an injanyous device an' pull th' cork out iv a bottle with a conthrivance that wud've made that frind that Hogan boasts about, that ol' boy Archy Meeds, think they was witchcraft in th' house. Science has been a gr-reat blessin' to me. But amidst all these granjoors here am I th' same ol' antiquated combination iv bellows an' pump I always was. Not so good. Time has worn me out. Th' years like little boys with jackknives has carved their names in me top. Ivry day I have to write off something f'r deprecyation. 'Tis about time f'r whoiver owns me to wurruk me off on a thrust. Mechanical science has done ivrything f'r me but help me. I suppose I ought to feel supeeryor to me father. He niver see a high buildin' but he didn't want to. He cudden's come here in five days but he was a wise man an' if he cud've come in three he'd have stayed in th' County Roscommon.

"Th' pa-apers tells me that midical science has kept pace with th' hop-skip-an'-a-jump iv mechanical inginooty. Th' doctors has found th' mickrobe iv ivrything fr'm lumbago to love an' fr'm jandice to jealousy, but if a brick bounces on me head I'm crated up th' same as iv yore an' put away. Rockyfellar can make a pianny out iv a bar'l iv crude ile, but no wan has been able to make a blade iv hair grow on Rockyfellar. They was a doctor over in France that discovered a kind iv a thing that if 'twas pumped into ye wud make ye live till people got so tired iv seein' ye around they cud scream. He died th' nex' year iv premachure ol' age. They was another doctor cud insure whether th' nex' wan wud be a boy or a girl. All ye had to do was to decide wud it be Arthur or Ethel an' lave him know. He left a fam'ly iv unmarredgeable daughters.

"I sometimes wondher whether pro-gress is anny more thin a kind iv a shift. It's like a merry-go-round. We get up on a speckled wooden horse an' th' mechanical pianny plays a chune an' away we go, hollerin'. We think we're thravellin' like th' divvle but th' man that doesn't care about merry-go-rounds knows that we will come back where we were. We get out dizzy an' sick an' lay on th' grass an' gasp: 'Where am I? Is this th' meelin-yum?' An' he says: 'No, 'tis Ar-rchey Road.' Father Kelly says th' Agyptians done things we cudden't do an' th' Romans put up sky-scrapers an' aven th' Chinks had tillyphones an' phony-grafts.

"I've been up to th' top iv th' very highest buildin' in town, Hinnissy, an' I wasn't anny nearer Hivin thin if I was in th' sthreet. Th' stars was as far away as iver. An' down beneath is a lot iv us runnin' an' lapin' an' jumpin' about, pushin' each other over, haulin' little sthrips iv ir'n to pile up in little buildin's that ar-re called sky-scrapers but not be th' sky; wur-rukin' night an' day to make a masheen that'll carry us fr'm wan jack-rabbit colony to another an' yellin', 'Pro-gress!' Pro-gress, oho! I can see th' stars winkin' at each other an' sayin': 'Ain't they funny! Don't they think they're playin' hell!'

"No, sir, masheens ain't done much f'r man. I can't get up anny kind iv fam'ly inthrest f'r a steam dredge or a hydraulic hist. I want to see sky-scrapin' men. But I won't. We're about th' same hight as we always was, th' same hight an' build, composed iv th' same inflammable an' perishyable mateeryal, an exthra hazardous risk, unimproved an' li'ble to collapse. We do make pro-gress but it's th' same kind Julyus Caesar made an' ivry wan has made befure or since an' in this age iv masheenery we're still burrid be hand."

"What d'ye think iv th' man down in Pinnsylvanya (George Baer) who says th' Lord an' him is partners in a coal mine?" asked Mr. Hennessy, who wanted to change the subject.

"Has he divided th' profits?" asked Mr. Dooley.

CHAPTER VI

LAW AND ORDER, AND OCCASIONAL CONTEMPT OF COURT

When the Republicans won the presidential election of 1900, it became clear that the U.S. would hang on to the territories acquired as a result of the Spanish — American War. Among other problems, it had to be determined whether or not the protection of the Constitution and the Bill of Rights would be extended to these new holdings; hence, the question of whether or not the Constitution followed the flag.

The administration did not want this, claiming that it would make governing (the Democrats called it exploiting) the territories more difficult, and the issue wound up in the lap of the Supreme Court. In 1901 the decision was handed down in favor of the administration's position, leading Mr. Dooley to one of his most famous observations: "... no matter whether th' Constitution follows th' flag or not, th' Supreme Coort follows th' illiction returns."

Although Dunne had a reverence for the law in the abstract, as a reporter who had covered the Chicago police beat he viewed its actual practice with a jaundiced eye. "I believe in the polis foorce, though not in polismen," he once said. As to the courts, he observed that "Th' best citizens is thim that th' statue iv limitations was made f'r." And on the equal administration of justice, "Niver steal a dure-mat. If ye do, ye'll be invistigated hanged, an' maybe rayformed. Steal a bank, me boy, steal a bank."

THE SUPREME COURT'S DECISION

"I see," said Mr. Dooley, "th' Supreme Coort has decided th' Constitution don't follow th' flag."

"Who said it did?" asked Mr. Hennessy.

"Some wan," said Mr. Dooley. "It happened a long time ago an' I don't raymimber clearly how it come up, but some fellow said that ivrywhere th' Constitution wint, th' flag was sure to go. 'I do't believe wan wurrud iv it,' says th' other fellow. 'Ye can't make me think th' Constitution is goin' thrapezin' around ivrywhere a young liftnant in th' ar-rmy takes it into his head to stick a flag pole. It's too old. It's a home-stayin' Constitution with a blue coat with brass buttons onto it, an' it walks with a goold-headed cane. It's old an' it's feeble an' it prefers to set on th' front stoop an' amuse th' childer. It wudden't last a minyit in thim thropical climes. 'Twud get a pain in th' fourteenth amindmint an' die befure th' doctors cud get ar-round to cut it out. No, sir, we'll keep it with us, an' threat it tenderly without too much hard wurruk, an' whin it plays out entirely we'll give it dacint buryal an' incorp'rate oursilves under th' laws iv Noo Jarsey. That's what we'll do,' says he. 'But,' says th' other, 'if it wants to thravel, why not lave it?' 'But it don't want to.' 'I say it does.' 'How'll we find out?' 'We'll ask th' Supreme Coort. They'll know what's good f'r it.'

"So it wint up to th' Supreme Coort. They'se wan thing about th' Supreme Coort, if ye lave annything to thim, ye lave it to thim. Ye don't get a check that entitles ye to call f'r it in an hour. The Supreme Coort iv th' United States ain't in any hurry about catchin' th' mails. It don't have to make th' las' car. I'd back th' Aujitoroom again it anny day f'r a foot race. If ye're lookin' f'r a game iv quick decisions an' base hits, ye've got to hire another empire. It niver gives a decision till th' crowd has dispersed an' th' players have packed their bats in th' bags an' started f'r home.

"F'r awhile ivrybody watched to see what th' Supreme Coort

wud do. I knew mesilf I felt I cudden't make another move in th' game till I heerd fr'm thim. Buildin' op'rations was suspinded an' we sthud wringin' our hands outside th' dure waiting' f'r information fr'm th' bedside. 'What're they doin' now?' 'They just put th' argymints iv larned counsel in th' ice box an' the chief justice is in a corner writin' a pome. Brown J. an' Harlan J. is discussin' th' condition iv th' Roman Empire befure th' fire. Th' r-rest iv th' Coort is considherin' th' question iv whether they ought or ought not to wear ruchin' on their skirts and hopin' crinoline won't come in again. No decision today!' An' so it wint f'r days, an' weeks an' months. Th' men that had argyied that th' Constitution ought to shadow th' flag to all th' tough resorts on th' Passyfic coast an' th' men that argyied that th' flag was so lively that no constitution cud follow it an' survive, they died or lost their jobs or wint back to Salem an' were f'rgotten. Expansionists contracted an' anti-expansionists blew up an' little childer was born into th' wurruld an' grew to manhood an' niver heerd iv Porther Ricky except whin some wan got a job there. I'd about made up me mind to thry an' put th' thing out iv me thoughts an' go back to wurruk when I woke up wan mornin' an' see be th' pa-aper that th' Supreme Coort had warned th' Constitution to lave th' flag alone an' tind to its own business.

"That's what th' pa-aper says, but I've r-read over th' decision an' I don't see annything iv th' kind there. They'se not a wurrud about th' flag an' not enough to tire ye about th' Constitution. 'Tis a matther iv limons, Hinnissy, that th' Supreme Coort has been settin' on f'r this gineration—a cargo iv limons sint fr'm Porther Ricky to some Eyetalian in Philydelphy. Th decision was r-read by Brown J., him bein' th' las' justice to make up his mind, an' ex-officio, as Hogan says, th' first to speak, afther a crool an' bitther contest. Says Brown J.: 'Th' question here is wan iv such gr-reat importance that we've been sthrugglin' over it iver since ye see us las' an' on'y come to a decision (Fuller C.J., Gray J., Harlan J., Shiras J., McKenna J., White J., Brewer J., an' Peckham J. dissentin' fr'm me an' each other) because iv th' hot weather comin' on. Wash'n'ton is a dhreadful place in summer (Fuller C.J. dissentin'). Th' whole fabric iv our government is threatened, th' lives iv our people an' th' progress iv civilization put to th' bad. Men ar-re excited. But why? We ar-re not. (Harlan J., 'I am.'' Fuller C.J. dissentin', but not f'r th' same reason.) This thing must be set-tled wan way or th' other undher that dear ol' Constitution be varchue iv which we are here an' ye ar-re there an' Congress is out West practicin' law. Now what does th' Constitution say? We'll look it up thoroughly whin we get through with this case (th' rest iv th' Coort dissentin'). In th' manetime we must be governed be th' ordnances iv th' Khan iv Beloochistan, th' laws iv Hinnery th' Eighth, th' opinyon iv Justice iv th' Peace Oscar Larson in th' case iv th' township iv Red Wing varsus Petersen, an' th Dhred Scott decision. What do they say about limons? Nawthin' at all. Again we take th' Dhred Scott decision. This is wan iv th' worst I iver r-read. If I cudden't write a betther wan with blindhers on, I'd leap off th' bench. This horrible fluke iv a decision throws a gr-reat, an almost dazzlin' light on th' case. I will turn it off. (McKenna J. concurs but thinks it ought to be blowed out.) But where was I? I must put on me specs. Oh, about th' limons. Well, th' decision iv th' Coort (th' others dissentin') is as follows: First, that th' Disthrict iv Col-umbya is a state; second, that it is not; third, that New York is a state; fourth, that it is a crown colony; fifth, that all states ar-re states an' all territories ar-re territories in th' eyes iv other powers, but Gawd knows what they ar-re at home. In th' case iv Hogan varsus Mullins, th' decision is he must paper th' barn. (Hinnery VIII, sixteen, six, four, eleven.) In Wiggins varsus et al. th' cow belonged. (Louis XIV, 90 in rem.) In E.P. Vigore varsus Ad Lib., the custody iv th' childer. I'll now fall back a furlong or two in me chair, while me larned but misguided col-lagues r-read th' Histhry iv Iceland to show ye how wrong I am. But mind ye, what I've said goes. I let thim talk because it exercises their throats, but ye've heerd all th' decision on this limon case that'll get into th' fourth reader.' A voice fr'm th' audjeence, 'Do I get me money back?' Brown J.: 'Who ar-re ye?' Th' Voice: 'Th' man that ownded th' limons.' Brown J.: 'I don't know.' (Gray J., White J., dissentin' an' th' r-rest iv th' birds concurrin' but f'r entirely diff'rent reasons.)

"An' there ye have th' decision, Hinnissy, that's shaken th' intellicts iv th' nation to their very foundations, or will if they thry to read it. 'Tis all r-right. Look it over some time. 'Tis fine spoort if ye don't care f'r checkers. Some say it laves th' flag up in th' air an' some say that's where it laves th' Constitution. Annyhow, something's in th' air. But there's wan thing I'm sure about."

"What's that?" asked Mr. Hennessy.

"That is," said Mr.Dooley, "no matther whether th' Constitution follows th' flag or not, th' Supreme Coort follows th' iliction returns."

ON CRIMINAL TRIALS

"I was r-readin' in th' pa-aper a hard kick again th' delay between th' time a criminal bumps some wan an' th' time he gets th' bump that is comin' to him accoordin' to th' law. This iditor feels bad because there's a diff'rence between this coun-thry an' England. Th' sentences like th' language ar-re th' same in th' two countries, but they're pronounced diff'rent. In England a man is presoomed to be innocent till he's proved guilty an' they take it f'r granted he's guilty. In this counthry a man is presoomed to be guilty ontil he's proved guilty an' af-ther that he's presoomed to be innocent.

"In th' oldher civilization th' judge reads th' news iv th' crime in th' mornin' pa-aper an' stops in at a hat shop on his way to coort an' buys a black cap to wear at th' approachin' fistivities. Whin he gets up on th' bench he calls th' shuriff to his side an' says he: 'Cap, go out an' grab a jury iv cross-lookin' marrid men to thry th' condimned.' The shuriff dhrags twelve indignant grocers fr'm their stores an' they come into coort protestin' because they will be bankrupted be sarvin' their counthry. But they ar-re soon restored to good humor be th' jovyal remarks iv th' coort, who makes thim laugh heartily at wanst be askin' thim if they ar-re opposed to capital punishmint.

"Th' pris'ner is thin hauled in in chains, an' th' judge, afther exprissin' his dislike iv his face with a look iv scorn, says: 'Murdhrer, ye ar-re entitled to a fair thrile. Ar-re ye guilty or not guilty? Not guilty, ye say? I thought ye wud. That's what th' likes iv ye always say. Well, let's have this disagreeable business over with in a hurry. I'll allow th' prosecution three hours to show ye up an' th' definse can have th' rest iv th' mornin'. Wake me up whin th' ividince is all in.'

"About noon his honor is woke be a note fr'm th' jury askin' how long they ar-re goin' to be kept fr'm their dinner. He hauls th' black cap out iv th' bandbox an' puttin' it on over his wig, says: 'Pris'ner at th' bar, it is now me awful jooty to lave ye'er fate to a British jury. I will not attimpt to infloonce thim in anny way. I will not take th' time to brush away th' foolish ividince put in in ye'er definse. Ye'er lawyers have done as well as they cud with nawthin' to go on. If anny iv th' jury believe ye innocent let thim retire to their room an' discuss th' matther over a meal iv bread an' wather while th' chops burn on th' kitchen stove an' their clerks are-re disthributin' groceries free to th' neighborhood.'

"But it's betther in this home iv th' free, mind ye. Afther th' polis have made up their mind that none iv th' polis foorce did it, they may or may not grab th' criminal. It depinds on th' weather. But supposin' it's a pleasant summer's day an' th' fugitive is in th' saloon nex' dure showin' th' revolver an' thryin' to thrade in a silver candlestick f'r a dhrink, an' th' polis foorce ar-re bendin' ivry effort to apprehind him an' ar-re combin' th' whole counthry f'r him, an' he doesn't know where to turn, but goes into th' station an' registhers an' gets his key an' ordhers his breakfast in th' cell an' gives a pair iv sugar tongs, a dimon necklace, a dozen knives an' forks, his autymatic an' other vallyables to th' sergeant to lock up in th' safe, an' laves wurrud not to be called, that's on'y th' begin—nin' iv th' exercises.

"Th' first year or two he passes away delightfully, havin' his pitchers took an' put in th' pa-apers an' bein' intherviewed while th' iditor iv th' Sob section sinds beautiful ladies out to talk with his wife an' describe his pretty little flat full iv keepsakes, but wan mornin' he wakes up an' gets th' pa-apers an' there's har'ly anny more mintion iv him thin if he was a meetin' iv th' Epworth league, or a debate in congress, or a speech iv th' prisidint, or a war in th' Ph'lipeens, an' that disturbs him. He fires his press agent, sinds f'r his lawyer an' demands a thrile. If th' fish ar-re not bitin' th' lawyer coaxes a judge to come into town, an' wanst more th' mallyfacther becomes a prom'nint citizen an' can read th' pa-apers without bein' disgusted at th' way they fill their colyums with news about nobodies.

"Th' first six months iv th' thrile ar-re usually taken in gettin' a jury that will be fair to both sides, but more fair to wan side thin to th' other. Th' state's attorney makes an effort to get twelve men who have no prejudices excipt a gin'ral opinyon that th' pris'ner is guilty. Th' lawyer f'r th' definse on'y asks that his client shall be thried be a jury iv his peers or worse, but wud compromise if all twelve were mimbers iv th' same lodge as himsilf. In due time twelve men iv intilligence who have r-read th' pa-apers an' can't remimber what they've r-read, or who can't r-read, or ar-re out iv wurruk, ar-re injooced to sarve, an' th' awful wheels iv justice begins to go round.

"Th' scene in th' coort is very beautiful an' touchin'. Th' pris'ner's wife rents a baby f'r th' winter an' sets where th' jury can see her whin her husband kicks her undher th' table an' she weeps. Th' table in front iv th' culprit is banked with flowers an' he comes into th' coort wearin' a geeranyum in his button-hole. Afther a flashlight iv th' august thribunal iv justice has been exploded an' th' masheen f'r takin' th' movies has been put up, th' dhread proceedure pro-ceeds. On th' first iv August th' prosecution succeeds in gettin' into th' record th' fact that such a person as th' victim iver lived in spite iv th' objictions iv th' definse on th' ground that it is immateeryal. Th' lawyer f'r th' definse objicts to all th' questions an' whin th' coort overrules him he takes an exciption. That is as much as to say to th' judge: 'I'll make a jack iv ye in th' supreem coort.' On th' twintieth iv Decimber afther a severe cross-examination iv th' principal witness th' jury asks the coort f'r a recess so they can lynch him.

"On th' fifteenth iv th' followin' April th' tistymony iv th' definse is submitted. It is, first, that th' pris'ner is insane an' five profissors fr'm th' infirmary swear that he was looney whin he done th' deed. Besides, he shot in self-definse, to protict his home an' th' honor iv American womanhood, while sthrugglin' with th' victim to keep him fr'm committin' suicide because th' pris'ner wudden't take his watch as a presint, th' gun accidintally wint off, a long an' a short man where seen leavin' th' premises afther th' crime, an' th' pris'ner was in Mitchigan City on that night, an' while on his way to see his sick child was stopped be an old lady who he rescued fr'm drownin' in th' park, who gave him all she had in her purse, a forty-four, a jimmy, a brace an' bit, an' a quantity iv silverware, clothing, curtains, an' joolry.

"So th' years roll brightly by an' day by day th' pris'ner sees his face on th' front page, th' fam'ly iv deceased is dhrove fr'm town be th' facts that has come out about his private life, an' most iv th' vallyable real estate in th' county is sold f'r taxes to pay th' bills iv th' short-hand writers f'r takin' down th' tistymony an' th' objictions iv th' definse.

"But though slow American justice, Hinnissy, is sure an' will overtake th' crim'nal if he'll on'y be patient an' not die, an' wan day all th' ividince is in. Th' disthrict attorney, who's a candydate f'r mayor, makes his closin' argymint, addhressin' th' jury as 'fellow Republicans.' Th' lawyer f'r th' pris'ner asks the jury on'y to consider th' law an' th' ividince an' to sind this innocent man home to his wife an' his starvin' childer. Afther th' judge has insthructed th' jury that he's all up in th' air about th' case an' doesn't know what he ought to say to thim, th' jury retires, charges its last meal to you an' me, an' discusses whether it ought to sind th' pris'ner home or somewhere's else. Afther askin' an' gettin' a description iv his home they decide on temperin' justice with mercy an' find him guilty. Th' pris'ner is brought into coort, smilin' an' cheerful, th' flashlights boom, th' cameras click, th' ladies swoon, an' th' judge says with a pleasant smile: 'It is me dhread jooty to sintince ye to th' Supreem Coort. Long life to ye.'

"Thin there's a lull in th' proceedin's. Th' seasons go swiftly by. Other things happen an' I can't remimber whether th' pris'ner was th' victim iv th' crime, th' witness f'r th' prosecution, or th' disthrict attorney. Manny times has blithe spring turned to mellow summer. Manny times has autumn reddened th' threes in th' parks. Men that were old durin' th' thrile ar-re dead. Men that were young ar-re old. Wan mornin' with decrepit fingers I open th' pa-aper an' r-read: 'Supreem Coort revarses th' Bill Sikes case. Th' coort yisterdah afthernoon held a long session fr'm two to a quarther to three an' cleared th' calendar up to eighteen sivinty-five be revarsin' th' lower coort f'r errors an ign'rance iv th' law in all th' cases appealed. In th' Sikes case th' decision is that while th' pris'ner was undoubtedly guilty, th' lower coort made a bone-head play to be allowin' th' disthrict attorney to open th' window an' expose th' pris'ner to a dhraft, be not asking Juryman Number Two whether he had iver been in th' dhry goods business, an' be omittin' a comma afther th' wurrud "so" on page fifty-three thousan' sivin hundred an' eighty in th' record.'

"An' th' pris'ner is brought back f'r a new thrile, Th' new thrile is always hurrid. Th' iditors refuse a requist fr'm th' pris'ner to sind around annywan to report it, th' iliventh assistant disthrict attorney appears f'r th' state in spite iv th' law on child labor, th' witnesses ar-re all dead an' burrid, an' th' onforchnit crim'nal is turned out on a wurruld that has f'rgotten him so completely that he can't aven get a job as an actor on th' vodyville stage."

"What happens to him if he hasn't got anny money?" asked Mr. Hennessy.

"He might as well be in England," said Mr. Dooley.

Justice Daniel P. Ward of the Illinois Supreme Court likes to read this essay aloud.

THE LAW'S DELAYS

"If I had me job to pick out," said Mr. Dooley, "I'd be a judge. I've looked over all th' others an' that's th' on'y wan that suits. I have th' judicyal timperamint. I hate wurruk.

"Ivrybody else is pushed an' hurrid in this tumulchuse age. Th' business man has to get to th' bank befure it closes an' th' banker has to get there befure th' business man escapes, an' th' high-priced actor has to kill off more gradyates iv th' school iv actin' thin iver he did, an' th' night editions iv th' pa-apers comes out arlier ivry mornin'. All is rush an' worry. Kings an' imprors duck about their jooties like bellhops, th' pampered son iv luxury at Newport is thryin' f'r a mile a minyit in his autymobill an' th' on'y leisure class left in th' wuruld is th' judicyary. Mind ye, Hinnissy, I'm not sayin' annything again' thim. I won't dhrag th' joodicyal ermine in th' mud though I haven't noticed that manny iv thim lift it immodestly whin they takes th' pollytical crossing. I have th' high rayspict f'r th' job that's th' alternative iv sixty days in jail. Besides, me boy, I invy thim.

"Somewhere a la-ad hits somewan on th' head with an axe or sinds him a bunch iv proosic acid done up to look like candy. Maybe he does an' maybe he don't; but annyhow that's what he's lagged f'r. Th' polis are in a hurry to get to th' pool-room befure th' flag falls in th' first race an' they carry th' case to th' gran' jury; th' gran' jury indicts him without a thought or a suspicion iv a har-rd feelin', th' judge takes his breakfast on th' bench to be there in time an' charges th' jury to be fair but not to f'rget th' man done it, an' th' jury rayturns a verdict iv guilty with three cheers an' a tiger. Th' pris'ner has hardly time to grab up his hat befure he's hauled off to his funeral obsequies, an' th' onprejudiced public feels happy about it. I don't believe in capital punishmint, Hinnissy, but'twill niver be abolished while th' people injye it so much. They're jus' squarin' thimsilves fr th' rayvoltin' details whin wurrud comes that Judge Tamarack iv Opolis has granted a stay iv proceedin's. Stays iv pro-ceedin's is devices, Hinnissy, be which th' high coorts keep in form. 'Tis a lagal joke. I med it up. Says Judge Tamarack: 'I know very little about this case excipt what I've been tol' be th' larned counsel fr th' dayfinse, an' I don't believe that, but I agree with Lord Coke in th' maxim that th' more haste th' less sleep. Therefore to all sheriffs, greetin': Fen jarrin' th' pris'ner till ye hear fr'm us.'

"So th' pris'ner waits an' dhreams he's alightnin' rod an' th' public waits an' ivrybody waits. Th' high coort is busy in its way. Ivry two to three years it is discovered takin' a nap at a county seat in th' corn belt, an' it hands down a decision fr th' defindant in a case fr damages growin' out if th' Shay rebillion. Then it dhrops off again. Th' judge that thried the case retires to a well-arned job with a railrood comp'ny, th' jury has ceased to look fr their pitchers in th' pa-apers an' th' insurance comp'nies insure young Cyanide's life fr the lowest known premyum. Occasionally a judge iv th' coort iv appeals walkin' in his sleep meets another judge, an' they discuss matthers. 'How ar-re ye gettin' on with th' Cyanide case, judge?' 'I'm makin' fair headway, judge. I r-read part iv th' vardict iv th' coroner's jury las' year an' nex' month whin th' fishin' is over, I expict to look into th' indictment. 'Tis a puzzlin' case. Th' man is not guilty.' 'Well, good bye, judge; I'll see ye in a year or two. Lave me know how ye'er gettin' on. Pleasant dhreams!' An' so they part. Th' higher up a coort is, th' less they see iv each other. Their office hours are fr'm a quarther to wan leap years. Ye take a lively lawyer that's wurruked twenty hours a day suin' sthreet railrood comp'nies an' boost him onto a high coort an' he can't think out iv a hammock. Th' more exalted what Hogan calls the joodicyal station, th' more it's like a dormitory. Th' years rowl by an' th' tillygraft op'rator that's been expictin' to sind a rush tillygram through young Cyanide sees his ohms an' his volts mouldin' an' no wurrud comes fr'm th' coort iv appeals but th' murmur iv th' chief justice discussin' th' nullification theery. But wan day, th' decision is wafted down. 'Th' coort finds,' it says, 'that th' vardict was conthry to th' law an' th' ividince. We seen this fr'm th' first. It's as plain as th' nose on ye'er face. Th' judge was prejudiced an' th' jury was ignorant. Th' ividince wasn't sufficient to hang a cat. We revarse th' decision an' ordher a new thrile that full justice may be done. We cannot help remarkin' at this time on th' croolty iv subjectin' this unforchnit man to all theses years iv torture an' imprisonment with a case again' him which we see at a glance durin' th' Mexican war cud not shtand th' test iv th' law.'

"But whin th' decision is carried to th' pris'ner, th' warden says 'Who?' 'P. Cyanide,' says th' clark iv th' coort. 'He's not here,' says th' warden. 'On consultin' me books, I find a man iv that name left in th' year sivinty-wan.' 'Did he escape?' 'In a sinse. He's dead.'

"So, Hinnissy, I'd like to be a judge iv a high coort, dhreamin' th' happy hours away. No hurry, no sthrivin' afther immejet raysults, no sprintin', no wan hollerin' 'Dooley J. hurry up with that ne exeat,' or 'Dooley, hand down that opinyion befure th' batthry gives out.' 'Tis th' thrue life iv aise an' gintlemanly comfort. 'Tis wait till th' clouds rowl by; 'tis time was meant for slaves; 'tis a long life an' a happy wan. Like th' Shamrock II, th' coort acts well in stays but can't run befure th' wind. A jury is f'r hangin' ivry man, but th' high coort says: 'Ye must die, but take ye'er time about it an' go out th' way ye like.' If I wanted to keep me money so that me gran'-childher might get it f'r their ol' age, I'd appeal to th' supreme coort. Oh, th' fine judge I'd make, f'r I can sleep anywhere, an' I'm niver impatient f'r annywan to get his jooes."

"I don't see," said Mr. Hennessy, "why they have anny

juries. Why don't they thry ivry man before th' supreme coort an' have done with it?''

"I have a betther way than that," said Mr. Dooley. "Ye see they're wurrukin' on time now. I wondher if they wudden't sthep livelier if they were paid be th' piece."

MAKING A WILL

"I niver made a will," said Mr. Dooley. "I didn't want t give mesilf a headache thinkin' iv something to put into it. A will iv mine wud be a puny little thing annyhow an' if anny wan thried to file it he'd be lible to be locked up f'r contimpt iv th' probate coort. Besides, I wuddn't like to cause anny onseemly wrangles an' maybe lawsuits among me heirs about who wud pay f'r th' express wagon to carry th' estate to th' city dump. An' annyhow I've always thought that if there's goin' to be ayether cheers or tears at me obsekees they shud spring fr'm th' heart, not fr'm mercinary motives. If anny fellow feels like cillybratin' me departure let him do it out iv his own pocket. Thin I'll know he's sincere. 'Twud grieve me if some wan broke into song at th' news an' a sthranger was to ask: 'Is that wan iv his inimies?' an' th' reply was, 'No, it's wan iv his heirs.'

"So f'r wan reason or another I've niver made a will, but I'll deny it must be considhrable spoort f'r thim that has th' names an' th' imagination to injye it. I'm pretty sure I'd burst into tears whin th' lawyers wrote down th' directions f'r somebody else to set in me rockin' chair, an' I can't think iv annything that wud brighten th' wurruld with me out iv it. But that wud be because I wuddn't go at it in th' right way. To be injyeable a will must be at wan an' th' same time a practical joke on th' heirs an' an advertisemint iv the man that made it. Manny a man niver has his own way till he has it through his will. Af-ther he's dead an' gone, he shoves his hat on th' back iv his head an' stalks up an' down through th' house, sayin, 'I'll show ye who's th' boss here. F'r th' first time in me life, now that I'm dead, I'm goin' to be obeyed.' No wondher that manny meek millyonaires comforts their declinin' years with this amusemint. It is as Hogan says, th' last infirmary f'r their noble minds. It's a chance f'r thim to tache th' fam'ly their proper place, an' blow their own horns without havin' anny wan interrupt th' solo. . . .

"Think iv th' throuble ye can cause an' the insults ye can hurl at ye'er inimies. I often though 'twud be a fine way iv gettin, aven with a man I didn't like. Supposin' Hogan an' me had a quarrul an' I didn't have time to write a frindly biography about him, or was afraid I might go first. Nawthin' wud be nater thin to put him in me will. 'I hereby cancel all bequests to me frind Terrence Hogan on account iv his bad habits.'

"I bet he'd be sorry I was gone. How he'd wish he cud have me back agin f'r a while.

"I niver see anny wan that entherd into th' spirit iv makin' a will so thurly as our ol' frind Dochney. Ye didn't like him, but I did. I liked him because he was so simple an' sincere. Prudent fellows like ye'ersilf, that spind ye'er lives pilin' up great stores iv good will an' affiction an' a comfortable conscience f'r ye'er old age don't apprecyate a spindthrift like Dochney, who threw all these things away in th' pursuit iv his pleasure, which was makin' money. Ye thought he was a bad man, but I knew him f'r a single-minded, innocint ol' la-ad who niver harmed anny wan excipt f'r gain an' was incapable iv falsehood outside iv business. To those who see him in th' rough battle iv life at home or among his neighbors, he may've seemed hard, but we who knew him in th' quiet seclusyon iv th' bank among his recreations, found another Dochney, a cheerful soul, who always had a smile on his face, wrote little verses to th' promissory notes an' cuddn't keep his feet still whin th' goold coin clatthered on th' counter. If Dochney had wan fault it was he was too sintimental about money. Men like ye ar-re th' ra-ally rapacyous wans. Ye have nawthin' but desire f'r money. Ye don't want to give it a home an' take care iv it. But Dochney had a tender feelin' f'r it. Tears come to his eyes as he watched it grow. He become so attached to it that no wan cud pry it away fr'm him. An' money reciprocated. Iv'ry dollar he had wurruked f'r him. It wint out an' decoyed another dollar an' aven if it come back ladin' nawthin' more thin a little chickenfeed Dochney wasn't cross about it. He wud pat a nickel on th' back an' say: 'Ye're small now, but with a little incouragemint we'll make a big sthrappin' dollar out iv ye yet.'

"Dochney lived to an old age, because as th' pote says, 'There's nawthin' like avarice to keep a man young.' Th' Spanyards knew that, whin they sarched f'r th' fountain iv perpetchool youth. They'd heerd th' Indyans had money. Annyhow, Dochney's cheeks wore th' bloom iv usury long afther manny philanthropists ar-re lookin' pale. But th' time come whin somethin' in th' eyes iv his financial frinds told him 'twud be betther not to go downtown agin unarmed, an' he retired. He planted his money th' way they do eyesthers an' let it breed, sindin' down wanst a week to haul out enough to sustain life an' puttin' th' rest back in agin.

"But this was no life f'r wan that had been an eyesther pirate in his day, an' Dochney begun to pine. I thried to amuse him. I had th' congressman sind him ivry day th' new currency bill; I cut out th' reports wanst a week iv th' bankruptcys in th' United States an' Canady an' wurruked th' cash registher f'r him be th' hour, because he liked th' old refrain. But nawthin' did him anny good ontil Dock O'Leary advised him to alter his will. Th' Dock says he always thries this prescription on aged millyonaires afther th' oxygen fails. Wan mornin' Dochney come in lookin' as cheerful as an advertisemint iv a breakfast food an' jinglin' his key ring in his pocket, f'r he niver carrid annything else to jingle, but made a practice iv exthractin' car fare out iv th' gran'childher's bank with a penknife ivry mornin'.

"'Ye're lookin' well, me ol' buccaneer,' said I. 'It's feelin' well I am,' says he, fillin' his pocket fr'm th' cheese bowl. 'I've been with me lawyer all mornin' revisin' me will. I find I've left out a good many ol' frinds. Ye haven't a middle inityal to ye'er name, have ye?' 'Give me a glass iv sas-prilly,' he says. Well, sir; though I knew th' crafty ol' pirate, th' thought suddenly lept into me head that maybe his heart or his brain had softened an' he'd put me in th' will. In that fatal sicond I bought two autymobills, a yacht, an' a goold watch an' chain an' shook me ol' frinds, an' whin I come to me sinses he'd gone an' hadn't settled f'r th' sas-prilly.

"Well, th' fun he had afther that. All day long he wint around makin' delicate inquiries about people's circumstances an' in th' mornin' he was downtown puttin' something new in his will. He hadn't been a popylar man. He had cashed in th' affictions iv his neighbors arly in life. An' prejudices ar-re hard to overcome. But grajaly—that is to say, within a week or ten days—people begun to see that a gr-reat injustice had been done to him. He didn't say annythin' about a will. But he had a way iv askin' people did they spell their name with an aitch or a zee an' puttin' it down in a notebook that was very consolin'. His rilitives begun to show a gr-reat inthrest in him an' some iv thim come fr'm as far as San Francisco to cheer his declinin' years an' form vigilance committees to protect him fr'm fortune hunters. He was niver alone, but always had th' most agreeable s'ciety. 'Twas 'Uncle, that's a fine cough ye have; wuddn't ye like to set in this cool draft?' Or 'Cousin Andhrew, tell us that joke ye made las' night. I nearly died laughin' at it, but no wan can tell it like ye'ersilf.'

"He niver took a meal at home. He stopped payin' all bills. He insisted on all babies born in th' ward bein' named afther him. He insulted people an' challenged thim to fight. By an' by th' pa-apers got hold iv him an' always spoke iv him as th' eccenthric philanthropist. Rows of carredges shtud at his dure an' inside iv his house he debated with th' thrustees iv binivolint institutions an' prisidints iv colledges about their plans f'r new buildin's. Wan iv th' ladin' univarsities sint th' glee club down to serenade him. He was ilicted vice prisidint iv Andhrew Carnaygie's peace comity, thrustee iv th' art museem, director in th' Home f'r Wan Eyed Owls, an' L. L. D. in Skowhegan univarsity.

"An' all th' time th' wurruld was talkin' about this gr-reat binifacthor all Mrs. Dochney cud find in her cold heart to say was, 'There's no fool like an ol' fool,' an' wint about her housewurruk an' made poultices f'r him whin he come home fr'm the meetin' iv th' s'ciety f'r pathronizin' th' poor, where they'd give him a cold in th' chest fr'm th' hankerchief salute.

"Well, sir, all times, good an' bad, has got to come to an end, an' wan day Dochney come in to see me. 'I think,' says he, 'I'll go home an' go to bed an' stay there. I've finished me will an' me life is no longer safe fr'm th' binificyants. There's a prisidint iv a college comin' to town. He's an eager idjacator, an' as I don't want to die with me boots on I think I won't see him. Here's 5 cints I owe ye f'r th' sas-prilly,' he says. An' he wint away an' I niver set eyes on him agin. He left a will in five lines, givin' all his money to th' good woman, an' sayin' that he thought he'd done enough f'r iv'rybody else by keepin' thim in hopes all these years, which is th' on'y pleasure in life."

"I niver cud undherstand a man like Dochney makin' money," said Mr. Hennessy.

"He made it," said Mr. Dooley, "because he honestly loved it with an innocint affiction. He was thrue to it. Th' reason ye have no money is because ye don't love it f'r itsilf alone. Money won't iver surrinder to such a flirt."

CHAPTER VII

THE SINGLE LIFE, LOVE AND/OR MARRIAGE

Mr. Dooley's comments on "Short Marriage Contracts" echo miles of newsprint appearing regularly today on "relationships" (a term that Dunne, with his devotion to the purity of the English language, would have loathed).

His essays on bachelorhood would haunt him when he finally married; some of his journalistic colleagues left behind were unkind enough to reprint them just before the nuptials.

As to divorce, in another essay, Dooley remarked that, "In me heart I think if people marry it ought to be for life. The Laws ar-re altogether too lenient with thim."

A BACHELOR'S LIFE

"It's always been a wondher to me," said Mr. Hennessy, "ye niver marrid."

"It's been a whonder to manny," Mr. Dooley replied haughtily. "Maybe if I'd been as aisy pleased as most—an' this is not sayin' annything again you an' ye'ers, Hinnisy, f'r ye got much th' best iv it—I might be th' father iv happy childher an' have money in th' bank awaitin' th' day whin th' intherest on th' morgedge fell due. 'Tis not f'r lack iv opporchunities I'm here alone, I tell ye that me bucko, f'r th' time was whin th' sound iv me feet'd brings more heads to th' windies iv Ar-rchey r-road thin'd bob up to see ye'er fun'ral go by. An' that's manny a wan."

"Ah, well," said Mr. Hennessy, "I was but jokin' ye." His

tone mollified his friend, who went on: "To tell ye th' truth, Hinnissy, th' raison I niver got marrid was I niver cud pick a choice f'r I look on all the sect as iligeable f'r me hand an' I'm on'y resthrained fr'm r-rentin' Lincoln Park f'r a home an' askin' them all to clave on'y to me, be me nachral modesty an' th' laws iv th' State iv Illinye. 'Twas always so with me an' I think it is so with most men that dies bachelors. Be r-readin' th' pa-apers ye'd think a bachelor was a man bor-rn with a depraved an' parvarse hathred iv wan iv our most cherished institootions, an' anti-expansionist d'ye mind. But 'tis no such thing. A bachelor's a man that wud extind his benificint rule over all th' female wurruld, fr'm th' snow-capped girls iv Alaska to th' sunny eileens iv th' Passyfic. A marrid man's a person with a limited affection—a protictionist an anti-expansionist, a mugwamp, be hivins. 'Tis th' bachelor that's keepin' alive th' rivrince f'r th' sect.

"I think marrid men gets on th' best f'r they have a home an' fam'ly to lave in th' mornin' an' a home an' fam'ly to go back to at night; that makes thim wurruk. Some men's domestic throubles dhrives thim to dhrink, others to labor. Ye r-read about a man becomin' a millyonaire an' ye think he done it be his own exertions whin 'tis much again little 'twas th' fear iv comin' home impty handed an' dislike iv stayin' ar-round th' house all day that make him rich. Misther Standard Ile takes in millyons in a year but he might be playin' dominoes in an injine house if it wasn't f'r Mrs. Standard Ile. 'Tis th' thought iv that dear quiet lady at home, in her white cap with her ca'm motherly face, waitin' patiently f'r him with a bell-punch that injooces him to put a shtick iv dinnymite in somebody else's ile well an' bury his securities whin th' assisor comes ar-round. Near ivry man's property ought to be in wife's name an' most iv it is.

"A marrid man gets th' money, Hinnissy, but a bachelor man gets th' sleep. Whin all me marrid frinds is off to wurruk poundin' th' ongrateful sand an' wheelin' th' rebellyous slag, in th' heat if th' afthernoon, ye can see ye'er onfortchnit bachelor frind perambulatin' up an' down th' shady side iv th' sthreet, with an umbrelly over his head an' a wurrud iv cheer fr'm young an' old to enliven his loneliness."

"But th' childer?" asked Mr. Hennessy slyly.

"Childer!" said Mr. Dooley. "Sure I have th' finest fam'ly in th' city. Without scandal I'm th' father iv ivry child in Ar-rchey r-road fr'm end to end."

"An' none iv ye'er own," said Mr. Hennessy.

"I wish to hell, Hinnissy," said Mr. Dooley savagely, "ye'd not lean against that mirror, I don't want to have to tell ye again."

SHORT MARRIAGE CONTRACTS

"Who is George Meredith?" asked Mr. Hennessy.

"Ye can search me," said Mr. Dooley. "What is th' charge again' him?"

"Nawthin'," said Mr. Hennessy; "but I see he's in favor iv short-term marredges."

"What d'ye mean? asked Mr. Dooley. "Reducin' th' terms f'r good behavyor?"

"No," said Mr. Hennessy. "He says people ought to get marrid f'r three or four years at a time. Thin, if they don't like each other, or if wan gets tired, they break up housekeepin'."

"Well," said Mr. Dooley, "it mightn't be a bad thing. Th' throuble about mathrimony, as I have obsarved it fr'm me seat in th' gran' stand, is that afther fifteen or twinty years it settles down to an endurance thrile. 'Women,' as Hogan says, 'are creatures iv such beaucheous mien that to be loved they have but to be seen; but,' he says, 'wanst they're seen an' made secure,' he says, 'we first embrace, thin pity, thin endure,' he says. Most iv th' ol' marrid men I know threat their wives like a rockin'-chair, a great comfort whin they're tired, but apt to be in th' way at other times.

"Now, it might be diff'rent if th' ladies, instead iv bein' secured f'r life, was on'y held on a short-term lease.

"I don't know how men propose. I niver thried it but wanst, an' th' hired girl said th' lady was not at home. No wan will iver tell ye. Most marrid men give ye th' impressyon that their wives stole thim fr'm their agonized parents. But, anyhow, we'll suppose that Archybald, layin' a silk handkerchief on th' carpet an' pullin' up th' leg iv his pantaloons, to prevint baggin', hurls himsilf impetchoosly at th' feet iv his adored wan a' cries: 'Belinda, I can on'y offer ye th' love iv an honest South Wather Sthreet commission merchant an' mimber iv th' Brotherhood iv Wholesale an' Retail Grocers. Will ye take me f'r life?' Belinda blushes a rosy red an' replies: 'Archybald, ye ask too much. I cannot take ye f'r life, but I'll give ye a five-year lease an' resarve th' right to renew at th' end iv that time,' she says. 'Will that do?' says she. 'I will thry to make ye happy,' says he. An' she falls on his bosom, an' between her sobs cries: 'Thin let us repair at wanst to th' Title Guarantee an' Thrust Comp'ny an' be made man an' wife,' she says.

"Well, after Archybald is safely marrid his good opinyon iv himsilf returns. Belinda does her share to encourage him, an' befure long he begins to wondher how as fine a fellow as him come to throw himsilf away. Not that she ain't a good creature, d'ye mind, an' slavishly devoted to him. He hasn't annything again' her; still, think iv what he might have done if he had on'y known his thrue worth. Whin a man gets a good repytation he doesn't have to live up to it. So bimeby Archybald, for knowin' fr'm what his wife says that he is handsome enough without anny artificyal aid, f'rgets th' mannycure an' th' hair-dhresser. Sometimes he shaves, an' sometimes he doesn't. So far as he is consarned, he thinks th' laundhry bill is too high. He advertises th' fact that he wears a red flannel chest-protictor. His principal convarsation is about his lumbago. He frequently mintions that he likes certain articles iv food, but they don't like him. Whin he comes home at night he plays with th' dog, talks pollyticks with his next-dure neighbor, puts his hat an' a pair iv cuffs on th' piannah, sets down in front iv th' fire, kicks off his boots, and dhraws on a pair iv carpet slippers, an' thin notices that the wife iv his bosom is on th' premises. 'Hello, ol' woman,' he says. 'How's all ye'er throubles?' he says.

"Wanst a year Belinda meets him at th' dure with a flower in her hair. 'Well,' he says, 'what are th' decorations about?' he says. 'Don't ye know what day this is?' says she. 'Sure,' says he, 'it's Choosdah.' 'No, but what day?' 'I give it up. St. Pathrick's day, Valentine's day, pay day. What's th' answer?' 'But think.' 'I give it up.' 'It's th' annyvarsary iv our weddin'.' 'Oh,' says he, 'so it is. I'd clean f'rgot. That's right. I raymimber it well, now that ye mintion it. Well, betther luck nex't time. There, take that,' he says. An' he salutes her on th' forehead an' goes down in th' cellar to wurruk on a patent skid that will rivoluchionize th' grocery business. If he suffers a twinge of remorse later he tells her to take two dollars out iv th' housekeepin' money an' buy herself a suitable prisint.

"He's pleasant in th' avenin'. At supper, havin' explained his daily maladies at full length, he relapses into a gloomy silence, broken on'y be such sounds as escape fr'm a man dhrinkin' hot coffee. Afther supper he figures on th' prob'ble market f'r rutybagy turnips, while his wife r-reads th' advertisements in th' theaytres. 'Jawn Drew is here this week,' says she. 'Is he?' says Archybald. 'That's good,' he says. 'I haven't been to a theaytre since Billy Emerson died,' he says. 'I hate th' theaytre. It ain't a bit like rale life as I see it in business hours,' he says. Afther a while, whin Belinda begins to tell him a thrillin' says-she about wan iv the neighbors, he lapses into a pleasant sleep, now an' thin arousin' himsilf to murmur: 'Um-m.' At nine o'clock he winds th' clock, puts th' dog out f'r the night, takes off his collar on th' stairs, an' goes to bed. Belinda sets up a little later an' dhreams Richard Harding Davis wrote a book about her.

"But th' five years ar-re up at last. Wan mornin' Archybald is glarin' fr'm behind a newspaper in his customary jaynial breakfast mood whin his wife says: 'Where will I sind ye'er clothes?' 'What's that?' says he. 'Where d'ye live to-morrah?'

'Don't be foolish, ol' woman. What d'ye mean?' says he. ' I mean,' says she, 'that th' lease has expired. At tin-thirty to-day it r-runs out. I like ye, Archybald, but I think I'll have to let ye go. Th' property has r-run down. Th' repairs haven't been kept up. Ye haven't allowed enough for wear an' tear. It looks too much like a boardin'-house. I'm goin' into th' market to prospect f'r a husband with all modhren improvements,' says she.

"Well, wudden't that be a jolt f'r Archybald? Ye bet he'd beat th' quarther-mile record to th' joolers. He'd haul out ol' pitchers iv himsilf as he was th' day he won his threasure, an' he'd hurry to a beauty upholsterer an' say: 'Make me as like that there Apollo Belvydere as ye can without tearin' me down altogether.' It wud be fine. He'd get her back, maybe, but it wud be a sthruggle. An' afther that, about a year befure th' conthract expired again, ye'd see him pickin' purple ties out iv th' shop window, buyin theaytre tickets be th' scoor, an' stoppin' ivry avenin' at a flower-shop to gather a bunch iv vilets. He'd hire a man to nudge him whin his birthday came around, an ivry time th' annyvarsary iv th' weddin' occurred he'd have a firewurruks display fr'm th' front stoop. Whin he'd succeeded in convincin' th' objeck iv his affictions that she cud put up with him f'r another five years they cud go on their weddin' journey. Ye'd read in th' pa-apers: 'Misther an' Mrs. Archybald Pullets were marrid again las' night be th' presidient iv th' First Naytional Bank. They departed on their twelfth weddin' journey, followed be a shower iv rice fr'm their gr-reat grandchilder.' It wud be fine. I hope George What's his-name puts it through."

"I don't believe wan wurrud ye say," said Mr. Hennessy.

"P'raps not," said Mr. Dooley. "In me heart I think if people marry it ought to be f'r life. Th' laws ar-re altogether too lenient with thim."

THE BACHELOR TAX

"This here pa-aper says," said Mr. Hennessy, "that they're goin' to put a tax on bachelors. That's r-right. Why shudden't there be a tax on bachelors? There's one on dogs."

"That's r-right," said Mr. Dooley. "An' they're goin' to make it five dollars a year. Th' dogs pay only two. It's quite a concession to us. They consider us more thin twice as vallyable, or annyhow more thin twice as dangerous as dogs. I suppose ye expect next year to see me throttin' around with a leather collar an' brass tag on me neck. If me tax isn't paid th' bachelor wagon'll come over an' th' bachelor catcher'll lassoo me an' take me to th' pound an' I'll be kept there three days an' thin, if still unclaimed, I'll be dhrowned onless th' pound keeper takes a fancy to me.

"Ye'll niver see it, me boy. No, Sir. Us bachelors ar-re a sthrong body iv men polytickally, as well as handsome and brave. If ye thry to tax us we'll fight ye to th' end. If worst come to worst we won't pay th' tax. Don't ye think f'r a minyit that light-footed heroes that have been eludin' onprincipled females all their lives won't be able to dodge a little thing like a five-dollar tax. There's no clumsy collector in th' wurruld that cud catch up with a man iv me age who has avoided the machinations iv th' fair f'r forty years an' remains unmarrid.

"An' why shud we be taxed? We're th' mainstay iv th' Constitution an' about all that remains iv liberty. If ye think th' highest jooty iv citizenzhip is to raise a fam'ly why don't ye give a vote to th' shad? Who puts out ye'er fire f'r ye, who supports th' Naytional Governmint be payin' most iv th' intarnal rivnoo jooties, who maintains th' schools ye sind ye'er ignorant little childer to, be payin' th' saloon licenses, who does th' fightin' f'r ye in th' wars but th' bachelors?

"Th' marrid men start all th' wars with loose talk whin they're on a spree. But whin war is declared they begin to think what a tur-ruble thing 'twud be if they niver come home to their fireside an' their wife got marrid again an' all their grandchilder an' their great-grandchilder an' their widow an' th' man that marrid her an' his divoorced wife an' their rilitives, descindants, friends, an' acquaintances wud have to live on af- ther father was dead and gone with a large piece iv broken iron in his stomach or back, as th' case might be, but a pension come fr'm th' Governmint. So, th' day war is declared ye come over here an' stick a sthrange-lookin' weepin in me hand an' I close down me shop an' go somewhere I niver was befure an' maybe lose me leg defindin' th' hearths iv me counthry, me that niver had a hearth iv me own to warm me toes by but th' oil stove in me bedroom. An' that's th' kind iv men ye'd be wantin' to tax like a pushcart or a cow. Onscrupulous villain!

"Whin ye tax th' bachelors ye tax valor. Whin ye tax th' bachelors ye tax beauty. Ye've got to admit that we're a much finer lookin' lot iv fellows thin th' marrid men. That's why we're bachelors. 'Tis with us as with th' ladies. A lady with an erratic face is sure to be marrid befure a Dhream iv Beauty. She starts to wurruk right away an' what Hogan calls th' doc- trine iv av'rages is always with thim that starts early an' makes manny plays. But th' Dhream iv Beauty figures out that she can wait an' take her pick an' 'tis not ontil she is bumpin' thir- ty that she wakes up with a scream to th' peril iv her position an' runs out an' pulls a man down fr'm th' top iv a bus. Man- ny a plain but determined young woman have I seen happily marrid an' doin' th' cookin' f'r a large fam'ly whin her frind who'd had her pitcher in th' contest f'r th' most beautiful woman in Brighton Park was settin' behind th' blinds waitin f'r some wan to take her buggy ridin'.

"So it is with us. A man with a face that looks as if some wan had thrown it at him in anger nearly always marries befure he is old enough to vote. He feels he has to an' he cultivates what Hogan calls th' graces. How often do ye hear about a fellow that he is very plain but has a beautiful nature. Ye bet he has. If he hadn't an' didn't always keep it in th' show-case where all th' wurruld cud see he'd be lynched be th' Society f'r Municipal Improvement. But 'tis diff'rent with us comely bachelors. Bein' very beautiful, we can afford to be haughty an' peevish. It makes us more inthrestin'. We kind iv look thim over with a gentle but supeeryor eye an' say to oursilves: 'Now, there's a nice, pretty atthractive girl. I hope she'll marry well.' By an by whin th' roses fade fr'm our cheeks an' our eye is dimmed with age we bow to th' inivitable, run down th' flag iv defiance, an' ar-re yanked into th' multichood iv happy an' speechless marrid men that look like flashlight pitchers. Th' best-lookin' iv us niver get marrid at all.

"Yes, Sir, there's no doubt we do a good deal to beautify th' landscape. Whose pitchers ar-re those ye see in th' advertisements iv th' tailorman? There's not a marrid man among thim. They're all bachelors. What does th' gents' furnishing man hang his finest neckties in th' front window f'r but to glisten with a livelier iris, as Hogan says, th' burnished bachelor? See th' lordly bachelor comin' down th' sthreet, with his shiny plug hat an' his white vest, th' dimon stud that he wint in debt f'r glistenin' in his shirt front, an' th' patent-leather shoes on his feet outshinin' th' noonday sun.

"Thin we see th' marrid man with th' wrinkles in his coat an' his tie undher his ear an' his chin unshaven. He's walkin' in his gaiters in a way that shows his socks ar-re mostly darned. I niver wore a pair iv darned socks since I was a boy. Whin I make holes in me hosiery I throw thim away. 'Tis a fine idee iv th' ladies that men are onhappy because they have no wan to darn their socks an' put buttons on their shirts. Th' truth is that a man is not onhappy because his socks ar-re not darned but because they ar-re.

"Whin a lady begins to wondher if I'm not onhappy in me squalid home without th' touch iv a woman's hand ayether in th' tidy on th' chair or in th' inside pocket iv th' coat, I say: "No, ma'am, I live in gr-reat luxury surrounded be all that money can buy an' manny things that it can't or won't. There ar-re Turkish rugs on th' flure an' chandyleers hang fr'm th' ceilins. There I set a night dhrinkin' absinthe, sherry wine, port wine, champagne, beer, whisky, rum, claret, kimmel, weiss

beer, cream de mint, curaso, an' binidictine, occas'nally takin'
a dhraw at an opeem pipe an' r-readin' a Fr-rinch novel. Th'
touch iv a woman' s hand wudden't help this here abode iv
luxury. Wanst, whin I was away, th' beautiful Swede slave that
scrubs out me place iv business broke into th' palachal
boodoor an' in thryin' to set straight th' ile paintin' iv th'
Chicago fire burnin' Ilivator B, broke a piece off a frame that
cost me two dollars iv good money.' If they knew that th' on'y
furniture in me room was a cane-bottomed chair an' a thrunk
an' that there was nawthin' on th' flure but oilcloth an' me
clothes, an' that 'tis so long since me bed was made up that it's
now a life-size plaster case iv me, I'd be dhragged to th' altar at
th' end iv a chain.

"Speakin' as wan iv th' few survivin' bachelors, an old
vethran that's escaped manny a peril an' got out iv manny a
difficult position with honor, I wish to say that fair woman is
niver so dangerous as whin she's sorry f'r ye. Whin th' wurruds
'Poor man' rises to her lips an' th' nurse light comes into her
eyes, I know 'tis time f'r me to take me hat an' go. An' if th'
hat's not handy I go without it.

"I bet ye th' idee iv taxin' bachelors started with th' dear
ladies, but I say to thim: 'Ladies, is not this petty revenge on
ye'er best finds? Look on ye'er own husbands an' think what
us bachelors have saved manny iv ye'er sisters fr'm. Besides
aren't we th' hope iv th' future iv th' instichoochion iv
mathrmony? If th' onmarrid ladies ar-re to marry at all, 'tis us,
th' bold bachelors, they must look forward to. We're not
bachelors fr'm choice. We're bachelors because we can't make
a choice. Ye all look so lovely to us that we hate to bring th'
tears into th' eyes iv others iv ye be marryin' some iv ye. Considher our onforchnit position an' be kind. Don't oppress us.
We were not meant f'r slaves. Don't thry to coerce us. Continue to lay f'r us an' hope on. If ye tax us there's hardly an old
bachelor in th' land that won't fling his five dollars acrost th'
counter at th' tax office an' say: 'Hang th' expense.'"

DIVORCE

"Well, sir," said Mr. Dooley, "I see they've been holdin' a Divoorce Congress."

"What's that?" asked Mr. Hennessy.

"Ye wudden't know," said Mr. Dooley. "Divoorce is th' on'y luxury supplied by th' law that we don't injye in Ar-rchey Road. Up here whin a marrid couple get to th' pint where 'tis impossible f'r thim to go on livin' together they go on livin' together. They feel that way some mornin' in ivry month, but th' next day finds thim still glarin' at each other over th' ham an' eggs. No wife iver laves her husband while he has th' breath iv life in him, an' anny gintleman that took a thrip to Reno in ordher to saw off th' housekeepin' expinses on a rash successor wud find throuble ready f'r him whin he come back to Ar-rchey Road.

"No, sir, whin our people grab hands at th' altar, they're hooked up f'river. There's on'y wan decree iv divoorce that th' neighbors will recognize, an' that's th' wan that entitles ye to ride just behind th' pall bearers. That's why I'm a batch. 'Tis th' fine skylark iv a timprary husband I'd make, bringin' home a new wife ivry Foorth iv July an' dischargin' th' old wan without a charackter. But th' customs iv th' neighbors are agin it.

"But 'tis diff'rent with others, Hinnissy. Down be Mitchigan Avnoo marredge is no more bindin' thin a dhream. A short marrid life an' an onhappy wan is their motto. Off with th' old love an' on with th' new an' off with that. 'Till death us do part," says th' preacher. 'Or th' jury,' whispers th' blushin' bride.

"Th' Divoorce Congress, Hinnissy, that I'm tellin' ye about was assembled to make th' divoorce laws iv all th' States th' same. It's a tur-rble scandal as it is now. A man shakes his wife in wan State on'y to be grabbed be her an' led home th' minyit he crosses th' border. There's no safety f'r anny wan. In some places it's almost impossible f'r a man to get rid iv his fam'ly onless he has a good raison. There's no regularity at all about it.

Ye can be divoorced f'r annything if ye know where to lodge th' complaint. Among th' grounds ar-re snorin', deefness, because wan iv th' parties dhrinks an' th' other doesn't, because wan don't dhrink an' th' other does, because they both dhrink, because th' wife is addicted to sick headaches, because he asked her what she did with that last $10 he give her, because he knows some wan else, because she injyes th' society iv' th' young, because he f'rgot to wind th' clock. A husband can get a divoorce because he has more money thin he had; a wife because he had less. Ye can always get a divoorce f'r what Hogan calls incompatibility iv temper. That's whin husband an' wife ar-re both cross at th' same time. Ye'd call it a tiff in ye'er fam'ly, Hinnissy.

"But, mind ye, none iv these raisons go in anny two States.

"It wud be a grand thing if it cud be straightened out. Th' laws ought to be th' same ivrywhere. In anny part iv this fair land iv ours it shud be th' right iv anny man to get a divoorce, with alimonhy, simply be goin' befure a Justice iv th' Peace an' makin' an affydavit that th' lady's face had grown too bleak f'r his taste. Be Hivens, I'd go farther. Rather than have people endure this sarvichood I'd let anny man escape be jumpin' th' conthract. All he'd have to do if I was r-runnin' this Governmint wud be to put some clothes in th' grip, write a note to his wife that afther thinkin' it over f'r forty years he had made up his mind that his warm nature was not suited to marredge with th' mother iv so manny iv his childer, an' go out to return no more.

"I don't know much about marrid life, except what ye tell me an' what I r-read in th' pa-apers. But it must be sad. All over this land onhappily mated couples ar-re sufferin' almost as much as if they had a sliver in their thumb or a slight headache. Th' sorrows iv these people ar-re beyond belief. I say, Hinnissy, it is th' jooty iv th' law to marcifully release thim.

"Ye take th' case iv me frind fr'm Mud Center that I was readin' about th' other day. There was a martyr f'r ye. Poor fellow! Me eyes filled with tears thinkin' about him. Whin a young man he marrid. He was a fireman in thim days, an' th' objict iv his etarnal affection was th' daughter iv th' most popylar saloon keeper in town. A gr-reat socyal gulf opened between thim. He had fine prospects iv ivinchooly bein' promoted to a two-fifty a day, but she was heiress to a cellar full iv Monongahela rye an' a pool table, an' her parents objicted, because iv th' diffrence in their positions. But love such as his is not to be denied. Th' bold suitor won. Together they eloped an' were marrid.

"F'r a short time all wint well. They lived together happily f'r twinty years an' raised wan iv th' popylous fam'lies iv people who expect to be supported in their old days. Th' impechuse lover, spurred on be th' desire to make good with his queen, slugged, cheated, an' wurruked his way to th' head iv th' railroad. He was no longer Greasy Bill, th' Oil Can, but Hinnery Aitch Bliggens, th' Prince iv Industhree. All th' diffrent kinds iv money he iver heerd iv rolled into him, large money an' small, other people's money, money he'd labored f'r an' money he'd wished f'r. Whin he set in his office countin' it he often left a call f'r six o'clock f'r fear he might be dhreamin' an' not get to th' roundhouse on time.

"But, bein' an American citizen, he soon felt as sure iv himsilf as though he'd got it all in th' Probate Coort, an' th' arly Spring saw him on a private car speedin' to New York, th' home iv Mirth. He was received with open ar-rms be ivry man in that gr-reat city that knew the combynation iv a safe. He was taken f'r yacht rides be his fellow Kings iv Fi-nance. He was th' principal guest iv honor at a modest but tasteful dinner, where there was a large artificyal lake iv champagne into which th' comp'ny cud dive. In th' on'y part iv New York ye iver read about—ar-re there no churches or homes in New York, but on'y hotels, night resthrants, an' poolrooms?—in th' on'y part iv New York ye read about he cud be seen anny night sittin' where th' lights cud fall on his bald but youthful head.

"An' how was it all this time in dear old Mud Center? It is painful to say that th' lady to whom our frind was tied f'r life had not kept pace with him. She had taught him to r-read, but he had gone on an' taken what Hogan calls th' postgrajate coorse. Women get all their book larnin' befure marredge, men afther. She'd been pretty active about th' childer while he was pickin' up more iddycation in th' way iv business thin she'd iver dhream iv knowin'. She had th' latest news about th' throuble in th' Methodist Church, but he had a private wire into his office.

"A life spint in nourishin' th' young, Hinnissy, while fine to read about, isn't anny kind iv a beauty restorer, an' I've got to tell ye that th' lady prob'bly looked diff'rent fr'm th' gazelle he use to whistle three times f'r whin he wint by on Number Il- iven. It's no aisy thing to rock th' cradle with wan hand an' on- dylate th' hair with another. Be th' time he was gettin' into th' upper classes in New York she was slowin' down aven f'r Mud Center. Their tastes was decidely dissimilar, says th' pa-aper. Time was whin he carrid th' wash pitcher down to th' corner f'r a quart iv malt, while she dandled th' baby an' fried th' round steak at th' same time. That day was past. She hadn't got to th' pint where she cud dhrink champagne an' keep it out iv her nose. Th' passin' years had impaired all possible founda- tions f'r a new crop iv hair. Sometimes conversation lagged.

"Mud Center is a long way fr'm th' Casino. Th' last suc- cessful exthravaganza that th' lady had seen was a lecture be Jawn B. Gough. She got her Eyetalian opry out iv a music box. What was there f'r this joynt intelleck an' this household tyrant to talk about? No wondher he pined. Think iv this Light iv th' Tendherloin bein' compelled to set down ivry month or two an' chat about a new tooth that Hiven had just sint to a fam'ly up th' sthreet! Nor was that all. She give him no rest. Time an' time again she asked him was he comin' home that night. She tortured his proud spirit be recallin' th' time whin she used to flag him fr'm th' window iv th' room where Papa had locked

her in. She aven wint so far as to dhraw on him th' last cow'rdly weapon iv brutal wives—their tears. One time she thravelled
to New York an' wan iv his frinds seen her. Oh, it was crool,
crool. Hinnissy, tell me, wud ye condim this gr-reat man to
such a slavery just because he'd made a rash promise whin he
didn't have a cent in th' wurruld? Th' law said no. Whin th'
Gr-reat Fi-nanceer cud stand it no longer he called upon th'
Judge to sthrike off th' chains an' make him a free man. He got
a divoorce.''

"I dare ye to come down to me house an' say thim things.''
said Mr. Hennessy.

"Oh, I know ye don't agree with me,'' said Mr. Dooley.
"Nayether does th' parish priest. He's got it into his head that
whin a man's marrid he's marrid, an' that's all there is to it. He
puts his hand in th' grab-bag an' pulls out a blank an' he don't
get his money back.

"'Ill-mated couples?' says he. 'Ill-mated couples? What ar-re
ye talkin' about? Ar-re there anny other kinds? Ar-re there anny
two people in th' wurruld that ar-re perfectly mated?' he says.
'Was there iver a frindship that was annything more thin a
kind iv suspension bridge between quarrels?' he says.

"'If people knew they cudden't get away fr'm each other
they'd settle down to life, just as I detarmined to like coal
smoke whin I found th' collection wasn't big enough to put a
new chimbley in th' parish house. I've acchally got to like it,'
he says. 'There ain't anny condition iv human life that's not
endurable if ye make ye'er mind that ye've got to endure it,' he
says. 'Th' throuble with th' rich,' he says, 'is this, that whin a
rich man has a perfectly nachral scrap with his beloved over
breakfast, she stays at home an' does nawthin' but think about
it, an' he goes out an' does nawthin but think about it, an' that
afthernoon they're in their lawyers' office,' he says. 'But whin a
poor gintleman an' a poor lady fall out, the poor lady puts all
her anger into rubbin' th' zinc off th' wash-boord an' th' poor
gintleman aises his be murdhrin' a slag pile with a shovel, an'
be th' time night comes ar-round he says to himsilf: "Well, I've

got to go home annyhow, an' it's no use I shud be onhappy because I'm misjudged,'' an' he puts a pound iv candy into his coat pocket an' goes home an' finds her standin' at the dure with a white apron on an' some new ruching ar-round her neck,' he says.

"An' there ye ar-re. Two opinions."

"I see on'y wan," said Mr. Hennessy. "What do ye raaly think?"

"I think," said Mr. Dooley, "if people wanted to be divoorced I'd let thim, but I'd give th' parents into th' custody iv th' childer. They'd larn thim to behave."

MARRIAGE AND POLITICS

"I see," said Mr. Hennessy, "that wan iv thim New York joods says a man in pollytics oughtn't to be marrid."

"Oh does he?" said Mr. Dooley. "Well, 'tis little he knows about it. A man in polytics has got to be marrid. If he ain't marrid where'll he go f'r another kind iv trouble?"

"Th' reason th' New York jood thinks pollytics is spoort. An' so it is. But it ain't amachoor spoort, Hinnissy. They don't give ye a pewter mug with ye'er name on it f'r takin' a chanst on bein' kilt. 'Tis a profissional spoort, like playin' base-ball f'r a livin' or wheelin' a thruck. Ye niver see an amachoor at annything that was as good as a profissional. No, sir, pollytics ain't dhroppin' into tea, an' it ain't wurrukin a scroll saw, or makin' a garden in a back yard. 'Tis gettin' up at six o'clock in th' mornin' an' r-rushin' off to wurruk, an' comin' home at night tired an' dusty. Double wages f'r overtime an' Sundahs."

"So a man's got to be a marrid to do it well. He's got to have a wife at home to make him oncomfortable if he comes in dhrunk, he's got to have little prattlin' childher that he can't sind to th' Young Ladies' academy onless he stuffs a ballot box properly, an' he's got to have a strong desire f'r to live in th' av'noo an' be seen dhrivin' down-town in an open carredge with his wife settin' beside him undher a r-red parasol. If he hasn't these things he won't succeed in a pollytics—or packin' pork. Ye niver see a big man in pollytics that dhrank hard, did ye? Ye niver will. An' that's because they're all marrid. Th' timptation's sthrong, but fear is sthronger.

"Th' most domestic men in th' wurruld ar-re pollyticians, an' they always marry early. An' that's th' sad part iv it, Hinnissy. A pollytician always marries above his own station. That's wan sign that he'll be a successful pollytician. Th' throuble is, th' good woman stays planted just where she was, an' he goes by like a fast thrain by a whistlin' station. D'ye mind O'Leary, him that's a retired capitalist now, him that was aldherman, an' dhrainage thrustee, an' state sinitor f'r wan term? Well, whin I first knew O'Leary he wurruked down on a railroad section tampin' th' thrack at wan-fifty a day. He was a sthrong, willin' young fellow, with a stiff right-hand punch an' a schamin' brain, an' anny wan cud see that he was intinded to go to th' fr-ront. Th' aristocracy iv th' camp was Mrs. Cassidy, th' widdy lady lady that kept th' boordin'-house. Aristocracy, Hinnissy, is like rale estate, a matther iv location. I'm aristocracy to th' poor O'Briens back in th' alley, th' brewery agent's aristocracy to me, his boss is aristocracy to him, an' so it goes, up to the czar of Rooshia. He's th' pick iv th' bunch, th' high man iv all, th' Pope not goin' in society. Well, Mrs. Cassidy was aristocracy to O'Leary. He niver see such a stylish woman as she was whin she turned out iv a Sundah afthernoon in her horse an' buggy. He'd think to himself, 'If I iver can win that I'm settled f'r life,' an' iv coorse he did. 'Twas a gran' weddin'; manny iv th' guests didn't show up at wurruk f'r weeks.

"O'Leary done well, an' she was a good wife to him. She made money an' kept him sthraight an' started him for constable. He won out, bein' a sthrong man. Thin she got him to r-run f'r aldherman, an' ye shud've seen her th' night he was inaugurated! Be hivins, Hinnissy, she looked like a fire pawnshop, fair covered with dimons an' goold watches an' chains. She was cut out to be an aldherman's wife, and it was worth goin' miles to watch her leadin' th' gran' march at th' Ar-rchy Road Dimmycratic Fife an' Dhrum Corps ball.

"But there she stopped. A good woman an' a kind wan, she cudden't go th' distance. She had th' house an' th' childher to care f'r an' her eddycation was through with. They isn't much a woman can learn afther she begins to raise a fam'ly. But with O'Leary 'twas diff'rent. I say 'twas diff'rent with O'Leary. Ye talk about ye'er colleges, Hinnissy, but pollytics is th' poor man's college. A la-ad without enough book larnin' to r-read a meal-ticket, if ye give him tin years iv polly-tical life, has th' air iv a statesman an' th' manner iv a jook, an' cud take anny job fr'm dalin' faro bank to r-runnin th' threasury iv th' United States. His business brings him up again' th' best men iv th' com-munity, an' their customs an' ways iv speakin' an' thinkin' an robbin' sticks to him. Th' good woman is at home all day. Th' on'y people she sees is th' childher an' th' neighbors. While th' good man in a swallow-tail coat is ad-dhressin' th' Commercial club on what we shud do f'r to reform pollytics, she's discussin' th' price iv groceries with th' plumber's wife an' talkin' over th' back fince to the milkman. Thin O'Leary moves up on th' boolyvard. He knows he'll get along all r-right on th' boolyvard. Th' men'll say: 'They'se a good deal of rugged common sinse in that O'Leary. He may be a robber, but they's mighty little that escapes him.' But no wan speaks to Mrs. O'Leary. No wan asts her opinion about our foreign policy. She sets day in an' day out behind th' dhrawn curtains iv her three-story brownstone risidence prayin' that somewan'll come in an' see her, an if annywan comes she's frozen with fear. An' 'tis on'y whin she slips out to Ar-rchey r-road an' finds th' plumber's wife, an' sets in th' kitchen over a cup iv tay, that peace comes to her. By an' by they offer O'Leary th' nommynation f'r congress. He knows he's fit for it. He's sthronger thin th' young lawyer they have now. Peo-ple'll listen to him in Wash'nton as they do in Chicago. He says: 'I'll take it.' An' thin he thinks iv th' wife an' they's no Wash'nton f'r him. His pollytical career is over. He wud niver have been constable if he hadn't marrid, but he might have been sinitor if he was a widower.

"Mrs. O'Leary was in to see th' Dargans th' other day. 'Ye mus' be very happy in ye'er gran' house, with Mr. O'Leary doin' so well,' says Mrs. Dargan. An' th' on'y answer th' foolish woman give was to break down an' weep on Mrs. Dargan's neck."

"Yet ye say a pollytician oughtn't to get marrid," said Mr. Hennessy.

"Up to a certain point," said Mr. Dooley, "he must be marrid. Afther that—well, I on'y say that, though pollytics is a gran' career f'r a man, 'tis a tough wan f'r his wife."

CHAPTER VIII
BRINGING UP BABY

Finley Peter and Margaret Abbott Dunne had four children: Finley Peter, Jr., born in 1903; Philip, in 1908; and twins, Margaret and Leonard, in 1910. However, Dunne's essays on childrearing began, as Mr. Dooley put it, long before he was an author, though he still felt he could be a critic. Not all are meant to amuse; "Shaughnessy," with its touching tale of the widower who finds himself with an empty nest, and "On Criminals," which raises questions as to why some children of devoted parents go to the bad, are just two examples. These columns were written during Dunne's Chicago years, and show more the dark side of the home life of the working class immigrants in the city.

Toward his own children in those pre-Spock days, Dunne seems to have been a loving, tolerant figure when they were babies, taking an increasing interest in them and spending more time with them as their personalities developed. As was the custom of the time, child-rearing was left to Mrs. Dunne, but he did see to it that the children were baptized Catholics and observed that church's feast days. That was about the limit of their religious training, however, as Dunne was not a practicing Catholic (a Chicago Catholic, he called himself), and Margaret Dunne was an Episcopalian. His feeling toward the Roman Catholic Church was much like that toward his family and the Irish: while he could express criticism, outsiders would do well not to join in.

THE BRINGING UP OF CHILDREN

"Did ye iver see a man as proud iv annything as Hogan is iv that kid iv his?" said Mr. Dooley.

"Wait till he's had iliven," said Mr. Hennessy.

"Oh, iv coorse," said Mr. Dooley. "Ye have contimpt f'r an

amachoor father that has on'y wan offspring. An ol' profis-
syonal parent like ye, that's practically done nawthin' all ye're
life but be a father to helpless childher, don't understand th'
emotions iv th' author iv a limited edition. But Hogan don't
care. So far as I am able to judge fr'm what he says, his is th'
on'y perfect an' complete child that has been projooced this
cinchry. He looks on you th' way Hinnery James wud look on
Mary Jane Holmes.

"I wint around to see this here projidy th' other day. Hogan
met me at th' dure. 'Wipe off ye'er feet,' says he. 'Why,' says I.
'Baby,' says he.· 'Mickrobes,' he says. He thin conducted me to
a basin iv water, an' insthructed me to wash me hands in a
preparation iv carbolic acid. Whin I was thurly perfumed he
inthrajooced me to a toothless ol' gintleman who was settin' up
in a cradle atin' his right foot. 'Ain't he fine?' says Hogan.
'Wondherful,' says I. 'Did ye iver see such an expressyon?' says
he. 'Niver,' says I, 'as Hiven is me judge, niver.' 'Look at his
hair,' he says. 'I will,' says I. 'Ain't his eyes beautiful?' 'They
ar-re,' I says. 'Ar-re they glass or on'y imitation?' says I. 'An'
thim cunning little feet,' says he. 'On close inspiction,' says I,
'yes, they ar-re. They ar-re feet. Ye'er offspring don't know it,
though. He thinks that wan is a doughnut.' He's not as old as
he looks,' says Hogan. 'He cudden't be,' says I. 'He looks old
enough to be a Dimmycratic candydate f'r Vice-Prisidint.
Why, he's lost most iv his teeth,' I says. 'Go wan,' says he;
'he's just gettin' thim. He has two uppers an' four lowers,' he
says. 'If he had a few more he'd be a sleepin'-car,' says I. 'Does
he speak?' says I. 'Sure,' says Hogan. 'Say poppa,' he says.
"Gah," says young Hogan. 'Hear that?' says Hogan; 'that's
poppa. Say momma,' says he. "Gah," says th' projidy. 'That's
momma,' says Hogan. 'See, here's Misther Dooley,' says he.
"Blub," says th' phenomynon. 'Look at that,' says Hogan; 'he
knows ye,' he says.

"Well, ye know, Hinnissy, wan iv th' things that has made
me popylar in th' ward is that I make a bluff at adorin'
childher. Between you an' me, I'd as lave salute a dish-rag as a

recent infant, but I always do it. So I put on an allurin' smile, an' says I, 'Well, little ol' goozy goo, will he give his Dooley-ums a kiss?' At that minyit Hogan seized me be th' collar an' drhagged me away fr'm th' cradle. 'Wud ye kill me child?' says he. 'How?' says I. 'With a kiss,' says he. 'Am I that bad?' says I. 'Don't ye know that there ar-re mickrobes that can be thransmitted to an infant in a kiss?' says he. 'Well,' says I, with indignation, 'I'm not proud iv mesilf as an antiseptic American,' I says, 'but in an encounther between me an' that there young cannibal,' I says, 'I'll lave it to th' board iv health who takes th' biggest chance,' I says, an we wint out, followed by a howl fr'm th' projidy. 'He's singin',' says Hogan. 'He has lost his notes,' says I.

"Whin we got down-stairs Hogan give me a lecture on th' bringin' up iv childher. As though I needed it, me that's been consulted on bringin' up half th' childher in Archey Road. 'In th' old days,' says he, 'childher was brought up catch-as-catch-can,' he says. 'But it's diff'rent now. They're as carefully watched as a geeranyum in a consarvatory,' he says. 'I have a book here on th' subjick,' he says. 'Here it is. Th' first thing that shud be done f'r a child is to deprive it iv its parents. Th' less th' infant sees iv poppa an' momma th' betther f'r him. If they ar-re so base as to want to look at th' little darlin' they shud first be examined be a competent physician to see that there is nawthin' wrong with thim that they cud give th' baby. They will thin take a bath iv suphuric acid, an' havin' carefully attired thimsilves in a sturlized rubber suit, they will approach within eight feet iv th' objeck iv their ignoble affection an' lave at wanst. In no case must they kiss, hug, or fondle their pro-jiny. Manny diseases, such as lumbago, pain in th' chest, premachoor baldness, senile decrepitude, which are privalent among adults, can be communicated to a child fr'm th' parent. Besides, it is bad f'r th' moral nature iv th' infant. Affection f'r its parents is wan iv th' mos' dangerous symptoms iv rickets. Th' parents may not be worthy iv th' love iv a thurly sturlized child. An infant's first jooty is to th' docthor, to whom it owes its bein' an' stayin'. Childher ar-re imitative, an' if they see much iv their parents they may grow up to look like thim. That wud be a great misfortune. If parents see their childher befure they enther Harvard they ar-re f'rbidden to teach thim foolish wurruds like "poppa" an' "momma." At two a properly brought up child shud be able to articulate distinctly th' wurrud "Docthor Bolt on th' Care an' Feedin' iv Infants," which is betther thin sayin' "momma," an' more exact.

" 'Gr-reat care shud be taken iv th' infant's food. Durin' th' first two years it shud have nawthin' but milk. At three a little canary-bur-rd seed can be added. At five an egg ivry other Choosdah. At siven an orange. At twelve th' child may ate a shredded biscuit. At forty th' little tot may have stewed prunes. An' so on. At no time, howiver, shud th' child be stuffed with greengages, pork an' beans, onions, Boston baked brown-bread, saleratus biscuit, or other food.

" 'It's wondherful,' says Hogan, 'how they've got it rayjooced to a science. They can almost make a short baby long or a blond baby black be addin' to or rayjoocin' th' amount iv protides an' casens in th' milk,' he says. 'Haven't ye iver kissed ye'er young?' says I. 'Wanst in a while,' he says, 'whin I'm thurly disinfected I go up an' blow a kiss at him through th' window,' he says.

" 'Well,' says I, 'it may be all right,' I says, 'but if I cud have a son an' heir without causin' talk I bet ye I'd not apply f'r a permit fr'm th' health boord f'r him an' me to come together. Parents was made befure childher, annyhow, an' they have a prire claim to be considhered. Sure, it may be a good thing to bring thim up on a sanitary plan, but it seems to me they got along all right in th' ol' days whin number two had just larned to fall down-stairs at th' time number three entered th' wur-ruld. Maybe they were sthronger thin they ar-re now. Th' docthor niver pretinded to see whether th' milk was properly biled. He cudden't very well. Th' childher was allowed to set up at th' table an' have a good cup iv tay an' a pickle at two. If there was more thin enough to go around, they got what nobody else wanted. They got plenty iv fresh air playin' in alleys an' vacant lots, an' ivry wanst in a while they were allowed to go down an' fall into th' river. No attintion was paid to their dite. Th' prisint race iv heroes who are now startlin' th' wurrould in finance, polytics, th' arts an' sciences, burglary, an' lithrachoor, was brought up on wathermillon rinds, specked apples, raw onions stolen fr'm th' grocer, an' cocoanut-pie. Their nursery was th' back yard. They larned to walk as soon as they were able, an' if they got bow-legged ivrybody said they wud be sthrong men. As f'r annybody previntin' a fond parent fr'm comin' home Saturdah night an' wallowin' in his beaucheous child, th' docthor that suggisted it wud have to move. No, sir,' says I, 'get as much amusemint as ye can out iv ye'er infant,' says I. 'Teach him to love ye now,' I says, 'before he knows. Afther a while he'll get onto ye an' it'll be too late.' "

"Ye know a lot about it," said Mr. Hennessy.

"I do," said Mr. Dooley. "Not bein' an author, I'm a gr-reat critic."

ON CRIMINALS

"Lord bless my sowl," said Mr. Dooley, "childher is a gr-reat risponsibility,—a gr-reat risponsibility. Whin I think iv it, I praise th' saints I niver was married, though I had opporchunities enough whin I was a young man; an' even now I have to wear me hat low whin I go down be Cologne Sthreet on account iv th' Widow Grogan. Jawn, that woman'll take me dead or alive. I wake up in a col' chill in th' middle iv th' night, dhreamin' iv her havin' me in her clutches.

"But that's not here or there, avick. I was r-readin' in th' pa-apers iv a lad be th' name iv Scanlan bein' sint down th' short r-road f'r near a lifetime; an' I minded th' first time I iver see him,—a bit iv a curly-haired boy that played tag around me place, an' 'd sing 'Blest Saint Joseph' with a smile on his face like an angel's. Who'll tell what makes wan man a thief an' another man a saint? I dinnaw. This here boy's father wurrked fr'm morn till night in th' mills, was at early mass Sundah mornin' befure th' alkalis lit th' candles, an' niver knowed a month whin he failed his jooty. An' his mother was a sweet-faced little woman, though fr'm th' County Kerry, that nursed th' sick an' waked th' dead, an' niver had a hard thought in her simple mind fr anny iv Gawd's creatures. Poor sowl, she's dead now. May she rest in peace!

"He didn't git th' shtreak fr'm his father or fr'm his mother. His brothers an' sisters was as fine a lot as iver lived. But this la-ad Petey Scanlan growed up fr'm bein' a curly-haired angel fr to be th' toughest villyun in th' r-road. What was it all, at all? Sometimes I think they'se poison in th' life iv a big city. Th' flowers won't grow here no more thin they wud in a tan-nery, an' th' bur-rds have no song; an' th' childher iv dacint men an' women come up hard in th' mouth an' with their hands raised again their kind.

"Th' la-ad was th' scoorge iv th' polis. He was as quick as a cat an' as fierce as a tiger, an' I well raymimber him havin' laid out big Kelly that used to thravel this post,—'Whistlin'' Kelly that kep' us awake with imitations iv a mockin' bur-rd, —I well raymimber him scuttlin' up th' alley with a score iv polismin laborin' afther him, thryin' fr a shot at him as he wint around th' bar-rns or undher th' thrucks. He slep' in th' coal-sheds afther that until th' poor ol' man cud square it with th' loot. But, whin he come out, ye cud see how his face had hardened an' his ways changed. He was as silent as an animal, with a sideways manner that watched ivrything. Right here in this place I seen him stand fr a quarther iv an' hour, not seemin' to hear a dhrunk man abusin' him, an' thin lep out like a snake. We had to pry him loose.

"Th' ol' folks done th' best they cud with him. They hauled him out iv station an' jail an bridewell. Wanst in a long while they'd dhrag him off to church with his head down: that was always afther he'd been sloughed up fr wan thing or another. Between times th' polis give him his own side iv th' sthreet, an' on'y took him whin his back was tur-rned. Thin he'd go in the wagon with a mountain iv thim on top iv him, swayin' an' swearin' an' sthrikin' each other in their hurry to put him to sleep with their clubs.

"I mind will th' time he was first took to be settled f'r good. I heerd a noise in th' ya-ard, an' thin he come through th' place with his face dead gray an' his lips just a turn grayer. 'Where ar-re ye goin', Petey?' says I. 'I was jus' takin' a short cut home,' he says. In three minyits th' r-road was full iv polismin. They'd been a robbery down in Halsted Sthreet. A man that had a grocery sthore was stuck up, an' whin he fought was clubbed near to death; an' they'd r-run Scanlan through th' alleys to his father's house. That was as far as they'd go. They was enough iv thim to've kicked down th' little cottage with their heavy boots, but they knew he was standin' behind th' dure with th' gun in his hand; an', though they was manny a good lad there, they was none that cared f'r that short odds.

"They talked an' palavered outside, an' telephoned th' chief iv polis, an' more pathrol wagons come up. Some was f'r settin' fire to th' buildin', but no wan moved ahead. Thin th' frront dure opened, an' who shud come out but th' little mother. She was thin an' pale, an' she had her apron in her hands, pluckin' at it. 'Gintlemin,' she says, 'what is it ye want iv me?' she says. 'Liftinant Cassidy,' she says, ''tis sthrange f'r ye that I've knowed so long to make scandal iv me befure me neighbors,' she says, 'Mrs. Scanlan,' says he, 'we want th' boy. I'm sorry, ma'am, but he's mixed up in a bad scrape, an' we must have him,' he says. She made a curtsy to thim an' wint indures. 'Twas less than a minyit befure she come out, clingin' to th' la-ads ar-rm. 'He'll go,' she says. 'Thanks be, though he's wild, they'se no crime on his head. Is there, dear?' 'No,' says he, like th' game kid he is. Wan iv th' polismin stharted to take hold iv him, but th' la-ad pushed him back; an' he wint to th' wagon on his mother's ar-rm."

"And was he really innocent?" Mr. McKenna asked.

"No," said Mr. Dooley. "But she niver knowed it. Th' ol' man come home an' found her: she was settin' in a big chair with her apron in her hands an' th' picture iv th' la-ad in her lap."

THE EDUCATION OF THE YOUNG

The troubled Mr. Hennessy had been telling Mr. Dooley about the difficulty of making a choice of schools for Packy Hennessy, who at the age of six was at the point where the family must decide his career.

" 'Tis a big question," said Mr. Dooley, "an' wan that seems to be worryin' th' people more thin it used to whin ivry boy was designed f'r th' priesthood, with a full undherstandin' be his parents that th' chances was in favor iv a brick yard. Nowadays they talk about th' edycation iv th' child befure they choose th' name. 'Tis: 'Th' kid talks in his sleep. 'Tis th' fine lawyer he'll make.' Or, 'Did ye notice him admirin' that photygraph? He'll be a gr-reat journalist.' Or, 'Look at him fishin' in Uncle Tim's watch pocket. We must thrain him f'r a banker.' Or, 'I'm afraid he'll niver be sthrong enough to wur-ruk. He must go into th' church.' Befure he's baptized too, d'ye mind. 'Twill not be long befure th' time comes whin th' soggarth'll christen th' infant: 'Judge Pathrick Aloysius Hin-nissy, iv th' Northern District iv Illinye,' or 'Profissor P. Aloysius Hinnissy, LL.D., S.T.D., P.G.N., iv th' faculty iv Nothre Dame.' Th' innocent child in his cradle, wondherin' what ails th' mist iv him an' where he got such funny lookin' parents fr'm, has thim to blame that brought him into th' wur-ruld if he dayvilops into a sicond story man befure he's twinty-wan an' is took up be th' polis. Why don't you lade Packy down to th' occylist an' have him fitted with a pair iv eyeglasses? Why don't ye put goloshes on him, give him a blue unbrelly an' call him a doctor at wanst an' be done with it?

"To my mind, Hinnissy, we're wastin' too much time thinkin' iv th' future iv our young, an' thryin' to larn thim ear-ly what they oughtn't to know till they've growed up. We sind th' childher to school as if 'twas a summer garden where they go to be amused instead iv a pinitinchry where they're sint f'r th' original sin. Whin I was a la-ad I was put at me ah-bee abs, th' first day I set fut in th' school behind th' hedge an' me head was sore inside an' out befure I wint home. Now th' first thing we larn th' future Mark Hannas an' Jawn D. Gateses iv our naytion is waltzin', singin', an' cuttin' pitchers out iv a book. We'd be much betther teachin' thim th' sthrangle hold, f'r that's what they need in life.

"I know what'll happen. Ye'll sind Packy to what th' Germans call a Kindygartin, an' 'tis a good thing f'r Germany, because all a German knows is what some wan tells him, an' his grajation papers is a certy-ficate that he don't need to think anny more. But we've inthrajooced it into this counthry, an' whin I was down seein' if I cud injooce Rafferty, th' Janitor iv th' Isaac Muggs Grammar School, f'r to vote f'r Riordan—an' he's goin' to—I dhropped in on Cassidy's daughter, Mary Ellen, an' see her kindygartnin'. Th' childher was settin' arround on th' flure an' some was moldin' dachshunds out iv mud an' wipin' their hands on their hair, an' some was carvin' figures iv a goat out iv paste-board an' some was singin' an' some was sleepin' an' a few was dancin' an' wan la-ad was pullin' another la-ad's hair. 'Why don't ye take th' coal shovel to that little barbaryan, Mary Ellen?' says I. 'We don't believe in corporeal punishment,' says she. 'School shud be made pleasant f'r th' childher,' she says. 'Th' child who's hair is bein' pulled is larnin' patience,' she says, 'an' th' child that's pullin' th' hair is discoverin' th' footility iv human indeavor,' says she. 'Well, oh, well,' says I, 'times has changed since I was a boy,' I says. 'Put thim through their exercises,' says I. 'Tommy,' says I, 'spell cat,' I says. 'Go to th' divvle,' says th' cheerub. 'Very smartly answered,' says Mary Ellen. 'Ye shud not ask thim to spell,' she says. 'They don't larn that till they get to colledge,' she says, 'an'' she says, 'sometimes not even thin,' she says. 'An' what do they larn?' says I. 'Rompin',' she says, 'an' dancin',' she says, 'an' indepindance iv speech, an' beauty songs, an' sweet thoughts, an' how to make home home-like,' she says. 'Well,' says I, 'I didn't take anny iv thim things at colledge, so ye needn't unblanket thim' I says. 'I won't put thim through anny exercise today,' I says. 'But whisper, Mary Ellen,' says I, 'Don't ye niver feel like bastin' th' seeraphims?' 'Th' teachin's iv Freebull and Pitzotly is conthrary to that,' she says. 'But I'm goin' to be marrid an' lave th' school on Choosdah, th' twinty-sicond iv Janooary,' she says, 'an' on Mondah, th' twinty-first, I'm goin' to ask a few iv th' little darlin's to th' house an',' she says, 'stew thim over a slow fire,' she says. Mary Ellen is not a German, Hinnissy.

"Well, afther they have larned in school what they ar-re licked f'r larnin' in th' back yard—that is squashin' mud with their hands—they're conducted up through a channel iv free an' beautiful thought till they're r-ready f'r colledge. Mamma packs a few doylies an' tidies into son's bag, an' some silver to be used in case iv throuble with th' landlord, an' th' la-ad throts off to th' siminary. If he's not sthrong enough to look f'r high honors as a middle weight pugilist he goes into th' thought departmint. Th' prisidint takes him into a Turkish room, gives him a cigareet an' says: 'Me dear boy, what special branch iv larnin' wud ye like to have studied f'r ye be our com-pitint profissors? We have a chair iv Beauty an' wan iv Puns an' wan iv Pothry on th' Changin' Hues iv the Settin' Sun, an' wan on Platonic Love, an' wan on Nonsense Rhymes, an' wan on Sweet Thoughts, an' wan on How Green Grows th' Grass, an' wan on th' Relation iv Ice to th' Greek Idee iv God,' he says. 'This is all ye'll need to equip ye f'r th' perfect life, onless,' he says, 'ye intind bein' a dintist, in which case,' he says, 'we won't think much iv ye, but we have a good school where ye can larn that disgraceful thrade,' he says. An' th' la-ad makes his choice, an' ivry mornin' whin he's up in time he takes a whiff iv hasheesh an' goes off to hear Profissor Maryan-na tell him that 'if th' dates iv human knowledge must be re-jicted as subjictive, how much more must they be subjicted as rejictive if, as I think, we keep our thoughts fixed upon th' in-anity iv th' finite in comparison with th' onthinkable truth with th' ondivided an' onimaginable reality. Boys ar-re ye with me?'

"That's at wan colledge—Th' Colledge iv Speechless Thought. Thin there's th' Colledge iv Thoughtless Speech, where th' la-ad is larned that th' best thing that can happen to annywan is to be prisident iv a railroad consolidation. Th' head iv this colledge believes in thrainin' young men f'r th' civic ideel, Father Kelly tells me. Th' on'y thrainin' I know f'r th' civic ideel is to have an alarm clock in ye'er room on iliction day. He believes 'young men shud be equipped with Courage, Discipline, an' Loftiness iv Purpose;' so I suppose Packy, if he wint there, wud listen to lectures fr'm th' Profissor iv Courage an' Erasmus H. Noddle, Doctor iv Loftiness iv Purpose. I loft, ye loft, he lofts. I've always felt we needed some wan to teach our young th' Courage they can't get walkin' home in th' dark, an' th' loftiness iv purpose that doesn't start with bein' hungry an' lookin' f'r wurruk. An' in th' colledge where these studies are taught, its undherstud that even betther thin gettin' th' civic ideel is bein' head iv a thrust. Th' on'y trouble with th' coorse is that whin Packy comes out loaded with loftiness iv purpose, all th' lofts is full iv men that had to figure it out on th' farm.''

"I don't undherstand a wurrud iv what ye're sayin','' said Mr. Hennessy.

"No more do I,'' said Mr. Dooley. "But I believe 'tis as Father Kelly says: 'Childher shudden't be sint to school to larn, but to larn how to larn. I don't care what ye larn thim so long as 'tis onpleasant to thim.' 'Tis thrainin' they need, Hinnissy. That's all. I niver cud make use iv what I larned in colledge about thrigojoomethry an' — an' — grammar an' th' welts I got on th' skull fr'm the schoolmaster's cane I have nivver been able to turn to anny account in th' business, but 'twas th' bein' there and havin' to get things to heart without askin' th' meanin' iv thim an' goin' to school cold an' comin' home hungry, that made th' man iv me ye see befure ye.''

"That's why th' good woman's throubled about Packy,'' said Hennessy.

"Go home,'' said Mr. Dooley.

The favorite column of Elmer Ellis, author of **Mr. Dooley's America**, *his excellent biography of Finley Peter Dunne.*

SHAUGHNESSY

"Jawn," said Mr. Dooley in the course of the conversation, "whin ye come to think iv it, th' heroes iv th' wurruld,—an' be thim I mean th' lads that've buckled on th' gloves, an' gone out to do th' best they cud,—they ain't in it with th' quite people nayether you nor me hears tell iv fr'm wan end iv th' year to another."

"I believe it," said Mr. McKenna; "for my mother told me so."

"Sure," said Mr. Dooley, "I know it is an old story. Th' wurruld's been full iv it fr'm th' beginnin'; an' 'll be full iv it till, as Father Kelly says, th' pay-roll's closed. But I was thinkin' more iv th' other night thin iver befure, whin I wint to see Shaughnessy marry off his on'y daughter. You know Shaughnessy,—a quite man that come into th' road befure th' fire. He wurruked fr Larkin, th' conthractor, fr near twenty years without skip or break, an' seen th' fam'ly grow up be candle-light. Th' oldest boy was intinded fr a priest. 'Tis a poor fam'ly that hasn't some wan that's bein' iddycated fr the priesthood while all th' rest wear thimsilves to skeletons fr him, an' call him Father Jawn 'r Father Mike whin he comes home wanst a year, light-hearted an' free, to eat with thim.

"Shaughnessy's lad wint wrong in his lungs, an' they fought death fr him fr five years, sindin' him out to th' Wist an' havin' masses said fr him; an', poor divvle, he kept comin' back cross an' crool, with th' fire in his cheeks, till wan day he laid down, an' says he: 'Pah,' he says, 'I'm goin' to give up,' he says. 'An' I on'y ask that ye'll have th' mass sung over me be some man besides Father Kelly,' he says. An' he wint, an' Shaughnessy come clumpin' down th' aisle like a man in a thrance.

"Well, th' nex' wan was a girl, an' she didn't die; but, th' less said, th' sooner mended. Thin they was Terrence, a big, bould, curly-headed lad that cocked his hat at anny man,—or woman f'r th' matter iv that,—an' that bruk th' back iv a polisman an' swum to th' crib, an' was champeen iv th' South Side at hand bell. An' he wint. Thin th' good woman passed away. An' th' twins they growed to be th' prettiest pair that wint to first communion; an' wan night they was a light in th' window of Shaughnessy's house till three in th' mornin'. I raymimber it; f'r I had quite a crowd iv Willum Joyce's men in, an' we wondhered at it, an' wint home whin th' lamp in Shaughnessy's window was blown out.

"They was th' wan girl left,—Theresa, a big clean-lookin' child that I see grow up fr'm hello to good avnin'. She thought on'y iv th' ol' man, an' he leaned on her as if she was a crutch. She was out to meet him in th' evnin'; an' in th' mornin' he, th' simple ol' man, 'd stop to blow a kiss at her an' wave his dinner-pail, lookin' up an' down th' r-road to see that no wan was watchin' him.

"I dinnaw what possessed th' young Donahue, fr'm th' Nineteenth. I niver thought much iv him, a stuck-up, aisy-come la-ad that niver had annything but a civil wurrud, an' is prisident iv th' sodality. But he came in, an' married Theresa Shaughnessy las' Thursdah night. Th' ol' man took on twinty years, but he was as brave as a gin'ral iv th' army. He cracked jokes an' he made speeches; an' he took th' pipes fr'm under th' elbow iv Hogan, th' blindman, an' played 'Th' Wind that Shakes th' Barley' till ye'd have wore ye'er leg to smoke f'r wantin' to dance. Thin he wint to th' dure with two iv thim; an' says he, 'Well,' he says, 'Jim, be good to her,' he says, an' shook hands with her through th' carredge window.

"Him an' me sat a long time smokin' across th' stove. Fin'lly, says I, 'Well,' I says, 'I must be movin'.' 'What's th' hurry?' says he. 'I've got to go,' says I. 'Wait a moment,' says he. 'Theresa 'll'—He stopped right there f'r a minyit, holdin' to th' back iv th' chair. 'Well,' says he, 'if ye've got to go, ye must,' he says. 'I'll show ye out,' he says. An' he come with me to th' dure, holdin' th' lamp over his head. I looked back at him as I wint by; an' he was settin' be th' stove, with his elbows on his knees an' th' empty pipe between his teeth."

THE AMERICAN FAMILY

"Is th' race dyin' out?" asked Mr. Dooley.

"Is it what?" replied Mr. Hennessy.

"Is it dyin' out?" said Mr. Dooley. "Th' ministhers an' me frind Dock Eliot iv Harvard say it is. Dock Eliot wud know diff'rent if he was a rale dock an' wint flying up Halsted Sthreet in a buggy, floggin' a white horse to be there on time. But he ain't, an' he's sure it's dyin' out. Childher ar-re disappearin' fr'm America. He took a squint at th' list iv Harvard gradjates th' other day, an' discovered that they had ivrything to make home happy but kids. Wanst th' wurruld was full iv little Harvards. Th' counthry swarmed with thim. Ye cud tell a Harvard man at wanst be a look at his feet. He had th' unmistakable cradle fut. It was no sthrange thing to see an ol' Harvard man comin' back to his almy mather pushin' a baby-carredge full iv twins an' ladin' a fam'ly that looked like an advertisemint in th' newspapers to show th' percintage iv purity iv bakin'-powdhers. Prisidint Eliot was often disturbed in a discoorse, pintin' out th' dangers iv th' counthry, be th' outcries iv th' progeny iv fair Harvard. Th' campus was full iv baby-carredges on commincemint day, an' specyal accomydations had to be took f'r nurses. In thim happy days some wan was always teethin' in a Harvard fam'ly. It looked as if ivinchooly th' wurruld wud be peopled with Harvard men, an' th' Chinese wud have to pass an Exclusion Act. But something has happened to Harvard. She is projoocin' no little rah-rahs to glad th' wurruld. Th' av'rage fam'ly iv th' Harvard gradjate an' th' jackass is practically th' same. Th' Harvard man iv th' prisint day is th' last iv his race. No artless prattle is heerd in his home.

"An' me frind Prisidint Eliot is sore about it, an' he has com-

municated th' sad fact to th' clargy. Nawthin' th' clargy likes
so much as a sad fact. Lave wan iv me frinds iv th' clargy know
that we're goin' to th' divvle in a new way an' he's happy. We
used to take th' journey be covetin' our neighbor's ox or his ass
or be disobeyin' our parents, but now we have no parents to
disobey or they have no childher to disobey thim. Th'
American people is becomin' as unfruitful as an ash-heap.
We're no betther thin th' Fr-rinch. They say th' pleasin'
squawk iv an infant hasn't been heerd in France since th'
Franco-Prooshun war. Th' governmint offers prizes f'r
families, but no wan claims thim. A Frinch gintleman who
wint to Germany wanst has made a good deal iv money lec-
turin' on 'Wild Babies I Have Met,' but ivry wan says he's a
faker. Ye can't convince anny wan in France that there ar're
anny babies. We're goin' th' same way. Less thin three millyon
babies was bor'rn in this counthry las' year. Think iv it, Hinnissy — less thin three millyon, hardly enough to consume wan-
tenth iv th' output iv pins! It's a horrible thought. I don't
blame ivry wan, fr'm Tiddy Rosenfelt down, f'r worryin'
about it.

"What's th' cause, says ye? I don't know. I've been readin'
th' newspapers, an' ivrybody's been tellin' why. Late marredges, arly marredges, no marredges, th' cost iv livin', th' luxuries iv th' day, th' tariff, th' thrusts, th' spots on th' sun, th'
difficulty iv obtainin' implyemint, th' growth iv culture, th'
pitcher-hat, an' so on. Ivrybody's got a raison, but none iv thim
seems to meet th' bill. I've been lookin' at th' argymints pro
an' con, an' I come to th' conclusion that th' race is dyin' out
on'y in spots. Th' av'rage size iv th' fam'ly in Mitchigan Avnoo is .000001, but th' av'rage size iv th' fam'ly in Ar-rchey
R-road is somewhat larger. Afther I r-read what Dock Eliot
had to say I ast me frind Dock Grogan what he thought about
it. He's a rale dock. He has a horse an' buggy. He's out so
much at night that th' polis ar-re always stoppin' him, thinkin'
he is a burglar. Th' dock has prepared some statistics f'r me,
an' here they ar're: Number iv twins bor-rn in Ar-rchey Road

fr'm Halsted Sthreet to Westhern Avnoo, fr'm Janooary wan
to Janooary wan, 355 pairs; number iv thrips iv thriplets in th'
same fiscal year, nine; number iv individjool voters, eighty-
three thousan' nine hundherd an' forty-two; av'rage size iv
fam'ly, fourteen; av'rage weight iv parents, wan hundherd an'
eighty-five; av'rage size iv rooms, nine be eight; av'rage height
iv ceilin', nine feet; av'rage wages, wan dollar sivinty-five;
av'rage duration iv doctor's bills, two hundherd years.

"I took th' statistics to Father Kelly. He's an onprejudiced
man, an' if th' race was dyin' out he wud have had a
soundin'-boord in his pulpit long ago. So that whin he mintioned th' wurrud 'Hell,' ivry wan in th' congregation wud
have thought he meant him or her. 'I think,' says Father Kelly,
'that Dock Grogan is a little wrong in his figures. He's
boastin'. In this parrish I allow twelve births to wan marredge.
It varies, iv coorse, bein' sometimes as low as nine, an'
sometimes as high as fifteen. But twelve is about th' av'rage,'
he says. 'If ye see Dock Eliot,' he says, 'ye can tell him th' race
ain't dyin' out very bad in this here part iv the wurruld. On th'
conthry. It ain't liable to, ayether,' he says, 'onless wages is
raised,' he says. 'Th' poor ar-re becomin' richer in childher,
an' th' rich poorer,' he says. ''Tis always th' way,' he says.
'Th' bigger th' house th' smaller th' fam'ly. Mitchigan Avnoo
is always thinnin' out fr'm itsilf, an' growin' fr'm th' efforts iv
Ar-rchey R-road. 'Tis a way Nature has iv gettin' even with th'
rich an' pow'rful. Wan part iv town has nawthin' but money,
an' another nawthin' but childher. A man with tin dollars a
week will have tin childher, a man with wan hundherd dollars
will have five, an' a man with a millyon will buy an
autymobill. Ye can tell Schwartzmeister, with his thirteen little
Hanses an' Helenas, that he don't have to throw no bombs to
make room f'r his childher. Th' people over in Mitchigan Avnoo will do that thimsilves. Nature,' he says, 'is a wild dimmycrat,' he says.

"I guess he's right. I'm goin' to ask Dock Eliot, Tiddy
Rosenfelt, an' all th' rest iv thim to come up Ar-rchey R-road

some summer's afthernoon an' show thim th' way th' r-race is
dyin' out. Th' front stoops is full iv childher; they block th'
throlley-cars; they're shyin' bricks at th' polis, pullin' up coal-
hole covers, playin' ring-around-th'-rosy, makin' paper dolls,
goin' to Sundah-school, hurryin' with th' sprinklin'-pot to th'
place at th' corner, an' indulgin' in other sports iv childhood.
Pah-pah is settin' on th' steps, ma is lanin' out iv th' window
gassin' with th' neighbors, an' a squad iv polis ar-re up at th'
church, keepin' th' christenin' parties fr'm mobbin' Father
Kelly while he inthrajooces wan thousan' little howlin' dimmycrats to Christyan s'ciety. No, sir, th' race, far fr'm dyin' out
in Ar-rchey R-road, is runnin' aisy an' comin' sthrong.''

"Ye ought to be ashamed to talk about such subjicks, ye, an
ol' batch," said Mr. Hennessy. "It's a seeryous question."

"How many childher have ye?" asked Mr. Dooley.

"Lave me see," said Mr. Hennessy. "Wan, two, four, five,
eight, siven, eight, tin, — no, that's not right. Lave me see. Ah,
yes, I f'rgot Terence. We have fourteen."

"If th' race iv Hinnissys dies out," said Mr. Dooley, "'twill
be fr'm overcrowdin'."

CHAPTER IX

KEEPING FIT

Dieting, food fads and exercise were a constant source of interest in Dooley's time. The standard of appearance was different then; it had not yet been said that one can neither be too rich or too thin. The styles allowed for ampler figures, Mr. Dooley himself (and in later years, Mr. Dunne) being given to "embinpint."

"The Food We Eat" was inspired by Upton Sinclair's book *The Jungle* about the horrors of meatpacking in Chicago's stockyards. Besides causing large numbers of the population to consider vegetarianism, it resulted in major federal legislation creating the Food and Drug Administration. "Alcohol as Food" was based on an absolutely serious suggestion by a U.S. Army doctor during the Spanish—American War. "Oats as Food" grew out of a preoccupation with starting the day the fibre way, which certainly has a familiar ring to it.

Dooley never shied from any subject, including modern medicine.

THE FOOD WE EAT

"What have ye undher ye'er arm there?" demanded Mr. Dooley.

"I was takin' home a ham," said Mr. Hennessy.

"Clear out iv here with it," cried Mr. Dooley. "Take that thing outside—an' don't lave it where th' dog might get hold iv it. Th' idee iv ye'er bringin' it in here! Glory be, it makes me faint to think iv it. I'm afraid I'll have to go an' lay down."

"What ails ye?" asked Mr. Hennessy.

"What ails me?" said Mr. Dooley. "Haven't ye r-read about th' investygation iv th' Stock Yards? It's a good thing f'r ye ye haven't. If ye knew what that ham—oh, th' horrid wur-rud—was made iv ye'd go down to Rabbi Hirsch an' be baptiz-ed f'r a Jew.

"Ye may think 'tis th' innocint little last left leg iv a porker ye're inthrajoocin' into ye'er innocint fam'ly, but I tell ye, me boy, th' pig that that ham was cut fr'm has as manny legs to-day as iver he had. Why did ye waste ye-er good money on it? Why didn't ye get the fam'ly into th' dining-room, shut th' windows, an' turn on th' gas? I'll be readin' in th' pa-aper to-morrah that wan Hinnissy took an overdose iv Unblemished Ham with suicidal intint an' died in a gr-reat agony. Take it away! It's lible to blow up at anny minyit, scattherin' death an' desthruction in its train.

"Dear, oh, dear, I haven't been able to ate annything more nourishin' thin a cucumber in a week. I'm grajally fadin' fr'm life. A little while ago no wan cud square away at a beefsteak with betther grace thin mesilf. To-day th' wurrud resthrant makes me green in th' face. How did it all come about? A young fellow wrote a book. Th' divvle take him f'r writin' it. Hogan says it's a grand book. It's wan iv th' gr-reatest books he iver r-read. It almost made him commit suicide. Th' hero is a Lithuanian, or as ye might say, Pollacky, who left th' barb'rous land iv his birth an' come to this home iv oppor-chunity where ivry man is th' equal iv ivry other man befure th' law if he isn't careful. Our hero got a fancy job poling food products out iv a catch-basin, an' was promoted to scrapin' pure leaflard off th' flure iv th' glue facthry. But th' binifits iv our gloryous civilyzation were wasted on this poor peasant. In-stead iv bein' thankful f'r what he got, an' lookin' forward to a day whin his opporchunity wud arrive an', be merely stubbin' his toe, he might become rich an' famous as a pop'lar soup, he grew cross an' unruly, bit his boss, an' was sint to jail. But it all tur-rned out well in th' end. Th' villain fell into a lard-tank an' was not seen again ontil he tur-rned up at a fash'nable resthrant in New York. Our hero got out iv jail an' was rewarded with a pleasant position as a porter iv an arnychist hotel, an' all ended merry as a fun'ral bell.

"Ye'll see be this that 'tis a sweetly sintimintal little volume to be r-read durin' Lent. It's had a grand success, an' I'm glad iv it. I see be th' publishers' announcemints that 'tis th' gr-reatest lithry hog-killin' in a peryod iv gin'ral lithry culture. If ye want to rayjooce ye'er butcher's bills buy *Th' Jungle*. It shud be taken between meals, an' is especially ricomminded to maiden ladies contimplatin' their first ocean voyage.

"Well, sir, it put th' Prisidint in a tur-ruble stew. Oh, Lawd, why did I say that? Think iv—but I mustn't go on. Annyhow, Tiddy was toying with a light breakfast an' idly turnin' over th' pages iv th' new book with both hands. Suddenly he rose fr'm th' table, an' cryin': 'I'm pizened,' begun thrownin' sausages out iv th' window. Th' ninth wan sthruck Sinitor Biv'ridge on th' head an' made him a blond. It bounced off, exploded, an' blew a leg off a secret-service agent, an' th' scatthred fagmints desthroyed a handsome row iv ol' oak-trees. Sinitor Biv'ridge rushed in, thinkin' that th' Prisidint was bein' assassynated be his devoted followers in th' Sinit, an' discovered Tiddy engaged in a hand-to-hand conflict with a potted ham. Th' Sinitor f'rm Injyanny, with a few well-directed wurruds, put out th' fuse an' rendered th' missile harmless. Since thin th' Prisidint, like th' rest iv us, has become a viggytaryan, an' th' diet has so changed his disposition that he is writin' a book called *Suffer in Silence*, didycated to Sinitor Aldrich. But befure doin' annything else, he selected an expert comity fr'm a neighborin' univarsity settlemint to prepare a thorough, onbiased rayport that day on th' situation an' make sure it was no betther thin th' book said. Well, what th' experts discovered I won't tell ye. Suffice it to say, that whin th' report come in Congress decided to abolish all th' days iv th' week except Friday.

"I have r-read th' report, an' now, whin I'm asked to pass th' corned-beef, I pass. Oh dear, th' things I've consumed in days

past. What is lard? Lard is annything that isn't good enough
for an axle. What is potted ham? It is made in akel parts iv
plasther iv Paris, sawdust, rope, an' incautious laborer. To
what kingdom does canned chicken belong? It is a mineral.
How is soup— Get me th' fan, Hinnissy.

"Thank ye. I'm betther now. Well, sir, th' packers ar-re gettin' r-ready to protect thimsilves again' *The Jungle.* It's on'y
lately that these here gin'rous souls have give much attintion to
lithrachoor. Th' on'y pens they felt an inthrest in was those
that resthrained th' rectic cow. If they had a blind man in th'
Health Departmint, a few competint frinds on th' Fedhral
bench, an' Farmer Bill Lorimer to protect th' cattle inthrests iv
th' Gr-reat West, they cared not who made th' novels iv our
counthry. But Hogan says they'll have to add a novel facthry to
their plant, an' in a few months ye'll be able to buy wan iv Nels
Morris's pop-lar series warranted to be fr'm rale life, like th'
pressed corned-beef.

"Hogan has wrote a sample f'r thim:

" ' Dear!' Ivan Ivanovitch was seated in th' consarvatory an'
breakfast-room pro-vided be Schwartzchild & Sulsberger f'r all
their employees. It was a pleasant scene that sthretched
beneath th' broad windows iv his cosey villa. Th' air was
redolent with th' aroma iv th' spring rendherin', an' beneath
th' smoke iv th' May mornin' th' stately expanse iv
Packin'town appeared more lovely that iver befure. On th'
lawn a fountain played brine incessantly an' melojously on th'
pickled pigs'-feet. A faint odor as iv peach blossoms come fr'm
th' embalmin' plant where kine that have perished fr'm joy in
th' long journey fr'm th' plains are thransformed into th'
delicacies that show how an American sojer can die. Thousan's
iv battle-fields are sthrewn with th' labels iv this justly pop'lar
firm, an' a millyon heroes have risen fr'm their viands an' gone
composedly to their doom. But to rayturn to our story. Th'
scene, we say, was more beautiful thin wurruds can describe.
Beyond th' hedge a physician was thryin' to make a cow show
her tongue, while his assistant wint over th' crather with a

stethoscope. Th' air was filled with th' joyous shouts iv dhrivers iv wagons heavily laden with ol' boots an' hats, arsenic, boric acid, bone-dust, sthricknine, sawdust, an' th' other ingreejents iv th' most nourishing food f'r a sturdy people. It was a scene f'r th' eye to dote upon, but it brought no happiness to Ivan Ivanovitch. Yisterdah had been pay-day at th' yards an' little remained iv th' fourteen thousan' dollars that had been his portion. There was a soupcan iv anger in his voice as he laid down a copy iv th' *Ladies' Home Journal* an' said: "Dear!" Th' haughty beauty raised her head an' laid aside th' spoon with which she had been scrapin' th' life-givin' proosic acid fr'm th' Deer Island sausage. "Dear," said Ivanovitch, "if ye use so much iv th' comp'ny's peroxide on ye'er hair there will be none left f'r th' canned turkey." Befure she cud lift th' buttherine dish a cheery voice was heerd at th' dure, an' J. Ogden Cudahy bounded in. Ivanovitch flushed darkly, an' thin, as if a sudden determination had sthruck him, dhrew on his overhalls an' wint out to shampoo th' pigs. [Th' continyaution iv this thrillin' story will be found in th' next issue iv *Leaf Lard*. F'r sale at all dellycatessen-stores.]'

"An' there ye ar-re, Hinnissy. It's a turr'ble situation. Here am I an' here's all th' wurruld been stowin' away meat since th' days iv Nebudcud—what-ye-may-call-him. 'Tis th' pleasant hour iv dinner. We've been waitin' half an hour, pretindin' we were in no hurry, makin' convarsation, an' lookin' at th' clock. There is a commotion in th' back iv th' house, an' a cheery perfume iv beefsteak an' onions comes through an open dure. Th' hired girl smilin' but triumphant flags us fr'm th' dinin'-room. Th' talk about th' weather stops at wanst. Th' story iv th' wondherful child on'y four years old that bit his brother is stowed away f'r future use. Th' comp'ny dashes out. There is some crowdin' at th' dure. 'Will ye sit there, Mrs. Casey?' 'Mrs. Hinnissy, squat down next to Mike.' 'Tom, d'ye stow ye'ersilf at th' end iv th' table, where ye can deal th' potatoes.' 'Ar-re ye all r-ready? Thin go.' There ar-re twinty good stories flyin' before th' napkins ar-re well inside iv th' collar. Th' platter comes in smokin' like Vesuvyous. I begin to play me fav'rite chune with a carvin'-knife on a steel whin Molly Donahue remarks: 'Have ye r-read about th' invistygations iv th' Stock Yards?' I dhrop me knife. Tom Donahue clutches at his collar. Mrs. Hinnissy says th' rooms seem close, an' we make a meal off potatoes an' wathercress. Ivrybody goes home arly without sayin' good-bye, an' th' next day Father Kelly has to patch up a row between you an' ye'er wife. We ate no more together, an' food bein' th' basis iv all frindship, frindship ceases. Christmas is marked off th' calendar an' Lent lasts f'r three hundherd an' sixty-five days a year.

"An', be Hivens, I can't stop with thinkin' iv th' way th' food is got r-ready. Wanst I'm thurly sick I don't care how much sicker I get, an' I go on wondherin' what food ra-ally is. An' that way, says Hogan, starvation lies. Th' idee that a Polish gintleman has danced wan iv his graceful native waltzes on me beefsteak is horrible to think, but it's on'y a shade worse thin th' thought that this delicate morsel that makes me th' man I am was got be th' assaynation iv a gentle animile that niver done me no harm but look kindly at me. See th' little lamb friskin' in th' fields. How beautiful an' innocint it is. Whin ye'er little Packy has been a good boy ye call him ye'er littl lamb, an' take him to see thim skippin' in th' grass. 'Aren't they cunnin', Packy?' But look! Who is this gr-reat ruffyanly man comin' acrost th' fields? An' what is that horrid blade he holds in his hands? Is he goin' to play with th' lamb? Oh, dhreadful sight. Take away th' little boy, Hinnissy. Ye have ordhered a leg iv lamb f'r supper.

"Th' things we eat or used to eat! I'll not mintion anny iv thim, but I'd like some pote to get up a list iv eatable names that wud sound th' way they taste. It's askin' too much f'r us to be happy whin we're stowin' away articles iv food with th' same titles as our own machinery. 'But why not ate something else?' says ye. Fish? I can't. I've hooked thim out iv th' wather. Eggs? What is an egg? Don't answer. Let us go on. Milk? Oh, goodness! Viggytables, thin? Well, if it's bad to take th' life iv a

cow or a pig, is it anny betther to cut off a tomato in th' flower
iv its youth or murdher a fam'ly iv baby pease in th' cradle? I
ate no more iv annything but a few snowballs in winter an' a
mouthful iv fresh air in th' summer-time.

"But let's stop thinkin' about it. It's a good thing not to
think long about annything—ye'ersilf, ye'er food, or ye'er
hereafther. Th' story iv th' nourishmint we take is on'y half
written in *Th' Jungle*. If ye followed it fr'm th' cradle to th'
grave, as ye might say—fr'm th' day Armour kicked it into a
wheelbarrow, through varyous encounters, th' people it met,
with their pictures while at wurruk, until it landed in th' care iv
th' sthrange lady in th' kitchen—ye'd have a romance that wud
make th' butcher haul down his sign. No, sir, I'm goin' to thry
to fight it. If th' millyonaire has a gredge again' me he'll land
me somehow. If he can't do me with sugar iv lead, he'll run me
down with a throlley-car or smash me up in a railroad accident.
I'll shut me eyes an' take me chance. Come into th' back room,
cut me a slice iv th' ham, an' sind f'r th' priest."

"They ought to make thim ate their own meat," said Mr.
Hennessy, warmly.

"I suggested that," said Mr. Dooley, "but Hogan says they'd
fall back on th' Constitution. He says th' Constitution f'rbids
crool an' unusual punishmints."

ALCOHOL AS FOOD

"If a man come into this saloon—" Mr. Hennessy was saying.

"This ain't no saloon," Mr. Dooley interrupted. "This is a
resthrant."

"A what?" Mr. Hennessy exclaimed.

"A resthrant," said Mr. Dooley. "Ye don't know, Hinnissy,
that liquor is food. It is though. Food—an' dhrink. That's
what a doctor says in the pa-apers, an' another doctor wants
th' gover'mint to sind tubs iv th' stuff down to th' Ph'lipeens.
He says 'tis almost issintial that people shud dhrink in thim hot

climates. Th' prespiration don't dhry on thim afther a hard
pursoot iv Aggynaldoo an' th' capture iv Gin'ral Pantaloons de
Garshy; they begin to think iv home an' mother sindin' down
th' lawn-sprinkler to be filled with bock, an' they go off
somewhere, an' not bein' able to dhry thimsilves with dhrink,
they want to die. Th' disease is called nostalgia or home-
sickness, or thirst.''

" ' What we want to do f'r our sojer boys in th' Ph'lipeens
besides killin' thim,' says th' ar-rmy surgeon, 'is make th' place
more homelike,' he says. 'Manny iv our heroes hasn't had th'
deleeryum thremens since we first planted th' stars an'
sthripes,' he says, 'an' th' bay'nits among th' people,' he says.
'I wud be in favor of havin' th' rigimints get their feet round
wanst a week, at laste.' he says. 'Lave us,' he says, 'reform th'
reg'lations,' he says, 'an' insthruct our sojers to keep their
powdher dhry an' their whistles wet,' he says.

"Th' idee ought to take, Hinnissy, f'r th' other doctor la-ad
has discovered that liquor is food. 'A man,' says he, 'can live
f'r months on a little booze taken fr'm time to time,' he says.
'They'se a gr-reat dale iv nourishment in it,' he says. An' I
believe him, f'r manny's th' man I know that don't think iv
eatin' whin he can get a dhrink. I wondher if the time will iver
come whin ye'll see a man sneakin' out iv th' fam'ly enthrance
iv a lunch-room hurridly bitin' a clove! People may get so
they'll carry a light dinner iv a pint iv rye down to their wurruk, an' a man'll tell ye he niver takes more thin a bottle iv
beer f'r breakfast. Th' cook'll give way to th' bartinder and th'
doctor 'll ordher people f'r to ate on'y at meals. Ye'll r-read in
th' pa-apers that 'Anton Boozinski, while crazed with ham an
eggs, thried to kill his wife an' childher.' On Pathrick's day
ye'll see th' Dr. Tanner Anti-Food Fife an' Drum corpse out at
th' head iv th' procession instead iv th' Father Macchews, an'
they'll be places where a man can be took whin he gets th'
monkeys fr'm immodhrate eatin'. Th' sojers'll complain that
th' liquor was unfit to dhrink an' they'll be inquiries to find out
who sold embammin' flood to th' ar-rmy. Poor people'll have

simple meals—p'raps a bucket iv beer an' a little crame de mint, an' ye'll r-read in th' pa-apers about a family found starvin' on th' North side, with nawthin' to sustain life but wan small bottle iv gin, while th' head iv th' family, a man well known to the polis, spinds his wages in a low doggery or bakeshop fuddlin' his brains with custard pie. Th' r-rich 'll inthrajoose novelties. P'raps they'll top off a fine dinner with a little hasheesh or proosic acid. Th' time'll come whin ye'll see me in a white cap fryin' a cocktail over a cooksthove, while a nigger hollers to me: 'Dhraw a stack iv Scotch,' an' I holler back: 'On th' fire.' Ye will not."

"That's what I thought," said Mr. Hennessy.

"No," said Mr. Dooley. "Whisky wudden't be so much iv a luxury if 'twas more iv a necissity. I don't believe 'tis a food, though whin me frind Schwartzmeister makes a cocktail all it needs is a few noodles to look like a biled dinner. No, whisky ain't food. I think better iv it thin that. I wudden't insult it be placin' it on th' same low plane as a lobster salad. Father Kelly puts it r-right, and years go by without him lookin' on it even at Hallowe'en. 'Whisky,' says he, 'is called the divvle, because,' he says, ''tis wan iv the fallen angels,' he says. 'It has it's place,' he says, 'but its place is not in a man's head,' says he. 'It ought to be th' reward iv action, not th' cause iv it,' he says. 'It's f'r th' end iv th' day, not th' beginnin',' he says. 'Hot whisky is good f'r a cold heart, an' no whisky's good f'r a hot head,' he says. 'Th' minyit a man relies on it f'r a crutch he loses th' use iv his legs. 'Tis a bad thing to stand on, a good thing to sleep on, a good thing to talk on, a bad thing to think on. If it's in th' head in th' mornin' it ought not to be in th' mouth at night. If it laughs in ye, dhrink; if it weeps, swear off. It makes some men talk like good women, an' some women talk like bad men. It is a livin' f'r orators an' th' death iv bookkeepers. It doesn't sustain life, but, whin taken hot with wather, a lump iv sugar, a piece iv lemon peel, and just th' dustin' iv a nutmeg-grater, it makes life sustainable.'"

"D'ye think ye'ersilf it sustains life?" asked Mr. Hennessy.

"It has sustained mine f'r many years," said Mr. Dooley.

BANTING

"I see th' good woman goin' by here at a gallop to-day," said Mr. Dooley.

"She's thryin' to rayjooce her weight," said Mr. Hennessy.

"Wat f'r?"

"I don't know. She looks all right," said Mr. Hennessy.

"Well," said Mr. Dooley, "'tis a sthrange thing. Near ivrybody I know is thryin' to rayjooce their weight. Why shud a woman want to be thin onless she is thin? Th' idee iv female beauty that all gr-reat men, fr'm Julius Caesar to mesilf, has held, is much more like a bar'l thin a clothes-pole. Hogan tells me that Alexander's wife an' Caesar's missus was no lightweights; Martha Wash'nton was short but pleasantly dumpy, an' Andhrew Jackson's good woman weighed two hundherd an' smoked a pipe. Hogan says that all th' potes he knows was in love with not to say fat, but ample ladies. Th' potes thimsilves was thin, but th' ladies was chubby. A pote, whin he has wurruked all day at th' typewriter, wants to rest his head on a shoulder that won't hurt. Shakespeare's wife was thin, an' they quarrelled. Th' lady that th' Eyetalian pote Danty made a fool iv himsilf about was no skeliton. All th' pitchers iv beautiful women I've iver see had manny curves an' sivral chins. Th' photty-graft iv Mary Queen iv Scots that I have in me room shows that she took on weight afther she had her dhress made. Th' collar looks to be chokin' her.

"But nowadays 'tis th' fashion to thry to emaciate ye'ersilf. I ate supper with Carney th' other day. It was th' will iv Hiven that Carney shud grow fat, but Carney has a will iv his own, an' f'r ten years he's been thryin' to look like Sinitor Fairbanks, whin his thrue model was Grover Cleveland. He used to scald himsilf ivry mornin' with a quart iv hot wather on gettin' up. That did him no good. Thin he thried takin' long walks. Th' long walk rayjooced him half a pound, and gave him a thirst that made him take on four pounds iv boodweiser. Thin he rented a horse, an' thried horseback ridin'. Th' horse liked his weight no more thin Carney did, an' Carney gained ten pounds in th' hospital. He thried starvin' himsilf, an' he lost two pounds an' his job f'r bein' cross to th' boss. Thin he raysumed his reg'lar meals, an' made up his mind to cut out th' sugar. I see him at breakfast wan mornin'. Nature had been kind to Carney in th' matther iv appytite. I won't tell ye what he consumed. It's too soon afther supper, an' th' room is close. But, annyhow, whin his wife had tottered in with th' last flap-jack an' fainted, an' whin I begun to wondher whether it wud be safe to stay, he hauled a little bottle fr'm his pocket an' took out a small pill. 'What's that?' says I. ''Tis what I take in place iv sugar,' says he. 'Sugar is fattenin', an' this rayjoocees th' weight,' says he. 'An' ar-re ye goin' to match that poor little tablet against that breakfast?' says I. 'I am,' says he. 'Cow'rd,' says I.

"Th' latest thing that Carney has took up to make th' fight again' Nature is called Fletching. Did ye iver hear iv it? Well, they'se a lad be th' name iv Fletcher who thinks so much iv his stomach that he won't use it, an' he tells Carney that if he'll ate on'y wan or two mouthfuls at ivry meal an' thurly chew thim he will invinchooly be no more thin skin an' bones an' very handsome to look at. In four weeks a man who Fletches will lose forty pounds an' all his frinds. Th' idee is that ye mumble ye'er food f'r tin minyits with a watch in front iv ye.

"This night Carney was Fletching. It was a fine supper. Th' table groaned beneath all th' indilicacies iv th' season. We tucked our napkins undher our chins an' prepared f'r a jaynial avenin'. Not so Carney. He laid his goold watch on th' table, took a mouthful iv mutton pie an' begun to Fletch. At first Hogan thought he was makin' faces at him, but I explained that he was crazy. I see be th' look in Carney's eye that he didn't like th' explanation, but we wint on th' supper. Well, 'twas gloryous. 'Jawn, ye'er health. Pass th' beefsteak,

Malachi. Schwartzmeister, ol' boy, can't I help ye to th' part that wint over th' fence last? What's that story? Tell it over here, where Carney can't hear. It might make him laugh an' hurt him with his frind Fletcher. No? What? Ye don't say? An' didn't Carney resint it? Haw, haw, haw! This eyesther sauce is th' best I iver see. Michael, this is like ol' times. Look at Schwartzmeister. He's Fletching, too. No, be gorry, he's chokin'. I think Carney's watch has stopped. No wondher; he's lookin' at it. Haw, haw, haw, haw, haw! A good joke on Carney. Did ye iver see such a face? Carney, me buck, ye look like a kinetoscope. What is a face without a stomach? Carney, ye make me nervous. If that there idol don't stop f'r a minyit I'll throw something at it. Carney, time's up. Ye win ye'er bet, but 'twas a foolish wan. I thought ye were goin' to push Fletcher in a wheelbarrow.'

"I've known Jawn Carney, man an' boy, f'r forty year, but I niver knew ontil that minyit that he was a murdhrer at heart. Th' look he give us whin he snapped his watch was tur-rble; but th' look he give th' dinner was aven worse. He set there f'r two mortal hours miditatin' what form th' assassynations wud take an' Fletchin' each wan iv us in his mind. I walked home with him to see that he came to no harm. Near th' house he wint into a baker's shop an' bought four pies an' a bag iv doughnuts. 'I've promised to take thim home to me wife,' he says. 'I thought she was out iv town,' says I. 'She'll be back in a week,' says he; 'an', annyhow, Misther Dooley, I'll thank ye not to be pryin' into me domestic affairs,' he says.

"An' there ye ar-re. What's th' use iv goin' up again' th' laws iv Nature, says I. If Nature intinded ye to be a little roly-poly, a little roly-poly ye'll be. They ain't annything to do that ye ought to do that 'll make ye thin an' keep ye thin. Th' wan thing in th' wurruld that 'll rejooce ye surely is lack iv sleeep, an' who wants to lose his mind with his flesh. I'll guarantee with th' aid iv an alarm-clock to make anny man a livin' skeliton in thirty days. A lady with a young baby won't niver get no chubbier, nor th' gintleman, its father. Th' on'y

ginooine anti-fat threatment is sickness, worry, throuble, an in-
somnya. Th' scales ain't anny judge iv beauty or health. To be
beautiful is to be nachral. Ye have gr-reat nachral skinny beauty, while my good looks is more buxom. Whin I see an ol' fool
in a sweater an' two coats sprintin' up' th' sthreet an' groanin'
at ivry step I want to join with th' little boys that ar-re throwin'
bricks at him. If he takes off th' flesh that Nature has wasted
on his ongrateful frame his skin won't fit him. They'se
nawthin' more heejous to look at than a fat man that has rayjooced his weight. He looks as though he had bought his
coverin' at an auction. It bags undher th' eyes an' don't fit in
th' neck.

"A man is foolish that thries to be too kind to his stomach,
annyhow. Fletcher's idee is that th' human stomach is a sort iv
little Lord Fauntleroy. If ye give it much to do it will pine
away. But Dock Casey tells me 'tis a gr-reat, husky, good-
natured pugilist that 'll take on most annything that comes
along. It will go to wurruk with grim resolution on a piece iv
hard coal. It will get th' worst iv it, but what I mane to say is
that it fears no foe, an' doesn't draw th' color-line. I wud put it
in th' heavy-weight class, an' it ought to be kept there. It requires plenty iv exercise to be at its best, an' if it doesn't get
enough it loses its power until a chocolate eclair might win
against it. It musn't be allowed to shirk its jooties. It shud be
kept in thrainin', an says Dock Casey, if its owner is a good
matchmaker, an' doesn't back it again' opponents that ar-re
out iv its class or too manny at wan time, it will still be doin'
well whin th' brain is on'y fit f'r light exercise."

"D'ye expict to go on accumylatin' flesh to th' end iv ye'er
days?" asked Mr. Hennessy.

"I do that," said Mr. Dooley. "I expict to make me frinds
wurruk f'r me to th' last. They'll be no gayety among th'
pallbearers at me obsequies. They'll have no sinycure. Befure
they get through with me they'll know they've been to a
fun'ral."

OATS AS A FOOD

"What's a breakfast food?" asked Mr. Hennessy.

"It depinds on who ye ar-re," said Mr. Dooley. "In ye're case it's annything to ate that ye're not goin' to have f'r dinner or supper. But in th' case iv th' rest iv this impeeryal raypublic, 'tis th' on'y amusement they have. 'Tis most iv th' advertisin' in th' pa-apers. 'Tis what ye see on th' bill-boords. 'Tis th' inspi-ration iv pothry an' art. In a wurrd, it's oats.

"I wint over to have breakfast New Year's mornin' at Joyce's. Th' air was sharp, an' though I'm not much given to reflectin' on vittles, regardin' thim more as meedjum f'r what dhrink I take with thim thin annything else, be th' time I got to th' dure I was runnin' over in me mind a bill iv fare an' kind iv wondhrin' whether I wud have ham an' eggs or liver an' bacon, an' hopin' I cud have both. Well, we set down at the table, an' I tucked me napkin into me collar so that I wudden't have to chase it down in me shoe if I got laughin' at annything funny durin' an egg, an' squared away. 'Ar-re ye hungry?' says Joyce. 'Not now,' says I. 'I've on'y been up two hours, an' I don't think I cud ate more thin a couple iv kerosene-lamps an' a bur-rd cage,' says I. 'But I'm li'ble to be hungry in a few minyits, an',' says I, 'p'raps 'twud be just as well to lock up th' small childer,' I says, 'where they'll be safe,' I says, thinkin' to start th' breakfast with a flow iv spirits, though th' rosy Gawd iv Day sildom finds me much betther natured thin a mustard plasther.

" 'What's ye'er fav'rite breakfast dish?' says Joyce. 'My what?' says I. 'Ye'er fav'rite breakfast dish?' says he. 'Whativer ye've got,' says I, not to be thrapped into givin' me suffrage to annything he didn't have in th' house. 'Anny kind iv food, so long as it's hot an' hurrid. Thank Hivin I have a mind about vittles, an' don't know half th' time what I'm atin',' says I. 'But I mane prepared food, says he. 'I like it fried,' says I; 'but I don't mind it broiled, roasted, stewed, or fricasseed. In a minyit or two I'll waive th' cookin' an' ate it off th' hoof,' I says. 'Well,' says he, 'me fav'rite is Guff,' he says. 'P'raps ye've seen th' advertisemint: "Out iv th' house wint Luck Joe; Guff was th' food that made him go." Mother prefers Almostfood, a scientific preparation iv burlaps. I used to take Sawd Ust, which I found too rich, an' later I had a peeroyd iv Hungareen, a chimically pure dish, made iv th' exterryor iv bath towels. We all have our little tastes an' enthusyasms in th' matther iv breakfast foods, depindin' on what pa-apers we read an' what billboords we've seen iv late. I believe Sunny Jim cud jump higher on Guff thin on Almostfood, but mother says she see a sign down on Halsted Sthreet that convinces her she has th' most stimylatin' tuck-in. Annyhow,' he says, 'I take gr-reat pains to see that nawthin' is sarved f'r breakfast that ain't well advertised an' guaranteed pure fr'm th' facthry, an' put up in blue or green pa-aper boxes,' he says. 'Well,' says I, 'give me a tub iv Guff,' I says. 'I'll close me eyes an' think iv an egg.'

"What d'ye suppose they give me, Hinnissy? Mush! Mush, be Hivens! 'What kind iv mush is this?' says I, takin' a mouthful. 'It ain't mush,' says Joyce. 'It's a kind iv scientific oatmeal,' says he. 'Science,' says I, 'has exthracted th' meal. Pass th' ink,' says I. 'What d'ye want ink f'r?' says he. 'Who iver heerd iv atin' blottin' pa-aper without ink?' says I. 'Ate it,' says he. 'Give me me hat,' I says. 'Where ar-re ye goin'?' he says. 'I f'rgot me nose-bag,' I says. 'I can't ate this off a plate. Give it to me an' I'll harness mesilf up in Cavin's buggy, have mesilf hitched to a post in front iv th' city hall, an' injye me breakfast,' I says. 'Ye have a delightful home here,' says I. 'Some day I'm goin' to ask ye to take me up in th' kitchen an' lave me fork down some hay f'r th' childer. But now I must lave ye to ye'er prepared oats,' I says. An' I wint out to Mulligan's resthrant an' wrapped mesilf around buckwheat cakes an' sausages till th' cook got buckwheat cake-makers'-paralysis.

"I don't know how people come to have this mad passion f'r oats. Whin I was a boy they was on'y et be horses, an' good horses rayfused thim. But some wan discovered that th' more ye did to oats th' less they tasted, an' that th' less annything tastes th' betther food it is f'r th' race. So all over th' counthry countless machines is at wurruk removin' th' flavor fr'm oats an' turnin' thim into breakfast food. Breakfast food is all ye see in th' cars an' on th' bill-boords. In th' small cities it's th' principal spoort iv th' people. Where childer wanst looked on th' boords to see whin th' misthrel show was comin' to town, they now watch f'r th' announcement iv th' new breakfast food. Hogan tol' me he was out in Decatur th' other day an' they was eighty-siven kinds iv oats on th' bill iv fare. 'Is they annything goin' on in this town?'' he ast a dhrummer. 'Nawthing' ontil th' eighth, whin Oatoono opens,' says th' man. People talk about breakfast food as they used to talk about bicycles. They compare an' they thrade. A man with th' 1906 model iv high-gear oats is th' invy iv th' neighborhood. All th' saw-mills has been turned into breakfast-food facthries, an' th' rip-saw has took th' place iv th' miller.

"Does it do anny harm, says ye? Ne'er a bit. A counthry that's goin' to be kilt be food is on its last legs, annyhow. Ivry race has its pecoolyarity. With th' Rooshyans it's 'Pass th' tallow candles'; with th' Chinese a plate iv rice an' a shark's fin. Th' German sets down to a breakfast iv viggytable soup, Hungaryan goolash, an' beer. Th' Frinchman is satisfied with a rose in his buttonhole an' tin minyits at th' pianny. An Irishman gets sthrong on potatoes, an' an Englishman dilicate on a sound breakfast iv roast beef, ham, mutton pie, eggs, bacon, an' 'alf-an'-'alf. Th' docthors bothers us too much about what we put into that mighty tough ol' man-iv-all-wurruk, th' human stomach. Hiven sint most iv us good digistions, but th' doctors won't let thim wurruk. Th' sthrongest race iv rough-an'-tumble Americans that iver robbed a neighbor was raised on pie. I'm f'r pie mesilf at anny time an' at all meals. If food makes anny diff'rence to people, how do I know that all our boasted prosperity ain't based on pie? Says I, lave well enough alone. It may be that if we sarched f'r th' corner-stone iv American liberty an' pro-gress, we'd find it was apple-pie with a piece iv toasted cheese.

"People don't have anny throuble with their digistions fr'm atin'. 'Tis thinkin' makes dyspepsy; worryin' about th' rent is twinty times worse f'r a man's stomach thin plum-puddin'. What's worse still, is worryin' about digistion. Whin a man gets to doin' that all th' oats between here an' Council Bluffs won't save him."

"Joyce tells me his breakfast food has made him as sthrong as a horse," said Mr. Hennessy.

"It ought to," said Mr. Dooley. "Him an' a horse have th' same food."

DRUGS

"What ails ye?" asked Mr. Dooley of Mr. Hennessey, who looked dejected.

"I'm a sick man," said Mr. Hennessey.

"Since th' picnic?"

"Now that I come to think iv it, it did begin th' day afther th' picnic," said Mr. Hennessey. "I've been to see Dock O'Leary. He give me this an' these here pills an' some powdhers besides. An' d'ye know, though I haven't taken anny iv thim yet, I feel betther already."

"Well, sir," said Mr. Dooley, " 'tis a grand thing to be a doctor. A man that's a doctor don't have to buy anny funny papers to enjye life. Th' likes iv ye goes to a picnic an' has a pleasant, peaceful day in th' counthry dancin' breakdowns an' kickin' a football in th' sun an' ivry fifteen minyits or so washin' down a couple of dill-pickles with a bottle of white pop. Th' next day ye get what's comin' to ye in th' right place an' bein' a sthrong, hearty man that cudden't be kilt be annything less thin a safe fallin' on ye fr'm a twenty-story buildin', ye know ye ar-re goin' to die. Th' good woman advises a mustard plasther but ye scorn th' suggestion. What good wud a mustard plasther be again this fatal epidemic that is ragin' inside iv ye? Besides a mustard plasther wud hurt. So th' good woman, frivilous crather that she is, goes back to her wurruk singin' a light chune. She knows she's goin' to have to put up with ye f'r some time to come. A mustard plasther, Hinnissy, is th' rale test iv whether a pain is goin' to kill ye or not. If the plasther is onbearable ye can be th' pain undherneath it is not.

"But ye know ye are goin' to die an' ye're not sure whether ye'll send f'r Father Kelly or th' doctor. Ye finally decide to save up Father Kelly f'r th' last an' ye sind f'r th' Dock. Havin' rescued ye fr'm th' jaws iv death two or three times befure whin ye had a sick headache th' Dock takes his time about comin', but just as ye are beginnin' to throw ye'er boots at th' clock an' show other signs iv what he calls rigem mortar, he rides up in his fine horse an' buggy. He gets out slowly, one foot at a time, hitches his horse an' ties a nose bag on his head. Thin he chats f'r two hundherd years with th' polisman on th' beat. He tells him a good story an' they laugh harshly.

"Whin th' polisman goes his way th' Dock meets th' good woman at th' dure an' they exchange a few wurruds about th' weather, th' bad condition iv th' sthreets, th' health iv Mary Ann since she had th' croup an' ye'ersilf. Ye catch th' wurruds, 'Grape Pie,' 'Canned Salmon,' 'Cast-iron digestion.' Still he doesn't come up. He tells a few stories to the childher. He weighs th' youngest in his hands an' says: 'That's a fine boy ye have, Mrs. Hinnissy. I make no doubt he'll grow up to be a polisman.' He examines th' phottygraft album an' asks if that isn't so-an-so. An' all this time ye lay writhin' in mortal agony an' sayin' to ye'ersilf: 'Inhuman monsther, to lave me perish here while he chats with a callous woman that I haven't said annything but "What?" to f'r twinty years.'

"Ye begin to think there's a conspiracy against ye to get ye'er money befure he saunters into th' room an' says in a gay tone: 'Well, what d'ye mane be tyin' up wan iv th' gr-reat in-dusthrees iv our nation be stayin' away fr'm wurruk f'r a day? 'Dock,' says ye in a feeble voice, 'I have a tur'ble pain in me abdumdum. It reaches fr'm here to here,' makin' a rough sketch iv th' burned disthrict undher th' blanket. 'I felt it comin' on last night but I didn't say annything f'r fear iv alarmin' me wife, so I simply groaned,' says ye.

"While ye ar-re describin' ye'er pangs, he walks around th' room lookin' at th' pictures. Afther ye've got through he comes over an' says: 'Lave me look at ye'er tongue. 'Hum,' he says, holdin' ye'er writs an' bowin' through th' window to a frind iv his on a sthreet car. 'Does that hurt?' he says, stabbin' ye with his thumbs in th' suburbs iv th' pain. 'Ye know it does,' says ye with a groan. 'Don't do that again. Ye scratched me.' He hurls ye'er wrist back at ye an' stands at th' window lookin' out at th' firemen acrost th' sthreet playin' dominoes. He says nawthin' to ye an' ye feel like th' prisoner while th' foremen iv th' jury is fumblin' in his inside pocket f'r th' verdict. Ye can stand it no longer. 'Dock,' says he, 'is it annything fatal? I'm not fit to die but tell me th' worst an' I will thry to bear it. 'Well,' says he, 'ye have a slight interioritis iv th' semi-colon. But this purscription ought to fix ye up all right. Ye'd betther take it over to th' dhrug sthore an' have it filled ye'ersilf. In th' manetime I'd advise ye to be careful iv ye'er dite. I wudden't ate annything with glass or a large percintage iv plasther iv Paris in it.' An' he goes away to write his bill.

"I wondher why ye can always read a doctor's bill and ye niver can read his purscription. F'r all ye know, it may be a short note to th' dhruggist askin' him to hit ye on th' head with a pestle. An' it's a good thing ye can't read it. If ye cud, ye'd say: 'I'll not cash this in at no dhrug store. I'll go over to Dooley's an' get th' rale thing.' So, afther thryin' to decipher this here corner iv a dhress patthern, ye climb into ye'er clothes f'r what may be ye'er last walk up Ar-rchy Road. As ye go along ye begin to think that maybe th' Dock knows ye have th' Asiatic cholery an' was onl'y thryin' to jolly ye with his man-ner iv dealin' with ye. As ye get near th' dhrug store ye feel sure iv it, an' 'tis with th' air iv a man without hope that ye hand th' paper to a young pharmycist who is mixin' a two-cent stamp f'r a lady customer. He hands it over to a scientist who is compoundin' an ice-cream soda f'r a child, with th' remark:

'O'Leary's writin' is gettin' worse an' worse. I can't make this out at all.' 'Oh,' says th' chemist, layin' down his spoon, 'that's his old cure f'r th' bellyache. Ye'll find a bucket iv it in th' back room next to th' coal scuttle.'

'It's a gr-reat medicine he give ye. It will do ye good no matther what ye do with it. I wud first thry poorin' some iv it in me hair. If that don't help ye see how far ye can throw th' bottle into th' river. Ye feel betther already. Ye ought to write to th' medical journals about th' case. It is a remarkable cure. 'M— H— was stricken with excruciating tortures in th' gastric regions followin' an unusually severe outing in th' counthry. F'r a time it looked as though it might be niciss'ry to saw out th' infected area, but as this wud lave an ugly space between legs an' chin, it was determined to apply Jam. Gin. ℥ VIII. Th' remedy acted instantly. Afther carryin' th' bottle uncorked f'r five minyits in his inside pocket th' patient showed signs iv recovery an' is now again in his accustomed health.'

"Yes, sir, if I was a doctor, I'd be ayether laughin' or cryin' all th' time. I'd be laughin' over th' cases that I was called into whin I wasn't needed an' cryin' over th' cases where I cud do no good. An' that wud be most iv me cases.

"Dock O'Leary comes in here often an' talks medicine to me. 'Ye'ers is a very thrying pro-fissyon,' says I. 'It is,' says he. 'I'm tired out,' says he. 'Have ye had a good manny desprit cases to-day?' says I. 'It isn't that,' says he, 'but I'm not a very muscular man,' he says, 'an' some iv th' windows in these old frame houses are hard to open,' he says. Th' Dock don't believe much in dhrugs. He says that if he wasn't afraid iv losin' his practice he wudn't give annybody annything but quinine an' he isn't sure about that. he says th' more he practises medicine th' more he becomes a janitor with a knowledge iv cookin'. He says if people wud on'y call him in befure they got sick, he'd abolish ivry disease in th' ward except old age an' pollyticks. He says he's lookin' forward to th' day whin th' tillyphone will ring an' he'll hear a voice sayin': 'Hurry up over to Hinnissy's. He niver felt so well in his life.' 'All right,

I'll be over as soon as I can hitch up th' horse. Take him away fr'm th' supper table at wanst, give him a pipeful iv tobacco an' walk him three times around th' block.'

"But whin a man's sick, he's sick an' nawthin' will cure him or annything will. In th' old days befure ye an' I were born, th' doctor was th' barber too. He'd shave ye, cut ye'er hair, dye ye'er mustache, give ye a dhry shampoo an' cure ye iv appindicitis while ye were havin' ye'er shoes shined be th' naygur. Ivry gineration iv doctors has had their favrite remedies. Wanst people were cured iv fatal maladies be applications iv blind puppies, hair fr'm the skulls iv dead men an' solutions iv bat's wings, just as now they're cured be dhrinkin' a tayspoonful iv a very ordhinary article iv booze that's had some kind iv a pizenous weed dissolved in it.

"Dhrugs, says Dock O'Leary, are a litte iv a pizen that a little more iv wud kill ye. He says that if ye look up anny poplar dhrug in th' ditchnry ye'll see that it is 'A very powerful pizen of great use in medicine.' I took calomel at his hands f'r manny years till he told me that it was about the same thing they put into Rough on Rats. Thin I stopped. If I've got to die, I want to die on th' premises.

"But, as he tells me, ye can't stop people from takin' dhrugs an' ye might as well give thim something that will look important enough to be inthrojuced to their important an' fatal cold in th' head. If ye don't, they'll leap f'r the patent medicines. Mind ye, I haven't got annything to say again patent medicines. If a man wud rather take thim thin dhrink at a bar or go down to Hop Lung's f'r a long dhraw, he's within his rights. Manny a man have I known who was a victim iv th' tortures iv a cigareet cough who is now livin' comfortable an' happy as an opeem fiend be takin' Doctor Wheezo's Consumption Cure. I knew a fellow wanst who suffered fr'm spring fever to that extent that he niver did a day's wurruk. To-day, afther dhrinkin' a bottle of Gazooma, he will go home not on'y with th' strenth but th' desire to beat his wife. There is a dhrug store on ivry corner an' they're goin' to dhrive out th' saloons onless th' govermint will let us honest merchants put a little co-caine or chloral in our cough-drops an' advertise that it will cure spinal minigitis. An' it will, too, f'r awhile."

"Don't ye iver take dhrugs?" asked Mr. Hennessy.

"Niver whin I'm well," said Mr. Dooley. "Whin I'm sick, I'm so sick I'd take annything."

CHAPTER X

ATHLETICS

In both 1885 and 1886, Chicago's White Stockings (later the Cubs) won championships, and the city went beserk over baseball. Until 1887, newspapers had covered the sport merely by publishing the results of the previous day's games. Responding to the craze, the *Evening News* assigned 20-year-old Finley Peter Dunne to cover both home and away games with veteran reporter Charles Seymour. Between the two of them, they developed a kind of coverage that all other papers quickly emulated and which set the standard for today. To Dunne also goes the credit for adding a word to the language: "southpaw," which originally meant a left-handed pitcher, and which has now come to mean a lefty in any profession.

Although a fan, Dunne was more interested in political reporting, and in early 1888, he joined the *Times* to accept such an assignment.

Dunne enjoyed sports, although he did have Mr. Dooley once admonish his friend President Roosevelt, who was aggressively athletic, that there was both "a strenuse life an' a sthrenuseless life."

Dunne played golf whenever he could, especially in later years, even to the extent of helping organize the Southampton Golf Club on Long Island. He was never more than a duffer, however, and no competition for his Olympic Gold Medalist wife.

ON GOLF

'But 'tis a gr-reat game, a gr-rand, jolly, hail-fellow-well-met spoort. With the exciption maybe iv th' theery iv infant damnation, Scotland has given nawthin' more cheerful to th' wurruld thin th' game iv goluf.'

"An' what's this game iv goluf like, I dinnaw?" said Mr.

Hennessy, lighting his pipe with much unnecessary noise. "Ye're a good deal iv a spoort, Jawnny: did ye iver thry it?"

"No," said Mr. McKenna. "I used to roll a hoop onct upon a time, but I'm out of condition now."

"It ain't like base-ball," said Mr. Hennessy, "an' it ain't like shinny, an' it ain't like lawn-teenis, an' it ain't like forty-fives an' it ain't" —

"Like canvas-back duck or anny other game ye know," said Mr. Dooley.

"Thin what is it like?" said Mr. Hennessy. "I see be th' pa-aper that Hobart What-d'ye-call-him is wan iv th' best at it. Th' other day he made a scoor iv wan hundherd an' sixty-eight, but whether 'twas miles or stitches I cudden't make out fr'm th' raypoorts."

"'Tis little ye know," said Mr. Dooley. "Th' game iv goluf is as old as th' hills. Me father had goluf links all over his place. an', whin I was a kid, 'twas wan iv th' principal spoorts iv me life, afther I'd dug the turf f'r th' avenin', to go out and putt" —

"Poot, ye mean," said Mr. Hennessy. "They'se no such wur-rud in th' English language as putt. Belinda called me down ha-ard on it no more thin las' night."

"There ye go!" said Mr. Dooley, angrily. "There ye go! D'ye think this here game iv goluf is a spellin' match? 'Tis like ye, Hinnissy, to be refereein' a twinty-round glove contest be th' rule iv three. I tell ye I used to go out in th' avenin' an' putt me mashie like hell-an'-all, till I was knowed fr'm wan end iv th' county to th' other as th' champeen putter. I putted two men fr'm Roscommon in wan day, an' they had to be took home on a dure.

"In America th' ga-ame is played more ginteel, an' is more like cigareet-smokin', though less onhealthy f'r th' lungs. 'Tis a good game to play in a hammick whin ye're all tired out fr'm social duties or shovellin' coke. Out-iv-dure golf is played be th' followin' rules. If ye bring ye'er wife f'r to see th' game, an' she has her name in th' paper, that counts ye wan. So th' first thing ye do is to find th' raypoorter, an' tell him ye're there. Thin ye ordher a bottle iv brown pop, an' have ye'er second fan ye with a towel. Afther this ye'd dhress, an' here ye've got to be dam particklar or ye'll be stuck f'r th' dhrinks. If ye'er necktie is not on sthraight, that counts ye'er opponent wan. If both ye an' ye'er opponent have ye'er neckties on crooked, th' first man that sees it gets th' stakes. Thin ye ordher a carredge" —

"Order what?" demanded Mr. McKenna.

"A carredge."

"What for?"

"F'r to take ye 'round th' links. Ye have a little boy followin' ye, carryin' ye'er clubs. Th' man that has th' smallest little boy it counts him two. If th' little boy has th' rickets, it counts th' man in th' carredge three. The little boys is called caddies; but Clarence Heaney that tol' me all this — he belongs to th' Foorth Wa-ard Goluf an' McKinley Club — said what th' little boys calls th' players'd not be fit f'r to repeat.

"Well, whin ye dhrive up to th' tea grounds" —

"Th' what?" demanded Mr. Hennessy.

"Th' tea grounds, that's like th' homeplate in base-ball or ordherin' a piece iv chalk in a game iv spoil five. Its th' be-ginnin' iv ivrything. Whin ye get to th' tea grounds, ye step out, an' have ye're hat irned be th' caddie. Thin ye'er man that ye're goin' aginst comes up, an' he asks ye, 'Do you know Pot-ther Pammer?' Well, if ye don't know Potther Pammer, it's all up with ye: ye lose two points. But ye come right back at him with an' upper cut: 'Do ye live on th' Lake Shore dhrive?' If he doesn't, ye have him in th' nine hole. Ye needn't play with him anny more. But, if ye do play with him, he has to spot three balls. If he's a good man an' shifty on his feet, he'll counter be askin' ye where ye spend th' summer. Now ye can't tell him that ye spent th' summer with wan hook on th' free lunch an' another on th' ticker tape, an' so ye go back three. That needn't discourage ye at all, at all. Here's yer chance to mix up, an' ye ask him if he was iver in Scotland. If he wasn't, it counts ye five. Thin ye tell him that ye had an aunt wanst that heerd th' Jook iv Argyle talk in a phonograph; an,' onless he comes back an' shoots it into ye that he was wanst run over be th' Prince iv Wales, ye have him groggy. I don't know whether th' Jook iv Argyle or th' Prince iv Wales counts f'r most. They're like th' right an' left bower iv thrumps. Th' best players is called scratch-men."

"What's that f'r?" Mr. Hennessy asked.

"It's a Scotch game," said Mr. Dooley, with a wave of his hand. "I wonder how it come out to-day. Here's th' pa-aper. Let me see. McKinley at Canton. Still there. He niver cared to wandher fr'm his own fireside. Collar-button men f'r th' goold standard. Statues iv Heidelback, Ickleheimer an' Company to be erected in Washington. Another Vanderbilt weddin'. That sounds like goluf, but it ain't. Newport society livin' in Mrs. Potther Pammer's cellar. Green-goods men declare f'r honest money. Anson in foorth place some more. Pianny tuners f'r McKinley. Li Hung Chang smells a rat. Abner McKinley supports th' goold standard. Wait a minyit. Here it is: 'Goluf in gay attire.' Let me see. H'm. 'Foozled his aproach,' — nasty thing. 'Topped th' ball.' 'Three up an' two to play.' Ah, here's the scoor. 'Among those prisint were Messrs. an' Mesdames'' —

"Hol' on!" cried Mr. Hennessy, grabbing the paper out of his friend's hands. "That's thim that was there."

"Well," said Mr. Dooley, decisively, "that's th' goluf scoor."

ON THE HIGHER BASEBALL

"D'ye iver go to a base-ball game?" asked Mr. Hennessy.

"Not now," said Mr. Dooley. "I haven't got th' intellick f'r it. Whin I was a young fellow nawthin' plazed me betther thin to go out to th' ball grounds, get a good cosy seat in th' sun, take off me collar an' coat an' buy a bottle iv pop, not so much, mind ye, f'r th' refrishment, because I niver was much on pop, as to have something handy to reprove th' empire with whin he give an eeronyous decision. Not only that, me boy, but I was a fine amachure ballplayer mesilf. I was first baseman iv th' Prairie Wolves whin we beat th' nine iv Injine Company five be a scoor iv four hundherd an' eight to three hundherd an' twinty-five. It was very close. Th' game started just afther low mass on a Sundah mornin' an' was called on account iv darkness at th' end iv th' fourth inning. I knocked th' ball over th' fence into Donovan's coal yard no less thin twelve times. All this talk about this here young fellow Baker makes me smile. Whin I was his age I wudden't count annything but home-runs. If it wasn't a home-run I'd say: 'Don't mark it down' an' go back an' have another belt at th' ball. Thim were th' days.

"We usen't to think base-ball was a science. No man was very good at it that was good at annything else. A young fellow that had a clear eye in his head an' a sthrong pair iv legs undher him an' that was onaisy in th' close atmosphere iv th' school room, an' didn't like th' pro-fissyon iv plumbing was like as not to join a ball team. He come home in th' fall with a dimon in his shirt front an' a pair iv hands on him that looked like th' boughs iv a three that's been sthruck be lightenin' an' he was th' hero in th' neighborhood till his dimon melted an' he took to drivin' a thruck. But 'tis far different nowadays. To be a ball-player a man has to have a joynt intilleck. Inside baseball, th' pa-apers calls it, is so deep that it'd give brain fever to a pro-fissor iv asthronomy to thry to figure it out. Each wan iv these here mathymatical janiuses has to carry a thousand mysteeryous signals in his head an' they're changed ivry day an' sometimes in th' middle iv th' game. I'm so sorry f'r th' poor fellows. In th' old days whin they were through with th' game they'd maybe sthray over to th' Dutchman's f'r a pint iv beer. Now they hurry home to their study an' spind th' avnin' poorin' over books iv allgibera an' thrigynomethry.

"How do I know? Hogan was in here last night with an article on th' 'Mysthries iv base-ball.' It's be a larned man. Here it is: Th' ordhinary observer or lunk-head who knows nawthin' about base-ball excipt what he larned be playin' it, has no idee that th' game as played to-day, is wan iv th' most inthricate sciences known to mankind. In th' first place th' player must have an absolute masthry iv th' theery iv ballistic motion. This is especially thrue iv th' pitcher. A most exact knowledge in mathymatics is required f'r th' position. What is vulgarly known as th' spit-ball on account iv th' homely way in which th' op'rator procures his effects is in fact a solution iv wan iv th' most inthricate problems in mechanics. Th' purpose iv th' pitcher is to project th' projectyle so that at a pint between his position an' th' batsman th' tindincy to pro-ceed on its way will be countheracted be an impulse to return whence it come. Th' purpose iv th' batsman is, afther judgin' be scientific methods th' probable coorse or thrajecthry iv th' missile to oppose it with sufficyent foorce at th' proper moment an' at th' most effi-cient point, first to retard its forward movement, thin to correct th' osseylations an' fin'ly to propel it in a direction approx-imately opposite fr'm its original progress. This, I am in-formed, is technically known as 'bustin' th' ball on th' nose (or bugle).' In a gr-reat number iv cases which I observed th' ex-periment iv th' batsman failed an' th' empire was obliged so to declare, th' ball havin' actually crossed th' plate but eluded th' (intended) blow. In other cases where no blow was attimpted or aven meditated I noted that th' empire erred an' in gin'ral I must deplore an astonishin' lack in thrained scientific observa-tion on th' part iv this officyal. He made a number iv grievous blundhers an' I was not surprised to larn fr'm a gintleman who set next to me that he (th' empire) had spint th' arly part iv his life as a fish in the Mammoth Cave iv Kentucky. I thried me best to show me disapproval iv his unscientific an' infamous methods be hittin' him over th' head with me umbrella as he left th' grounds. At th' requist iv th' editor iv th' magazine I in-therviewed Misther Bugs Mulligan th' pitcher iv th' Kangaroos afther th' game. I found th' cillybrated expert in th' rotundy iv th' Grand Palace Hotel where he was settin' with other players polishin' his finger nails. I r-read him my notes on th' game an' he expressed his approval addin' with a show at laste iv enthusyasm: 'Bo, ye have a head like a dhrum.' I requested him to sign th' foregoin' statement but he declined remarkin' that th' last time he wrote his name he sprained his wrist an' was out iv the game f'r a week.

"What'd I be doin' at th' likes iv a game like that? I'd come away with a narvous headache. No, sir, whin I take a day off, I take a day off. I'm not goin' to a baseball game. I'm goin' to take a bag iv peanuts an' spind an afthernoon at th' chimical labrytory down at th' colledge where there's something goin' on I can undhrstand."

"Oh, sure," said Mr. Hennessy, "if 'twas as mysteryous as all that how cud Tom Donahue's boy Petie larn it that was fired fr'm th' Brothers School because he cuddn't add?"

"Well, I dinnaw," said Mr. Dooley, "I thought iv it th' last time he was in here. I'd been readin' an article be Pro-fissor Slapgood an' I har'ly knew how to addhress th' young scientist though 'tis not so many years since I chased him away fr'm in front iv th' place with th' hose. I'd lost thrack iv him since he left home so I says: 'I suppose ye've studied hard,'' says I, 'since I seen ye last.' I says, 'How long a coorse iv science did ye take befure ye enthered th' pro-fissyon?' seys I. 'Put 'em lower,' seys he. 'Th' sun's in me eyes,' he seys. 'Well,' says I, 'where did ye larn base-ball?' I says. 'In th' back yard with a bed slat an' a woolen ball,' he says. 'Thin it isn't thrue ye wint to Heidleberg whin ye left here?' says I. 'I niver heerd iv th' team. I wint as substichoot sicond base on th' Baryboo nine an' thin was thraded to Cedar Rapids,' he says. 'This here pa-aper,' seys I, 'seys ye pitch a wonderful ball that ye prejooce be disturbin' th' relations iv th' radyus iv th' ball to th' cir- cumference,' seys I. 'How about it?' 'It's thrue,' seys he. 'He's thryin' to tell ye in simple language about th' ol' spitter. Ye see it's this way, ol' hoss. On some days I can peg it so it crosses the turkey like a poached egg an' Ty Cobb cuddn't hit it with a snow-shovel. That's th' day I've got th' smoke onto it. Thin

another day whin I feel just as good, ivrything I toss across
looks like a thrunk covered with electhric lights. What's th'
name iv that fellow, that wrote th' article ye was readin'?' says
he. 'What d'ye want to know f'r?' says I. 'I want to find out
how I do it whin I do it an' why I don't do it whin I don't,'
says he. I ast him about th' science iv battin'; he said it was in
hittin' on'y th' good wans. His idee iv th' mathymaticks iv
fieldin' was niver to thry to catch a ground ball with th' ankle
or a fly ball with th' nose. 'Whin,' says I, 'd'ye pitch best?' 'A
day or two,' says he, 'befure I sign me conthract,' he seys. I
asked about his thrainin'. It is simple but severe. Afther
breakfast he goes to dinner. His dinner is usually intherupted
in th' middle iv the fifth pie be th' summons to th' game. Afther th' game he goes to supper. Afther supper he sits in a
rockin' chair in front iv th' hotel till th' manager goes to bed
whin him an' th' other athleets sojourn to a rathskellar. He is
invaryably in bed befure th' manager gets up. In return f'r all
their sufferin' these heroes ar-re threated like white slaves. His
sal'ry is on'y nine thousan' dollars a year an' f'r this he is often
compelled to pitch ev'ry other week.

"That's all I cud get out iv him an' there ye ar-re. I know no
more about th' subjeck now at th' end iv me investigation thin
I did before.

"Annyhow 'tis a gr-rand game, Hinnissy, whether 'tis played
th' way th' pro-fissor thinks or th' way Petie larned to play it in
th' back yard an' I shuddent wondher if it's th' way he's still
playin'. Th' two gr-eat American spoorts are a good deal alike
— pollyticks an' base-ball. They're both played be pro-
fissyonals, th' teams ar-re r-run be fellows that cudden't throw
a base-ball or stuff a ballot-box to save their lives an' ar-re on'y
intherested in countin' up th' gate receipts, an' here ar-re we
settin' out in th' sun on th' bleachin' boords, payin' our good
money f'r th' spoort, hot an' uncomfortable but happy, injying
ivry good play, hootin' ivry bad wan, knowin' nawthin' about
th' inside play an' not carin', but all jinin' in th' cry iv 'Kill th'
empire.' They're both grand games.''

"Speakin' iv pollyticks," said Mr. Hennessy, "who d'ye think'll be ilicted?"

"Afther lookin' th' candydates over," said Mr. Dooley, "an' studyin' their qualifications carefully I can't thruthfully say that I see a prisidintial possibility in sight."

FOOTBALL

"Ye see," said Mr. Dooley, "when 'tis done be la-ads that wur-ruks at it an' has no other occupation it's football, an' whin it's done in fun an' be way iv joke it's disorderly conduct, assault an' batthery an' rite."

Mr. Dooley had been explaining the pious Thanksgiving exercise, and that was his conclusion. He went on: "Still, ye know, if it wasn't f'r football they'd be no Thanksgivin' Day, an' if they wasn't a Thanksgivin' Day they'd be no chanst f'r Big Steve to issue a pro-clamation fr'm Wash'nton. I niver wint much on thim proclamations annyhow. They come to this: 'Whereas I've had a good job at fifty thousan' dollars a year f'r four years an' th' ilictions come my way an' I don't have to wurruk anny more as long as I live, therefore, those iv ye that have gone hungry an' need clothes f'r th' childher an' got on th' short side iv politics three weeks ago, praise Gawd fr'm whom my blessin's flow or I'll r-run ye in.' I wondher what Bryan's got to be thankful f'r! Mebbe it is that afther th' ice wagon r-run over him it didn't back down on him.

"Be that as it may, I'd give th' eye out iv me head to see th' first Thanksgivin' on Plymouth rock. It was a cold an' frosty mornin', an', as Bill Nugent says iv it, th' ocean waves leaped high again th' stern an' rock-bound grandstand. Prom-ply at il-iven o'clock th' two teams lined up. Cotton Mather, th' demon halfback captain iv th' Lambs, won th' toss an' took th' ball. Th' first play was a r-run around th' end be Praisegod Simpson, but he was downed in his thracks be Preserved Fish, th' terrific fullback iv th' Arks. A revolving wedge was thin thried again th' center f'r a gain iv five yards. Following this up Jawn

Eliot, th' frightful tackle, made a hole bechune Canned Salmon an' Elihu Bradberry f'r a gain iv three yards. On th' next play Cotton Mather fumbled an' th' ball wint to th' Arks. A series iv frightful center r-rushes followed an' slowly but surely th' ball was carrid down to'rd th' Lambs' goold. 'Tear 'em into ribbons,' roared Jawn Eliot, as th' Arks again an' again broke through th' defense. Cotton Mather urged his men to stand together, an' fin'lly they succeeded in holdin' their opponents. Then th' signal was given f'r a kick. Th' punt was accurate, but th' ball fell into Cotton Mather's hands. Honest ol' Cotton was there, all right. With th' inergy bor-rn iv despair he started down th' field, protected be th' superb tacklin' iv Bradbury Standish, Holy Smoke an' other saints. Th' gigantic Arks thried to stop him, but he hurled thim to wan side or th' other, breakin' collar bones an' ribs an' th' tin commandmints as he wint. Down th' field he tore like a steam ingine that he knew nothin' about, his long hair flyin' in th' air, his sweater in ribbons, th' mud rainin' fr'm his heels. At last there was on'y wan man bechune him an' th' pricious an' valyable goold. That was Preserved Fish, th' demonyac fullback. Th' hearts iv th' Ark rooters rose to their throats as th' two men come together. Wud Cotton be stopped be Preserved or wud he make a sucker iv Fish? was th' question ivry wan asked himsilf. Th' darin' fullback blew at his man like a tiger an' grabbin' him be his ankles threw him heavily forward. 'Down,' roared th' spectators. 'Not on ye'er Westminster confession,' roared Cotton, as playfully kickin' th' demonyac child iv iniquity in th' face he dashed on an' scored a touchdown amid th' r-roars iv th' inthrested spectators. Th' Lambs thin gathered in th' centher iv th' field an' give their well-known cry: 'Ivry time we buck th' line we go, we go,' to th' chune iv th' long meter doxology.

"What ar-re ye givin' us?" asked Mr. Hennessy who had listened to the fancy sketch with much bewilderment displayed on his face. "Thim puritans didn't know anny more about football thin about—about pin pool."

"Ye'er mistaken, Hinnissy," returned Mr. Dooley calmly.

"It's a puritan custom, as ye'd know if ye r-read th' histhry iv th' people that you an' I an' Billy Lorimer an' Ole Oleson is descinded fr'm. It's to honor th' la-ads that founded th' counthry an' whose spirit r-runs it now on Sundays an' holidays, that th' people cillybrate it with th' pious customs iv their ancistors. If that there young woman Priscilla what-d'ye-call-her wasn't out on top iv th' tally-ho seein' her lover sustainin' compound fractures, she was no thrue puritan ancestress iv mine, an' I'll have to back to where I was befure th' Frinch got licked be th' Proosians an' claim Jones of Ark on me father's side.

"On'y we're not allowed f'r to cillybrate th' day properly south iv th' river an' wist iv th' thracks. Downtown it's football; out here it's th' Irish killin' each other. Downtown th' spectators sees it f'r a dollar a piece; out here it costs th' spectators ne'er a cent, but th' players has to pay tin dollars an' costs."

ON WOMEN AND ATHLETICS

"We're gettin' to be th' gr-reatest spoortin' nation in th' wurruld," said Mr. Hennessy, who had been laboring through pages of athletic intelligence which he could not understand.

"Oh, so we ar-re," said Mr. Dooley. "An' I wondher does it do us anny good. 'Tis impoorted fr'm th' English. They have a sayin' over there that th' jook iv Wellinton said first or somebody said f'r him an' that's been said a number iv times since, that th' battle iv Watherloo was won on th' playin' fields iv Eton, that bein' a school where th' youth iv England an' Noo York is sint f'r idjycation. It was not. Th' battle iv Watherloo was won on th' potato fields iv Wexford an' th' bog patches iv Connock, that's where 't was won. Th' Fr-rinch arre a good fightin' people an' a Fr-rinchman cudden't hit a goluf ball with a scoop shovel. Th' Germans is a hardy race an' they thrain on Wesphalyan ham an' Boodweiser an' the' on'y exercise they have is howlin' at a sangerfest. Th' Rooshyans is a tur-rble crowd an' they get their strenth by standin' on th' corner askin' if ye have anny ol' clothes ye'd like to seel or be matchin' kopecks f'r th' vodkies. Ar-re we anny betther, tell me, f'r bein' th' high tinnis experts, th' intherprisin' rowsmen, th' champeen yachters iv th' wurruld thin we were whin we were on'y th' champeen puddlers, milkers, ploughers, an' sewin' machine agents? Why is England losin' her supreemacy, Hinnissy? Because Englishmen get down to their jobs at iliven o'clock figurin' a goluf scoor on their cuffs an' lave at a quarther to twelve on a bicycle. We bate thim because 't was th' habit iv our joynt iv commerce f'r to be up with th' cock an' down to th' damper befure th' cashier come; an' in his office all day long in his shirt sleeves an' settin' on th' safe till th' las' man had gone. Now, if ye call up wan iv these captains iv industhree at wan o'clock iv a Saturdah afthernoon, th' office boy answers th' tillyphone. Th' Titan iv Commerce is out in a set iv green an' blue knee breeches, batin' a hole in a sand pile an' cur-rsin' th' evil fate that made him a millyionaire whin nature intinded him f'r a goluf champeen. Ye can't keep ye'er eye on th' ball an' on th' money at th' same time. Ye've got to be wan thing or another in this wurruld. I niver knew a good card player or a great spoortsman that cud do much iv annything else. They used to tell me that Napoleon Bonyparte, th' imp'ror iv th' Frinch, was a champeen chess player, but Hogan says he was on'y good because annybody that bate him might as well do down an' be measured f'r his ball an' chain. A rale high class chess player, without room f'r annything else in his head, cud close his eyes, an' put th' dhrinks on Napoleon Bonyparte in three moves. Did ye iver hear iv Grant wearin' anny medals f'r a hundherd yard dash? Did annywan iver tell ye iv th' number iv base hits made be Abraham Lincoln? Is there anny record iv George Wash'nton doin' a turn on a thrapeze or Thomas Jifferson gettin' th' money f'r throwin' th' hammer?

"In me younger days 't was not considhered rayspictable f'r to be an athlete. An athlete was always a man that was not sthrong enough f'r wurruk. Fractions dhruv him fr'm school an' th' vagrancy laws dhruv him to base-ball. We used to go out to th' ball game to see him sweat an' to throw pop bottles at th' empire but none iv his fam'ly was iver proud iv him except his younger brother. A good seat on th' bleachers, a bottle handy f'r a neefaryous decision at first base an' a bag iv crackerjack was as far as iver I got tow'rd bein' a spoortin' character an' look at me now! Ye can't have ye'er strength an' use it too, Hinnissy. I gredge th' power I waste in walkin' upstairs or puttin' on me specs."

"But 't is good f'r th' women," said Mr. Hennessy.

"Is it, faith?" said Mr. Dooley. "Well, it may be, but it's no good f'r th' woman f'r th' men. I don't know annything that cud be more demoralizin' thin to be marrid to a woman that cud give me a sthroke a shtick at goluf. 'Tis goin' to be th' roon iv fam'ly life. 'Twill break up th' happy home. I'm a man, we'll say, that's down town fr'm th' arly mornin' bendin' over a ledger an' thryin' to thrap a dollar or two to keep th' landlord fr'm th' dure. I dispise athletes. I see that all th' men that have a metallic rattle whin they get on a movin' sthreet car are pounds overweight an' wud blow up if they jogged around th' corner. Well, I come home at night an' no matther how I've been 'Here-you-d' all day, I feel in me heart that I'm th' big thing there. What makes me feel that way, says ye? 'Tis th' sinse iv physical supeeryority. Me wife is smarter thin I am. She's had nawthin' to do all day but th' housewurruk an' puttin' in th' coal an' studyin' how she can make me do something I don't want to do that I wud want to do if she didn't want me to do it. She's thrained to th' minyit in havin' her own way. Her mind's clearer, mine bein' full iv bills iv ladin'; she can talk betther an' more frequent; she can throw me fam'ly in me face an' whin har-rd put to it, her starry eyes can gleam with tears that I think ar-re grief, but she knows diff'rent. An' I give in. But I've won, just th' same. F'r down in me heart I'm sayin': 'Susette, if I were not a gentleman that wud scorn to smash a lady, they'd be but wan endin' to this fracas. Th' right to th' pint iv th' jaw, Susette.' I may niver use it, d'ye mind.

We may go on livin' together an' me losin' a battle ivry day f'r fifty year. But I always know 'tis there an' th' knowledge makes me a proud an' haughty man. I feel me arm as I go out to lock th' woodshed again, an' I say to mesilf: 'Oh, woman, if I iver cut loose that awful right.' An' she knows it too. If she didn't she wudden't waste her tears. Th' sinse of her physical infeeryority makes her weep. She must weep or she must fight. Most anny woman wud rather do battle thin cry, but they know it's no use.

"But now how is it? I go home at night an' I'm met at th' dure be a female joynt. Me wife's th' champeen lady golufess iv th' Ivy Leaf Goluf club; th' finest oarslady on th' canal; a tinnis player that none can raysist without injury. She can ride a horse an' I cudden't stay on a merry-go-round without clothespins. She can box a good welter weight an' she's got medals f'r th' broad jump. Th' on'y spoorts she isn't good at is cookin' an' washin'. This large lady, a little peevish because she's off her dhrive, meets me at th' dure an' begins issuin' or- dhers befure I have me shoes off. 'Tis just th' same as if I was back on th' hoist. She doesn't argy, she doesn't weep. She jus' says 'Say you,' an' I'm off on th' bound. I look her over an' say I to mesilf: 'What's th' good? I cudden't cross that guard,' an' me reign is ended. I'm back to th' ranks iv th' prolitory.

"It won't do, Hinnissy. It's a blow at good governmint. 'T will disrupt th' home. Our fathers was r-right. They didn't risk their lives an' limbs be marryin' these female Sharkeys. What they wanted was a lady that they'd find settin' at home whin they arrived tired fr'm th' chase, that played th' harp to thim an' got their wampum away fr'm thim more like a church fair thin like a safe blower. In th' nex' eighty or ninety years if I make up me mind to lave this boistherous life an' settle down, th' lady I'll rayquist to double me rent an' divide me borrowin' capacity will wear no medals f'r athletic spoorts. F'r, Hinnissy, I'm afraid I cud not love a woman I might lose a fight to."

"I see be th' pa-aper," said Mr. Hennessy, "th' athletic girl is goin' out, what iver that means."

"She had to," said Mr. Dooley, "or we wud."

CHAPTER XI

WOMEN, MINORITIES, AND OTHER TROUBLEMAKERS

In his youth—he was only 26 when he began writing dialect essays—Dunne had a tendency to take the women's movement less than seriously, bowing to the conventional wisdom that women didn't need rights when they had privileges. As he matured, this changed, in no small part because Mrs. Dunne was an avid feminist.

He wrote several essays on racial problems when most columnists chose to leave the topic alone, and his support of Theodore Roosevelt was nothing short of courageous during the storm that broke when the President invited Booker T. Washington to dine at the White House (the first black ever to do so as a guest).

His columns on immigration and the third world were similarly on target. With regard to the former, he used Dooley to point out how ludicrous it was for a nation of recent immigrants to fear other newcomers. As to the latter, he pointed out that we started it when we sent Commodore Perry in to open the door to Japan. "Th' throuble is, whin the gallant Commodore kicked open th' door, we didn't go in. They come out." Dunne predicted war with Japan almost forty years before it happened, as well as the problems that would arise from Japan's economic aggressiveness.

Now, as then, the servant girl problem is of concern to only the privileged few, but the unwillingness of even the most recent arrivals to work for low pay and in difficult or unpleasant surroundings is the subject of articles and a topic of conversation among those unwilling to pay a living wage. Congressional arguments over immigration policy rage on, with the immigrant all too frequently receiving the same welcome that awaited Mr. Dooley — open arms that ended in a clinch.

THE SERVANT GIRL PROBLEM

When this essay was written, the Congress was debating whether to extend the so-called open door policy to China, as well as to whether or not to seat a much-married Mormon Congressman.

"Whin Congress gets through expellin' mimbers that believes so much in mathrimony that they carry it into ivry relation iv life an' opens th' dure iv Chiny so that an American can go in there as free as a Chinnyman can come into this refuge iv th' opprissed iv th' wurruld, I hope 'twill turn its attention to th' gr-reat question now confrontin' th' nation—th' question iv what we shall do with our hired help. What shall we do with thim?"

"We haven's anny," said Mr. Hennessy.

"No," said Mr. Dooley. "Ar-rchey Road has no servant girl problem. Th' rule is ivry woman her own cook an' ivry man his own futman, an' be th' same token we have no poly-gamy problem an' no open dure problem an' no Ph'lippeen problem. Th' on'y problem in Ar-rchey Road is how many times does round steak go into twelve at wan dollar-an-a-half a day. But east iv th' r-red bridge, Hinnissy, wan iv th' most cryin' issues iv th' hour is: 'What shall we do with our hired help?' An' if Congress don't take hold iv it we ar're a rooned people.

"'Tis an ol' problem an' I've seen it arise an' shake its gory head ivry few years whiniver th' Swede popylation got wurruk an' begun to get married, thus rayjoocin' th' visible supply iv help. But it seems 'tis deeper thin that. I see be letters in th' pa-apers that servants is insolent, an' that they won't go to wurruk onless they like th' looks iv their employers, an' that they rayfuse to live in th' counthry. Why anny servant shud rayfuse to live in th' counthry is more thin I can see. Ye'd think that this disreputable class'd give annything to lave th' crowded

tinimints iv a large city where they have frinds be th' hundherds an' know th' polisman on th' bate an' can go out to
hateful dances an' moonlight picnics—ye'd think these un-
forchnate slaves'd be delighted to live in Mulligan's subdivi-
sion, amid th' threes an' flowers an' bur-rds. Gettin' up at four
o'clock in th' mornin' th' singin' iv th' full-throated alarm
clock is answered be an invisible chorus iv songsters, as
Shakespere says, an' ye see th' sun rise over th' hills as ye go
out to carry in a ton iv coal. All day long ye meet no wan as ye
thrip over th' coalscuttle, happy in ye'er tile an' ye'er heart is
enlivened be th' thought that th' childher in th' front iv th'
house ar-re growin' sthrong on th' fr-resh counthry air. Besides
they'se always cookin' to do. At night ye can set be th' fire an'
improve ye'er mind be r-readin' half th' love story in th' part iv
th' pa-aper that th' cheese come home in, an' whin ye're
through with that, all ye have to do is to climb a ladder to th'
roof an' fall through th' skylight an' ye're in bed.

"But wud ye believe it, Hinnissy, manny iv these misguided
women rayfuse f'r to take a job that ain't in a city. They prefer
th' bustle an' roar iv th' busy marts iv thrade, th' sthreet car,
th' saloon on three corners an' th' church on wan, th' pa-apers
ivry mornin' with pitchers iv th' s'ciety fav'rite that's just
thrown up a good job at Armours to elope with th' well-known
club-man who used to be yard-masther iv th' three B's,
G.L.&N., th' shy peek into th' dhry-goods store, an' other base
luxuries, to a free an' healthy life in th' counthry between iliven p.m. an' four a.m. Wensdahs and Sundahs. 'Tis worse
thin that, Hinnissy, f'r whin they ar-re in th' city they seem to
dislike their wurruk an' manny iv thim ar-re givin' up splindid
jobs with good large families where they have no chanst to
spind their salaries, if they dhraw thim, an' takin' places in
shops, an' gettin' marrid an' adoptin' other devices that will
give thim th' chanst f'r to wear out their good clothes. 'Tis a
horrible situation. Riley th' conthractor dhropped in here th'
other day in his horse an' buggy on his way to the drainage
canal an' he was all wurruked up over th' question. 'Why,' he

says, "'tis scand'lous th' way servants act,' he says. 'Mrs. Riley
has hystrics,' he says. 'An' ivry two or three nights whin I come
home,' he says, 'I have to win a fight again' a cook with a stove
lid befure I can move me family off th' fr-ront stoop,' he says,
'We threat thim well too,' he says. 'I gave th' las' wan we had
fifty cints an' a cookbook at Chris'mas an' th' next day she left
befure breakfast,' he says. 'What naytionalties do he hire?' says
I. 'I've thried thim all,' he says, 'an',' he says, 'I'll say this in
shame,' he says, 'that th' Irish ar-re th' worst,' he says. 'Well,'
says I, 'ye need have no shame,' I says, 'fr 'tis on'y th' people
that ar-re good servants that'll niver be masthers,' I says. 'Th'
Irish ar-re no good as servants because they ar-re too good,' I
says. 'Th' Dutch ar-re no good because they ain't good
enough. No matther how they start they get th' noodle habit. I
had wan, wanst, an' she got so she put noodles in me tay,' I
says. 'Th' Swedes ar-re all right but they always get marrid th'
sicond day. Ye'll have a polisman at th' dure with a warrant fr
th' arrist iv ye'er cook if ye hire a Boheemyan,' I says.
'Coons'd be all right but they're liable fr to hand ye'er food in
ragtime, an' if ye ordher pork-chops fr dinner an' th' hall is
long, 'tis little ye'll have to eat whin the platter's set down,' I
says. 'No,' says I, 'they'se no naytionality now livin' in this
counthry that're nathral bor-rn servants,' I says. 'If ye want to
save throuble,' I says, 'Ye'll import ye'er help. They'se a race
iv people livin' in Cinthral Africa that'd be jus' right. They
niver sleep, they can carry twice their weight on their backs,
they have no frinds, they wear no clothes, they can't read, they
can't dance an' they don't dhrink. Th' fact is they're
thoroughly oneddycated. If ye cud tache thim to cook an' take
care iv childher they'd be th' best servants,' says I. 'An' what
d'ye call thim?' says he. 'I frget,' says I. An' he wint away
mad."

"Sure an' he's a nice man to be talkin' iv servants," said Mr.
Hennessy. "He was a gintleman's man in th' ol' counthry an' I
used to know his wife whin she wurruked fr——"

"S-sh," said Mr. Dooley. "They're beyond that now. Besides

they speak fr'm experyence. An' mebbe that's th' throuble. We're always harder with our own kind thin with others. 'Tis I that'd be th' fine cinsor iv a bartinder's wurruk. Th' more ye ought to be a servant ye'ersilf th' more difficult 'tis f'r ye to get along with servants. I can holler to anny man fr'm th' top iv a buildin' an' make him tur-rn r-round, but if I come down to th' sthreet where he can see I ain't anny bigger thin he is, an' holler at him, 'tis twinty to wan if he tur-rns r-round he'll hit me in th' eye. We have a servant girl problem because, Hinnissy, it isn't manny years since we first begun to have servant girls. But I hope Congress'll take it up. A smart Congress like th' wan we have now ought to be able to spare a little time fr'm its preparation iv new jims iv speech f'r th' third reader an' rig up a bill that'd make keepin' house a recreation while so softenin' th' spirit iv th' haughty sign iv a noble race in th' kitchen that cookin' buckwheat cakes on a hot day with th' aid iv a bottle iv smokeless powdher'd not cause her f'r to sind a worthy man to his office in slippers an' without a hat."

"Ah," said Mr. Hennessy, the simple democrat. "It wud be all r-right if women'd do their own cookin'."

"Well," said Mr. Dooley. "'Twud be a return to Jacksonyan simplicity, an' 'twud be a gr-reat thing f'r th' resthrant business."

ON THE NEW WOMAN

"Molly Donahue have up an' become a new woman!

"It's been a good thing f'r ol' man Donahue, though, Jawn. He shtud ivrything that mortal man cud stand. He seen her appearin' in th' road wearin' clothes that no lady shud wear an' ridin' a bicycle; he was humiliated whin she demanded to vote; he put his pride under his ar-rm an' ma-arched out iv th' house whin she committed assault-an'-batthry on th' piannah. But he's got to th' end iv th' rope now. He was in here las' night, how-come-ye-so, with his hat cocked over his eye an' a look iv risolution on his face; an' whin he left me, he says, says he,

'Dooley,' he says, 'I'll conquir, or I'll die,' he says.

"It's been comin f'r months, but it on'y bust on Donahue las' week. He'd come home at night tired out, an' afther supper he was pullin' off his boots, whin Mollie an' th' mother begun talkin' about th' rights iv females. ''Tis th' era iv th' new woman,' says Mollie. 'Ye're right,' says th' mother. 'What d'ye mean be the new woman?' says Donahue, holdin' his boot in his hand. 'Th' new woman,' says Mollie, ''ll be free fr'm th' opprision iv man,' she says. 'She'll wurruk out her own way, without help or hinderance,' she says. 'She'll wear what clothes she wants,' she says, 'an' she'll be no man's slave,' she says. 'They'll be no such thing as givin' a girl in marredge to a clown an' makin' her dipindant on his whims,' she says. 'Th' women'll earn their own livin',' she says; 'an' mebbe,' she says, 'th' men'll stay at home an' dredge in th' house wurruk,' she says. 'A-ho,' says Donahue, 'An' that's th' new woman, is it?' he says. An' he said no more that night.

"But th' nex' mornin' Mrs. Donahue an' Mollie come to his dure. 'Get up,' says Mrs. Donahue, 'an' bring in some coal,' she says. 'Ye drowsy man, ye'll be late f'r ye'er wurruk.' 'Divvle th' bit iv coal I'll fetch,' says Donahue. 'Go away an' lave me alone,' he says. 'Ye're inthruptin' me dreams.' 'What ails ye, man alive?' says Mrs. Donahue. 'Get up.' 'Go away,' says Donahue, 'an lave me slumber,' he says. 'Th' idee iv a couple iv big strong women like you makin' me wurruk f'r ye,' he says. 'Mollie'll bring in th' coal,' he says. 'An' as f'r you, Honoria, ye'd best see what there is in th' cupboord an' put it in ye'er dinner-pail,' he says. 'I heerd th' first whistle blow a minyit ago,' he says; 'an' there's a pile iv slag at th' mills that has to be wheeled off befure th' sup'rintindint comes around,' he says. 'Ye know ye can't afford to lose ye'er job with me in this dilicate condition,' he says. 'I'm going to sleep now,' he says. 'An', Mollie, do ye bring me in a cup iv cocoa an' a pooched igg at tin,' he says. 'I ixpect me music-teacher about that time. We have to take a wallop out iv Wagner an' Bootoven befure noon.' 'Th' Lord save us fr'm harm,' says

Mrs. Donahue. 'Th' man's clean crazy.' 'Divvle's th' bit,' says Donahue, wavin' his red flannel undhershirt in th' air. 'I'm the new man,' he says.

"Well, sir, Donahue said it flured thim complete. They didn't know what to say. Mollie was game, an' she fetched in th' coal; but Mrs. Donahue got nervous as eight o'clock come around. 'Ye're not goin' to stay in bed all day an' lose ye'er job,' she says. 'Th' 'ell with me job,' says Donahue. 'I'm not th' man to take wurruk whin they'se industhrees women with nawthin' to do,' he says. 'Show me th' pa-apers,' he says. 'I want to see where I can get an eighty-cint bonnet f'r two and a half.' He's that stubborn he'd've stayed in bed all day, but th' good woman weakened. 'Come,' she says, 'don't be foolish,' she says. 'Ye wudden't have th' ol' woman wurrukin' in th' mills,' she says. ''Twas all a joke,' she says. 'Oh-ho, th' ol' woman!' he says. 'Th' ol' woman! Well, that's a horse iv another color,' he says. 'An' I don't mind tellin' ye th' mills is closed down to-day, Honoria.' So he dhressed himsilf an' wint out; an' says he to Mollie, he says: 'Miss Newwoman,' says he, 'ye may find wurruk enough around th' house,' he says. 'An', if ye have time, ye might paint th' stoop,' he says. 'Th' ol' man is goin' to take th' ol' woman down be Halsted Sthreet' an' blow himsilf f'r a new shawl f'r her.'

"An' he's been that proud iv th' victhry that he's been a reg'lar customer f'r a week."

WOMAN SUFFRAGE

"I see be th' pa-apers that th' ladies in England have got up in their might an' demanded a vote."

"A what?" cried Mr. Hennessy.

"A vote," said Mr. Dooley.

"Th' shameless viragoes," said Mr. Hennessy. "What did they do?"

"Well, sir," said Mr. Dooley, "an immense concoorse iv for-ty iv thim gathered in London an' marched up to th' House iv

Commons, or naytional dormytory, where a loud an' almost universal snore proclaimed that a debate was ragin' over th' bill to allow English gintlemen to marry their deceased wife's sisters befure th' autopsy. In th' great hall iv Rufus some iv th' mightiest male intellects in Britain slept undher their hats while an impassioned orator delivererd a hem-stitched speech on th' subject iv th' day to th' attintive knees an' feet iv th' ministhry. It was into this here assimbly iv th' first gintlemen iv Europe that ye see on ye'er way to France that th' furyous females attimpted to enter. Undaunted be th' stairs iv th' building or th' rude jeers iv th' multichood, they advanced to th' very outside dures iv th' idifice. There an overwhelmin' force iv three polismen opposed thim. 'What d'ye want, mum?' asked the polis. 'We demand th' suffrage,' says th' commander iv th' army iv freedom.

"The brutal polis refused to give it to thim an' a desp'rate battle followed. Th' ladies fought gallantly, hurlin' cries iv 'Brute,' 'Monster,' 'Cheap,' et cethry, at th' constablry. Hat pins were dhrawn. Wan lady let down her back hair; another, bolder thin th' rest, done a fit on th' marble stairs; a third, p'raps rendered insane be sufferin' f'r a vote, sthruck a burly ruffyan with a Japanese fan on th' little finger iv th' right hand. Thin th' infuryated officers iv th' law charged on th' champeens iv liberty. A scene iv horror followed. Polismen seized ladies be th' arms and' led thim down th' stairs; others were carried out fainting by th' tyrants. In a few minyits all was over, an' nawthin' but three hundherd hairpins remained to mark th' scene iv slaughter. Thus, Hinnissy, was another battle f'r freedom fought an' lost."

"It sarves thim right," said Mr. Hennessy. "They ought to be at home tindin' th' babies."

"A thrue statement an' a sound argymint that appeals to ivry man. P'raps they havn't got any babies. A baby is a good substichoot f'r a ballot, an' th' hand that rocks th' cradle sildom has time f'r anny other luxuries. But why shud we give thim a vote, says I. What have they done to injye this impeeryal

suffrage that we fought an' bled f'r? Whin me forefathers were
followin' George Wash'nton an' sufferin' all th' hardships that
men endure campin' out in vacation time, what where th'
women doin'? They were back in Matsachoosetts milkin' th'
cow, mendin' socks, followin' th' plow, plantin' corn, keepin'
store, shoein' horses, an' pursooin' th' other frivvlous follies iv
th' fair but fickle sect. Afther th' war our brave fellows come
back to Boston an' as a reward f'r their devotion got a vote
apiece, if their wives had kept th' Pilgrim fathers that stayed at
home fr'm foreclosin' th' morgedge on their property. An'
now, be hivens, they want to share with us what we won.

"Why, they wudden't know how to vote. They think it's an
aisy job that anny wan can do, but it ain't. It's a man's wurruk,
an' a sthrong man's with a sthrong stomach. I don't know annything that requires what Hogan calls th' exercise iv manly
vigor more thin votin'. It's th' hardest wurruk I do in th' year.
I get up befure daylight an' thramp over to th' Timple iv
Freedom, which is also th' office iv a livery stable. Wan iv th'
judges has a cold in his head an' closes all th' windows.
Another judge has built a roarin' fire in a round stove an' is
cookin' red-hots on it. Th' room is lit with candles an'
karosene lamps, an' is crowded with pathrites who haven't
been to bed. At th' dure are two or three polismen that maybe
ye don't care to meet. Dock O'Leary says he don't know annything that'll exhaust th' air iv a room so quick as a polisman
in his winter unyform. All th' pathrites an', as th' pa-apers call
thim, th' high-priests iv this here sacred rite, ar-re smokin' th'
best seegars that th' token money iv our counthry can buy.

"In th' pleasant warmth iv th' fire, th' harness on th' walls
glows an' puts out its own peculiar aromy. Th' owner iv th'
sanchooary iv Liberty comes in, shakes up a bottle iv liniment
made iv carbolic acid, pours it into a cup an' goes out. Wan iv
th' domestic attindants iv th' guests iv th' house walks through
fr'm makin' th' beds. Afther a while th' chief judge, who
knows me well, because he shaves me three times a week, gives
me a contimchous stare, asks me me name an' a number iv

scand'lous questions about me age.

"I'm timpted to make an angry retort, whin I see th' polisman movin' nearer, so I take me ballot an' wait me turn in th' booth. They're all occupied be writhin' freemen, callin' in sthrangled voices f'r somewan to light th' candle so they'll be sure they ain't votin' th' prohybition ticket. Th' calico sheets over th' front iv th' booths wave an' ar-re pushed out like th' curtains iv a Pullman car whin a fat man is dhressin' inside while th' thrain is goin' r-round a curve. In time a freeman bursts through, with perspyration poorin' down his nose, hurls his suffrage at th' judge an' staggers out. I plunge in, sharpen an inch iv lead pencil be rendin' it with me teeth, mutilate me ballot at th' top iv th' dimmycratic column, an' run f'r me life.

"Cud a lady do that, I ask ye? No, sir, 'tis no job f'r th' fair. It's men's wurruk. Molly Donahue wants a vote, but though she cud bound Kamachatka as aisily as ye cud this percint, she ain't qualified f'r it. It's meant f'r gr-reat sturdy American pathrites like Mulkowsky th' Pollacky down th' sthreet. He don't know yet that he ain't votin' f'r th' King iv Poland. He thinks he's still over there pretindin' to be a horse instead iv a free American givin' an imytation iv a steam dhredge.

"On th' first Choosday afther th' first Monday in November an' April a man goes ar-round to his house, wakes him up, leads him down th' sthreet, an' votes him th' way ye'd wather a horse. He don't mind inhalin' th' air iv liberty in a livery stable. But if Molly Donahue wint to vote in a livery stable, th' first thing she'd do wud be to get a broom, sweep up th' flure, open th' windows, disinfect th' booths, take th' harness fr'm th' walls, an' hang up a pitcher iv Niagary be moonlight, chase out th' watchers an' polis, remove th' seegars, make th' judges get a shave, an' p'raps invalydate th' iliction. It's no job f'r her, an' I told her so.

"We demand a vote,' says she. 'All right,' says I, 'take mine. It's old, but it's trustworthy an' durable. It may look a little th' worse f'r wear fr'm bein' hurled again a republican majority in this counthry f'r forty years, but it's all right. Take my vote an' use it as ye please,' says I, 'an' I'll get an hour or two exthry sleep iliction day mornin',' says I. 'I've voted so often I'm tired iv it annyhow,' says I. 'But,' says I, 'why shud anny wan so young an' beautiful as ye want to do annything so foolish as to vote?' says I. 'Ain't we intilligent enough?' says she. 'Ye're too intilligent,' says I. 'But intilligence don't give ye a vote.'

" ' What does, thin,' says she. 'Well,' says I, 'enough iv ye at wan time wantin' it enough. How many ladies ar-re there in ye're Woman's Rights Club?' 'Twinty,' says she. 'Make it three hundherd,' says I, 'an' ye'll be on ye'er way. Ye'er mother doesn't want it, does she? No, nor ye'er sister Katie? No, nor ye'er cousin, nor ye'er aunt? All that iliction day means to thim is th' old man goin' off in th' mornin' with a light step an' fire in his eye, an' comin home too late at night with a dent in his hat, news-boys hollerin' exthries with th' news that fifty-four votes had been cast in th' third precint in th' sivinth ward at 8 o'clock, an' Packy an' Aloysius stealin' bar'ls fr'm th' groceryman f'r th' bone-fire. If they iver join ye an' make up their minds to vote, they'll vote. Ye bet they will.'

" 'Ye see, 'twas this way votin' come about. In th' beginnin' on'ly th' king had a vote, an' ivrybody else was a Chinyman or an Indyan. Th' king clapped his crown on his head an' wint down to th' pols, marked a cross at th' head iv th' column where his name was, an' wint out to cheer th' returns. Thin th' jooks got sthrong, an' says they: "Votin' seems a healthy exercise an' we'd like to thry it. Give us th' franchise or we'll do things to ye." An' they got it. Thin it wint down through th' earls an' th' markises an' th' rest iv th' Dooley fam'ly, till fin'lly all that was left iv it was flung to th' ign'rant mases like Hinnissy, because they made a lot iv noise an' threatened to set fire to th' barns.'

" 'An' there ye ar-re. Ye'll niver get it be askin' th' polis f'r it. No wan iver got his rights fr'm a polisman, an' be th' same token, there ar-re no rights worth havin' that a polisman can keep ye fr'm gettin'. Th' ladies iv London are followin' the right coorse, on'y there ain't enough iv thim. If there were forty thousand iv thim ar-rmed with hat pins an' prepared to plunge th' same into th' stomachs iv th' inimies iv female suffrage, an' if, instead iv faintin' in th' ar-rms iv th' constablry, they charged an' punctured thim an' broke their way into th' House iv Commons, an' pulled th' wig off the speaker, an' knocked th' hat over th' eyes iv th' prime ministher it wudden't be long befure some mimber wud talk in his sleep in their favor. Ye bet! If ye'er suffrage club was composed iv a hundhred thousand sturdy ladies it wudden't be long befure Bill O'Brien wud be sindin' ye a box iv chocolate creams f'r ye'er vote.'

" 'Some day ye may get a vote, but befure ye do I'll read this in th' pa-apers: "A hundhred thousand armed an' detarmined women invaded th' capital city to-day demandin' th' right to vote. They chased th' polis acrost th' Pottymac, mobbed a newspaper that was agin th' bill, an' tarred an' feathered Sinitor Glue, th' leader iv th' opposition. At 10 o'clock a rumor spread that th' Prisident wud veto th' bill, an' instantly a huge crowd iv excited females gathered in front of the White House, hurlin' rocks an' cryin' 'Lynch him!' Th' tumult was on'y quelled whin th' Prisident's wife appeared on th' balcony an' made a brief speech. She said she was a mimber iv th' local suffrage club, an' she felt safe in assuring her sisters that th' bill wud be signed. If nicissry, she wud sign it hersilf. (Cheers.) Th' Prisident was a little onruly, but he was frequently that way. Th' marrid ladies in th' aujeence wud undherstand. He meant nawthin'. It was on'y wan iv his tantrums. A little moral suasion wud bring him ar-round all right. At prisint th' Chief Magistrate was in th' kitchen with his daughter settin' on his head.

" 'Th' speech was received with loud cheers, an' th' mob proceeded down Pinnsylvanya Avnoo. Be noon all enthrances to th' capital were jammed. Congressmen attimptin' to enter were seized be th' hair iv th' head an' made to sign a pa-aper promisin' to vote right. Immejately afther th' prayer th' Hon'rable Clarence Gumdhrop iv Matsachoosettts offered th' suffrage bill f'r passage. 'Th' motion is out iv ordher,' began th' Speaker. At this minyit a lady standin' behind th' chair dhrove a darning needle through his coat tails. 'But,' continued th' Speaker,' reachin' behind him with an agnized expression, 'I will let it go annyhow.' 'Mr. Speaker, I protest,' began th' Hon'rable Attila Sthrong, 'I protest—' At this a perfeck tornado iv rage broke out in th' gall'ries. Inkwells, bricks, combs, shoes, smellin' bottles, hand mirrors, fans, an' powdher puffs were hurled at th' onforchnit mimber. In the midst iv th' confusion th' wife iv Congressman Sthrong cud be seen wavin' a par'sol over her head an' callin' out: 'I dare ye to come home to-night, polthroon.'

" 'Whin th' noise partially subsided, th' bold Congressman, his face livid with emotion, was heard to remark with a sob: 'I was on'y about to say I second th' motion, deary.' Th' bill was carried without a dissintin' voice, an' rushed over to th' Sinit. There it was opposed be Jeff Davis but afther a brief dialogue with th' leader iv th' suffrageites, he swooned away. Th' Sinit fin'lly insthructed th' clerk to cast th' unanimous vote f'r th' measure. To-night in th' prisince iv a vast multichood th' Prisident was led out be his wife. He was supported, or rather pushed, be two iv his burly daughters. He seemed much confused, an' his wife had to point out th' place where he was to sign. With tremblin' fingers he affixed his signature an' was led back.

" 'The night passed quietly. Th' sthreets were crowded all avenin' with good-natured throngs iv ladies, an' in front iv th' dry goods stores, which were illuminated f'r th' occasion, it was almost impossible to get through. Iv coorse there were th' usual riochous scenes in th' dhrug stores, where th' bibulous gathererd at th' sody-wather counthers an' cillybrated th' victory in lemon, vanilla, an' choc'late, some iv thim keepin' it up till 9 o'clock, or aven later.' "

" 'Whin that comes about, me child,' says I, 'ye may sheathe ye'er hat pins in ye'er millinary, f'r ye'll have as much right to vote as th' most ignorant man in th' ward. But don't ask f'r rights. Take thim. An' don't let anny wan give thim to ye. A right that is handed to ye f'r nawthin' has somethin' th' matther with it. It's more than likely it's on'y a wrong turned inside out,' says I. 'I didn't fight f'r th' rights I'm told I injye though to tell ye th' truth I injye me wrongs more; but some wan did. Some time some fellow was prepared to lay down his life, or betther still, th' other fellows', f'r th' right to vote.' "

"I believe ye're in favor iv it ye'ersilf," said Mr. Hennessy.

"Faith," said Mr. Dooley, "I'm not wan way or th' other. I don't care. What diff'rence does it make? I wudden't mind at all havin' a little soap an' wather, a broom an' a dusther applied to pollyticks. It wudden't do anny gr-reat harm if a man cudden't be illicted to office onless he kept his hair combed an' blacked his boots an' shaved his chin wanst a month. Annyhow, as Hogan says, I care not who casts th' votes iv me counthry so long as we can hold th' offices. An' there's on'y wan way to keep the women out iv office, an' that's to give thim a vote."

THE RISING OF THE SUBJECT RACES

"Ye'er frind Simpson was in here a while ago," said Mr. Dooley, "an' he was that mad."

"What ailed him?" asked Mr. Hennessy.

"Well," said Mr. Dooley, "it seems he wint into me frind Hip Lung's laundhry to get his shirt an' it wasn't ready. Followin' what Hogan calls immemoryal usage, he called Hip Lung such names as he cud remimber and thried to dhrag him around th' place be his shinin' braid. But instead iv askin' f'r mercy, as he ought to, Hip Lung swung a flatiron on him an' thin ironed out his spine as he galloped up th' stairs. He come to me f'r advice an' I advised him to see th' American consul. Who's th' American consul in Chicago now? I don't know. But Hogan, who was here at th' time, grabs him be th' hand an' says he: 'I congratulate ye, me boy,' he says. 'Ye have a chance to be wan iv th' first martyrs iv th' white race in th' gr-reat sthruggle that's comin' between thim an' th' smoked or tinted races iv th' wurruld,' he says. 'Ye'll be another Jawn Brown's body or Mrs. O'Leary's cow. Go back an' let th' Chink kill ye an' cinchries hence people will come with wreathes and ate hard-biled eggs on ye'er grave,' he says.

"But Simpson said he did not care to be a martyr. He said he was a retail grocer be pro-fissyon an' Hip Lung was a customer iv his, though he got most iv his vittles fr'm th' taxydermist up th' sthreet an' he thought he'd go around to-morrah an' concilyate him. So he wint away.

"Hogan, d'ye mind, has a theery that it's all been up with us blondes since th' Jap'nese war. Hogan is a prophet. He's wan iv th' gr-reatest prophets I know. A prophet, Hinnissy, is a man that foresees throuble. . . . He cudden't find a goold mine f'r ye but he cud see th' bottom iv wan through three thousand feet iv bullyon. He can peer into th' most blindin' sunshine an' see th' darkness lurkin' behind it. He's predicted ivry war that has happened in our time and eight thousand that haven't happened to happen. If he had his way th' United States navy wud be so big that there wudden't be room f'r a young fellow to row his girl in Union Park. He can see a war cloud where I can't see annything but somebody cookin' his dinner or lightin' his pipe. He'd make th' gr-reat foreign iditor an' he'd be fine f'r th' job f'r he's best late at night.

"Hogan says th' time has come f'r th' subjick races iv th' wurruld to rejooce us fair wans to their own complexion be batin' us black and blue. Up to now 'twas: 'Sam, ye black rascal, tow in thim eggs or I'll throw ye in th' fire.' 'Yassir,' says Sam. 'Comin',' he says. 'Twas: 'Wow Chow, while ye'er idly stewin' me cuffs I'll set fire to me upaid bills.' 'I wud feel repaid be a kick,' says Wow Chow. 'Twas: 'Maharajah Sewar, swing th' fan swifter or I'll have to roll over f'r me dog whip.' 'Higgins Sahib,' says Maharajah Sewar, 'Higgins Sahib, beloved iv Gawd an' Kipling, ye'er punishments ar-re th' nourishment iv th' faithful. My blood hath served thine f'r manny ginerations. At laste two. 'Twas thine old man that blacked me father's eye an' sint me uncle up f'r eighty days.

How will ye'er honor have th' accursed swine's flesh cooked
f'r breakfast in th' mornin' when I'm through fannin' ye?'

"But now, says Hogan, it's all changed. Iver since th'
Rooshyans were starved out at Port Arthur and Portsmouth,
th' wurrud has passed around an' ivry naygur fr'm lemon col-
or to coal is bracin' up. He says they have aven a system of
tilly-graftin' that bates ours be miles. They have no wires or
poles or wathered stock but th' population is so thick that whin
they want to sind wurrud along th' line all they have to do is f'r
wan man to nudge another an' something that happens in
Northern Chiny is known in Southern Indya befure sunset.
And so it passed through th' undherwurruld that th' color line
was not to be dhrawn anny more, an' Hogan says that almost
anny time he ixpicts to see a black face peerin' through a window an' in a few years I'll be takin' in laundhry in a basement
instead iv occupyin' me present impeeryal positon, an' ye'll be
settin' in front iv ye'er cabin home playin' on a banjo an'
watchin' ye'er little pickahinnissies rollickin' on th' ground an'
wondhern' whin th' lynchin' party'll arrive. . . .

"I don't see what th' subjick races got to kick about, Hinnissy. We've been awfully good to thim. We sint thim missionaries to teach thim th' error iv their relligyon an' nawthin'
cud be kinder thin that f'r there's nawthin' people like betther
thin to be told that their parents are not be anny means where
they thought they were but in a far more crowded an' excitin'
locality. An' with th' missionaries we sint sharpshooters that
cud pick off a Chinyman beatin' th' conthribution box at five
hundherd yards. We put up palashal goluf-coorses in the
cimitries an' what was wanst th' tomb iv Hung Chang, th' gr-
reat Tartar Impror, rose to th' dignity iv bein' th' bunker
guardin' th' fifth green. No Chinyman cud fail to be pleased at
seein' a tall Englishman hittin' th' Chinyman's grandfather's
coffin with a niblick. We sint explorers up th' Nile who
raypoorted that th' Ganzain flows into th' Oboo just above
Lake Mazap, a fact that th' naygurs had known f'r a long time.
Th' explorer announces that he has changed th' names iv these

wather-coorses to Smith, Blifkins an' Winkinson. He wishes to deny th' infamyous story that he iver ate a native alive. But wan soon succumbs to th' customs iv a counthry an' Sir Alfred is no viggytaryan. . . .

"It's no laughin' matther, I tell ye. A subjick race is on'y funny whin it's raaly subjick. About three years ago I stopped laughin' at Jap'nese jokes. Ye have to feel supeeryor to laugh an' I'm gettin' over that feelin'. An' nawthin' makes a man so mad an' so scared as whin something he looked down on as infeeryor tur-rns on him. If a fellow man hits him he hits him back. But if a dog bites him he yells 'mad dog' an' him an' th' neighbors pound th' dog to pieces with clubs. If th' naygurs down South iver got together an' flew at their masters ye'd hear no more coon songs f'r awhile. It's our conceit makes us supeeryor. Take it out iv us an' we ar-re about th' same as th' rest. . . .

"An' I sigh f'r th' good old days befure we become what Hogan calls a wurruld power. In thim days our fav'rite spoort was playin' solytare, winnin' money fr'm each other, an' no wan th' worse off. Ivrybody was invious iv us. We didn't care f'r th' big game goin' on in th' corner. Whin it broke up in a row we said: 'Gintlemen, gintlemen!' an' maybe wint over an' grabbed somebody's stake. But we cudden't stand it anny longer. We had to give up our simple little game iv patience an' cut into th' other deal. An' now, be Hivins, we have no peace iv mind. Wan hand we have wan partner; another hand he's again us. This minyit th' Jap an' me ar-re playin' together an' I'm tellin' him what a fine lead that was; th' next an' he's again me an' askin' me kindly not to look at his hand. There ar-re no frinds at cards or wurruld polyticks. Th' deal changes an' what started as a frindly game iv rob ye'er neighbor winds up with an old ally catchin' me pullin' an ace out iv me boot an' denouncin' me."

"Sure thim little fellows wud niver tackle us," said Mr. Hennessy. "Th' likes iv thim!"

"Well," said Mr. Dooley, " 'tis because they ar-re little ye've got to be polite to thim. A big man knows he don't have to fight, but whin a man is little an' knows he's little an' is thinkin' all th' time he's little an' feels that ivrybody else is thinkin' he's little, look out f'r him."

THE NEGRO PROBLEM

"What's goin' to happen to th' naygur?" asked Mr. Hennessy.

"Well," said Mr. Dooley, "he'll ayther have to go to th' north an' be a subjick race, or stay in th' south an' be an objick lesson. 'Tis a har-rd time he'll have, annyhow. I'm not sure that I'd not as lave be gently lynched in Mississippi as baten to death in New York. If I was a black man, I'd choose th' cotton belt in prifrince to th' belt on th' neck fr'm th' polisman's club. I wud so.

"I'm not so much throubled about th' naygur whin he lives among his opprissors as I am whin he falls into th' hands iv his liberators. Whin he's in th' south he can make up his mind to be lynched soon or late an' give his attintion to his other pleasures iv composin' rag-time music on a banjo, an' wur-rukin' f'r th' man that used to own him an' now on'y owes him his wages. But 'tis th' divvle's own hardship f'r a coon to step out iv th' rooms iv th' S'ciety f'r th' Brotherhood iv Ma-an where he's been r-readin' a pome on th' 'Future of th' Moke' an' be pursooed be a mob iv abolitionists till he's dhriven to seek polis protection, which, Hinnissy, is th' polite name f'r fracture iv th' skull.

"I was f'r sthrikin' off th' shackles iv th' slave, me la-ad. 'Twas thrue I didn't vote f'r it, bein' that I heerd Stephen A. Douglas say 'twas onconstitootional, an' in thim days I wud go to th' flure with anny man f'r th' constitootion. I'm still with it, but not sthrong. It's movin' too fast f'r me. But no matther. Annyhow I was f'r makin' th' black man free, an' though I shtud be th' south as a spoortin' proposition I was kind iv glad in me heart whin Gin'ral Ulyss S. Grant bate Gin'ral Lee an' th' rest iv th' Union officers captured Jeff Davis. I says to mesilf, 'Now,' I says, 'th' coon'll have a chanst f'r his life,' says I, 'an' in due time we may injye him,' I says.

"An' sure enough it looked good f'r awhile, an' th' time come whin th' occas'nal dollar bill that wint acrost this bar on pay night wasn't good money onless it had th' name iv th' naygur on it. In thim days they was a young la-ad—a frind iv wan iv th' Donohue boys—that wint to th' public school up beyant, an' he was as bright a la-ad as ye'd want to see in a day's walk. Th' larnin' iv him wud sind Father Kelly back to his grammar. He cud spell to make a hare iv th' hedge schoolmasther, he was as quick at figures as th' iddycated pig they showed in th' tint las' week in Haley's vacant lot, an in joggerphy, asthronomy, algybbera, jommethry, chimisthry, physiojnomy, bassoophly an' fractions, I was often har-rd put mesilf to puzzle him. I heerd him gradyooate an' his composition was so fine very few cud make out what he meant.

"I met him on th' sthreet wan day afther he got out iv school. 'What ar-re ye goin' to do f'r ye'ersilf, Snowball,' says I—his name was Andhrew Jackson George Wash'n'ton Americus Caslateras Beresford Vanilla Hicks, but I called him 'Snowball,' him bein' as black as coal, d'ye see—I says to him: 'What ar-re ye goin' to do f'r ye'ersilf?' I says. 'I'm goin' to enther th' profission iv law,' he says, 'where be me acooman an' industhry I hope,' he says, 'f'r to rise to be a judge,' he says, 'a congrissman,' he says, 'a sinator,' he says, 'an' p'raps,' he says, 'a prisidint iv th' United States,' he says. 'They'se nawthin to prevint,' he says. 'Divvle a thing,' says I. 'Whin we made ye free,' says I, 'we opened up all these opporchunities to ye,' says I. 'Go on,' says I, 'an' enjye th' wealth an' position conferred on ye be th' constitootion,' I says. 'On'y,' I says, 'don't be too free,' I says. 'Th' freedom iv th' likes iv ye is a good thing an' a little iv it goes a long way,' I says, 'an' if I ever hear iv ye bein' prisidint iv th' United States,' I says, 'I'll take me whitewashing' away fr'm ye'er father, ye excelsior hair, poached-egg eyed, projiny iv tar,' I says, f'r me Anglo-Saxon feelin' was sthrong in thim days.

"Well, I used to hear iv him afther that defindin' coons in th' polis coort, an' now an' thin bein' mintioned among th' scatthrin' in raypublican county con-vintions, an' thin he dhropped out iv sight. 'Twas years befure I see him again. Wan day I was walkin' up th' levee smokin' a good tin cint seegar whin a coon wearin' a suit iv clothes that looked like a stained glass window in th' house iv a Dutch brewer an' a pop bottle in th' fr-ront iv his shirt, steps up to me an' he says: 'How dy'e do, Mistah Dooley,' says he. 'Don't ye know me—Mistah Hicks?' he says. 'Snowball,' says I. 'Step inside this dureway,' says I, 'less Clancy, th' polisman on th' corner, takes me f'r an octoroon,' I says. 'What ar-re ye do-in'?' says I. 'How did ye enjye th' prisidincy?' says I. He laughed an' told me th' story iv his life. He wint to practisin' law an' found his on'y clients was coons, an' they had no assets but their vote at th' prim'ry. Besides a warrant f'r a moke was the same as a letther iv inthroduction to th' warden iv th' pinitinchry. Th' on'y thing left f'r th' lawyer to do was to move f'r a new thrile an' afther he'd got two or three he thought ol' things was th' best an' ye do well to lave bad enough alone. He got so sick iv chicken he cudden't live on his fees an' he quit th' law an' wint into journalism. He r-run 'Th' Colored Supplimint,' but it was a failure, th' taste iv th' public lanin' more to quadhroon publications, an' no man that owned a resthrant or theaytre or dhrygoods store'd put in an adver-tisemint f'r fear th' subscribers'd see it an' come ar-round. Thin he attimpted to go into pollyticks, an' th' best he cud get was carryin' a bucket iv wather f'r a Lincoln Club. He thried to larn a thrade an' found th' on'y place a naygur can larn a thrade is in prison an' he can't wurruk at that without committin' burglary. He started to take up subscriptions f'r a sthrugglin' church an' found th' profission was overcrowded. 'Fin'ly,' says he, ''twas up to me to be a porther in a saloon or go into th' on'y business,' he says, 'in which me race has a chanst,' he says. 'What's that?' says I. 'Craps,' says he. 'I've opened a palachal imporyium,' he says, 'where,' he says, "twud please me very much,' he says, 'me ol' abolitionist frind,' he says, 'if ye'd dhrop in some day,' he says, 'an' I'll roll th' sweet, white bones f'r ye,' he says. "Tis th' hope iv me people,' he says. 'We have an even chanst at ivry other pursoot,' he says, 'but 'tis on'y in craps we have a shade th' best iv it,' he says.

"So there ye ar-re, Hinnissy. An' what's it goin' to come to, says ye? Faith, I don't know an' th' naygurs don't know, an' be hivins, I think if the lady that wrote th' piece we used to see at th' Halstead Sthreet Opry House come back to earth, she wudden't know. I used to be all broke up about Uncle Tom, but cud I give him a job tindin' bar in this here liquor store? I freed th' slave, Hinnissy, but, faith, I think 'twas like tur-rnin' him out iv a panthry into a cellar."

"Well, they got to take their chances," said Mr. Hennessy. "Ye can't do annything more f'r thim than make thim free."

"Ye can't," said Mr. Dooley; "On'y whin ye tell thim they're free they know we're on'y sthringin' thim."

THE BOOKER WASHINGTON INCIDENT

"What ails th' prisidint havin' a coon to dinner at th' White House?" asked Mr. Hennessy.

"He's a larned man," said Mr. Dooley.

"He's a coon," said Mr. Hennessy.

"Well, annyhow," said Mr. Dooley, "it's goin' to be th' roonation iv Prisidint Tiddy's chances in th' South. Thousan's iv men who wudden't have voted f'r him undher anny circumstances has declared that under no circumstances wud they now vote f'r him. He's lost near ivry state in th' South. Th' gran' ol' commonwealth iv Texas has deserted th' banner iv th' raypublican party an' Mississippi will cast her unanimous counted vote again him. Onless he can get support fr'm Matsachoosetts or some other state where th' people don't care annything about th' naygur excipt to dislike him, he'll be beat sure.

"I don't suppose he thought iv it whin he ast me cultured but swarthy frind Booker T. They'd been talkin' over th' race problem an' th' Cubian war, an' th' prospects iv th' race an' th' Cubian war, an' th' future iv th' naygro an' th' Cubian war, an' findin' Booker T. was inthrested in important public subjects like th' Cubian war, th' prisidint ast him to come up to th' White House an' ate dinner an' have a good long talk about th' Cubian war. 'Ye'll not be th' first Wash'nton that's et here,' he says. 'Th' other was no rilitive, or at laste,' says Booker T., 'he'd hardly own me,' he says. 'He might,' says th' prisidint, 'if ye'd been in th' neighborhood iv Mt. Vernon in his time,' he says. 'Annyhow,' he says, 'come up. I'm goin' to thry an experiment,' he says. 'I want to see will all th' pitchers iv th' prisidints befure Lincoln fall out iv th' frames whin ye come in,' he says. An' Booker wint. So wud I. So wud annywan. I'd go if I had to black up.

"I didn't hear that th' guest done annything wrong at th' table. Fr'm all I can larn, he hung his hat on th' rack an' used proper discrimination between th' knife an' th' fork an' ast f'r nawthin that had to be sint out f'r. They was no mark on th' table cloth where his hands rested an' an invintory iv th' spoons after his departure showed that he had used gintlemanly resthraint. At th' con-clusion iv th' fistivities he wint away, lavin' his ilusthrees friend standin' on th' top iv San Joon hill an' thought no more about it. Th' ghost iv th' other Wash'nton didn't appear to break a soop tureen over his head. P'raps where George is he has to assocyate with manny mimbers iv th' Booker branch on terms iv akequality. I don't suppose they have partitions up in th' other wurruld like th' kind they have in th' cars down south. They can't be anny Crow Hivin. I wondher how they keep up race supreemacy. Maybe they get on without it. Annyhow I wasn't worried about Booker T. I have me own share iv race prejudice, Hinnissy. Ne'er a man an' brother has darkened this threshold since I've had it or will but th' whitewasher. But I don't mind sayin' that I'd rather ate with a coon thin have wan wait on me. I'd sooner he'd handle his food thin mine. F'r me, if anny thumb must be in th' gravy, lave it be white if ye please. But this wasn't my dinner an' it wasn't my house an' I hardly give it a thought.

"But it hit th' Sunny Southland. No part iv th' counthry can be more gloomy whin it thries thin th' Sunny Southland an' this here ivint sint a thrill iv horror through ivery newspaper fr'm th' Pattymack to th' Sugar Belt. 'Fr'm time immemoryal,' says wan paper I read, 'th' sacred rule at th' White House has been, whin it comes to dinner, please pass th' dark meat. It was a wise rule an' founded on thrue prin- ciples. Th' supreemacy iv th' white depinds on socyal supeeryority an' socyal supeeryority depinds on makin' th' coon ate in th' back iv th' house. He raises our food f'r us, cooks it, sets th' table an' brings in th' platter. We are liberal an' we make no attimpt to supplant him with more intilligent an' wage labor. We encourage his industhry because we know that f'r a low ordher iv intilligence, labor is th' on'y panacee. It is no good f'r a thoughtful man. We threat him right. He has plenty to do an' nawthin' to bother him an' if he isn't satisfied he be hanged. We are slowly givin him an' id- jacation. Ivry year wan or more naygurs is given a good id- jacation an' put on a north bound freight with a warnin.' But whin it comes to havin' him set down at th' table with us, we dhraw th' color line an' th' six shooter. Th' black has manny fine qualities. He is joyous, light-hearted, an' aisily lynched. But as a fellow bong vivant, not be anny means. We have th' highest rayspict f'r Booker T. Wash'nton. He's an idjacated coon. He is said to undherstand Latin an' Greek. We do not know. But we know that to feed him at th' White House was an insult to ivry honest man an' fair woman in th' Sunny Southland and' a blow at white supreemacy. That must be av- inged. Th' las' enthrinchmint iv socyal supeeryority in th' South is th' dinin' room an' there we will defind it with our sacred honor. We will not on'y defind our own dinin' room but ivry other man's, so that in time, if th' prisidint iv th'

United States wants to ate with a naygur, he'll have to put on a coat iv burnt cork an' go to th' woodshed. Manetime we hear that th' white man in Alabama that voted f'r Rosenfelt las' year has come out again him. Th' tide has turned.'

"So there ye are. An' f'r th' life iv me, I can't tell which is right. But I think th' prisidint's place is a good dale like mine. I believe that manny an honest heart bates beneath a plaid vest, but I don't like a naygur. Howiver, Hinnissy, if Fate, as Hogan said, had condemned me to start in business on th' Levee, I'd sarve th' black man that put down th' money as quick as I wud th' white. I feel I wudden't, but I know I wud. But bein' that I'm up here in this Cowcasyan neighborhood, I spurn th' dark coin. They'se very little iv it annyhow an' if anny iv me proud customers was f'r to see an unshackled slave lanin' again this bar, it'd go hard with him an' with me. Me frinds has no care f'r race supeeryority. A raaly supeeryor race niver thinks iv that. But black an' white don't mix, Hinnissy' an' if it wint th' rounds that Dooley was handin' out rayfrishmint to th' colored popylation, I might as well change me license. So be th' prisidint. They'se nawthin' wrong in him havin' me frind Booker T. up to dinner. That's a fine naygur man, an' if me an' th' prisidint was in a private station, d 'ye mind, we cud f'rget th' color iv th' good man an' say, 'Booker T. stretch ye'er legs in front iv th' fire, while I go to th' butcher's f'r a pound iv pork chops.' But bein' that I — an' th' prisidint—is public sarvants an' manny iv our customers has onrais'nable prejoodices, an' afther all 't is to thim I've got to look f'r me support, I put me hand on his shouldher an' says I: 'Me colored frind, I like ye an' ye're idjacation shows ye're a credit to th' South that it don't desarve, an' I wud swear black was white f'r ye; but swearin' it wudden't make it so, an' I know mos' iv me frinds thinks th' thirteenth amindmint stops at th' dure shtep, so if ye don't mind, I'll ast ye to leap through th' dure with ye'er hat on whin th' clock sthrikes sivin.' 'Tis not me that speaks, Hinnissy, 't is th' job. Dooley th' plain citizen says, 'Come in, Rastus.'

Dooley's job says: 'If ye come, th' r-rest will stay away.' An' I'd like to do something f'r th' naygur, too.''

"What wud ye do?" asked Mr. Hennessy.

"Well," said Mr. Dooley, "I'd take away his right to vote an' his right to ate at th' same table an' his right to ride on th' cars an' even his sacred right to wurruk. I'd take thim all away an' give him th' on'y right he needs nowadays in th' South."

"What's that?"

"Th' right to live," said Mr. Dooley. "If he cud start with that he might make something iv himsilf."

IMMIGRATION

"Well, I see Congress has got to wurruk again," said Mr. Dooley.

"The Lord save us fr'm harm," said Mr. Hennessy.

"Yes, sir," said Mr. Dooley, "Congress has got to wurruk again, an' manny things that seems important to a Congressman 'll be brought up befure thim. 'Tis sthrange that what's a big thing to a man in Wash'nton, Hinnissy, don't seem much account to me. Divvle a bit do I care whether they dig th' Nicaragoon Canal or cross th' Isthmus in a balloon; or whether th' Monroe docthrine is enfoorced or whether it ain't; or whether th' thrusts is abolished as Teddy Rosenfelt wud like to have thim or encouraged to go on with their neefaryous but magnificent entherprises as th' Prisidint wud like; or whether th' water is poured into th' ditches to reclaim th' aird lands iv th' West or th' money f'r thim to fertilize th' arid pocket-books iv th' conthractors; or whether th' Injun is threated like a depindant an' miserable thribesman or like a free an' indepindant dog; or whether we restore th' merchant marine to th' ocean or whether we lave it to restore itsilf. None iv these here questions inthrests me, an' be me I mane you an' be you I mane ivrybody. What we want to know is, ar-re we goin' to have coal enough in th' hod whin th' cold snap comes; will th' plumbin' hold out, an' will th' job last.

"But they'se wan question that Congress is goin' to take up that you an' me are inthrested in. As a pilgrim father that missed th' first boats, I must raise me claryon voice again' th' invasion iv this fair land be th' paupers an' arnychists iv effete Europe. Ye bet I must — because I'm here first. 'Twas diff'rent whin I was dashed high on th' stern an' rockbound coast. In thim days America was th' refuge iv th' oppressed iv all th' wurruld. They cud come over here an' do a good job iv oppressin' thimsilves. As I told ye I come a litle late. Th' Rosenfelts an' th' Lodges bate me be at laste a boat lenth, an' be th' time I got here they was stern an' rockbound thimsilves. So I got a gloryous rayciption as soon as I was towed off th' rocks. Th' stars an' sthripes whispered a welcome in th' breeze an' a shovel was thrust into me hand an' I was pushed into a sthreet excyvatin' as though I'd been born here. Th' pilgrim father who bossed th' job was a fine ol' puritan be th' name iv Doherty, who come over in th' Mayflower about th' time iv th' potato rot in Wexford, an' he made me think they was a hole in th' breakwather iv th' haven iv refuge an' some iv th' wash iv th' seas iv opprission had got through. He was a stern an' rockbound la-ad himsilf, but I was a good hand at loose stones an' wan day — but I'll tell ye about that another time.

"Annyhow, I was rayceived with open arms that sometimes ended in a clinch. I was afraid I wasn't goin' to assimilate with th' airlyer pilgrim fathers an' th' instichoochions iv th' counthry, but I soon found that a long swing iv th' pick made me as good as another man an' it didn't require a gr-reat intellect, or sometimes anny at all, to vote th' dimmycrat ticket, an' befure I was here a month, I felt enough like a native born American to burn a witch. Wanst in a while a mob iv intilligint collajeens, whose grandfathers had bate me to th' dock, wud take a shy at me Pathrick's Day procission or burn down wan iv me churches, but they got tired iv that befure long; 'twas too much like wurruk.

"But as I tell ye, Hinnissy, 'tis diff'rent now. I don't know why 'tis diff'rent but 'tis diff'rent. 'Tis time we put our back again' th' open dure an' keep out th' savage horde. If that cousin iv ye'ers expects to cross, he'd betther tear f'r th' ship. In a few minyits th' gates 'll be down an' whin th' oppressed wurruld comes hikin' acrost to th' haven iv refuge, they'll do well to put a couplin' pin undher their hats, f'r th' Goddess iv Liberty 'll meet thim at th' dock with an axe in her hand. Congress is goin' to fix it. Me frind Shaughnessy says so. He was in yisterdah an' says he: ' 'Tis time we done something to make th' immigration laws sthronger,' says he. 'Thrue f'r ye, Miles Standish,' says I; 'but what wud ye do?' 'I'd keep out th' off-scourin's iv Europe,' says he. 'Wud ye go back?' says I. 'Have ye'er joke,' says he. ' 'Tis not so seeryus as it was befure ye come,' says I. 'But what ar-re th' immygrants doin' that's roonous to us?' I says. 'Well,' says he, 'they're arnychists,' he says; 'they don't assymilate with th' counthry,' he says. 'Maybe th' counthry's digestion has gone wrong fr'm too much rich food,' says I; 'perhaps now if we'd lave off thryin' to digest Rockyfellar an' thry a simple diet like Schwartzmeister, we wudden't feel th' effects iv our vittels,' I says. 'Maybe if we'd season th' immygrants a little or cook thim thurly, they'd go down betther,' I says.

" 'They're arnychists, like Parsons,' he says. 'He wud've been an immygrant if Texas hadn't been admitted to th' Union,' I says. 'Or Snolgosh,' he says. 'Has Mitchigan seceded?' I says. 'Or Gittoo,' he says. 'Who come fr'm th' effete monarchies iv Chicago, west iv Ashland Av'noo,' I says. 'Or what's-his-name, Wilkes Booth,' he says. 'I don't know what he was—maybe a Boolgharyen,' says I. 'Well, annyhow,' says he, 'they're th' scum iv th' earth.' 'They may be that,' says I; 'but we used to think they was th' cream iv civilization,' I says. 'They're off th' top annyhow. I wanst believed 'twas th' best men iv Europe come here, th' la-ads that was too sthrong and indepindant to be kicked around be a boorgomasther at home an' wanted to dig out f'r a place where they cud get a chanst to make their way to th' money. I see their sons fightin' into politics an' their daughters tachin' young American idee how to shoot too high in th' public school, an' I thought they was all right. But I see I was wrong. Thim boys out there towin' wan heavy foot afther th' other to th' rowlin' mills is all arnychists. There's warrants out f'r all names endin' in 'inski, an' I think I'll board up me windows, f'r,' I says, 'if immygrants is as dangerous to this counthry as ye an' I an' other pilgrim fathers believe they are, they'se enough iv thim sneaked in already to make us aborigines about as infloointial as the prohibition vote in th' Twinty-ninth Ward. They'll dash again' our stern an' rock-bound coast till they bust it,' says I.

" 'But I ain't so much afraid as ye ar-re. I'm not afraid iv me father an' I'm not afraid iv mesilf. An' I'm not afraid iv Schwartzmeister's father or Hinnery Cabin Lodge's grandfather. We all come over th' same way, an' if me ancestors were not what Hogan calls rigicides, 'twas not because they were not ready an' willin', on'y a king niver come their way. I don't believe in killin' kings, mesilf. I niver wud've sawed th' block off that curly-headed potintate that I see in th' pitchers down town, but, be hivins, Presarved Codfish Shaughnessy, if we'd begun a few years ago shuttin' out folks that wudden't mind handin' a bomb to a king, they wudden't be enough people in Mattsachoosetts to make a quorum f'r th' Anti-Impeeryal S'ciety,' says I. 'But what wud ye do with th' offscourin' iv Europe?' says he. 'I'd scour thim some more,' says I.

"An' so th' meetin' iv th' Plymouth Rock Assocyation come to an end. But if ye wud like to get it together, Deacon Hinnissy, to discuss th' immygration question, I'll sind out a hurry call f'r Schwartzmeister an' Mulcahey an' Ignacio Sbarbaro an' Nels Larsen an' Petrus Gooldvink, an' we 'll gather tonight at Fanneilnoviski Hall at th' corner iv Sheridan an' Sigel sthreets. All th' pilgrim fathers is rayquested f'r to bring interpreters."

"Well," said Mr. Hennessy, "divvle th' bit I care, on'y I'm here first, an' I ought to have th' right to keep th' bus fr'm bein' overcrowded."

"Well," said Mr. Dooley, "as a pilgrim father on me gran' nephew's side, I don't know but ye're right. An' they'se wan sure way to keep thim out."

"What's that?" asked Mr. Hennessy.

"Teach thim all about our instichoochions befure they come," said Mr. Dooley.

CHAPTER XII

PHILOSOPHER AND CRITIC OR EVERYTHING OLD IS NEW AGAIN

These essays cover a wide range of topics, providing the ultimate proof that Mr. Dooley's wit and wisdom is up to the minute and valuable to us as it was to his original readers. With a mere change of names, dates and/or places, Dooley's inspired nonsense could pass for commentary on the nightly news.

Airborne, "The Comforts of Travel" may be translated from the passenger train to modern airlines. Scarcely a week goes by without some one or some institution selecting the 100 most famous or important individuals; Mr. Dooley puts such fame and glory in their perspective, as he does the pretensions of the intellectual life.

The subject of revolution was of great concern in Dunne's time as in our own, and involved many of the same countries, including Ireland. Dunne, while proud of his Irish heritage, never cared for the professional Irishmen of his day, and tended to ridicule their efforts on behalf of the Irish freedom he himself strongly supported. As Mr. Dooley said, "Be hivins, if Ireland cud be freed be a picnic, it'd not on'y be free today, but an impire." To a born satirist, nothing is sacred, and he sometimes incurred the wrath of other Americans of Irish descent.

In the brief essay "On the End of Things," Mr. Dooley observes that "No man is a hayro to his undertaker." When Dunne died, the crush at his funeral in New York's cavernous St. Patrick's Cathedral proved that he was a hero to many. His passing was mourned across America, even though Mr. Dooley had been in retirement for over a decade.

ON BOOKS

"They're on'y three books in th' wurruld worth readin',—Shakespeare, th' Bible, an' Mike Ahearn's histhry iv Chicago. I have Shakespeare on thrust, Father Kelly r-reads th' Bible f'r me, an' I didn't buy Mike Ahearn's histhry because I seen more thin he cud put into it. Books is th' roon iv people, specially novels."

"Life, says ye! There's no life in a book. If ye want to show thim what life is, tell thim to look around thim. There's more life on a Saturdah night in th' Ar-rchy Road thin in all th' books fr'm Shakespeare to th' rayport iv th' drainage thrustees."

COLLEGES AND DEGREES

"I see," said Mr. Dooley, "that good ol' Yale, because it makes us feel so hale, dhrink her down, as Hogan says, has been cillybratin' her bicintinry."

"What's that?" asked Mr. Hennessy.

"'Tis what," said Mr. Dooley, "if it happened to you or me or Saint Ignatyus Colledge'd be called our two hundherdth birthday. From th' Greek, bi, two, cintinry, hundherd, two hundherd. Do ye follow? 'Tis th' way to make a colledge wur-rud. Think iv it in English, thin think it back into Greek, thin thranslate it. Two hundherd years ago, Yale Colledge was founded be Eli Yale, an Englishman, an' dead at that. He didn't know what he was doin' an' no more did I till I r-read iv these fistivities. I knew it nestled undher th' ellums iv New Haven, Connecticut, but I thought no more iv it thin that 't was th' name iv a lock, a smokin' tobacco an' a large school nestlin' undher th' ellums iv New Haven where ye sint ye'er boy if ye cud afford it an' be larned th' Greek chorus an' th' American an' chased th' fleet fut ball an' th' more fleet aorist, a spoort that Hogan knows about, an' come out whin he had to an' wint to wurruk. But, ye take me wurrd f'r it. Yale's more thin that, Hinnissy. I get it sthraight fr'm th' thruthful sons iv Yale thimsilves that if it hadn't been f'r this dear bunch iv dormitories nestlin' undher th' ellums iv New Haven, our beloved counthry an' th' short end iv th' wurruld too, might to-day be no betther thin they should be. Ivry great invintion fr'm th' typewriter to th' V-shaped wedge can be thraced to this prodigal instichoochion. But f'r Yale, we'd be going' to Europe on th' decks iv sailin' vessels instead iv comin' away in th' steerage iv steamships or stayin' at home; we'd be dhrivin' horses, as manny iv the' unlarned iv us do to this day instead iv pushin' th' swift autymobill up hill; we'd be writin; long an' amusin' letters to our frinds instead iv tillyphonin' or tillygraftin' thim.

"What's a degree, says ye? A degree is a certyficate fr'm a ladin' university entitlin' ye to wear a mother Hubbard in spite iv th' polis. It makes ye doctor iv something an' enables ye to practise at ye'er pro-fission. I don't mind tellin' ye, Hinnissy, that if I was a law which I'm not, I'd have to be pretty sick befure I'd call in manny iv th' doctors iv laws I know, an' as f'r American lithrachoor, it don't need a doctor so much as a coroner. But annyhow degrees is good things because they livils all ranks. Ivry public man is entitled ex-officio to all th' degrees there are. An' no public or private man escapes. Ye haven't got wan, ye say? Ye will though. Some day ye'll see a polisman fr'm th' University iv Chicago at th' dure an' ye'll hide undher th' bed. But he'll get ye an' haul ye out. Ye'll say: 'I haven't done annything,' an' he'll say: 'Ye'd betther come along quite. I'm sarvin' a degree on ye fr'm Prisidint Harper.' Some iv th' thriftier univarsities is makin' a degree th' alternytive iv a fine. Five dollars or docthor iv laws.

"They was manny handed out be Yale, an' to each man th' prisidint said a few wurruds explainin' why he got it, so's he'd know. I r-read all th' speeches: 'Kazoo Kazama, pro-fissor iv fan paintin' at th' Univarsity iv Tokeeo, because ye belong to an oldher civilization thin ours but are losin' it,' to 'Willum Beans, wanst iditor iv th' Atlantic Monthly but not now,' to 'Arthur Somerset Soanso who wrote manny long stories but some short,' to 'Markess Hikibomo Itto because he was around,' to 'Fedor Fedorvitch Fedorivinisky because he come so far.'

"An' thin they was gr-reat jubilation, an' shootin' off iv firewurruks an' pomes be ol' gradyates with th' docthors iv lithrachoor sittin' in th' ambulances waitin' f'r a hurry call. An' thin ivry wan wint home. I was glad to r-read about it, Hinnissy. It done me heart good to feel that boys must be boys even whin they're men. An' they'se manny things in th' wurruld that ye ought to believe even if ye think they're not so."

"D'ye think th' colledges has much to do with th' progress iv th' wurruld?" asked Mr. Hennessy.

"D'ye think," said Mr. Dooley, "'tis th' mill that makes th' wather run?"

ORATORY

"I guess a man niver becomes an orator if he has anything to say, Hinnissy. If a lawyer thinks his client is innocint he talks to th' jury about th' crime. But if he knows where th' pris'ner hid th' plunder, he unfurls th' flag, throws out a few remarks about th' flowers an' th' bur-rds, an' asks th' twelve good men an' thrue not to break up a happy Christmas, but to sind this man home to his wife an' childer, an' Gawd will bless thim if they ar-re iver caught in th' same perdicymint. Whiniver I go to a pollytical meetin', an' th' laad with th' open-wurruk face mentions Rome or Athens I grab f'r me hat. I know he's not goin' to say anything that ought to keep me out iv bed. I also bar all language about bur'rds an' flowers; I don't give two cints about th' Oregon, whether it rolls or staggers to th' sea; an' I'll rap in th' eye anny man that attimpts to wrap up his sicond-hand oratory in th' American flag. There ought to be a law against usin' th' American flag f'r such purposes. I hope to read in th' pa-aper some day that Joe Cannon was arrested f'r usin' th' American flag to dicorate a speech on th' tariff, an' sintinced to two years solitary confinemint with Sinitor Berridge. An' be hivens, I don't want anny man to tell me that I'm a mimber iv wan iv th' grandest races th' sun has iver shone on. I know it already. If I wasn't, I'd move out.

"No, sir, whin a man has something to say an' don't know how to say it, he says it pretty well. Whin he has something to say an' knows how to say it he makes a gr-reat speech. But whin he has nawthin' to say an' has a lot iv wurruds that come with a black coat, he's an orator. There's two things I don't want at me fun'ral. Wan is an oration, an' th' other is waxflowers. I class thim alike."

REVOLUTION

"I'm sthrong f'r anny rivolution that ain't goin' to happen in me day But th' thruth is, me boy, that nawthin' happens, annyhow. I see gr-reat changes takin place ivry day, but no change at all ivry fifty years. What we call this here counthry iv ours pretinds to want to thry new experiments, but a sudden change gives it a chill. It's been to th' circus an' bought railroad tickets in a hurry so often that it thinks quick change is short change. Whin I take me mornin' walk an' see little boys an' girls with their dinner-pails on their arms goin' down to th' yards I'm th' hottest Socialist ye iver see. I'd be annything to stop it. I'd be a Raypublican, even. But whin I think how long this foolish old buildin' has stood, an' how manny a good head has busted again' it, I begin to wondher whether 'tis anny use f'r ye or me to thry to bump it off th' map. Larkin here says th' capitalist system is made up iv th' bones iv billions iv people, like wan iv thim coral reefs that I used to think was pethrified sponge. If that is so, maybe th' on'y thing I can do about it is to plant a few geeranyums, injye thim while I live, an' thin conthribute me own busted shoulder-blades f'r another Rockyfellar to walk on.''

THE INTELLECTUAL LIFE

"Well, sir," said Mr. Dooley, "it must be a grand thing to be a colledge profissor.''

"Not much to do," said Mr. Hennessy.

"But a gr-reat deal to say," said Mr. Dooley. "Ivry day th' minyit I pick up me pa-aper afther I've read th' criminal an' other pollytical news, th' spoortin' news, th' rale-estate advertisemints, th' invytation fr'm th' cultured foreign gent to meet an American lady iv some means, th' spoortin' news over again, thin th' iditoryals, I hasten to find out what th' colledge pro-fissor had to say yisterdah. I wish th' iditor wud put it in th' same column iv the pa-aper ivry day. Thin he wudden't have to collect anny other funny column. 'Humorous: Profissor Windhaul iv Harvard makes a savidge attack on Abraham Lincoln.' As it is, I sometimes have to hunt through th' pa-aper fr'm th' Newport scandal on page wan to th' relligious notes on page two hundherd an' four befure I come acrost me fav'rite funny sayin's iv funny fellows.

"I've been collictin' these wurruds iv wisdom f'r a long time, Hinnissy an' I'm now prepared to deliver ye a sample colledge lecture on all subjicks fr'm th' creation iv th' wurruld: 'Young gintlemen: I will begin be sayin' that I have me doubts about th' varyous stories consarnin' th' creation iv th' wurruld. In th' first place, I dismiss with a loud laugh th' theery that it was created in six days. I cud make such a poor wurruld as this in two days with a scroll-saw. Akelly preposterous is th' idee that it wasn't made at all, but grew up out iv nawthin'. Me idee is that th' wurruld is a chunk iv th' sun that was chipped off be a collisyon with th' moon, cooled down, an' advertised f'r roomers. As to its age, I differ with th' Bible. Me own opinyon iv th' age iv th' arth is that it is about twinty-eight years old. That is as far as I go back.

"'Speakin' iv th' Bible, it is an inthrestin' wurruk, but th' English is poor. I advise all iv ye not to injure ye'er style be readin' th' prisint editions, but if ye want rale good English ye will read th' Bible thranslated into Hoosier d'lect be Pro-fissor Lumsum Jiggs iv th' Univarsity iv Barry's Corner, wan iv our gr-reatest lithrachoors, whose loss to th' sody-wather business was a gloryous gain to relligion an' letthers. If ye want to make a comparison to show ye how lithrachoor has improved, compare th' wurruks iv Homer an' Jiggs. Homer nodded. He niver nodded to me, but he nodded. But has Jiggs nodded? Niver. He hasn't time. He is on his four thousandth book now, an' has larned to wurruk a second typewriter with his feet. Read Jiggs an' f'rget about Homer. As f'r Shakespeare, he is a dead wan. Th' opinyon I have iv Shakespeare is so low that I will not express it befure ladies. I ain't sayin' that his wurruks have not been pop'lar among th' vulgar. An' he might have amounted so something if he had been ijjacated, but his language is base, an' he had no imagination. Th' gr-reatest potes th' wurruld has projooced are Ransom Stiggs an' J.B. Mulcoon iv Keokuk. Th' Keokuk school iv pothry has all others badly stung. J.B. Mulcon has discovered more rhymes f'r dear thin Al Tinnyson iver heerd iv.

"'Me opinyon iv pollyticks, if ye shud ask me f'r it, is that we might as well give up th' experimint. A govermint founded be an ol' farmer like George Wash'nton an' a job-printer like Bin Franklin was bound to go down in roon. It has abandoned all their ideels—which was a good thing—an' made worse wans. Look at Lincoln. There's a fellow ivrybody is always crackin' up. But what did he amount to? What did he do but carry on a war, free th' slaves, an' run this mis'rable counthry? But who asked him to free th' slaves? I didn't. A man utterly lackin' in principle an' sinse iv humor, he led a mob an' was conthrolled be it. An' who ar-re th' mob that direct this counthry? A lot iv coarse, rough people, who ar-re sawin' up lumber an' picklin' pork, an' who niver had a thought iv th' Higher Life that makes men aspire to betther things an' indijestion. They ar-re ye'er fathers an' mine, young gintlemen. Can I say worse thin that? An' to think iv th' likes iv thim runnin' this govermint! By Jove, if I had raymimbered las' Choosdah that it was iliction day I'd have larned fr'm me milkman how to vote an' gone down to th' polls an' dhriven thim fr'm power. Well, there's wan consolation about it all: th' counthry won't last long. I noticed th' other day it had begun to crack. Whin it sinks ye'ers thruly will be near th' edge, ready to jump off. An-nyhow, it don't matther much. Th' American people ar-re all gettin' to be Indyans again. Walkin' down to-day, I obsarved twinty-two people who looked to me like Indyans. Next week I intind to verify me conclusyons be buyin' a picture iv an In-dyan. But I'm intirely convinced that in three or four years at laste we'll all be livin' in wickey-ups an' scalpin' each other. With these few remarks, let us inquirers f'r knowledge go out an' commit suicide on th' futball field. Ruh-ruh-ruh-ruh! Baz-zybazoo!''

"I like it, Hinnissy. What I like most about it is that a col-ledge pro-fissor niver speaks fr'm impulse. He thinks ivrything out thurly befure announcin' his opinyon. Th' theery iv me larned frind down in Rockyfellar's colledge that very soon ye'd seen me r-rushin' down Archey Road with a tommyhawk in me hand, thryin' to thrade off a pony f'r a wife an' a wife f'r a bottle iv wood alcohol, didn't leap out iv his gr-reat brain in a scandalous hurry. He pondered it long an' carefully. Th' idee sthruck him at breakfast while he was eatin' his prunes, an' did not machure till he was half through with th' ham an' eggs. So with Pro-fissor Windhaul. He didn't land on Lincoln till he was sure iv his ground. He first made inquiries, an' found out that there was such a man. Thin he looked f'r his name among th' gradjates iv Harvard. Thin he bumped him. It's a good thing Lincoln was dead befure he was assaulted. He niver wud have survived th' attack.

"It's a fine thing f'r th' young men who set at th' feet iv these

larned ducks. A little boy is chased away fr'm home an' enthers wan iv these here siminaries. He was licked yisterdah f'r
neglectin' to scrub below the chin, but to-morroh he will be
cheerin' wildly while Pro-fissor Bumpus tells him universal suffrage was a bad break. If he has a weak chest, an' can't play
futball, he goes on imbibin' wisdom ontil he arrives at th' dew
pint, whin his alma mather hurls him at th' onforchnit wurruld. He knows fifty thousan' things, but th' on'y wan iv thim
that he cud prove is that Heffelfinger was a gr-reat futball
player. Thin begins his rale colledge career. Th' post-gradjate
coorse is th' best in th' wurruld. Th' enthrances fee is all he
has. Th' wurruld takes it away fr'm him th' minyit he thries to
apply his colledge pro-fissor's idee that undher th' doctrine iv
probabilities two pair ought to beat three iv a kind. He hasn't
on'y wan new pro-fissor, but twinty millyon, old an' young,
rich an' poor, men an' women, especyally women. He can't
shirk his lessons. He has to be up in th' mornin' bright an' arly
larnin' an' passin' examinations. He's on'y told annything
wanst. If he don't raymimber it th' next time he is asked, some
pro-fissor gives him a thump on th' head. Anny time he don't
like his dear ol' alma mather he can quit. Th' wurruld ain't
advertisin' f'r anny students. It has no competitors, an' th' lists
are always full. Th' coorse lasts fr'm wan to sixty years, an' it
gets harder to'rd th' commincemint day. If he's a good scholar,
an' behaves himsilf, an' listens to th' pro-fissors, an wurruks
hard, he can gradjate with honors. In anny case, he is allowed
to write out his own diploma. He knows best what he is entitled to."

"If ye had a boy wud ye sind him to colledge?" asked Mr.
Hennessy.

"Well," said Mr. Dooley, "at th' age whin a boy is fit to be
in colledge I wudden't have him around th' house."

*Eric Severeid of CBS news, one of America's premiere political
journalists and a prominent observer of contemporary heroes*

and current events, admires all of Mr. Dooley, but is par-
ticularly partial to the following:

ON HEROES

"There's on'y wan thing that wud make me allow mesilf to
be a hero to th' American people, an' that is it don't last long.
A few columns in th' newspaper, a speech in Congress, assault
an' batthry be a mob in th' sthreet, a flatthrin' offer fr'm a
dime museem, an' thin ye sink back into th' discard an' are not
mintioned again onless ye get into jail, whin ye have a more ex-
tinded notice thin ye'er crime entitles ye to."

HISTORY

"I know histhry isn't thrue, Hinnessy, because it ain't like
what I see ivry day in Halsted Sthreet. If any wan comes along
with a histhry iv Greece or Rome that'll show me th' people
fightin', gettin' dhrunk, makin' love, gettin' married, owin' th'
grocery man an' bein' without hard-coal, I'll believe they was a
Greece or Rome, but not befure. Historyans is like doctors.
They are always lookin' f'r symptoms. Those iv them that
writes about their own times examines th' tongue an' feels th'
pulse an' makes a wrong dygnosis. Th' other kind iv histhry is
a post-mortem examination. It tells ye what a counthry died iv.
But I'd like to know what it lived iv."

THE COMFORTS OF TRAVEL

"D'ye know," said Mr. Hennessy, "ye can go fr'm Chicago
to New York in twinty hours? It must be like flyin'."
"It's something like flyin'," said Mr. Dooley, "but it's also
like fallin' off a roof or bein' clubbed be a polisman."
"It's wondherful how luxuryous modhren thravel is," said
Mr. Hennessy.
"Oh, wondherful," said Mr. Dooley. "It's almost a dhream.

Ye go to bed at night in Kansas City an' ye ar-re still awake in Chicago in th' mornin'. Ye have New York to-day an' nex' Thursdah ye ar-re in San Francisco an' can't get back. An' all th' time ye injye such comforts an' iligances as wud make th' Shah iv Persha invious if he heerd iv thim. I haven't thravelled much since I hastily put four thousan' miles iv salt wather an' smilin' land between me an' th' constabulary, but I've always wanted to fly through space on wan iv thim palace cars with th' beautiful names. Th' man that names th' Pullman cars an' th' pa-aper collars iv this counthry is our greatest pote, whoiver he is. I cud see mesilf steppin' aboard a palace on wheels called Obulula or Onarka an' bein' fired fr'm wan union deepo to another. So las' month, whin a towny iv mine in Saint Looey asked me down there, I determined to make th' plunge. With th' invitation come a fine consarvitive article be th' gin'ral passenger agent indivrin', Hinnissy, to give a faint idee iv th' glories iv th' thrip. There was pitchers in this little pome showin' how th' thrain looked to th' passenger agent. Iligantly dhressed ladies an' gintlemen set in th' handsomely up-holstered seats, or sthrolled through th' broad aisles. Says I mesilf: 'here is life. They'll have to dhrag me fr'm that rollin' home iv bliss feet foremost,' says I.

"An' I wint boundin' down to th' deepo. I slung four dollars at th' prisidint iv th' road whin he had con-cluded some impor-tant business with his nails, an' he slung back a yard iv green paper, by which I surrindered me rights as an American citizen. With this here deed in me hand I wint through a line iv haughty gintlemen in unyform, an' wan afther another looked at th' ticket an' punched a hole in it. Whin I got to th' thrain th' last iv these gr-reat men says: 'Have ye got a ticket?' 'I had,' says I. 'This porous plasther was a ticket three minyits ago!' 'Get aboard,' says he, givin' me a short, frindly kick, an' in a minyit I found mesilf amid a scene iv Oryental splendhor an' no place to put me grip-sack.

"I stood dhrinkin' in th' glories iv th' scene until a proud man, who cud qualify on color f'r all his meals at th' White

House, come up an' ordhered me to bed. 'Where,' says I, 'do I sleep?' 'I don't know where ye sleep, cap,' says he, 'but ye'er ticket reads f'r an upper berth.' 'I wud prefer a thrapeze,' says I, 'but if ye'll call out th' fire department maybe they can help me in,' I says. At that he projooced a scalin' laddher, an' th' thrain goin' around a curve at that minyit I soon found mesilf on me hands an' knees in wan iv th' cosiest little up-stairs rooms ye iver saw. He dhrew th' curtains, an' so will I. But some day whin I am down-town I am goin' to dhrop in on me frind th' prisidint iv th' Pullman Company an' ask him to publish a few hints to th' wayfarer. I wud like to know how a gintleman can take off his clothes while settin' on thim. It wud help a good deal to know what to do with th' clothes whin ye have squirmed out iv thim. Ar-re they to be rolled up in a ball an' placed undher th' head or dhropped into th' aisle? Again, in th' mornin' how to get into th' clothes without throwin' th' thrain off th' thrack? I will tell ye confidintially, Hinnissy, that not bein' a contortionist th' on'y thing I took off was me hat.

"Th' thrain sped on an' on. I cud not sleep. Th' luxury iv thravel kept me wide awake. Who wud coort slumber in such a cosey little bower. There were some that did it; I heerd thim coortin'. But not I. I lay awake while we flew, or, I might say, bumped through space. It did not seem a minyit befure we were in Saint Looey. It seemed a year. On an' iver on we flew past forest, river, an' plain. Th' lights burned brightly just over me left ear, th' windows was open an' let in th' hoarse, exultant shriek iv th' locymotive, th' conversation iv th' baggageman to th' heavy thrunk, th' bammy night air, an' gr-reat purple clouds iv Illinye coal smoke. I took in enough iv this splindid product iv our prairie soil to qualify as a coal-yard. Be th' time th' sun peeked, or, I may say, jumped into me little roost, I wud've made a cheerful grate-fire an' left a slight deposit iv r-red ashes.

"Th' mornin' came too soon. With th' assistance iv th' stepladdher, th' bell-rope, an' th' bald head iv th' man in th' lower berth, I bounded lightly out iv me little nook an' rose fr'm th' flure with no injury worse thin a sprained ankle. I thin walked th' long an' splindid aisle, flanked be gintlemen who were writhin' into their clothin', an' soon found mesilf in th' superbly app'inted washroom.

"What hasn't American ingenuity done f'r th' wurruld? Here we were fairly flyin' through space, or stoppin' f'r wather at Polo, Illinye an' ye cud wash ye'ersilf as comfortably as ye cud in th' hydrant back iv th' gas-house. There were three handsome wash-basins, wan piece iv soap, an' towels galore—that is, almost enough to go round. In front iv each wash-basin was a dilicately nurtured child iv luxury cleansin' himsilf an' th' surroundin' furniture at wan blow. Havin' injyed a very refreshin' attimpt at a bath, I sauntered out into th' car. It looked almost like th' pitchers in th' pamphlet, or wud've if all th' boots had been removed. Th' scene was rendered more atthractive be th' prisince iv th' fair sect. A charmin' woman is always charmin', but niver more so thin on a sleepin'-car in th' mornin' afther a hard night's rest an' forty miles fr'm a curlin'-ir'n. With their pretty faces slightly sthreaked be th' right iv way, their eyes dancin' with suppressed fury, an' their hair almost sthraight, they make a pitcher that few can f'rget—an' they're lucky.

"But me eyes were not f'r thim. To tell ye th' thruth, Hinnissy, I was hungry. I thought to find a place among th' coal in me f'r wan iv thim sumchous meals I had r-read about, an' I summoned th' black prince who was foldin' up th' beddin' with his teeth. 'I wud like a breakfast fr'm ye'er superbly equipped buffay,' says I. 'I got ye,' says he. 'We have canned lobster, canned corn-beef, canned tomatoes, canned asparygus, an' wather fresh fr'm th' company's own spring at th' Chicago wather wurruks,' he says. 'Have ye annything to eat?' says I. 'Sind me th' cook,' I says. 'I'm th' cook,' says he, wipin' a pair iv shoes with his sleeve. 'What do ye do ye'er cookin' with?' says I. 'With a can-opener,' says he, givin' a hearty laugh.

"An so we whiled th' time away till Saint Looey was reached. O'Brien an' his wife nursed me back to life; I ray-

turned on th' canal-boat, an' here I am, almost as well as
befure I made me pleasure jaunt. I'm not goin' to do it again.
Let thim that will bask in their comforts. I stay at home.
Whiniver I feel th' desire to fly through space I throw four
dollars out iv th' window, put a cinder into me eye, an' go to
bed on a shelf in th' closet.

"I guess, Hinnissy, whin ye come to think iv it, they ain't anny such thing as luxury in thravel. We was meant to stay where
we found oursilves first, an' thravellin' is conthry to nature. I
can go fr'm Chicago to New York in twinty hours, but what's
th' matther with Chicago? I can injye places betther be not
goin' to thim.

"They ain't anny easy way iv thravellin'. Our ancesthors
didn't have anny fast thrains, but they didn't want thim. They
looked on a man thravellin' as a man dead, an' so he is. Comfort is in havin' things where ye can reach thim. A man is as
comfortable on a camel as on a private car, an' a man who cud
injye bouncin' over steel rails at sixty miles an hour cud go to
sleep on top iv a donky-injine. Th' good Lord didn't intind us
to be gaddin' around th' wurruld. Th' more we thry to do it
th' harder 'tis made f'r us. A man is supposed to take his meals
an' his sleep in an attichood iv repose. It ain't nachral to begin
on a biled egg at Galesburg an' end on it at Bloomington. We
weren't expected to spread a meal over two hundred miles, an'
our snores over a thousand. If th' Lord had wanted San Francisco to be near New York he'd have put it there. Th' railroads
haven't made it anny nearer. It's still tin thousan' miles, or
whativer it is, an' ye'd be more tired if ye reached it in wan day
thin ye wud if ye did it in two months in a covered wagon an'
stopped f'r sleep an' meals. Th' faster a thrain goes th' nearer
th' jints iv th' rails ar-re together. Man was meant to stay where
he is or walk. If Nature had intinded us to fly she wud've fixed
us with wings an' taught us to ate chicken-feed."

"But th' railroads assist Nature," said Mr. Hennessy.

"They do," said Mr. Dooley. "They make it hard to
thravel."

FAMOUS MEN

"I see," said Mr. Dooley, "that a lot iv people has been asked to make out a list iv th' hundherd gr-reatest men in th' wurruld that ar-re now dead."

"I didn't know there were that manny," said Mr. Hennessy.

"No more did I," said Mr. Dooley. "But judgin' be what's been turned in be th' boys as their pick iv th' wurruld's champeenship team there's not a hundherd—there's a millyon. I don't know most iv thim. They done things in thrades that I know nawthin' about. Ye see, ivry wan that's asked puts down names iv la-ads in their own business. They all start with Shakespeare, Wash'nton, an' Lincoln, but they're lible to wind up with Ephraim Perkins, who was th' champeen calcyminer iv his time.

"'Twas Andhrew Carnaygie started it, iv coorse. There's a man I like. He's good comp'ny. Whin nobody is talkin' an' some people ar-re thinkin' iv goin' home, he's always ready to jump in an get up some kind iv parlor intertainmint, whether 'tis reyformed spellin', or a peace conference, or a hundhred gr-reatest men compytition.

"Well, he'd no sooner suggested this rough but injyable spoort thin th' whole wurruld set down an' begun makin' out lists. Ivry man to his graft, as th' sayin' is. A pote picks out a hundherd potes who he thinks ar-re in his class, or nearly so. A banker can't see annybody but Shakespeare, Wash'nton, an' Lincoln excipt th' boys that can separate money with their thumbs. A bartinder tells ye that th' customers he wud like to see on a dull avenin' ar-re Shakespeare, Wash'nton, Lincoln, an' th' janiuses that has had cocktails named afther thim. That's a crowded ordher, but 'tis as sure a way to fame as anny I know. Cinchris fr'm now Col. Rickey will be cillybrated whin people can't raymimber whether it was Roodyard Kipling or Laura Jean Libbey that lived in Brooklyn. A mannyfacthrer iv furniture acknowledges that th' men that have had most influence on his life were Shakespeare, Wash'nton, Lin-

coln, an' th' invintor iv curled hair. A grocery man says that
his eyes ar-re dimmed with tears ivry time he thinks iv
Shakespeare, Wash'nton, Lincoln, an' th' author iv dhried apples. Cassidy, who goes out to Celtic park ivry Sundah an'
sprains his back thryin' to throw th' hammer over his feet,
thinks that nex' to th' athaleets mentioned Flanagan, who cud
throw th' hammer over th' moon if he wanted to, is th' head iv
th' list. Ye'er little boy thinks it's th' dhriver iv Hook an' Laddher Five. Ye'er oldest boy thinks it's Cap Chance. Ye'er
daughter thinks it's Jawn Dhrew. An author heads th' list with
th' two Dutchmen that invinted printin', though Father Kelly
says authors was just as well off whin they chalked their own
novels on a piece iv slate an' charged people so much a head to
look at thim. They were their own publisher in thim days.

"Ask a Chinyman to put down th' hundherd gr-reatest men
he iver heerd iv an' ye won't recognize a name onless it
reminds ye iv where ye lost a shirt. A German will pack th' list
as full iv Germans as a brass band. There'll be nawthin' but
Shakespeare an' Fr-rinch in th' Fr-rinch list, an' th' Rooshyan
list wud make th' chief iv polis sind out a riot call.

"An' they're right, all iv thim. If Shakspeare goes on th' list
because he cud throw a pome farther thin anny man befure or
since, Flanagan ought to go on because he can throw th' hammer. Jack Johnson is as gr-reat a man in his way as Prisidint
Eliot. They've both got th' punch, but 'tis in a diff'rent way.
Look out iv th' window at that fellow acrost th' sthreet
climbin' up a derrick with a hammer in wan hand, a monkey
wrench between his teeth, an' a bag iv spikes hangin' fr'm his
neck. Cud Hogan's frind Milton do that? He cud not no more
thin that acrobat cud write 'Shurdan's Ride' or whativer it
was. Manny a man that cud capture this here city with wan
hand cudden't bate a carpet. Manny a man that cud rule a
hundherd millyon sthrangers with an ir'n hand is careful to
take off his shoes in th' front hallway whin he comes home late
at night.

"What makes a man gr-reat annyhow? It isn't because he's

good, though it may be because he isn't. Manny a hero iv an-
tikity has a pitcher iv somewan else in th' goold watch th' boys
in th' office give him f'r Chris'mas. It ain't because he's betther
iddycated thin others. There ar-re fellows tachin' school in
Waukegan that cud spell better thin Alexandher th' Gr-reat. It
ain't because he's pretty. An album filled with pitchers iv th'
gr-reatest cud on'y be opened afther dark. It ain't because
they're brave. Manny a man has voted th' Raypublican tickey
in Mississippi without aven gettin' his name on th' tally sheet.
It ain't because they're forchnit. Th' on'y fellows ye remimber
who wint up in flyin' masheens last year ar-re thim that come
down too quick. An' it ain't because they plan things in ad-
vance, f'r there was Columbus, whose name is on manny lamp
posts, an' he didn't find what he wint lookin' f'r, Hogan tells
me, an' it wasn't America he discovered at first but a place
called Watling's island that he bumped into on his way to
Chiny, th' poor deluded Eyetalyan thinkin' Chiny was
somewheres near Phillydelphy.

"So there ye ar-re. Befure ye pick out th' gr-reatest men ye've
got to tell me what is ye'er idee iv a gr-reat man. Father Kelly
says a man's gr-reat who can do th' wan thing he knows how
to do betther thin most annywan else. That is, if he has th' luck
to cash in. Be that rule I can prove ye're th' akel iv Joolyus
Cayzar, f'r I've obsarved ye'er scientific handlin' iv a shovel,
me boy, though I've niver mentioned it f'r fear iv turnin' ye'er
head.

"But whin I look over these lists I'm disappinted in not
seein' th' mintion iv manny a binifactor iv humanity that I've
always looked up to. I'm goin' to make out me own list. I've as
good a right as annywan. An' th' name I'll put down fourth is
th' fellow that invinted suspinders. I've often talked to ye
about him. He's wan iv me gr-reatest heroes. I don't know his
name, but ivry time I look down at me legs an' see they're properly dhraped I think kindly iv this janius. I wanst had an idee
that suspinders was wan iv th' oldest iv human institutions. I
suppose ivrybody did. That's th' careless way we take th' gr-

reat gifts iv science. We think there niver was a time whin there weren't all these convayniences. We have no thought iv th' lone student settin' undher th' midnight lamp an' dopin' thim out f'r th' benefit iv a thankless race. I supposed that th' second thing Adam bought afther he become ashamed iv himself—an' he'd ought not to be goin' around that way aven if 'twas on'y his own fam'ly that cud see him—was a pair iv suspinders to hold thim up.

"But it ain't so. Fr'm what Hogan tells me they're almost what ye might call a modhren invintion. F'r eight thousan' years, accoordin' to Father Kelly's count, or f'r eight thousan' millyon years th' way they add it up in th' colledges, th' wurruld wint without thim till this modest frind iv man come along with an invintion that has made it possible f'r mankind to fight th' battles iv th' wurruld with both hands free. Iver since Hogan told me this I can't read histhry without puttin' in lines that make me shiver. 'Give me liberty or give me death,' says Pathrick Hinnery, raisin' his hands above his head with a passyonate gesture, accordin' to histhry. 'Give me liberty or give me death,' says Pathrick Hinnery, raisin' wan hand above his head, accordin' to me. No wondher sojers in th' old times were brave. They cudden't run away comfortably. An' I've always wondhered how th' Fr-rinch cud talk at all in thim dark days.

"Who else wud I put on me list? Faith, I don't know. Manny gr-reat devilopments has been made in me line iv business since liquor merchants used to go ar-round sellin' pints out iv a leather bag. I wud mention th' creators iv th' beer pump, th' cash registher, th' combynation cheese, cracker, an' coffee plate, th' seegar lighter, an' th' injanyous device f'r cuttin' off th' ends iv seegars which in oncivilized peeroyds was bit off. But I'm willin' to accipt anny man's list so long as it don't include th' invintor iv th' alarm clock an' th' gas meter. I've got thim on me other list.

"'Tis a good sign whin people acknowledge that other people ar-re gr-reat. It shows self-resthraint. It's far aisier to say no man was gr-reat. An' ye can always prove that, f'r there's

somethin' th' matther with ivry man, an' if there wasn't he'd
be lynched. I wondher who'll be th' gr-reat men iv to-day a
hundherd years fr'm now. Lookin' over me contimpraries, I
shud say that almost annywan has a chanst. Posterity, Hinnissy, sometimes likes to vote f'r th' dark horse. There's wan
thing ye may be sure iv, an' that is that manny a boy that
thinks he's got th' diploma in his bag won't figure in th'
biographical ditchnries. Faith, I wudden't be surprised at all if
ye got in ye'ersilf. A hundherd years fr'm now a man may pick
up a histhry iv our counthry an' read: 'At this peeryod there ar-
rose a remarkable figure in th' person iv Malachi Hinnissy. F'r
cinchries th' wurruld had been full iv talk. Now f'r th' first
time there appeared a man who cud listen. He was th' foundher iv th' pow'rful school that includes at th' prisint day most
iv th' thoughtful men iv th' wurruld.'"

"But I haven't been listenin'," said Mr. Hennessy.

"Well," said Mr. Dooley, "if ye won't talk an' ye won't
listen ye can have ye'er thrunk checked to th' Hall iv Fame to-
night. Ye'er ilicted."

ON THE DESCENT OF MAN

"What ar-re ye readin'?" asked Mr. Hennessy.

"A comical little piece in th' Sunday pa-aper on th' Descent
iv Man," said Mr. Dooley. "Ye get a good dale iv knowledge
out iv th' pa-apers whin ye're not lookin' f'r it, an' a fellow
that's paid five cents to find out where Gyp th' Blood spint his
vacation, if he doesn't stop there but goes on r-readin', is li'ble
to end up as an idjacated man.

"Maybe ye'd like me to read ye something out iv this here
fable in slang. Well, thin, listen to th' pro-fissor: 'Such habits
not on'y tended to develop the motor cortex itsilf,' he says, 'but
thrained th' tactile an' th' kin—th' kin—I'll spell it f'r ye —
k-i-n-a-e-s-t-h-e-t-i-c—pronounce anny way ye plaze—senses an'
linked up their cortical areas in bonds iv more intimate
assocyations with th' visyool cortex——'"

"What kind iv a language is that?" Mr. Hennessy interrupted.

"It's scientific language," said Mr. Dooley. "I've been
thryin' to wurruk it out mesilf with th' aid iv a ditchnry, but I
cudden't put it together till Dock O'Leary, who's great at these
puzzle pitchers, come in. Fr'm what he said I guess that th'
pro-fissor that wrote it meant to say that th' raison man is betther thin th' other animals is because iv what's in his head. I
suspicted as much befure an' have often said so. But nobody
has iver ast me to go befure a larned society an' have me chest
dhraped with medals f'r sayin' it. I cudden't fill up me time on
th' program. All I cud say wud be: 'Fellow pro-fissors, th'
thing that give ye an' me a shade over th' squrl an' th'
grasshopper is that we have more marrow in th' bean.
Thankin' ye again f'r ye'er kind attintion, I will now lave ye
while ye thranslate this almost onfathomable thought into a
language that on'y a dhrug clerk can undherstand.'

"Fr'm what Dock O'Leary says, this here profissor has seen
Darwin an' histed him a couple iv billyon years. If ye'd like to
hear about it I'll tell ye. Well, thin, it was this way: Some time
befure th' big fire, whin I was wurrukin' f'r Mullaney, th' conthractor, dhrivin' a team, a fellow be th' name iv Darwin come
along an' made a monkey iv man. He showed that th' principal
diff'rence between us an' th' little frinds iv Italy was that we
had lost our tails. We had to lave th' old entailed estates an' th'
ancesthral bamboo threes where our fam'ly had spint so many
happy millyons iv years an' come down to earth an' be men.
Our first ancestor had his tail docked, an', havin' lost this here
member which was at wanst his manes iv rapid thransit an' his
aisy chair, th' old gintleman cud no longer swing fr'm th'
branch iv th' three an' amuse th' childher be pickin' things off
thim, but had to go to wurruk. In ordher to apply f'r a job he
was forced to larn to walk an' to talk. He manicured his front
feet an' made hands iv thim, an', so he cud win th' affections iv
th' fair, he was compelled to shed his comfortable an' nachral
hairy coat an' buy clothes. Th' fam'ly all took afther th' old

man an' improved on him through th' cinchries, till to-day ye
have th' magnificent jooks ye see all ar-round ye, dhressed up
in quare garmints, puttin' on supeeryor airs, wearin' crowns,
runnin' f'r office, killin' each other, dancin' th' turkey throt,
an' gin'rally behavin' so foolish that whin th' father iv a fam'ly
iv monkeys sees a human bein' comin' along in th' woods he
calls out: 'Mother, bring th' little wans to th' end iv this
branch. Here comes wan iv our poor relations who has to wurruk f'r a livin'. He wud've been just as well off as we ar-re if
his fam'ly hadn't squandered their tails. Dhrop a cocynut on
his head an' see him jump. Ain't he the funny sight?'

"I can well remimber how hot ivrybody was agan Darwin on
account iv what he wrote. Nobody had been very proud iv
Adam as an ancesthor, but still ye cud put up with him if ye
took into account that he was dalin' with new problems an'
was th' first married man. But it hurted a good manny proud
people to think that but f'r th' luck iv th' game they might all
be up in Lincoln park makin' faces through th' glass at little
boys an' girls. So Darwin was excymunicated fr'm manny a
church that he'd niver been in, an' expelled fr'm th' Knights iv
Pythias, an' gin'rally threated as he desarved f'r a long time.
But afther awhile people begun to take more kindly to th' idee
an' to say: 'Well, annyhow, it's more comfortable to feel that
we're a slight improvement on a monkey thin such a fallin' off
fr'm th' angels. F'r awhile it looked as though we weren't
holdin' our own. But now it looks as if we are on our way,' an'
thought no more about it. An' th' monkeys had no access to
th' press, so they cudden't write in kickin' letthers signed 'Indignant Monkey' or th' live iv that.

"But this pro-fissor has gone further thin Darwin in pursooin' our lineege down to its disgraceful start. He has run
acrost a lot iv old town records, marredge certyficates, birth
registhers, an' so on an' has discovered that our original pro-
ginitor, th' boy that give us our push tords respectability, th'
first mimber iv th' fam'ly that moved uptown, th' survivor iv
th' Fort Dearborn massacree, th' pilgrim father that came out

iv th' jungle, th' foundher iv th' fam'ly fortune was—what d'ye think? Ye'll niver guess is I give ye a thousand guesses. It was th' jumpin' shrew iv South America. It's as I tell ye. Here ye see it in black an' white befure ye'er eyes: 'Man descinded fr'm th' jumpin' shrew.' Hence our sunny dispositions an' th' presint campaign. I niver cud undherstand why if mankind come down fr'm th' monkey we weren't more janyal. But now I know. It's th' old shrew blood that still coorses through our veins that makes us so cross with each other.

"Yes, sir; this la-ad with th' aid iv a microscope, a knife, an' perhaps a dhream book has thraced us back to this inthrestin' little crather. Prob'ly ye niver see a jumpin' shrew. Ye wudden't? There ar-re very few jumpin' shrews in this neighborhood. But back in th' old estate in South Africa they ar-re numerous an' highly respicted. Manny iv th' mimbers iv th' original branch iv our fam'ly still live in th' homes iv our ancistors an' keep up th' thraditional customs like th' old fam'lies iv Boston. This scientific dock gives us a plazin' pitcher iv their lives. 'These three shrews,' says he, 'ar-re small squrl like animals which feed on insects an' fruit. Whin feedin' they often set on their haunches, holdin' their food, afther th' manner iv squrls, in their front paws.' There, Hinnissy, ye have a view iv ye'ersilf as ye were befure th' flood. Ye've often told me ye were descinded fr'm th' kings iv Ireland, an' manny is th' time I've wondhered how ye'd look in a soot iv ir'n an' bull skin, settin' on a horse, holdin' on to th' mane with wan hand an' to a spear with th' other. But I injye more th' thought iv ye still further back, perched on th' branch iv a three makin' a light lunch iv a peanut an' an ant. Some day I'm goin' to take a stepladdher an' go to South Africa an' visit these relations iv ye'ers an' mine. An' why not? If a man be the name iv Jones will spind money thryin' to prove that he's descinded fr'm a cillibrated holdup man iv th' same name in th' reign iv Queen Elizabeth why shudden't he look up his rilitives, th' jumpin' shrews iv South Africa, an' be took over th' fam'ly residence be a caretaker, f'r a shillin', an' see where th' ol' jook died defindin' his threasures iv huckleberries an' weevils against th' night attack iv th' ant eater an' th' banded armydillo? Tell me why. An' why, now that this prof has thraced out th' line, shuden't we resume th' fam'ly name? Be rights we'd all be called jumpin' shrews. There's a chance f'r a hyphen there that manny a mimber iv th' stock exchange wud welcome.

"But I don't think this here prof wint far enough in lookin' f'r our start. Th' jumpin' shrews ar-re all right enough, but what come befure them? Accordin' to this article it's har'ly thirty billyon years since this gallant little fellow first hopped up a three. Ar-re we to f'rget our arlier ancestors? What about th' patient lobster, th' ca'm eyesther, th' cheerful jelly fish, an' back through th' cinchries th' first onobtrusive microbe, an' befure that th' viggytables, an' befure thim th' mud at th' bottom iv th' sea? Rash, upstart jumpin' shrew, d'ye niver ralize that it's an own cousin ye're atin' fried on th' beefsteak an' maybe a shovelful iv th' original stock ye're hurlin' into th' barrow to give a ride down to th' dump?

"But don't feel bad about it. There's always wan encouragin' thing about th' sad scientific facts that comes out ivry week in th' pa-apers. They're usually not thrue. I know there niver was a Dooley that lived in a three, because I niver see wan that cud climb a three. An' annyhow I don't care. Divvle th' bit iv attintion I give to a fellow lookin' at a glass iv wather through an eyeglass an' guessin' what happened in South Africa eighty-three billyon years ago. Mind ye, I don't blame this dock f'r thryin' to make us all—th' Dooleys, an' th' Honezollerns, an' th' Vere de Veres—members iv th' same fam'ly. His name is Smith. But if he'd f'rget about th' origin iv th' race an' tell us not where man comes fr'm but where he's goin' to I'd take an intherpeter aroun' an' listen to him."

"These men ar-re inimies iv religion," said Mr. Hennessy.

"P'raps," said Mr. Dooley. "But they'll niver be dangerous ontil some wan comes along an' thranslates their lectures into English. An' I don't think there's a chance that cud be done."

GLORY

Hogan has been in here this afthernoon, an' I've heerd more scandal talked thin I iver thought was in the wurrld."

"Hogan had betther keep quiet," said Mr. Hennessy. "If he goes circulatin' anny stories about me I'll——"

"Ye needn't worry," said Mr. Dooley. "We didn't condiscend to talk about annywan iv ye'er infeeryor station. If ye want to be th' subjick iv our scand'lous discoorse ye'd betther go out an' make a repytation. No, sir, our talk was entirely about th' gr-reat an' illusthrees an' it ran all th' way fr'm Julius Cayzar to Ulysses Grant.

"Dear, oh dear, but they were th' bad lot. Thank th' Lord nobody knows about me. Thank th' Lord I had th' good sinse to retire fr'm pollyticks whin me repytation had spread as far as Halsted Sthreet. If I'd let it go a block farther I'd've been sorry f'r it th' rest iv me life an' some years afther me death.

"I wanted to be famous in thim days, whin I was young an' foolish. 'Twas th' dhream iv me life to have people say as I wint by: 'There goes Dooley, th' gr-reatest statesman iv his age,' an' have thim name babies, sthreets, schools, canal boats, an' five-cent seegars afther me, an' whin I died to have it put in th' books that 'at this critical peeryod in th' history of America there was need iv a man who combined strenth iv charackter with love iv counthry. Such a man was found in Martin Dooley, a prom'nent retail liquor dealer in Ar-rchey Road.'

"That's what I wanted, an' I'm glad I didn't get me wish. If I had, 'tis little attintion to me charackter that th' books iv what Hogan calls bi-ography wud pay, but a good deal to me debts. Though they mintioned th' fact that I resked death f'r me adopted fatherland, they'd make th' more intherestin' story about th' time I almost met it be fallin' down stairs while runnin' away fr'm a polisman. F'r wan page they'd print about me love iv counthry, they'd print fifty about me love iv dhrink.

"Th' things thim gr-reat men done wud give thim a place in Byrnes's book. If Julius Caysar was alive to-day he'd be doin' a lockstep down in Joliet. He was a corner loafer in his youth an' a robber in his old age. He busted into churches, fooled arround with other men's wives, curled his hair with a poker an' smelled iv perfumery like a Saturday night car. An' his wife was a suspicyous charackter an' he turned her away.

"Napolyon Bonypart. impror iv th' Fr-rinch, was far too gay aven f'r thim friv'lous people, an' had fits. His first wife was no betther than she shud be, an' his second wife didn't care f'r him. Willum Shakespeare is well known as an author of plays that no wan can play, but he was betther known as a two-handed dhrinker, a bad actor, an' a thief. His wife was a common scold an' led him th' life he desarved.

"They niver leave th' ladies out iv these stories iv th' grreat. A woman that marries a janius has a fine chance iv her false hair becomin' more immortal thin his gr-reatest deed. It don't make anny diff'rence if all she knew about her marital hero was that he was a consistent feeder, a sleepy husband, an' indulgent to his childher an' sometimes to himsilf, an' that she had to darn his socks. Nearly all th' gr-reat men had something th' matther with their wives. I always thought Mrs. Wash'nton, who was th' wife iv th' father iv our counthry, though childless hersilf, was about right. She looks good in th' pitchers, with a shawl ar-round her neck an' a frilled night-cap on her head. But Hogan says she had a tongue sharper thin George's soord, she insulted all his frinds, an' she was much older thin him. As f'r George, he was a case. I wish th' counthry had got itsilf a diff'rent father. A gr-reat moral rellijous counthry like this desarves a betther parent.

"They were all alike. I think iv Bobby Burns as a man that wrote good songs, aven if they were in a bar'brous accint, but Hogan thinks iv him as havin' a load all th' time an' bein' th' scandal iv his parish. I remimber Andhrew Jackson as th' man that licked th' British at Noo Orleans be throwin' cotton bales at thim, but Hogan remimbers him as a man that cudden't spell an' had a wife who smoked a corncob pipe. I remimber Abraham Lincoln f'r freein' th' slaves, but Hogan remimbers how he used to cut loose yarns that made th' bartinder shake th' stove harder thin it needed. I remimber Grant f'r what he done ar-round Shiloh whin he was young, but Hogan remimbers him f'r what he done arr-ound New York whin he was old.

"An' so it goes. Whin a lad with nawthin' else to do starts out to write a bi-ography about a gr-reat man, he don't go to th' war departmint or th' public library. No, sir, he begins to search th' bureau dhrawers, old pigeon-holes, th' records iv th' polis coort, an' th' recollections iv th' hired girl. He likes letters betther thin annything else. He don't care much f'r th' kind beginnin': 'Dear wife, I'm settin' in front iv th' camp fire wearin' th' flannel chest protector ye made me, an' dhreamin' iv ye,' but if he can find wan beginnin': 'Little Bright Eyes: Th' old woman has gone to th' counthry,' he's th' happiest bi-ographer ye cud see in a month's thraval.

"Hogan had wan iv thim books in here th' other day. 'Twas written by a frind, so ye can see it wasn't prejudiced wan way or another. 'At this time,' says the book, 'an ivint happened that was destined to change th' whole coorse iv our hero's life. Wan day, while in a sthreet car, where he lay dozin' fr'm dhrink, he awoke to see a beautiful woman thryin' to find a nickle in a powder puff. Th' brutal conductor towered over her, an' it was more thin th' Gin'ral cud bear. Risin' to his feet, with an oath, he pulled th' rope iv th' fare register an' fell off th' car.

"'Th' incident made a deep impression on th' Gin'ral. I have no doubt he often thought iv his beautiful Madonna iv th' throlly, although he niver said so. But wan night as he staggered out iv th' dinin'-room at th' German Ambassadure's, who shud he run acrost but th' fair vision iv th' surface line. She curtsied low an' picked him up, an' there began a frindship so full iv sorrow an' happiness to both iv thim. He seldom mintioned her, but wan night he was heard to mutter: 'Her face is like wan iv Rembrand's saints.' A few historyans contind that what he said was: 'Her face looks like a remnant sale,' but I cannot believe this.

"They exchanged brilliant letters f'r manny years, in fact on-til th' enchanthress was locked up in an insane asylum. I have not been able to find anny iv his letters, but her's fell into th' hands iv wan iv his faithful servants, who presarved an' published thim. (Love an' Letters iv Gin'ral Dhread-naught an' Alfaretta Agonized; Stolen, Collected an' Edited be James Snooper.) * * * Next year was mim'rable f'r his gloryous vic-thry at Punkheim, all th' more wondherful because at th' time our hero was sufferin' fr'm deleeryyum thremens.

"'It shows th' fortitude iv th' Gen'ral an' that he was as gr-reat a liar as I have indicated in th' precedin' pages, that with th' cheers iv his sojers ringin' in his ears, he cud still write home to his wife: 'Ol' girl—I can't find annything fit to dhrink down here. Can't ye sind me some cider fr'm th' farm.' * * * In 1865 he was accused iv embezzlemint, but th' charges niver reached his ears or th' public's ontil eight years afther his death. * * * In '67 his foster brother, that he had neglected in Kansas City, slipped on his ballroom flure an' broke his leg. * * * In '70 his wife died afther torturin' him f'r fifty years. They were a singularly badly mated couple, with a fam'ly iv fourteen childher, but he did not live long to enjoy his hap-piness. F'r some reason he niver left his house, but passed away within a month, one of th' gr-reatest men th' cinchry has pro-jooced. For further details iv th' wrong things he done see th' notes at th' end iv th' volume.'

"It seems to me, Hinnissy, that this here thing called bi-ography is a kind iv an offset f'r histhry. Histhry lies on wan wide, an' bi-ography comes along an' makes it rowl over an' lie on th' other side. Th' historyan says, go up; th' bi-ographer says, come down among us. I don't believe ayether iv thim.

"I was talkin' with Father Kelly about it afther Hogan wint out. 'Were they all so bad, thim men that I've been brought up to think so gloryous?' says I. 'They were men,' says Father Kelly. 'Ye mustn't believe all ye hear about thim, no matther who says it,' says he. 'It's a thrait iv human nature to pull down th' gr-reat an' sthrong. Th' hero sthruts through histhry with his chin up in th' air, his scipter in his hand an' his crown on his head. But behind him dances a boot-black im- itatin' his walk an' makin' faces at him. Fame invites a man out iv his house to be crowned f'r his gloryous deeds, an' sarves him with a warrant f'r batin' his wife. 'Tis not in th' nature iv things that it shudden't be so. We'd all perish iv humilyation if th' gr-reat men iv th' wurruld didn't have nachral low-down thraits. If they don't happen to possess thim, we make some up f'r thim. We allow no man to tower over us. Wan way or another we level th' wurruld to our own height. If we can't reach th' hero's head we cut off his legs. It always makes me feel aisier about mesilf whin I r-read how bad Julius Cayzar was. An' it stimylates compytition. If gr- reatness an' goodness were hand in hand 'tis small chance an- ny iv us wud have iv seein' our pitchers in th' pa-apers.'

"An' so it is that the battles ye win, th' pitchers ye paint, th' people ye free, th' childher that disgrace ye, th' false step iv ye'er youth, all go thundherin' down to immortality together. An' afther all, isn't it a good thing? Th' on'y bi-ography I care about is th' one Mulligan th' stone-cutter will chop out f'r me. I like Mulligan's style, f'r he's no flatthrer, an' he has wan model iv bi-ography that he uses f'r old an' young, rich an' poor. He merely writes something to th' gin'ral effect that th' deceased was a wondher, an' lets it go at that."

"Which wud ye rather be, famous or rich?" asked Mr. Hen- nessy.

"I'd like to be famous," said Mr. Dooley, "an' have money enough to buy off all threatenin' bi-ographers."

FAME

"'Tis a gr-reat rayciption they do be givin' Bryan down in New York state," said Mr. Hennessy.

"A fine rayciption f'r a dimmycrat in New York state," said

Mr. Dooley, "is that he's not dangerously wounded. Annything short iv death is regarded as a frindly an' inthrested rayciption, an' a mild kind iv death, like suffycation be chloroform, wud be considhered a rayspictful hearin'. All ye can say about Willum Jennings Bryan's rayciption is that he got by Wall sthreet without bein' stoned to death with nuggets fr'm th' goold resarve. Annyhow, what ar-re ye dhraggin' pollytics into this peaceful abode f'r, Hinnissy? Isn't it bad enough f'r me to have to stand here all day long listenin' to sthrangers rayjoocin' th' constitootynal questions now befure th' people to personal insult without havin' me frinds makin' me nights mis'rable with chatther about th' fleetin' problems iv th' hour? Th' votes is as good as cast an' counted. Ayether th' counthry is rooned or its rooned. An' it ain't, annyhow. Ayether we ar-re delivered over hand an' foot to th' widdies an' orphans that've had thrust stocks sawed off on thim be th' ex-icutors, or th' gover'mint abandons a policy iv brutal, crool, murdhrous conquist iv th' cow'rdly assassins iv th' land iv etarnal sunshine an' shadow. Two weeks fr'm today we'll be ayether neglectin' to pay our debts in th' standard money iv th' nations iv th' earth or in a debased an' wretched cienage that no wan has iver got enough iv. An' what th' divvle diff'rence does it make, me boy? Th' mornin' afther iliction, 'tis Hinnissy to th' slag pile an' Dooley to th' beer pump an' Jawn D. Rockefellar to th' ile can, an' th' ol' flag floatin' over all iv us if th' wind is good an' th' man in charge has got up in time to hist it. Foolish man, th' fun'rals don't stop f'r ilictions, or th' christenin's or th' weddin's. Be hivins, I think th' likes iv ye imagines this counthry is something besides a hunk iv land occypied be human bein's. Ye think it a sort iv an autymobill that'll run down onless ye charge it with ye'er partic'lar kind i gas. Don't ye expict Hinnissy that anny throop iv angels will dhrop fr'm Hiven to chop ye'er wood on th' mornin' iv th' siventh iv Novimber if Bryan is ilicted, an' don't ye lave Jawnny McKenna think that if th' raypublicans gets in, he'll have to put a sthrip iv ile-cloth on th' dure sill to keep pluthycrats fr'm shovin' threasury notes undher th' dure. No, sir; I used to hink that was so—wanst, in th' days whin I pathronized a lothry. Now I know diff'rent.

"Where'll they be a hundhred years fr'm now? Debs an' Mark Hanna, an' Web Davis, an' Croker an' Bill Lorimer — where'll they be? I was r-readin' th' other day about a vote cast be a lot iv distinguished gazabs through th' counthry f'r occypants iv a hall iv fame. A Hall iv Fame's th' place where th' names iv th' most famous men is painted, like th' side iv a barm where a little boy writes th' name iv th' little girl he loves. In a week or two he goes back an' rubs it out. But in this matther 't was detarmined to lave out th' question to a lot iv sthrong laads an' have thim vote on it an' on'y th' dead wans iligeable. I r-read th' list today, Hinnissy, an' will ye believe me or will ye not, much as I know I cudden't recall more thin half th' names. George Wash'nton was ilicted, iv coorse, unaminously an' without a contistin' dillygation an' proud he'll be to larn iv it. Thin there was Ulyss S. Grant an' Thomas Jefferson an' Robert E. Lee. I know all iv thim as though we'd been raised in th' same lot. But near all th' others got by me. Wan man was famous because he made a cotton gin, though th' author iv more common dhrinks was cut out. Another man got by th' flag on th' ground that he manyfacthered a clock. A third passed th' stand because he made a ditchnary, which is a book that tells ye how manny diff'rent things th' same wurrud means. They was potes I niver r-read an' statesmen I niver heard iv, an' gin'rals I niver knew fought, an' fought, an' invintors iv bluein', an' discov'rers iv things that had been discovered befure an' things that had to be undiscovered later. An' th' list was as onfamilyar to me as th' battin' ordher iv th' Worcester ball team iv eighteen hundhred an' siventy-six. 'Bedad,' says I, 'if this is fame, I'll dhraw cards mesilf. Some day whin th' owner iv a new Hall iv Fame tells th' janitor to climb up an' white-wash over th' names on th' wall an' make out a new list, some wan may vote f'r th' gr-reat soul that discovered how to make both ends meet in th' year nineteen hundhred.' That's a gr-reat invintion, Hinnissy. Thank th' Lord th' Standard Ile Comp'ny hasn't got a patent on it.

"What's fame, afther all, me la-ad? 'Tis as apt to be what some wan writes on ye'er tombstone as annything ye did f'r ye-ersilf. It takes two to make it, but on'y wan has much iv a hand. 'Tis not a man's life in wan volume be himsilf, but his 'Life' in three volumes be wan iv his frinds. An' be th' way th' jury voted f'r th' lodgers in this tiniment house iv fame, manny that cud pay their scoor at th' desk is left on th' dure step because th' bunks is filled with th' frinds iv th' managers. I think *I'll* hire a large buildin' f'r th' rayjicted. I wudden't be surprised if manny iv th' star boardhers come out iv th' other Hall iv Fame f'r th' conjanial comp'ny in mine.

"Whin ye think iv it, whin ye considher how manny men have done things or thried to do thim f'r wan hundhred years in this counthry, an' now whin it comes to pick th' winners about half th' list is on'y famous to th' men that voted f'r thim, how ar-re ye goin' to figure that anny iv th' la-ads that ye're wastin' ye'er lungs f'r will bring up r-right? A hundhred years fr'm now Hogan may be as famous as th' Impror Willum, an' annyhow they'll both be dead an' that's th' principal ingreejent iv fame. Go home an' think that over."

THE END OF THINGS

"The raison no wan is afraid iv Death, Hinnessy, is that no wan ra-ally undherstands it. If anny wan iver come to undher-stand it he'd be scared to death. If they is anny such thing as a cow'rd, which I doubt, he's a man that comes nearer realizin' thin other men, how seeryous a matther it is to die. I talk about it, an' sometimes I think about it. But how do I think about it? It's me lyin' there in a fine shoot iv clothes an' listenin' to all th' nice things people are sayin' about me. I'm dead, mind ye, but I can hear a whisper in the furthest corner iv th' room. Ivry wan is askin' ivry wan else why did I die. 'It's a gr-reat loss to th' counthry,' says Hogan. 'It is,' says Donahue. 'He was a fine man,' says Clancy. 'As honest a man is iver dhrew th' breath iv life,' says Schwartzmeister. 'I hope he forgives us all th' harm we attempted to do him,' says Donahue. 'I'd give annything to have him back,' says Clancy. 'He was this and that, th' life iv th' party, th' sowl iv honor, th' frind iv th' disthressed, th' boolwark iv th' constichoochion, a pathrite, a gintleman, a Christyan an' a scholard.' 'An' such a roguish way with him,' says th' Widow O'Brien.

"That's what I think, but if I judged fr'm expeeryence I'd know it'd be, 'It's a nice day f'r a dhrive to th' cimitry. Did he lave much?' No man is a hayro to his undertaker."

CASUAL OBSERVATIONS

These short takes were written by Dunne himself to stand alone; other brief excerpts from Dooley essays similarly have become epigrammatic. Mike Royko, best selling writer and *Chicago Tribune* columnist, whom Dunne would be proud to claim as a literary descendant, is partial to "Politics ain't bean-bag," as well as to other Dooleyisms that follow. Art Seidenbaum, OPINION Editor of the *Los Angeles Times*, prefers, "Th' past always looks better than it was. It's on'y pleasant because it isn't here." According to Kennedy Library Curator David Paivers, President John F. Kennedy included the following in his handwritten collection of quotable quotes: "When ye build ye'er triumphal arch to yer conquerin' hero, Hinnissy, build it out of bricks so th' people will have somethin' convenient to throw at him as he passes through." As indicated, other dedicated Dooley fans join in this preference for the pithy.

To most people a savage nation is wan that doesn't wear oncomf'rtable clothes.

Manny people'd rather be kilt at Newport thin at Bunker Hill.

If ye live enough befure thirty ye won't care to live at all afther fifty.

As Shakespere says, be thrue to ye'ersilf an' ye will not thin
be false to ivry man.

Play actors, orators an' women ar-re a class be thimsilves.

Among men, Hinnissy, wet eye manes dhry heart.

Th' nearest anny man comes to a con-ciption iv his own
death is lyin' back in a comfortable coffin with his ears cocked
f'r th' flatthrin' remarks iv th' mourners.

A fanatic is a man that does what he thinks th' Lord wud do
if He knew th' facts iv th' case. (Social Historian J. C. Furnas)

A millionyaire—or man out iv debt—wanst tol' me his
dhreams always took place in th' farm-house where he was
bor-rn. He said th' dhreamin' part iv his life was th' on'y part
that seemed real.

'Tis no job to find out who wrote an anonymous letter. Jus'
look out iv th' window whin ye get it. 'Tis harder to do evil
thin good be stealth.

A German's idee iv Hivin is painted blue an' has cast-iron
dogs on th' lawn.

No man was iver so low as to have rayspict f'r his brother-in-
law.

Th' modhren idee iv governmint is 'Snub th' people, buy th'
people, jaw th' people.'

I wisht I was a German an' believed in machinery.

A vote on th' tallysheet is worth two in the box.

I care not who makes th' laws iv a nation if I can get out an injunction. (Union Leader Robert Walz)

An Englishman appears resarved because he can't talk.

What China needs is a Chinese exclusion act.

All th' wurruld loves a lover—excipt sometime th' wan that's all th' wurruld to him.

A nation with colonies is kept busy. Look at England! She's like wan iv th' Swiss bell-ringers.

Th' paramount issue f'r our side is th' wan th' other side doesn't like to have mintioned.

If ye put a beggar on horseback ye'll walk ye'ersilf.

It takes a sthrong man to be mean. A mean man is wan that has th' courage not to be gin'rous. Whin I give a tip 'tis not because I want to but because I'm afraid iv what th' waiter'll think. Russell Sage is wan iv Nature's noblemen.

An autocrat's a ruler that does what th' people wants an' takes th' blame f'r it. A constitootional ixicutive, Hinnissy, is a ruler that does as he dam pleases an' blames th' people.

'Tis as hard f'r a rich man to enther th' kingdom iv Hiven as it is f'r a poor man to get out iv Purgatory.

Evil communications corrupt good Ph'lippeens.

Ivry man has his superstitions. If I look at a new moon over me shoulder I get a crick in me neck.

Thrust iverybody—but cut th' ca-ards. (Mike Royko)

If Rooshia wud shave we'd not be afraid iv her.

Some day th' Ph'lippeens 'll be known as th' Standard Isles iv th' Passyfic.

A woman's since iv humor is in her husband's name.

Most women ought niver to look back if they want a following.

If ye dhrink befure siven ye'll cry befure iliven.

A man that'd expict to thrain lobsters to fly in a year is called a loonytic; but a man that thinks men can be tur-rned into angels be an iliction is called a rayformer an' remains at large.

Th' throuble with most iv us, Hinnissy, is we swallow pollytical idees befure they're ripe an' they don't agree with us.

Dhressmakers' bills sinds women into lithrachoor an' men into an early decline.

A bur-rd undher a bonnet is worth two on th' crown.

People tell me to be frank, but how can I be whin I don't dare to know mesilf?

People that talk loud an' offind ye with their insolence are usu'lly shy men thryin' to get over their shyness. 'Tis th' quite, resarved, ca'm spoken man that's mashed on himsilf.

If men cud on'y enjye th' wealth an' position th' newspapers give thim whin they're undher arrest! Don't anny but prominent clubman iver elope or embezzle?

Miditation is a gift con-fined to unknown philosophers an' cows. Others don't begin to think till they begin to talk or write.

A good manny people r-read th' ol' sayin' "Larceny is th' sincerest form iv flatthry."

'Tis a good thing th' fun'ral sermons ar-re not composed in th' confissional.

Most vigitaryans I iver see looked enough like their food to be classed as cannybals.

I don't see why anny man who believes in medicine wud shy at th' faith cure.

Miracles are laughed at be a nation that r-reads thirty millyon newspapers a day an' supports Wall sthreet. (Mike Royko again)

All men are br-rave in comp'ny an' cow'rds alone, but some shows it clearer thin others.

I'd like to tell me frind Tiddy that they'se a strenuse life an' a sthrenuseless life.

I'd like to've been ar-round in th' times th' historical novelists writes about—but I wudden't like to be in th' life insurance business.

I wondher why porthrait painters look down on phrenologists.

Di-plomacy is a continyual game iv duck on th' rock — with France th' duck.

Whin we think we're makin' a gr-reat hit with th' wurruld
we don't know what our own wives thinks iv us.

INDEX

Title   **Page(s)**